REVIEWS for
LEARNING TO WALTZ

A well-conceived saga with a complex and compelling cast. *Learning to Waltz* reminds us that our forebears also grappled with "modern" issues of abuse, angst, and aching hearts. This well-researched and beautiful Regency romance will appeal to anyone who has ever loved and (almost) lost. A stunning and refreshing novel in the Regency genre.
　　—*Barbara Bamberger Scott for Chanticleer Book Reviews*

Reid excels at the slow, careful picture of two complex personalities... The tensions and issues of the historical backdrop are drawn with more vividness and well-researched detail than is usually the case, but it is the convincingly-drawn characters who are the main attraction of this extremely promising debut.
　　—*Steve Donoghue for Historical Novels Review*

The perfect historical romantic novel... a beautiful journey of family and love. Flawless... a sure fire winner; do not pass it by.
　　—*Readers' Favorite*

Stunning... The author weaves a delightfully suspenseful tale that kept me on the edge of my seat. I love, absolutely love Regency and thought I knew all the tales by heart, but this one is different.
　　—*The Romance Reviews*

I adored this book! It is absolutely beautifully written... a gentle love story, but also a story of family love and values. A real gem!
　　—*Online Book Club*

KERRYN REID

LEARNiNG
TO WALTZ

Published by Wrackwater Press
Copyright © 2020, 2013 by Kerryn Reid
ISBN: Print 978-1-7350179-2-1
Ebook 978-1-7350179-3-8
Cover Design by Fiona Jayde Media

Learning to Waltz was previously released with a different cover. Minor modifications have been made to the original text.

LEARNING TO WALTZ
by KERRYN REID

Deborah Moore has learned her lessons well—feel nothing, reveal less, and trust no one. Now widowed with a child of her own, she leads a lonely, cloistered existence, counting her farthings and thinking she is safe. When five-year-old Julian is lost one bitter December day, she discovers how tenuous that safety is.

Evan Haverfield has lived thirty carefree years, hunting, laughing, and dancing among London's high society. His biggest problem has been finding excuses not to marry. But his life changes when he finds Julian Moore half-frozen under a hedge and carries him home to his mother. The young widow hides behind a mask, hard and reserved, but Evan sees glimpses of another woman, wistful, intelligent, and passionate. She's vulnerable, desirable—and completely unsuitable for the heir to Northridge.

Alone in the earliest hours of a new year, Evan teaches Deborah to waltz—that's child's play. Can he teach her joy and laughter? Can his love sweep away the shadows of her past and reveal the luminous woman she was meant to be?

~ To Mom and Dad ~

My introduction to romance,
on and off the page

ACKNOWLEDGMENTS

To Doris Lemcke and Karen Dean Benson, my long-time critique partners, I send my love and thanks for their time and honest comments—sometimes tactful, usually right, always appreciated!

And to my unpaid consultants from Southwest Florida Romance Writers and beyond, who taught me everything I know so far about publishing my own books! In alphabetical order, because I couldn't possibly decide on any other sequence, Sarah Andre, Jacie Floyd, Evelyn Lederman, Becca St. John, and Tara September.

All these ladies write great books. Look 'em up!

"Julian!" She tried to call out but had no breath to carry the sound. *God, please let this be a nightmare.* She had plenty of experience with those.

The lane stretched longer with each gasp, each stumbling step. She would never reach Whately. The stitch in her side tore her ribs apart. Her skirts were wet to the thighs, tangling themselves around her knees and ankles. Her old boots, soaked and broken, scooped up dirt and pebbles from the road, making her stagger. Thankfully, her feet were numb—her bare hands too, torn by snags and brambles. Not that it mattered. If she didn't find Julian, nothing would matter.

Just a couple of hours ago Deborah had sent her maid to fetch some eggs from the dairy farther out this same road. The weather was cold and blustery, but Julian had begged to go along and she gave in, bundling him into his coat and sturdy shoes, chiding him for his fidgets as she smoothed the mittens over his hands. He was bound to lose at least one of them. *What a trivial, stupid thing to worry about. Oh, why did I let him go?*

Molly and the eggs had come home. Julian had not.

"Oh, ma'am, I didn't know what else to do! We looked all over, me and John, but couldn't find any sign of 'im at all. John went back to the farm to see if maybe he went back there, and I come on home to get you."

Deborah had snatched her woolen cloak from its peg by the kitchen door, knotting it around her neck as they flew out the back gate.

"I'm so sorry, ma'am, I could die," Molly blubbered. "John was—we were—"

Deborah could just imagine. Molly, only fourteen, had been sweet on the dairyman's son for months. "It doesn't matter now." Later, if they found him, would be time enough for anger.

Molly had stopped, her chest heaving and one hand pressed to her side. "This here's about where I saw 'im last. One o' the dogs followed us from the farm an' they was playing with a stick. He was right there, an' then I—"

"Julian!" Deborah had called, and then whipped around and called again. Ran on a bit and called again, and again. All the way to the farm they ran. No news of him there, though some of the men were still searching the area.

Molly was spent, gasping and sobbing. "Go on inside and get warm," Deborah told her, "then get John to walk you home. And by heaven, keep your eyes open on the way!"

It had been raining when she left the farm, a frigid wind-blown drizzle that glazed the leaves and grasses. She'd pushed through a stand of trees to the river, called, and called again. Julian loved the river, especially in rough weather like today when it seemed twice the stream it really was, tumbling and shouting. Even screaming as loud as she could, she could hardly hear her own voice.

Slipping on the muddy bank, she'd sloshed up to her knees and bashed her leg against a rock. Julian was not much taller than her knees. There were rocks everywhere. It was so easy to slip, and if he did, it would be his head…

That image drove her now, back toward the village, lungs burning and legs like wood. The squire's estate lay clear on the other side. He could organize a search so easily. If he would. *Surely* he would? She cut across a field, tripped and fell, got up and ran some more.

He was not at home. She must have looked a fright because the footman answered her desperate query without hesitation.

"He was to meet with some men at the inn, ma'am. You might look for him there. If you'll wait—"

But she was off, running again. Another half mile, needles of rain mixing with her tears. She stopped before turning into the high street, her back pressed against the stone wall of Whately's bakery. The smell of yeast made her nauseous.

She could not run like a rabid dog through the village—*would* not beg Squire Reston for help looking like a madwoman. Her breath rasping in her throat, she adjusted her cloak and wrapped it tight to hide the state of her gown, pulled up her hood and tucked her hair inside it with hands she couldn't feel.

She squeezed her eyes shut, dug her teeth into her lower lip, and forced her face to stillness. When her breathing no longer sounded like a death rattle, she pushed herself away from the wall. Her knees tried to buckle, but she commanded them to carry her around the corner. She could see the inn sign, so familiar. Just yesterday, Julian had stopped for the hundredth time to exclaim over the painted boar that ran across it. Not so far away…

She nearly fell through the doorway, tripping over the torn sole of her boot. The innkeep's wife, passing through the hallway with a tray full of dirty dishes, said something sharp, but Deborah paid no heed.

A rumble of voices came from the public room. But as she paused in the doorway to locate Squire Reston, all fell silent. As if they'd frozen in place, mouths open with whatever they'd been saying, eyes turned on her. Was her appearance so shocking? She almost looked down to make sure this was not one of those dreams where she found herself naked in public. Of course, ladies did not frequent public taprooms alone, but she hardly considered herself a lady anymore and did not suppose the townspeople did, either.

3

The air in here was far too warm, suffocating her with the smell of wet wool coats and mufflers hanging by the big fireplace. She shoved the hood back from her face.

There he was. Seated with his back to the door, Sir James was turning toward her, no doubt to see what sort of creature had invaded the room. He rose to his considerable height, his blue eyes startled and graying brows raised in surprise. Then a frown creased his forehead as she hurried to his table.

"Why, Mrs. Moore—"

"Please, I must speak with you. Julian—my son—is lost along the river road somewhere. Please, sir…"

A murmur rose around the room, punctuated by the *shushes* of those avid for gossip. How hateful they were! Humiliating enough that she had to come begging; she did not need an audience thirsty for tragedy.

Except she *did* need them, every one of them that the squire could bring to her aid.

Sir James offered her his chair. "Sit down, ma'am, and tell me…"

She shook her head. "No! No, there's no time."

"But you must tell me what's happened before I can take appropriate measures. Sit down and catch your breath while you do so."

Every instinct screamed to keep moving, keep running. But the other men at the table had risen along with the squire—she could not keep them all on their feet. So she sat, rigid as the chair itself, her hands clenched tight on the table in front of her. Sir James folded himself into the chair beside her.

She might as well have shouted out her dread—some version of it would go home with each one of these ghouls—but she forced herself to speak softly. Until she neared the end of the tale. "We've been looking but can't find any trace of him. The river is wild today, and it's so cold, I can't bear to think what might…" She broke off with a gasp and bit into her lip to silence herself. It would be so easy to give in to hysteria.

Sir James had been kind enough in the year since her husband's death, in his perfunctory way. She already owed him too much, and now this…

He patted her tense hands. "There, there. We'll find him, don't you worry."

Her legs had stiffened as she sat, but she forced them to straighten as she pushed herself to her feet. Sir James circled the room, addressing all the local men. Several of them promised help, and she made a mental list of these further obligations. Mr. Corbett, who grew hay on the squire's land. Another tenant farmer, whose name she did not know. The brewer, seated at Squire Reston's table.

But more waved Sir James away. Even Viscount Latimer, with all those servants at his disposal… Well, that should be no surprise. He'd never shown any liking for her husband and probably did not know she existed.

"Come now, my lord, surely you can give us something," the squire insisted. In the end the viscount offered up a couple of grooms from his stables and turned back with a huff to the young man seated across the table, staring at her. Shocked, no doubt, at the pathetic picture of humanity she presented.

She could expect nothing from him, either. A stranger, no doubt cut from the same cloth as Viscount Latimer. The last table was a better bet, a pair of winter-idle farm laborers…

"I'll be there as well," she heard, and turned back to the viscount's friend. His gaze was still fixed on her face.

"Good man, Haverfield." Sir James moved on, but the man stepped toward her and held out his steaming mug.

"A hot drink, ma'am? It's just cider. Or maybe some coffee?"

She eyed the cup with revulsion. She couldn't even think of swallowing—her own saliva sat thick and cloying in her throat. "No, sir."

The squire began collecting the search party together. Ten or a dozen of them, donning their outer garments, calling for carriages and discussing where they should begin the hunt. Deborah stumbled to the door to wait for them, discovering just how much her feet hurt. No matter, soon they'd be numb again. *Let's go, let's go!* Sir James rested a hand on her shoulder. "Leave this to us, Mrs. Moore. You'll die of pneumonia if you don't get warm and dry. And when we find your boy, he will need you ready at home."

She would have argued, but she was shivering too hard to say anything at all.

2

W hat in bloody hell am I doing out here?

The December cold bit through Evan's greatcoat and huddled round his ankles. He couldn't feel his face, and his toes were just a memory. With each hoofbeat, he feared his teeth would crack. There were more pleasurable ways to cure the restlessness that ailed him—Latimer had the right of it, sitting home by his fireside.

Grady, who'd been Evan's groom and companion for fifteen years and accompanied him through plenty of uncomfortable situations, didn't look much happier. Each exhalation of man and horse added to the gray mist that surrounded them. They should have moved to Italy long ago—*southern* Italy. Or Greece. There, at least, if he took a chivalrous notion to go searching for some little boy who'd been mislaid, they would be in no danger of freezing to death.

As Evan's discomfort increased, each field they traversed seemed a bit larger, and his sympathy for the boy's mother receded a bit further. He hoped he would feel a similar compassion for any child in hazard, but no use denying it was the woman's face that had spurred him to join the little troop of villagers scouring the countryside. If one of his own nieces or nephews went missing, there would be a battalion of servants and tenants to search every square inch of ground three times over. That face made a few hours of discomfort seem a paltry sacrifice. Or it had a few hours ago.

The squire had sent them out along the river lane into the partitioned farmlands that surrounded Whately. But searchers already roved up and down the lane, and Evan had decided to leave the roadway, cutting through the hedgerow into a series of fields that ran alongside. They kept the impatient horses to a walk, riding the perimeter of each enclosure as they worked their way out from town.

Several fields later, he doubted his wisdom.

"That's quite a frown you're wearing, Mr. Haverfield," said Grady, glancing up to check the bare branches of a beech tree. "What're you thinking?"

"A number of things, none of them pleasant." Except, possibly, what her face might look like wearing a smile. "Are we wasting our time, Grady? Why would a child play here in these empty fields when there are farms and a river on the other side of the road? I suppose you *were* a child once, Grady?"

A chuckle sounded from behind Grady's muffler. "Aye, sir. But it's hard to remember what it was like, isn't it?" He turned his horse and opened the gate into the next field. "Can't really know, sir. He could've been following some animal, or thought he might find his way home cross-country."

Like all the others they'd inspected, this field was empty but for the frost-coated stubble of whatever crop had grown there. Evan sighed in frustration. With each passing minute, rescue became more imperative, yet seemed more unlikely. Already it was almost dark with those heavy clouds hunkered in the treetops.

"Don't s'pose they've found him, do you?" Grady asked.

Evan shook his head. "We'd have heard the horn." He whipped at a low-hanging branch with his riding crop to make sure there was no one hiding behind it. "But surely only a fool would go searching after dark for a small child in a black coat."

They passed through another gate into yet another enclosure. It looked just like the previous one, and the one before that, and the three or thirty before that, except for the back end of a dog jutting from the hawthorn brambles, snuffling and pawing at something under the hedge. "Don't s'pose he's got anything more 'n a dead bird or whatnot," muttered Grady.

Evan grunted in agreement. Just a farm dog hunting up an extra meal.

The animal looked up and barked.

"Stupid beast," said Grady. "We don't want yer stinkin' carrion."

"You're not hungry, Grady?"

Another cackle of amusement. "Oh, a nice slab of mutton would taste just fine. But he's welcome to whatever rotting critter he's got."

Evan frowned as they rode closer. "Don't know, Grady. He looks mighty happy to share." The dog dived under the hedge, backed out, and barked again, his scraggly tail wagging his whole hind end.

Evan dismounted and passed his reins to Grady. "What have you found, fella?" He squatted down to peer under the branches. And there he saw no bird, no mouse, but a boy who matched the description they'd been given. Evan gave the dog a quick pat on the head and crawled into the child's cave. The urchin lay not six feet from the lane, but he would never have been found from that side. He would not have been found at all without the dog.

Curled up on his side facing the entrance of the cave, his hands shoved under his arms for warmth, the child looked very pale and small and—well, dead. Evan groaned. The boy's skin was cold, and he did not respond to touch or voice, but under the collar Evan detected a faint pulse. He dragged him out as gently as he could and stood up with his limp parcel. Dark eyes flickered open for a moment, unseeing —Evan's heart thudded faster and he forgot about the cold.

Mounted again, he nestled the little body against his side, pulling his greatcoat closed again around them both. Icy feet, one of them bare, rested against Evan's thigh. Perhaps he had, indeed, spent some part of the afternoon by the river as his mother feared. They cut through to the lane and spurred the horses to a canter, bearing their precious cargo back toward Whately.

Some half-mile from town they met Squire Reston, huddled inside his greatcoat wearing a scowl. His face brightened at the sight of them. "By God, man, you found him!" He held a hunting horn to his lips and sounded a double blast to call off the search. "I was just about to put an end to it, anyway—it's all but dark. How is he?"

"He's unconscious and his feet are like ice, but he is alive." Sir James reached out to take the child, but Evan shook him off. "I know where he lives. I suggest you ride for the doctor."

In front of the widow's little cottage that Latimer had pointed out on their drive home earlier, Evan slid carefully down from the saddle, hoping his numbed feet would support him. He sent Grady and the horses up the road to the inn and turned toward the house. The gate stood open. Three short steps took him to the front door. A lantern hung beside it, rocking on its peg. Smoke from the burning lard blew into Evan's face, and he coughed as he pounded on the door.

She had changed her gown and tidied her hair, but her face was pale and pinched, and one hand gripped the doorjamb as though clutching the reins on a runaway horse. The other went to her throat as she scanned the inert form of her child. Then her eyes darted to Evan's face, burning, begging for an answer.

He managed the ghost of a reassuring smile. "He'll be all right." He hoped it was true.

Evan had never seen a woman faint, but he was surely about to do so. Those fevered eyes went blank, her face slack. Before he had any chance to react, she recovered herself and reached anxious arms for her son.

"I'll carry him, ma'am—only show me where."

"Molly!" she called over her shoulder as she hurried Evan into a small parlor off the tiny entrance hall. The warmth of the room felt alien after so long out in the cold.

"Thank the Lord!" cried a plump matron, jumping up from her chair by the fire. Evan had visited Whately many times, hunted and dined with the squire; this was the man's wife. Good to see a familiar face, and to know Mrs. Moore had reliable female support.

"Why, it's Mr. Haverfield. I didn't know you were in town."

"I arrived yesterday," Evan said with a nod of acknowledgment. Small hands clutched at his coat as he lowered the boy to the sofa.

He spoke to the widow. "He took shelter under a hedge and must have fallen asleep."

"On the river road? I searched all along there, twice."

"I don't know Whately well enough to tell you precisely where. But he was well-hidden. We found him from the fields, not the road. If it weren't for the dog..." Evan helped her pull off the boy's coat. "I'm afraid his feet are quite frozen. Sir James has gone for the doctor."

A maidservant rushed into the room, wringing her hands. She was very young, and her face was red and swollen with crying. She burst into fresh tears when she saw her young master.

"Oh my God, he's dead! Oh, it's all my fault!"

"Be quiet, girl!" said Lady Reston, authoritative in her expensive silks. "He's not dead and not going to be." Her eyes met Evan's, and she shook her head at the girl's stupidity. "I hope you have better luck with your servants, Mr. Haverfield."

As far as Evan could tell, Mrs. Moore did not resent Lady Reston's assumption of authority, but neither did she yield her own. She sent the maid off to the kitchen for warm water and stripped off her son's trousers, shirt, and underclothes. She said nothing, but her hands shook as she took gentle hold of each small foot. The skin was flushed except for a white gloss that colored portions of his toes. The boy stirred and opened his eyes, muttering something unintelligible before sliding back into unconsciousness. Lady Reston helped to put him into a warm, woolen nightshirt.

Evan retreated to a table at the far end of the room, laid with books and writing paper. The women were busy, and he saw no way he could be of use. Probably he should leave—a stranger could not be welcome. He told himself there might be need of a messenger or some other assistance he could provide. But mostly he wanted to hear, first-hand, the doctor's report on the child he had found.

He watched the widow as she worked. She was not fashionable. Her hair was not the preferred blonde, nor cut short in the current mode, but a dark chestnut, pulled back into a thick plait and neatly pinned up. Evan missed the wayward curls from earlier in the day—so feminine, so vulnerable. He was happy to see her warm and dry, however, in a gray woolen gown that *might* have been in style at one time, though he was positive his sisters would consider it suitable only for their maids. Her pallor had lessened, and in the heat from the fire, her skin glowed with a richness that had little to do with the cream and peach-fuzz complexion so admired by the *ton*.

"What can possibly be keeping that girl so long?" exclaimed Lady Reston. "I'm sorry I sent her to you, but her mother has given us such good service over the years…"

"She is very upset," Mrs. Moore replied quietly.

"*Molly* is upset? She loses your son because she can't keep her eyes off the dairyman's boy for five minutes—heaven knows where her hands were, or his!—and you make excuses for her?"

The widow pressed her lips tight, but her eyes remained on the child.

"*You* are the one who should be upset," Lady Reston went on. "Irate, in fact!"

"Molly is fully aware of her negligence, Lady Reston, and of my disappointment in her. Ranting about it will not help."

"I can scarce believe how calm you are!"

One brief glance she gave Lady Reston. Then her attention returned to her son. "Perhaps you might see if you can hurry her along."

Lady Reston rustled out of the room and returned in a few minutes, scolding the girl who trailed behind her carrying a wash-tub. This she set on a stool Lady Reston pulled up in front of the sofa.

Mrs. Moore carefully checked the water temperature and settled herself, pulling Julian close against her side so his little legs reached the water. She submerged his feet, and almost immediately he began to fidget, crying out as the frozen tissue began to thaw. Very soon he was fully conscious and wailing, kicking out against the pain. Water splashed on every surface within three feet.

Molly struggled to hold the child's feet still, and Lady Reston retreated to a safe distance. "Come, girl, can't you do any better than that? You'll flood the whole house."

Mrs. Moore continued murmuring to her son, but her hands shook and her chin trembled. Abandoning his dry corner, Evan strode across the room.

"Here, let me try." The widow gaped up at him in surprise—no doubt she'd forgotten his existence.

"Oh, Mr. Haverfield," Lady Reston exclaimed. "You'll ruin your coat!" But Molly, who had just been kicked in the face, was only too eager to pass her responsibility off to someone else. Down on one knee, Evan pressed the boy's feet deep into the tub. There was not much water left, and it was barely warm.

A tremor in her voice, Mrs. Moore spoke. "Molly, I need you to fetch the laudanum and a cup, and—Lady Reston, you'll tell her what we need." The girl fairly ran from the room. The squire's wife followed more sedately, swiping at her wet skirts. "Pardon me, sir, you *did* say the doctor was coming?"

"Yes indeed," Evan replied. "I would guess Sir James did not find him at home."

Lady Reston returned with a glass of water and the bottle of laudanum. Mrs. Moore eyed it doubtfully. "I'm not sure how much to give him..."

Lady Reston chuckled. "Believe me, dear, with nine children, I've had plenty of experience. Let me see—Isabella broke her arm falling from the saddle at age two, and Charles fell in the river and nearly drowned, and Harry's broken more bones than I can remember. And they've *all* had the toothache at one time or another." She added a few drops to the water.

Evan stared up at her. "I'm amazed that you've kept them all alive, ma'am." Perhaps it was not age so much as motherhood that had grayed her hair and lined her face.

"I *am* rather proud of that. And young Master Moore will be fine too. Now let's see if we can get this into the poor lad." It took both women and tight swaddling with the blankets, but in the end, the feat was accomplished. And Evan was wet from shoulder to knee.

A knock sounded. Lady Reston started toward the hall, but Molly was already there. "Humph. About time she did something useful."

"Sir James Reston and Doctor Overley," Molly announced in a subdued voice and prepared to efface herself once again.

"Stay, girl," commanded Lady Reston, "and take Mr. Haverfield's place." She pointed at Evan on the floor by her feet. Sniffling, Molly did as she was told. Mrs. Moore spoke gently to her and received a watery look of gratitude in return.

As Doctor Overley approached, Evan moved to one side of the fireplace, the squire and his lady to the other. The physician had been dining with a family some way out of town, and though his words apologized for the delay, his expression said he was not pleased about the interruption of his evening. He also smelled strongly of spirits.

He sat down on the sofa and curtly told Molly to dry the child's feet. While she did so, he perused Mrs. Moore in a way that struck Evan as far too familiar. "My dear, how nice to see you out of—*No, you idiot, don't rub them, just pat gently!*—out of black gloves. I never did think black showed off your many attractions to best advantage."

Good heavens. Could the man really be pursuing a flirtation at such a wildly inappropriate time? Mrs. Moore flushed.

Evan had to satisfy himself with analyzing everything that made the doctor ridiculous. Though not an ill-looking man, everything about him spoke his conceit. His hair was teased on top and curled tortuously around his face *a la Brutus*, and his clothing proclaimed an ambition to be more than a small-town physician. His high, starched shirt-points and cravat might have drawn the envy of a London dandy. The style he favored did nothing to flatter his round figure, despite the stays that creaked audibly as he moved.

His lip curling with disgust, Overley inspected Julian's frozen toes without touching them. Blisters had formed as the skin thawed, but the boy had quieted, his eyes blurred with the drug, and was sleepily turned in to his mother's side. Mrs. Moore pulled one tiny arm from the blankets, and Overley felt for the pulse in his wrist.

The man rose. "A minor case of frostbite. You seem to have done everything right, as usual, my dear. Just leave the blisters alone, and you must keep him off his feet for a few days. He should be merry as a grig in short order. I shall stop by soon to see how he does—ahem, how *both* of you do." Overley bowed over her hand and kissed it with quite unnecessary zeal.

Evan was gratified to see the widow wipe her hand on the blankets as soon as the doctor turned toward the door. Sir James saw Doctor Overley out, and Evan prepared to take his leave as well. The relief of the diagnosis had left Mrs. Moore looking weary. In the bustle of heating bricks for the beds and getting the sleeping boy upstairs to his bedchamber, Evan took himself off unnoticed by the others.

It was nearly nine o'clock and he was suddenly, ravenously hungry. He strode up the street to retrieve Grady, and they rode back to Viscount Latimer's estate on a road crusted with ice. A sprinkling of stars now shone here and there between the clouds. Tomorrow promised to be brighter, if not warmer—and he would see her again. He could not remember when he had so looked forward to a new morning.

3

The fire roared in welcome as Evan strolled into Latimer's library half an hour later. It was his favorite room in Whately Manor, the place that had been almost a second home since he and Frank first became school chums at Rugby. *Gad, that was twenty years ago.*

"Good God, look what the cat dragged in." Latimer returned the poker to its hook on one side of the hearth. His sister rose from a chair on the other side. It was the first Evan had seen of Amanda since his arrival the previous day—she appeared taller every time he visited.

"You're so cold," she scolded as he took her hands and kissed her cheek. "I'll have you know, I dined at home on purpose to act the hostess, and *you* run off to play knight-errant. I've half a mind to send you to bed without any supper."

"'*Of all wild beasts preserve me from a tyrant,*'" Evan replied. "In any case, your excellent butler already offered food. I wouldn't want to waste it."

Amanda snorted. "Nothing edible goes to waste in this household. Pull over another chair and tell us all about your adventure. We know from the stable hands that the child was found, but no more than that."

Frank poured a brandy and pushed it across the table. "But you were gone a hell of a long time, so I suppose you managed to involve yourself in the rescue."

"Well of course he did. He makes a perfect knight. You're being rude, Frank."

Evan made her a formal bow. "Thank you, Miss Latimer. Though I must apologize for my deplorable appearance. I did wonder if the bath should come before the food, but hunger won out. I washed my hands, I assure you."

Amanda surveyed the moisture beaded on his boots and dusting his hair, the dirt on his knees. "*Marmion* doesn't say, but I suppose Lochinvar was soiled when he arrived at Netherby. I hope *you* did not have to swim?"

Evan laughed. "No, thankfully." He stood up when a footman put his head around the door to say that supper was ready.

"Well, I want to hear the whole story, Evan." Amanda rose as well and slipped her arm through his. "I'll keep you company while you stave off starvation. Are you coming, Frank?"

"I'll be along."

"My, he's been moody," Amanda murmured as they moved across the hall into the breakfast parlor. "What's wrong with him now?"

"He thought we should let the villagers take care of their own. Perhaps it was rude of me to desert him."

"That's nonsense. A host should do what his guests want to do."

Evan shrugged and tackled the roast beef. "Frank tells me you're betrothed to the squire's son. Tell me about that while I eat. I talk better when I'm not chewing."

Nibbling at a bowl of grapes, her elbows on the table, Amanda regaled Evan with the tale of her courtship. "I've been bosom-bows with Isabella Reston since we could walk, but I hardly spared a thought for Charles. When he came home wounded from Belgium, she wanted to spend every minute with *him*. If I wanted to see *her*, I had to see him too. He seemed so much older, more mature, more... interesting, somehow. A far cry from those fribbles in London." She made a face. "You know better than anyone how unsuited I was to marry any of *them*."

Evan did know. He had squired her about town during her first and only season, partly out of loyalty and partly because she was safe and undemanding company, the same horse-mad tomboy she'd always been under a thin veneer of society polish. A pretty enough fortune ensured that she would receive offers, but not from him. He'd known her too long—it would have been like marrying one of his sisters.

"And at least Charles is taller than me." She grinned. "Maybe an inch. I don't know what he saw in me, but I wasn't going to let him change his mind. I accepted him on the spot."

"So unfashionable," Evan murmured.

She giggled. "But enough of my affairs. Did you earn a knighthood today?"

He pushed his plate away and refilled his glass. Then he gave her an abbreviated account of the afternoon's search and the evening in Mrs. Moore's parlor.

"God, I hate the cold," he finished. "Thought I might get frostbite myself." He watched the claret swirling in his glass. "I've just come here from my sister's in Yorkshire. Elizabeth has a boy much the same age as Julian Moore, and seeing him so recently… well, I thought of all the resources my sister would have if Alexander were lost, while this woman had to go to the squire begging for help. One useless child-maid, whose negligence apparently caused the crisis in the first place." Another pause, and then he looked up at Amanda. "Tell me, what do you know of her? Frank says she was married to your vicar?"

Amanda nodded and popped another grape into her mouth. "I can't claim to know her well. I've met her any number of times, but she is so quiet, so… so *still*. I can never tell what she's thinking."

"I know what you mean, I think." Even in the throes of panic today, she had wrapped herself in a sort of desperate dignity that only made her seem more vulnerable.

"Her husband was a different sort. Far easier to know, though I didn't like him much. They made a handsome couple, but very distant from one another, at least in public."

"That's hardly unusual. Quite the fashion, in fact."

"That doesn't mean he should tell everyone at a party how stupid she is or call for the carriage and leave her to walk home."

"Lord, no."

"After she got in the family way, the gossip was that he took up with some woman over in Ashby. And through all that, she never said a word of complaint. Or praise, either."

Latimer wandered into the room, poured himself some port, and sat down. "Did I miss the whole melodramatic saga?"

The long delay, the patent disinterest in the day's anxieties, the failure to offer Evan a drink—Evan figured all that was an attempt to punish him for his charity. Well, he didn't care what Frank thought, didn't care if he'd made his friend look bad. He could mete out a little punishment of his own.

Ignoring Frank, he addressed Amanda again. "Did he make provision for her and the child?"

Amanda scoffed and helped herself to Evan's uneaten custard. "A fair provision of debts, I should imagine. I'm sure his income didn't support his stables." She gazed at Evan while she savored a spoonful. "So you... like her?"

"Oh yes," said the viscount, "our Evan has finally fallen. The coldest fish in the pond has been hooked, the wildest colt broken."

"Goddamn it, Latimer, I'm not falling in love. I feel sorry for her, that's all. Is the concept beyond your comprehension?"

Frank emitted a skeptical snort. "I have nothing against love, Haverfield. Unlike you, I've been there. But you're the heir to North-ridge, for God's sake—you could hardly find anyone less eligible. At least I choose women of my own station."

"I seem to recall a serving girl once in Oxford—"

"That was a decade ago!"

"And Mrs. Moore is no serving girl. Haven't you heard the way she speaks, seen how she carries herself?"

Latimer yawned and got to his feet. "Never paid that much attention, Haverfield." He ambled out of the room again.

Evan slammed his hand down on the table. "How did I lose my temper? I apologize for my language."

Amanda said nothing, merely looked at him, her eyebrows lifted and a knowing little smile on her face.

He pointed a finger at her. "I'm not, you know."

Her smile grew wider.

"I've not spoken more than a dozen words to her. But I mean to call on her tomorrow to see how the boy goes on. Will you come?"

"Of course I will. We should by all means check on the boy. And if you're lucky, you might exchange another dozen words with his mother."

4

Deborah sat on the sofa the following day with Julian and a book, trying to keep the child quiet. He insisted his feet didn't hurt, and as the day wore on, keeping him happily contained became a struggle. When they heard the sounds of arrival from the hallway, she had to physically restrain him from running to see who had come.

She was curious herself to get a long, clear look at the gentleman Molly delivered into the parlor with Miss Latimer, stumbling over the name on his card. She'd received only vague impressions in all the turmoil of the previous day.

Deborah dropped the book into Julian's lap and jumped up to greet the callers. She took the man's proffered hand between both of hers. "I am so glad you came. I was dreadfully remiss last evening; I did not even find out your name, much less thank you properly, Mr.— Haverfield, is it?"

She was bound to admire him had he been hunch-backed and scarred with a patch over one eye, for he had saved her son's life. But in fact, he stood straight and handsome, with curly dark hair and warm brown eyes. His hand, still holding one of hers, was cool from the outdoors. He was dressed for riding, yet impeccably neat and beautifully tailored. A bit tongue-tied, perhaps...

He cleared his throat. "Evan Haverfield, ma'am. It was—is—a pleasure to be of service."

She slid her hand gently away. Pulling her eyes from his was not as simple.

Turning to his companion, she made a slight bow. "Good afternoon, Miss Latimer. I've not had a chance to offer my congratulations on your betrothal. It's nice to know you will not be leaving Whately."

"Thank you, Mrs. Moore. That's sweet of you. And speaking of sweet, we brought you some cakes. Your girl took them to the kitchen."

"You are far too generous, Miss Latimer."

"Nonsense," Miss Latimer replied, smiling. She moved toward the sofa, where Julian clambered about. He'd been forbidden to touch the floor. "I do hope this young fellow is recovering from his adventure."

"Yes, thanks to Mr. Haverfield." Deborah smiled again at him. "The doctor said he should stay off his feet, but as you see..." Normally her son was only too happy to spend all his time looking at books. Today, of all days, he wanted to go outside and crack the ice on the puddles.

"It is a lot to expect of a five-year-old." Miss Latimer shook his hand. "Good afternoon, Master Moore." Bashful, Julian muttered something that might have been a greeting.

Deborah gestured toward the room's only upholstered chair, beside the fire. "Mr. Haverfield?" But Mr. Haverfield, smiling at Julian, sat down beside him on the sofa. Miss Latimer got the chair instead and commenced the usual small talk.

Molly carried in tea and the cakes the visitors had brought, and the conversation resumed. Deborah struggled through it as well as she could—she was far more interested in what was happening beside her on the sofa.

Mr. Haverfield had taken no part in her conversation with Miss Latimer, devoting himself to Julian. Her son had had limited contact with men since his father's death and needed little encouragement. He stared, fascinated, as Mr. Haverfield pulled out his watch. Julian took it in both hands like it was something holy and examined it at length, and then did the same with the attached fob, a miniature globe. Deborah saw Mr. Haverfield point something out to him—England, perhaps? Could such a tiny thing even show England?

The man surprised her. Hartley had been a good father in some ways, but always more inclined to spend money than time. No man she knew had any interest whatsoever in other people's offspring.

"I think you must have children of your own, Mr. Haverfield," she said.

"No, ma'am, not even a wife. Seven nieces and nephews have taught me a few things, however."

A bachelor. *And what possible difference can that make to you, you fool?*

When the proper half hour had elapsed, Miss Latimer rose to take her leave. As Mr. Haverfield followed suit, Julian's little hands clutched at his sleeve, and a very small voice asked, "Would you read me a story? Please?" The blood rose hot to Deborah's cheeks.

"I would be delighted, but we must ask your mother."

Two pairs of eyes turned toward Deborah, one pleading, the other amused. Busy noticing the way his eyes crinkled up at the corners, she did not say *no* fast enough.

Mr. Haverfield pressed the negotiations. "Perhaps if we promise to entertain ourselves and not keep her from her chores…"

"We cannot possibly take such advantage of your good nature, Mr. Haverfield."

"Oh, pooh," Miss Latimer said. "My brother's out shooting and won't be back for hours, and I'll be at Isabella's the rest of the day. What better way for him to spend the afternoon?" Deborah saw her wink at him, and Mr. Haverfield smiled blindingly back.

Deborah blinked. What a smile he had!

"Shall I take your horse to the Restons, Evan?" Miss Latimer asked him. "It's too cold to leave him standing in the street. If you're willing to walk home…"

Another obligation. They'd backed her into a corner where further objection would have seemed discourteous. And it would be callous to make him walk home.

"There's a shed in the yard. For your horse, I mean." It had formerly sheltered her own carthorse; now it was only the goat.

"But just one story," she cautioned her son. "We must not take advantage of Mr. Haverfield's good nature."

❧

EVAN HAD THOUGHT her lovely yesterday, distracted and distraught, dressed in little better than homespun. He'd waited all morning for proper visiting hours so he could have those dozen words with her that Amanda had promised—but when she looked up at him, her eyes and smile alight, speech deserted him.

Her dark hair was braided and coiled neatly at the nape of her neck. Her eyes were not gray but green, with silver sparks lit up by the sunshine pouring through the windows. Though only wool, and still not in the latest mode, the dark blue of her gown flattered her. Today she looked very much a lady.

Slender and graceful, she walked out of the room with Amanda. Evan turned his attention to Julian, watching him with eyes like his mother's.

They looked through the pile of books on the table by the sofa. These were items likely to appeal to children: nursery rhymes, *Robin Hood*, a little chapbook about King Arthur and his knights. There was a well-used copy of *Little Goody Two-Shoes* inscribed with the name Deborah Carlington in a child's painstaking hand, and an old edition of *Pilgrim's Progress*, dedicated:

14 October 1804

   To my dear Deborah on your 14th birthday. May you one day have all the books you can possibly read.

   With much love, Aunt Matilda

Evan glanced over his shoulder at the large bookcase behind him, filled to overflowing. It was an impressive collection for a widow in straitened circumstances. Few ladies of his acquaintance—or gentlemen, for that matter—seemed interested in much beyond the latest literary sensations and popular poets. Never mind that they stocked their libraries with volumes that were never touched by anything but a dusting cloth. *She puts us to shame.*

He stood when Mrs. Moore returned to the room, *Pilgrim's Progress* in his hand. "I ran across the inscription here." Then he gestured toward the bookshelves. "It seems your hopes have been fulfilled. Unless you've read all these?"

Mrs. Moore blushed, but her voice was cool as she replied. "No, but I intend to do so. I confess I love books."

"I thought perhaps they were your husband's."

She shook her head. "My husband was not a reader. And you, Mr. Haverfield?"

"I fear I must disappoint you, ma'am. I've read the classics, of course, and some of the current novels, but I'm afraid my only regular reading is the newspaper and a bit of poetry." He put down *Pilgrim's Progress* and picked up another volume. "But I do enjoy learning about exotic places, and Julian wants to introduce me to these *Tales of the East*. They've not yet come my way."

He looked back at her where she stood, one hand on the back of a chair, eyeing him uncertainly. She was so serious. Evan smiled. "I'm quite happy to look after your boy for an hour. I'm sure you have things to do, even if it's only to spend some time with a book of your own."

All sorts of feelings flitted across her face in succession, too quickly to identify. Then it was as though she slipped on a mask, showing the same face but made of wood. She replied in a voice to match, "I will be in the kitchen if you need me."

"Mr. Haffield?" The little voice was accompanied by a tentative tug on his breeches. Evan turned from his woolgathering and sat down again. "Do you have any horses, Mr. Haffield?" The boy sounded shy, but his gaze was direct and curious.

"The only horses I have with me in Whately are my two carriage horses."

"What color are they?"

"They're gray with a bit of dappling on the hindquarters. Very handsome."

"Is it a barouche?" Julian pronounced the word carefully, as though he'd just learned it.

Evan quelled a laugh. From an adult, those same questions would constitute an inquiry into his financial status. "No, merely a phaeton."

"We used to have a gig and a brown pony to pull it. He was handsome too." The corners of his mouth turned down. "Mama sold them."

"That must have been a disappointment. I gather you like horses?"

"I *love* horses. And dogs and kittens. And cows too. The dairy is my favorite place in the whole world."

The whole square mile of world the child had seen. "Are there any animals you *don't* like?

"Geese." Julian wrinkled up his nose. "And turkeys."

"No, they're not good for much, are they? Except at dinnertime."

"I'd rather just eat strawberries for dinner."

Evan chuckled. "I expect you'd want some variety before long." He rubbed his chin. Despite all those nieces and nephews, he'd never really conversed with a child, seldom been alone with one. "What do you do with your friends?"

Julian picked at his bandages, his brow creased in thought. "I climbed a tree once with Harry."

Evan waited for more, but it didn't come. "That's all? No games? No sports?" Incredulous, Evan spoke without thinking and regretted it. The child looked bewildered.

"Sometimes Mama plays fox and geese with me, or spillikins."

Good Lord. "What about Molly?" She was still a child herself, after all.

"She's silly, and she can't even read. I can read as good—as *well*—as her, and I'm only five." He held up one hand, displaying the five digits.

"Perhaps she didn't have a room full of books when she was five." Evan spread his fingers to match.

"Humph," was the boy's only response. Evan opened up *Tales of the East,* the book Julian had insisted upon.

Evan had his doubts. Exotic places were all well and good, but this was no book of nursery rhymes—there were no illustrations, and the text was dense on the page. It certainly would have daunted *him* at age five. He chose the shortest story he could find.

The boy listened quietly for the most part, coughing occasionally. But he used his finger to follow along as best he could and asked "Mr. Haffield" to identify several words. He lasted through the first tale, but as they continued into a second, the child's weight grew heavy against Evan's side, and he slept.

After a few minutes, Evan slipped off the sofa and inserted a pillow under Julian's dark head. Surely the boy's skin was rather warm? Should he go find Mrs. Moore? He'd promised her an hour... No, probably it was just the fire. He adjusted the screen a bit and surveyed the room.

It had looked better last night. At the highest levels of society, one heard *the noble cottage* proclaimed as the most romantic of residences, but by daylight this cottage fell far short of nobility. Wretched would exaggerate its faults, but humble it certainly was. She'd made an effort, hanging drapes at the windows and bird prints on the walls. But the ceiling fairly hit his head when he stood up straight and was stained with damp besides. If it weren't so depressing, he might have laughed at the image of his sisters living here. They wouldn't last the afternoon unless they found something good to read.

He strolled over to the bookcase, rough-built like the dining table where he had sat last evening. It held an eclectic mix of titles—essays and poetry, some Shakespeare, and plenty of more serious volumes on history, nature, and religion. They were far from new, with broken spines and a faint smell of mildew. He wasn't sure what his sisters read these days, but anyone should be able to find something to amuse them for a few hours.

There was little else in the room to attract his interest. But a fine mahogany writing table stood by the door, incongruous among the other furnishings, and on it sat one silver-framed miniature. It depicted a plain young woman with a mild, kindly face, not quite smiling, but thinking of something pleasant. Mrs. Moore herself? The coloring was similar, but the features... No, he thought not.

Julian spoke, abrupt and unintelligible, and Evan turned to respond. But the child's eyes remained closed, though he shifted restlessly. The picture still in one hand, Evan checked his forehead again —hotter. *Damn.*

As he turned toward the hall to find her, Mrs. Moore returned to the room, pushing the door wide. She shied away from him, avoiding collision but losing her balance. He reached out to catch her arm, juggling the picture. When she was steady on her feet, he placed it back on the table.

"I thought at first it was you," he said.

"My aunt," she replied with the economy of words he was coming to expect from her.

"Matilda? The one who gives you books? She looks... kind."

"Oh, she was!" The fervency of her reply took Evan by surprise. Mrs. Moore too, perhaps—she bit her lip, looked down at her hands clenched together at her waist. "At least to me," she muttered, and stepped quickly away to Julian's side.

Evan followed her. "I'm no expert—could he be feverish? And he's been coughing."

Mrs. Moore frowned as she smoothed the hair back from her son's forehead. "Oh, sweetling." He muttered something but did not awake.

"Shall I carry him up to his bed, ma'am?"

"No, it's easier for me to have him here. I can keep an eye on him while I do some sewing."

"You did not accomplish all your chores during the last hour?"

Her gaze jerked up to meet his, hard and angry. "I think you do not quite understand my circumstances, sir. I am very glad to have Molly, but she is only fourteen, which is why I can afford to keep her. And while she is much better than I at keeping the fires going, and quite capable of doing the washing and plucking those fine pheasants you brought, she is no cook, and certainly no seamstress." She stopped with a gasp, lowering her eyes to the floor, one hand fluttering as though to wave away her speech. "Forgive me."

Evan caught her hand, reddened and rough, crossed and recrossed with scratches. "No, I am the one who must apologize. It was a

30

thoughtless question. I know you've been wishing me at Jericho all afternoon. May I call again tomorrow to see how the boy goes on?"

She pulled her hand away and glanced up, but her eyes got no farther than his cravat. "Of course." Hardly louder than a whisper.

After a glance at Julian, she led Evan into the hall, helped him shrug into his greatcoat, and handed him his hat, gloves, and riding crop. Nodding toward an open door at the end of the hall, she said, "Molly is in the kitchen. She can help you with your horse."

Evan sighed as she disappeared into the parlor. He'd gotten his dozen words and more, but she seemed mighty eager to get rid of him.

Molly escorted him to the yard. The stone wall continued around the corner from the high street, with a convenient gate opening onto the road that led to Latimer's estate. A massive chestnut tree dominated the space from its spot beyond the back wall. Beneath its bare branches stood a large shed with an attached chicken coop, both cowering as though they feared the tree would topple them—the stone wall already showed cracks and a few coping stones lay in the tall grass. The shed door screeched in protest as the girl hauled it open.

It was cozy enough inside. Evan's borrowed mount had been relieved of saddle and bridle, rubbed down, covered with a blanket, and ensconced with water and hay. The girl was good with livestock, at least.

"You do good work."

Molly bobbed a curtsy. "Me granddad used to be head groom up at the inn, so I spent a lot o' time with horses. This here's a real nice fella."

"His name is Lookout. Belongs to Viscount Latimer." He watched as she laid the sheepskin pad in place. "Master Julian said your mistress had a horse and gig until recently."

"Aye, the lad was fair tore up over that, he was. Wouldn't hardly speak to his mum for a week." Molly chatted easily out of the house and away from her employer's supervision. "Afore he died, Mr. Moore kept a fine carriage and three or four horses for riding an' hunting.

But o' course, the mistress, she had to let 'em all go. There's no place for 'em here and no money for a groom, neither. I saw to the one carriage horse meself, but what with feed 'n all... She sold him 'n the gig, back last spring." Molly threw the saddle onto Lookout's back.

"Did you work at the vicarage, then, before Mr. Moore died?" Evan asked, reaching under the horse's belly to pass her the girth.

"Oh no, sir, I just came to Missus Moore last January when she moved here to make way for the new vicar. But o' course I seen 'em around town. I lived with me mum at Squire's and helped out there, 'specially when they had company and such, an' I used to sneak out to the stables and check out all the fancy horses."

"Were Mr. Moore's horses—er, fancy?"

"Ooh, yes sir. I heard his coachman tell Squire's that he paid £250 for one of his hunters! And the mistress's mare was a pretty, lively thing too."

"She rides herself, then? It must have been difficult to part with her horse."

"Well, meself, I think the gig was more of a loss." Molly eased the bit into Lookout's mouth and looped the bridle over his ears. "A ridin' horse just gets you someplace, where a carriage is good for carryin' parcels and all sorts o' reasons."

Evan agreed it was as he checked the girth. "I don't suppose your mistress has much time to ride for pleasure. She helps with the housework, I think?"

"Yes, sir. I seen her scrub till her hands bled, and then there's the chickens and the garden and meals 'n all. She spends a lot o' time with the child too, learnin' him his letters 'n I don't know what besides."

"She's teaching you to read also, Julian tells me."

She blushed. "Aye, but I'm not near so quick as the young master."

Decidedly precocious in other ways, though—bright and engaging and very feminine, her talents as a groom notwithstanding.

He'd thought her a child, but already Molly was a young woman whose preoccupation with her sweetheart had led to Julian's misadventure. At fourteen, Alberta and Elizabeth had still been learning their stitches and French verbs in the schoolroom.

He thanked her for her help and pressed a shilling into her hand. Nothing out of the ordinary in society stables, but Molly opened her eyes wide, grinned, and curtsied, and held the stirrup for him as he mounted. Then she ran back to the house with her unexpected wealth.

Evan smiled at the irony as he rode away toward the Manor. In a conversation aimed at learning more about Mrs. Moore, he knew the maid more intimately than the mistress. Would that a paltry shilling could win *her* good will.

𝕾 5 𝕾

Deborah returned to the parlor after Mr. Haverfield left the house and watched out the side window until he rode through the gate and out of sight toward the Manor, hoping he *would* return while wishing he would not.

Why had she thought him tongue-tied? On the contrary, he was lamentably persistent. No doubt he would be leaving Whately soon— all the better for her peace of mind.

Julian awakened from his nap fretful and fevered, with heavy eyes, sore throat, and a deepening cough. He ate nothing, Deborah and Molly not much more. Deborah spent the evening coddling him, applying cool cloths to his hot face, and replacing the blankets he continually kicked off.

Finally she sent Molly off to bed in her little room off one end of the kitchen. She gave Julian a dose of laudanum, undressed for bed, and lay down with him in her own room, which boasted a fireplace. Though quieter, he continued restless, coughing and moaning, and toward dawn he grew agitated and fearfully hot. As soon as there was sufficient light for the girl to see her way, Deborah woke Molly and sent her for the doctor.

It was several hours before Doctor Overley put in an appearance. Deborah paced the floor, teeth clenched so hard her head ached. *Probably busy with his fancy toilette.* Julian was restless too, tossing and turning in the bed. She picked him up and sat down to wait in the big upholstered chair by the fire.

Finally footsteps sounded on the stairs. Molly appeared in the doorway, and the doctor oozed in behind her, stinking of musk. Julian began fidgeting again.

"My dear Mrs. Moore, I am so sorry to hear that your little fellow is ailing. I confess I was concerned after his prolonged exposure the other day that some illness might accrue from the experience. Let's see what we have here, shall we?"

Deborah carried Julian to the bed and unwrapped the arms that clung around her neck. The doctor listened to all she had to say about the child's symptoms and felt his forehead in a cursory fashion, listened to his breathing through an ear trumpet, and pronounced a serious inflammation of the lungs.

"I will send the apothecary a list of medications, and his man will bring them by." He glanced at the bottle on the night table. "You'll be needing more laudanum—'tis best to keep the patient quiet. A saline draught for the fever, and a wash for cooling the skin. For the cough, Powell's Balsam of Aniseed. Also, he must be bled—"

"Oh, Doctor. Surely, such a small child—"

He frowned. "Well, well, we might wait until tomorrow, perhaps, and see how he goes on. But if there is no improvement, I shall have to insist. It is crucial to rid the body of toxins in this manner, as I am sure you know. If the illness does not respond to that, we shall have to consider blistering as well. "Now, Mrs. Moore, if you would be so kind as to grant me a moment of your time…"

Deborah felt far from kind, but she left Molly with Julian and escorted the doctor downstairs. In the hall, he took one of her hands between both of his. They were thick and soft, clammy like a plucked chicken.

"I shall not pretend, Mrs. Moore, that your son's illness is not quite serious. He will without doubt require intensive nursing from you, as well as daily visits from me, for many days. Now, my dear, I have a fair notion of your current circumstances, and I would be pleased to suggest an alternative to monetary payment."

Deborah tried to draw her hand away, but he held it firm. She swallowed hard. "And what might that be, sir?"

He turned her hand palm up and rubbed the inside of her wrist with his thumb. She watched with horrified fascination as his thumb moved back and forth, turning the blood in her veins to ice. His other hand held her arm above the wrist—a deceptively light grip, she discovered when she tried again to withdraw.

"Let us just say, Mrs. Moore—may I call you Deborah?—that I have admired your—ah—beauty for quite some time, and have been eagerly awaiting your emergence from mourning. Nothing, you see—"

"You mistake—"

"No, let me finish, my dear. Nothing could bring me to intrude upon that sacred and vulnerable state. But now that is past, Deborah —" he fixed his eyes on her bosom, "—I feel quite sure we could find a great deal of enjoyment in each other's—ah—company."

No more! Deborah snatched her hand away and backed out of his reach. She itched to slap him but dared not. She needed him too badly. *Julian* needed him.

"You presume too much, sir. Believe me, my circumstances do not compel me to consider your proposition. Rest assured that your bill will be paid promptly, in full." How she would accomplish that, she had no idea. And by heaven, he'd better give her no reason to doubt that he'd done his best!

"Ah, Deborah, so proud," he murmured. "Think of all the worthwhile things you could obtain with that money. New gowns for yourself, a decent education for your son. I do hope you will reconsider, my dear."

"The only thing I'm likely to reconsider, sir," she responded through clenched teeth, "is my decision not to slap you."

He laughed. Deborah trembled, furious and impotent. The effrontery of the man!

"Well, well, we shall see." He reached for his expensive greatcoat. She made no move to help him, so he shrugged himself into it and headed toward the door. Deborah held it open for him—she could not wait to be rid of him.

As he passed her he stopped, too close, and stroked her cheek. She jerked her head away. He curled around his fat finger a tendril of hair that had escaped from her hastily-made bun and whispered into one unwilling ear. "Ah, the touch of a lover, Deborah. I know you miss it..."

He went through the door chuckling, and she stood with clenched fists, watching as his groom handed him into his phaeton, got up behind and took the reins. The doctor smiled upon her beatifically and tipped his hat as they drove off. All those capes, as though he were some Corinthian, yet he didn't even drive his own horses.

Deborah slammed the door and leaned against it for support. She shut her eyes and bit her lip, willing herself to ignore his final words. They were true enough; there were nights when... But heaven forbid she should *ever* be so desperate as to let that slimy, vainglorious *worm* into her bed. *New gowns, he says. What mother would think of new gowns at a time like this!*

She would have given much to escape into the cold and walk until her rage abated, or failing that, to sleep for three days. But those things were impossible. She went to the kitchen and splashed some cold water on her face, took several deep breaths, and returned to the sickroom.

The day seemed quite long enough without callers. Half asleep, Deborah was startled when Molly came in and announced that Mr. Haverfield was below. She almost denied herself, but his timing was fortunate as Julian slept quietly for the moment. She tidied her hair, smoothed down her old wool dress, and made her appearance in the parlor while Molly sat with the boy.

Mr. Haverfield turned from the window to greet her. His eyes widened and then puckered with concern, giving her a pretty clear idea what she must look like.

"I fear I am not at my best today, Mr. Haverfield."

He took her hands. "Julian is no better, then?"

"No, much worse."

"I'm sorry to hear that. Molly is with him?"

"Yes. He's sleeping, or I couldn't leave him."

"I shan't keep you for long. Can you sit with me for a few minutes?"

Deborah nodded. It occurred to her that she felt no compulsion to escape from *his* grasp. He sat next to her on the sofa. "You've had the doctor to him?"

"Yes." She looked down at her hands in her lap. She didn't want to think about the doctor. "Inflammation of the lungs. He sent some medications, but I think it must be several days before... And he talks of bleeding him, but I don't know if I can bear that."...

"Why so? It's accepted practice."

"I know that. But he is so young. I'm afraid..." They'd bled Hartley so many times while he was ill, bled him until he had no blood left, a white wraith that shriveled and faded away.

"I'm sure it will not come to that," he said. He was no physician; he could not possibly know that. Why should his words comfort her?

He rose to take his leave. "I'll let you get back to your invalid. But is there any way I can be of assistance? I know Lord Latimer could spare a servant for a few days. Or perhaps Miss Reston could bear you company? I would be pleased to make the arrangements."

"I thank you, but no. Molly can do all that's necessary outside the sickroom. While Julian is confined, we are confined as well, and our needs will be small."

He looked dissatisfied. But it was hardly his place to insist, and he did not. "I will stop by again tomorrow, if I may."

"Of course, sir. I know you'll understand if I cannot see you, that I am unable to leave Julian."

He would not allow her, today, to call Molly to his assistance. "I'm entirely capable of saddling a horse on my own, you know." She hardly heard him. He took her hand and kissed it as she let him out the kitchen door and hurried back to her son.

Mr. Haverfield dropped from her mind soon enough.

Yet she noticed, sometime later, that she could still feel the touch of his lips on the back of her hand.

eborah and Molly hovered by the bed the following morning while Doctor Overley examined his patient. Deborah's skin crawled every time he looked at her, which was far too often. He had kissed her hand when he arrived—his kiss lingered as Mr. Haverfield's had, but it felt like a cancer planted beneath her skin.

Someone pounded on the door downstairs, and Molly turned to go. *No!* Deborah did not want to be alone with him, chaperoned only by a half-conscious child. Brushing past her maid, Deborah went to answer the door herself.

Mr. Haverfield stood on the step, his back to the door, surveying the fancy high-perch phaeton that waited in the street. He turned to her and said, "Good morning."

She all but dragged him into the hall, muttering something, she hardly knew what, as she took his hat, gloves, scarf, and riding crop, piling them all unceremoniously on the table. He made no complaint, though he hung up his own greatcoat rather than delivering it into her hands.

"Is it the doctor's carriage outside? It seems a rather elaborate vehicle for a village physician."

"Yes, it is his." Her voice was strained. He studied her, a crease between his eyebrows.

He took her hand. "What is it? Bad news?"

"No—I don't know yet." It was humiliating to find herself in need of a knight, but she asked anyway. "Would you step upstairs with me, Mr. Haverfield?"

His brows rose. "Of course, ma'am, if you wish it."

He looked baffled. She was sorry for it but could not possibly explain. She preceded him up the dark, narrow stairs.

They nearly collided with Molly, who was leaving the bedchamber with the reeking chamber pot filled with soiled rags. Entering the room, they found Doctor Overley peering into the little mirror over her dressing table, shaking out his lace cuffs, and straightening his complicated cravat. He smiled at Deborah's reflection as she came through the doorway, but it was quickly replaced by a frown when he saw Mr. Haverfield behind her.

"Ah, there you are, my dear." He took hold of her elbow as though he had some claim on her, in case Mr. Haverfield had misunderstood the endearment. "If I might confer with you downstairs, Mrs. Moore?"

"Mr. Haverfield is a friend of the family, sir. I depend upon his experience and advice."

The doctor dropped his hand, his manner shifting abruptly from ingratiating to glacial—a decided improvement.

"I see. Are you a physician, sir?"

"No."

"Well, then." He dismissed Mr. Haverfield with a wave of his hand. "Madam, I must tell you that I see no improvement in your son's condition. On the contrary, I find him in a considerably worse state than yesterday. His lungs are extremely congested, and I am sure you have taken note of the blood in his phlegm." Deborah drooped but said nothing. Mr. Haverfield laid a hand on her back. "I must tell you that without releasing the poisons through bloodletting, there is very little likelihood of recovery."

If he was trying to punish her, he had the perfect means to do so. He must love playing God. Her hands hurt, one gripping the fist of the other inside it. She pressed them against her lips and turned toward the bed.

Mr. Haverfield stepped past her, shielding her from the doctor's gaze. "Surely there's some alternative, Overley," Mr. Haverfield suggested. "Some new medication, or—"

"There is not."

Deborah's hands fell to her sides and then spread wide in submission. All night she had dreaded this, braced herself for it. Yet she did not feel braced at all.

"The surgeon will come in the morning, then. Now, Mrs. Moore, if you'll just—"

"I will see you out, Overley," Mr. Haverfield said, propelling him out of the room as the doctor shot an indignant look over his shoulder.

You should be relieved, Doctor. I might kick you down the stairs, watch you roll to the bottom, and brush my hands at a job well done.

But then she'd have to walk back into the sickroom, and there would be no doctor to call on.

Every nerve stretched to breaking point, her stomach roiling, she clung to the bedpost, listening for the door downstairs. *What could they possibly be doing?* She waited for what felt like an hour, and finally it snapped shut.

She exhaled. Smoothed the hair from Julian's forehead. Tucked his arms under the covers. Straightened the sheet, then the blanket, and pulled them to his chin. *A man's footsteps on the stairs.* She turned to the table beside the bed and lined up the medicine bottles in order by height. Wiped a wet spot with her apron. Shifted the doctor's written instructions so they lined up perfectly with the edge of the table. Picked out the bottle she needed and slid it out of its military formation.

Mr. Haverfield must have been watching her because he prodded from the doorway, "What is it?"

Oh, why hadn't he gone away? She wanted to scream, cry, break something. But he was standing there, watching her. "I... oh, he is so detestable! I cannot stand to be in the same room with him."

"I'd find him rather laughable in different circumstances. But he upsets *you*, which is reason enough to... I wasn't sure what you wanted me to do."

"It's enough that you were here." She'd have liked him to throw the man out the window, but she could hardly say that. It would make her sound as irrational as she felt.

She poured a draught for Julian, but he roused himself to fight the vile stuff. Half of it ended on the boy's chin and half on the sheets. Deborah's hands shook as she swiped at the tears that rolled down her cheeks.

Calmly Mr. Haverfield held out his hand for the spoon. "Let me see what I can do." His voice sounded hoarse.

She measured out another dose and watched with resentment as Julian swallowed the medicine with only a muttered complaint. He might as well have said "Yes, sir." *She* was his mother—why should he obey Mr. Haverfield? She could not even tell that he recognized the man, yet he graced him with a wan smile as they laid his head back on the pillow.

Mr. Haverfield took his leave a few minutes later. Finally she was alone again, alone with her nightmares.

"Mama!" Waking in her cold room from a restless, fevered sleep, it felt as though she'd been calling forever. Why didn't she come?

She focused on the familiar furnishings so she wouldn't have to think about the shadows in the corners. There was the little table with its child-size chairs where they sat to do lessons when Mama had the time. There was her little window seat where the cold winter moon peeked in. There she would put her bed pillow for a cushion and sit for ages, looking out over their wild little garden, and beyond that the pasture where Mr. Johnstone kept his dreadful bull. Beyond the fence lay a piece of moorland, and away beyond that a glimpse of the very top of Lydford Castle where Papa said naughty children were put in prison and made to drink molten tin. Mrs. Maddox said that wasn't true, they were criminals and it was hundreds of years ago, but it haunted her, nevertheless.

There, hung on the wall, was the little pouch Mrs. Maddox had sewn from the fancy brocade they'd used for the draperies in Papa's library, and in it, "for better luck someday, child," a real penny from the ancient Lydford mint. There on the shelves were her two books, dog-eared from use; and filling the space, all her treasures collected from the outdoors—dried flowers and pine cones, some rocks, a butterfly wing, half of a blackbird's egg, feathers from robin, chaffinch, and kestrel, a wren's nest, even the skull of a mouse or some similar creature. Mama didn't like that one at all.

"Mama!" Why didn't she come? Her rushlight had gone out, and the room was all shadows now. The bed was wet with sweat and urine, her pillow was wet with tears. It was so cold. Turning the pillow over took all the energy she had. Too weak and dizzy to get up and strip the sheets, she curled up small in the driest corner, pulled the blanket up to cover everything but her eyes and nose, and lay staring blindly at the boarded-up fireplace where the good-luck penny hung, waiting for daylight and Mama.

DEBORAH AWOKE with a start and turned to check her own sick child, tossing in the bed beside her. Had Julian cried out as she had in her dream? His eyes glittered strangely in the dim light from the fire. She got up and stoked the smoldering coals back to life. Then she lit the candle by the bed and looked at Hartley's watch that she kept on the table there: half past three. She had slept for two hours, the longest stretch in the past two days, though it could hardly have been called restful. Thirty minutes yet until the next round of medicines was due.

Julian called out plaintively. She lay down again on her side and drew him into the curve of her body, kissing his lank hair and murmuring in his ear until he relaxed again into a half sleep.

Her thoughts returned to the dream. One of many nights, hidden for so long yet remembered still, right down to the excruciating desolation. Now a mother herself, she'd come to recognize the sacrifices her mother had made. She could see now how her mother had drawn her father's anger to herself, as a rabbit leads the fox away from its burrow to protect its young, even at the risk of its own life. She never knew why Mama had not come to her sickbed that particular lonely night, but no doubt there had been reasons, probably painful ones.

Her father's hatred had been a mystery to her. At six, she had only known that staying quiet and out of his way gave her the best chance of avoiding his wrath. She was Jack, hiding in the cupboard, carefully scouting each corridor before entering it, always ready to bolt for that safe place where the Giant could not penetrate.

Gradually she became aware that some families behaved differently, that other children laughed and ran and climbed trees and went on outings and were taught to ride by indulgent fathers. That knowledge came from the conversation of the household servants and from the vastly different treatment accorded to the boy Robert after he came to live with them. Deborah rarely met him face-to-face, for he lived in the front of the house and she in the back, but she saw him from her window, playing with the dogs or riding his pony, and she heard him below, running up the stairs and banging doors, making all the noise she dared not make.

Oh, the Giant sometimes took a cane to Robert too, but Robert had a working fireplace and a nursemaid, and was allowed privileges Deborah never imagined. Taught always to refer to him as her brother, she knew always that he was not quite. She'd learned much later that her father had sired him by some woman other than her mother and foisted him onto society as his heir.

From the day the attending physician informed the impatient father that his wife would bear no more children, Deborah was relegated to nursery and kitchens until she was old enough to help with the cooking, cleaning, and laundry—skills that had served her well since Hartley's death. And her mother had turned from wife to housekeeper.

The people of Lydford probably thought Mrs. Carlington fortunate. They saw the new carpet in the drawing room, the silver epergne on the dining table, and the fashionable clothes her mother wore. They did not see the family's private rooms, stripped of everything saleable, or the clothes Mrs. Carlington changed into as soon as they left. And they did not see, as Deborah did, the bruises and scars her mother wore under those clothes.

Deborah was trapped as well, even now, but she no longer had to hide from the Giant, or listen to her mother's stifled tears, or check to make sure her sleeves covered her own bruises. Her snare was merely financial. So long as she had Julian and funds enough to keep them both after some fashion, she was content.

She rose to prepare the boy's medicines. He was limp and lethargic, without the energy to do more than cry weakly in protest. Later in the day she supposed—almost hoped—he would fight her as he had the previous afternoon. He'd been so docile with Mr. Haverfield—and *she* had been criminally ungrateful. Regardless, she could hardly expect Mr. Haverfield to stand in as nurse. The thought was laughable. Seductive. Perilous. Impossible.

In any case, he and Viscount Latimer had gone to enjoy a couple of days' shooting with a friend near Nuneaton. He'd promised to call upon his return, but probably she would never see him again. Promises meant nothing.

7

"I'll leave you two to your port." Amanda rose from the table. "And in case I don't see you before you leave tomorrow, have a pleasant visit."

Evan stood as well. "Good night, then." When the door had closed behind her, he sat down again.

Latimer poured a glass for each of them and took a sip. "You're mighty quiet tonight, Haverfield. Is it something to do with your widow? I'm surprised m' sister didn't ask at dinner."

Amanda hadn't needed to ask—she'd gotten his report earlier. "About the trip tomorrow... I can't go, Frank."

Latimer brought his fist down on the table. "Damn it, Haverfield. You said at breakfast you would go. I'm counting on your company."

"I know." He'd cogitated on it all afternoon and finally made up his mind. "But the boy is near death."

"And is there any earthly thing you can do to stop it?"

Evan pressed his fingertips against his eyelids until he saw stars. Then he rubbed his hands down his face and returned the only possible answer. "No."

"Of course not. So why—"

"She's so alone." He got up again, wandered over to the window, and spoke into the darkness beyond. "They're going to bleed him tomorrow."

"So what? Prinny does it for fun."

Evan spun to face him. "Prinny's not five years old. And they could take twenty pounds of blood without putting a dent in his bulk."

Latimer let out a crack of laughter. "True enough. But the fact remains, it's done all the time. Why the drama?"

Evan turned back to the window. "She's afraid of it. I'm not sure why."

"Just one of those maggots women get in their heads, I expect." Glassware clinked as Latimer poured himself more port. "Do you love her, Evan?"

Evan jumped. "What? Are you crazy? I've only just met her. I…" He jabbed one hand through his hair. "I don't know."

"Surely you ain't thinking marriage?"

Evan sighed and came back to the table. "Lord no. It's impossible, even if I wanted it."

Latimer leaned forward, hands slapping down on the polished mahogany. "Then what do you think you're doing, man?" he exploded. "There's already gossip. Does that help her? How long do you think she'd survive in this town on your *carte blanche*, or even the appearance of it? Or are you planning to move her to London? Or maybe Northridge. Your family would love that!"

Evan surged to his feet. "I'm not *planning* anything, you crackbrain. And if you think I'd—"

"And what if she gets another maggot in her head and decides *she* loves *you*? Does that help her after you leave town?"

Evan glowered at his friend for a long moment. It was all true, every blasted word of it. He dropped back into his chair and downed his port. He needed something stronger, something to knock him out for a week, or a year.

When Latimer spoke again, his voice was gentle. "That's just it, man. You're not planning, you're not thinking. It can't work the way you want it to, and it can't work the way you *don't* want it to. Best to let it go." He refilled Evan's glass and stood up, yawning. "I'll see you in the morning. We leave at eight."

Evan was ready in plenty of time. What sleep he'd had made him wish he hadn't gone to bed at all. So he was in place, seated behind the leader with reins in hand, when Latimer arrived in the stable yard.

"Hey," Latimer exclaimed, "that's my curricle and my horses."

"Yes, well, the early bird gets to drive." It wasn't very funny, but at least it showed his good will. One did not discard twenty years of friendship over a bit of truth-telling, no matter how unpalatable it was. And he much preferred to do the driving—it gave him something to think about besides what might be happening in a certain humble cottage on Whately's high street. Cervantes had called absence *that common cure of love*—well, that remained to be seen. If it even *was* love.

It was an easy two-hour drive to Mr. Sherill's estate. They could not talk about those unpalatable truths with the groom up behind them, and it was a subject best avoided in any case. Latimer was full of chatter but thankfully did not require much of Evan's attention. An occasional chuckle or grunt seemed to satisfy him.

They spent the afternoon shooting with a congenial group of fellows, houseguests like themselves. Here too, Evan found his mind was largely free to wander. The conversation consisted of muted words like "Look, over there," followed by a gunshot, then "Oh, jolly good shot!"

The birds had nothing to say but an occasional squawk.

But the evening's dinner party was agony. If Dante had needed another circle for hell, he might have chosen tedium. Mr. Sherill and his mother had invited everyone they knew, it seemed, most of them strangers to Evan. The gentlemen talked of nothing but hunting and horses—which should have made him happy but didn't—and the ladies appeared peculiarly undistinguished in beauty, conversation, and accomplishments.

Was that merely because of his fixation on a woman who was not there? Deborah Moore could claim no greater talent for conversation than his fellow guests and no superior accomplishments, either, unless one counted cooking and mending and teaching children to read. More practical than playing the harp or painting mediocre watercolors, but hardly lady-like. And beauty? *He* saw it, but Latimer did not.

So why do I find her so captivating?

The following afternoon, they headed home behind Latimer's new team of bays, purchased from Mr. Sherill. They proved strong and fast, if not fast enough to suit Evan.

He'd hoped to reach Whately early enough for a brief visit to Mrs. Moore, but there was scarcely time to seek out Amanda before dressing for dinner.

He found her in the library. "The favor I asked of you—I hope it was not too great an imposition?"

"Heavens, no. I was thrilled to have something to do. They threw me out of Reston Park. Thought Meg and Julia had head colds, but the doctor says it's influenza. Most of the household has it now. I wanted to help, but I think they wanted to get rid of me. Can you imagine?"

Evan could. Amanda was much too high-spirited for a sickroom. "Is it serious?"

"Oh no, the girls are already on the mend. The ball is just two weeks away. You may be sure they'll be healthy by then."

"Tell me, how did you find Mrs. Moore?"

"She couldn't see me when I first called, but I had better luck today. We visited for ten minutes, but I think it was just out of courtesy. She looked every bit as ill as the Restons, only she can't blame it on influenza."

Evan opened his mouth to ask after the boy, but the viscount walked in and he dropped the subject.

Much of the dinner conversation revolved around the Latimers' upcoming house party. It had been Frank's plan, which meant there *was* no plan to speak of. "I was in London last month and invited most everyone I saw. Including your sister Lady Witney and the earl. Other than that, let me think: Walton and Westwood and Lord Hartwell and—"

"A fine collection of rakes and gamblers," Evan said, working his way through the stewed rabbit. "Don't you know any respectable people, Latimer?"

The viscount set down his fork and leaned forward. "Well, this is interesting. I ran into Sudbury and his eldest sister in Bond Street, and when I mentioned *your* name, what do you think *she* said?"

"I can't begin to imagine."

"She said '*Indeed!*' in *such* a tone, and then she lifted her eyebrows at Sudbury and said, 'Lowell, dear, we don't have any plans for New Year's, do we?'" He grinned, wiggling his eyebrows up and down. "She's a beautiful girl, don't you think?"

Evan choked on his wine. "Lady Blythe? She's pretty enough, but hardly *respectable*. She's a flirt and a tease, and sooner or later she's going to compromise some poor gent. Scares me to death. She's coming here?"

"Don't know yet." Latimer turned to his sister, a gleam of excitement in his eyes. "Did anything come in the mail while we were gone?"

"Not from Lady Blythe," said Amanda.

"Anyway," Evan said, "why would she be angling for me? You've got a title—she should try for you. Why don't you court her and put the rest of us out of harm's way?"

Latimer cleared his throat. "Well—have you met the younger sister? Lady Honora?"

"No." Evan sat back with his wine glass and a sigh of discontent. "Is she prettier than Blythe?"

"Oh, you know I prefer fair women."

"When do all these people descend upon us?" Evan asked.

"Over New Year's. We'll celebrate New Year's Eve at the village ball."

Evan grunted and drained his burgundy.

"I had to invite Sudbury," Latimer said, on the defensive. "He's the best of good fellows." Evan shook his head. In Latimer's book, that merely meant he was a clipping rider and an intrepid sportsman. "And I figured you might at least enjoy an innocent flirtation!"

"I do, Frank. But there's nothing innocent about Blythe. She's like a particularly bloodthirsty hawk."

"Well, maybe some of those rakes you object to will come through. Don't know Westwood that well, but perhaps Hartwell—"

"Sorry to disappoint you," Amanda interrupted. "We did get a letter from *him*. He's engaged and wants to bring his fiancée."

"Damn!" Latimer growled. "When did marriage become a contagious disease?"

Amanda ignored him. "And your sister sent an acceptance as well, Evan." She sorted through a small pile of mail beside her plate and handed him a letter. "Here, you can read it for yourself."

He skimmed his older sister's familiar handwriting. She and Theo were spending Christmas with Mama and Papa but would be delighted to celebrate the New Year and Twelfth Night at Whately Manor. Why, in heaven's name? Theo, the Earl of Witney, moved in a different realm than Latimer—politics, not horses, were the center of his world.

Alberta must have some reason for dragging her husband here other than the pleasure of Evan's company. They'd seen each other quite recently. Probably she was hoping there would be some titled lady—or at least a rich one—she could talk Evan into marrying. It had become a family project.

8

He let the horse pick its way through the darkness toward Mrs. Moore's cottage. Regardless of Latimer's objections, he had to see her, however briefly, and put his mind at rest. Yet oddly, he was not eager to arrive. He'd chased an almond around his plate for ten minutes while Amanda described all the preparations for the ball. Finally she asked about Frank's new horses. *That* subject had already consumed more of Evan's attention than he could stand, and he left them to it. Rude, no doubt, but no more so than sitting there in a brown study, absorbed in a depressing little world of his own.

Marriage! Ugh. If only he could be sure of finding himself in Elizabeth's sort of marriage. She and Philip were proof that one could be married *and* happy, even in Yorkshire. Thank heavens *he* would never have to live there. Evan supposed he would wind up settling down with Melanie Littleton, just as Mama wanted. The thought was disheartening. They would be comfortable and respectful, civilized in every way. And he would always wonder if he had missed his own *bright, particular star* somewhere along the road.

It sometimes seemed he must have met every eligible woman in England, but of course he had not. No doubt, among those some were pretty, some smart, some alluring; some might make him laugh, some might make him sing—though they'd regret that soon enough—and one of them might make him blissfully happy... if only he could find her.

Deborah Moore was pretty, and smart, and alluring. The first woman to deal him a knockout punch. But there was that other, ugly word, the one Latimer kept invoking—*eligible.* Whatever her birth and education might be, her current situation made her completely, definitively unacceptable. He bit down hard on the irony of it.

Despite her status, she was still subject to society's rules. That was one of Frank's truths the other evening. Evan had given Overley a tongue-lashing the other day for *his* improper attentions, but he was guilty himself. An unmarried woman receiving in her home a single, unaccompanied gentleman always risked ruin. How much more so in the dark of night. He would be doing Mrs. Moore no favors by exposing her to gossip.

He needn't have worried. He never even saw the high street, so no one saw him except Molly. A lantern wobbled about in the yard as Evan approached the side gate. In its erratic light, he saw the girl returning from the far end of the garden, lantern in one hand and empty washtub in the other. She jumped when the gate creaked open, dropping the metal tub with a clatter onto the rocks that edged the little garden. But she ran to hold Lookout, bobbing a curtsy.

"Evenin', sir."

Evan swung to the ground, responding in kind. "How does the boy go on, Molly?"

Her face fell. "Ooh, not well at all, sir. He's coughin' up blood and rants like old King George half the time." Evan frowned. "And your mistress?"

"About dead on her feet, she is. She ain't hardly left his bedside while you was away, nor ate, nor slept."

Damn. He shouldn't have gone. "I know it's late. Do you think she'd see me for a few minutes?"

"I 'spect she would if I take you up so she don't have to come downstairs." They led the horse into the shed, but aside from removing the bit from his mouth and throwing a blanket over saddle and all, left him ready for the return ride to the Manor. Then they entered the house through the kitchen.

Evan followed Molly up the stairs, lit by a single candle in a sconce. Tallow, by the smell of it. On the landing, he waited while the maid informed her mistress of his visit.

At Molly's nod, he entered to find mother and son in the chair by the fire. Mrs. Moore turned toward him, her face white and haggard. Julian's lay on his mother's shoulder, hidden in shadow. Evan could see little more than the glitter of his eyes and one thin arm wrapped around his mama's neck.

"I must apologize for disturbing you so late, ma'am. Miss Latimer's report of you left me uneasy."

"It's good of you to venture out in the cold for our sakes, sir." Her voice was distant, toneless.

Evan squatted down to look directly into Julian's face. "How are you, my young friend?" The boy lifted a languid hand, which Evan took and held. *So hot.* "Not quite up to snuff today? Have you been behaving for your mama?"

Julian coughed, wracking his little body, and turned his head away.

He shifted his gaze to Mrs. Moore. "Does that mean no?"

She lifted a hand to her mouth to conceal a yawn. "To tell the truth, I would prefer him to fight me. He is alarmingly docile."

Evan pulled a stool from the dressing table over to the bed, sitting with his back against the mattress.

His hostess bit her lip. "I'm sorry to receive you here. The accommodations leave much to be desired."

"Nonsense. It is a bedchamber, after all." Never mind that his mother's and sisters' bedchambers had dressing rooms this size and attached sitting rooms with sofas and chairs to seat a dozen in comfort. The few other "ladies" whose private quarters he had infiltrated were high-class courtesans whose rooms were business suites, after all, though decorated—and scented—for frivolity.

They spent several minutes discussing Julian's condition, but Evan learned little. He asked about the bloodletting, expecting to see a shudder or a grimace, perhaps a spurt of rage. But she merely laid her head against the back of the chair, expressionless, looking down to adjust Julian's blanket. "I saw no change, for good or ill. He's to repeat the procedure tomorrow."

"Did Overley say—"

"How was your visit to Nuneaton?"

Evan didn't believe she cared a whit, but it seemed any questions about the doctor would go unanswered. Impossible to sit still and watch the two of them—he'd tear his hair out. Instead, he stood up and prowled the room while describing the petty details of their sojourn, doing his best to make them diverting. Of his own impatience to return to Whately, he said nothing.

She was half asleep when Evan finished. He stood beside her chair watching the firelight play across her hollowed cheeks, the dejected droop of her mouth, the shadows beneath her eyes. His mouth twisted. So much for his attempt at entertainment.

She jerked awake. "I am so sorry." She reached out her free hand as though to touch him but hurriedly withdrew it again. "You must think me—"

"I think you are worn out. Can you not put him in bed and get some sleep yourself?"

She shook her head. "He is restless in bed, and it is worst at night. I get more sleep this way—but I assure you I do not usually sleep when we have company."

"Then don't think of me as company." He paused, undecided. "Let me take your seat for a while, if he will accept me. You don't look at all well yourself, and it will do Julian no good if you—"

"No." Anger flared in her face. "That's not necessary."

"Pardon me, but I think it is." She squeezed her eyes shut.

Evan wanted to kiss those bruised eyelids, take her in his arms and comfort her. But it was indisputably the wrong time, and unthinkable in any event. Instead he lifted Julian from his mother's lap. The boy made no protest, wrapping his arms quite naturally around Evan's neck.

This might be the most honorable thing I've ever done.

It might also be the most foolish.

§

IT WAS dark when Deborah awoke. She drifted on the edge for some minutes, barely aware that she was in Julian's little bed rather than her own, hesitant to leave the blessedly mindless void that enveloped her. No worries, no emotion, no uncertainty. Then her feet bumped against the unfamiliar footboard as she stretched beyond the warm circle where she had lain unmoving for—how long?

Oh God, too long, surely! Her candle had burned out. She scrambled into her gown in the darkness, tying the ribbons any which way, but could find only one shoe. After opening the door to let in a little light from the hallway, she spotted it deep under the bed and pulled it out. She allowed herself one minute to restore a semblance of order to her hair.

She must have looked a mess as she pushed open the door to the sickroom—oh, the stench! Happily, Mr. Haverfield was rumpled as well. In wrinkled shirtsleeves, with waistcoat askew and cravat crushed beyond repair, he stood by the nightstand perusing the collection of vials that lived there now. Julian lay in bed watching him through slitted eyes, his hands fidgeting with his little stuffed pony.

"I am so sorry," Deborah exclaimed. Hartley's watch told her it was past midnight. "I never meant to…" More than two hours she had slept while her guest tended her child, even apparently helping him to use the chamber pot. "Let me just…" She moved the offending article into Julian's room and closed his door.

Mr. Haverfield stared at her as she flustered about, his lips compressed in a straight line, his brows drawn together. He must resent her sleeping so long, and no wonder.

"I apologize again, sir. I don't know how I came to…" She hastened toward him, expecting him to move aside, but he did not.

Instead, he smiled. Just a softening of his face, really, but she could swear there was sympathy in it. And he did not *sound* resentful. "I'm glad you slept. If you would just sit with Julian, and perhaps help me interpret these rather cryptic instructions. The doctor must be a devotee of riddles."

"Never mind. I know the dosages by heart."

Deborah held Julian's head while Mr. Haverfield administered the medicines. She kissed her son's forehead and laid him down again. And still the man lingered.

"I'm afraid you had a difficult time with him while I was asleep."

"Not so bad. He slept as well for part of the time."

At last he picked up his coat. "I suppose I should be heading back."

Julian appeared to be asleep, but she whispered anyway in his ear. "I'll be right back." She accompanied Mr. Haverfield downstairs, taking the candle from her bedchamber to light their way through the dark kitchen. Once the door closed behind him, she rinsed her face and filled a pitcher to take upstairs.

The house felt empty without him. She had made assumptions about him at first sight based on his association with Viscount Latimer, his deportment, and his attire. Yet Mr. Haverfield had bothered himself to search for Julian while his friend had not. She knew nothing about him—where he was from, how he lived, what his fortune was, what family he had—yet when he looked into her eyes, she felt soothed... yet perturbed too.

Her father, her brother, her husband—all her limited experience with men told her they could not be trusted. Though her heart might tell her Mr. Haverfield was different, she could not afford to take that chance.

She was keenly aware of her loneliness, there in the dark, though it was a creature that lived with her always. Mostly it just kept her company, sitting at her feet or walking by her side, climbing the stairs with her as it did now. Sometimes, though, it leaped onto her chest and ripped open an old wound that never quite healed. *If Julian should die...*

She would not think it, *could* not think it. She stood in the doorway and watched him, drugged with laudanum, more unconscious than asleep. Such a serious child, as she herself had been. And lonely, as well. Her little Jack did not face the giant she herself had feared, yet here they were, confronting the biggest giant of them all. And she could do no more to protect him than her mother had done for her.

She had been thirteen when Matilda arrived, a fairy godmother-aunt dropped to Earth to rescue her from desolation. Matilda spent four years in Lydford instructing Deborah in literature, geography, history, and natural science, boldly taking her to see the dreaded castle and the fabulous gorge of which she had heard so much. Deborah saw that it was possible to defy her father's tyranny and began to despise her mother's weakness. And when Mama refused to come away with them, despite all their entreaties and exhortations, that betrayal had torn her apart.

Julian broke out in a fresh paroxysm of coughing. Deborah slapped the pitcher onto her dressing table, water sloshing over the rim, and returned to her place beside him. She drew his head and shoulders into her lap face-down to make the coughing a bit easier. None of Doctor Overley's remedies had effected any improvement whatsoever. These fits left him utterly weakened, too exhausted even to weep.

They sat that way until the candles guttered and another cold gray day seeped into the room. Deborah rubbed her son's back, held him together when he coughed, and kept him warm as the cold dread crept into every part of her.

Aunt Matilda had wrested her from the grip of one beast, but Deborah always suspected she had won only a temporary reprieve. If Julian died now, his death would be the price she paid for cheating fate.

A very high price, indeed.

✤ 9 ✤

fter sleeping until mid-morning, Evan strolled into the drawing room to find Amanda entertaining Whately's elderly vicar and his wife. "Refused to see us, Miss Latimer," Mrs. Hepplewhite was saying, "refused us absolutely. I am told the boy is near death. One would think the poor woman would be eager to receive our prayers and blessings. If she has turned away from the Lord since her husband's passing, then I must say it will not be surprising if He turns His face from her as well."

She turned to Evan, nostrils distended as though sniffing out evil. "I am also told that she has received *this* young man, into her bedchamber, no less. It is an abomination that a woman who served as this town's moral preceptress should now be so lost to all sense of propriety."

The woman faded from Evan's view—instead he saw Julian's pinched white face. The vicar said something—Evan heard only his own blood boiling in his ears, and then Amanda, uttering words he did not comprehend. Fury sizzling in his mouth like acid, he locked onto Mrs. Hepplewhite's sanctimonious blue gaze. "Were you also told, madam, that *Wherein thou judgest another, thou condemnest thyself?*"

The woman flushed an ugly red and opened her mouth to respond, but the vicar intervened, patting his wife's arm. "I understand from the good doctor that Mrs. Moore's bedchamber is currently serving as a sickroom. And we must remember, too, that Mr. Haverfield saved the child's life. I think we can grant Mrs. Moore some leniency, don't you, my dear?"

Her eyes continued to shoot sparks of malice Evan's way, but her mouth snapped shut into a thin, bloodless line, and she did not speak again. They left almost immediately. Evan held his breath until he heard the outer door close behind them.

Amanda drew a hand across her forehead. "Phew! I'm glad *he* is the vicar and not she. I promise you they would never see my face at church again. One might almost believe they worship different gods."

Evan had never been so glad to see the back of someone. Still simmering, he uttered some choice epithets as he strode across the room and back. "Who gave her the authority to pass judgment on anyone?"

Amanda giggled. "Can this really be mild-mannered Evan Haverfield? I thought you were going to explode."

"I thought I did." Evan came to a halt in front of her. "Tell me, did she come here just to berate Deborah Moore?"

"Oh no, there were some other matters. They wanted to assure themselves of flowers from our hothouses for the Christmas service. Not that we have very much, but—"

"I'd stuff the flowers down their self-righteous throats!" He took another angry turn around the room.

"Do stop pacing, Evan. That rug is quite ancient, you know. You might wear a hole right through it."

"Sorry." He stopped and took a deep breath. "The devil of it is, I cannot stay away. I feel responsible for the boy, and—" He raked a hand through his hair and nodded toward the door. "But that woman could make things very uncomfortable indeed for Mrs. Moore. Are there more like her?"

Amanda lifted one eyebrow. "It's an English village, Evan. But between us, I think we can paint quite a rosy picture of propriety for

Mrs. Hepplewhite and her kind." She propped her chin on one hand. "Now, let me think…"

In the drizzly dusk, they set out down the lane to visit Mrs. Moore. Amanda sat ensconced in Latimer's best carriage, and Evan rode Lookout alongside. She laughed through the open window, mischief in her face.

"I always wanted to be an actress," she said. "This big old carriage, and four horses, and the men in livery—it's hilarious for just a mile."

"Coachman's enjoying it as much as you are," Evan replied.

"Oh yes. Poor chap, he never gets to drive this contraption anymore."

As they approached the junction with the high street, Amanda giggled again and put up the window. Evan dropped behind and slipped through the side gate into Mrs. Moore's yard. He led Lookout into the shed as the coach lumbered around the corner, harness jangling. He made the horse comfortable as quickly as he could and emerged again into the evening. The carriage, standing in front of the cottage, hid him from the street.

He opened the kitchen door but recoiled on the threshold. *What the hell?* Were those *ghosts* cavorting in the murk?

He reached out and touched the coarse, damp cloth of a cheap bedsheet. It was merely laundry, a profusion of towels and bed linens hung to dry on lines strung across the room. He breathed again and began weaving his way through the maze.

He heard Molly come in. She screeched in fright when she saw him step around the other edge of a sheet and clapped a hand over her mouth.

"I'm so sorry," Evan said. "Did Miss Latimer not tell you I would be here?"

"Aye, but—" She glanced nervously over her shoulder. "I put her in the parlor, sir, is that right? She says I'm to see her out in twenty minutes." A cricket chirped somewhere near the hearth and Molly jumped. "Oh, sir, I'm so scared. It's been so quiet, like—like the house is just waitin' for death to come."

The bedroom door was ajar, the room beyond lit only by the fire and what light still filtered through two small windows. He tapped as he entered.

Mrs. Moore sat against the headboard, one hand cupping Julian's cheek and the other slack in her lap. She looked dull, limp, spiritless—neat, as usual, but as though she had spent not one unnecessary minute on her appearance. Her shoes lay on the floor by the bed, her hair was pulled back very simply, and she had on the same plain gray gown she'd worn the previous day.

She gazed directly into his face for some seconds. She said nothing, showed no surprise, no annoyance, nothing at all. Then she returned to her contemplation of Julian's still form. A slight wheeze as he breathed through dry, cracked lips was the only thing to tell the boy was alive. Evan saw no movement, no perceptible rise and fall of the bedclothes, no fevered muttering as in the past few days.

Half of him wanted to turn around and walk out again, ride back to Latimer's, collect Grady and his horses, and drive off somewhere. Most anywhere would do.

His other half—the better half, he supposed—made him walk quietly to the side of the bed and lay his hand on the boy's burning forehead. Why should he care so much about a child he'd known so briefly? A child unrelated to him, whom he had never seen healthy or happy?

Perhaps that was why. "How is he?"

"He's dying."

Just that bald statement in a voice like iron, hard and cold. Evan looked sharply at her, but her face was turned from him. Her callousness was appalling, unnatural. Could this be the same woman who'd come running into the inn a week ago with mud past her knees and panic in her eyes?

He jerked upright and strode angrily about the small room. He wanted to throw something. Surely any woman should demonstrate some emotion when saying such words of her own child! Had he misjudged her so grossly? He was angry with himself, furious with her, and enraged that God could think of stealing this child Evan thought he had saved and delivered into his mother's care six short days ago.

He turned back to the bed to find her eyeing him warily, like a cornered fox facing the baying hounds. He spoke through gritted teeth. "You take it mighty calmly, ma'am."

Color rushed to her face, suddenly twisted with passion. She thrust forward, her free hand clenched into a fist that dug into her thigh. Julian whimpered, and Evan could see the effort she made to relax. "No doubt I should be wailing and tearing out my hair. Perhaps I should throw myself into the river. But will you permit me to wait until he's actually dead?"

It was little more than a whisper for Julian's sake, yet it throbbed with defiance and sarcasm. And something else bled into her voice. *Terror.*

Evan's anger evaporated, and he moved to her side. He touched his fingers lightly to her cheek. "I'm sorry. I think you must be the strongest person I've ever met."

She gazed up at him, eyes wide, lips parted. A tremor in her voice sounded almost like laughter. "No, no, surely you have that wrong."

He resumed his pacing about the room, fidgeting with one thing and then another. "I don't mean that you feel less than anyone else. But you don't run from your difficulties, you just stare them in the face and keep going." He glanced into the mirror above her dressing table and quickly away again. "I, on the other hand, have made a practice of avoiding anything I don't want to think about."

"Believe me, I've done my share of running away." The hard edge was back in her voice. She looked down and said, more softly, "And you haven't run from us."

"Leaving you all alone in this crisis? I think not!" Yet he had thought about it, to his shame.

Mrs. Moore shook her head. "It's a crisis for me, of course. It need not be for you. We have absolutely no claim on you."

Evan picked up her little perfume bottle and cupped it in his palm. "But you do. There is a very sweet attraction at the center of this crisis. I can't seem to think about anything else." He kept his voice light, his eyes on the bottle. *God, my timing is atrocious.*

❧

DEBORAH'S FACE BURNED, and she ducked her head. He *must* mean his concern for Julian—that was natural enough under the circumstances. He had no earthly reason to like *her*. She had shown him the worst she had to offer, had been rude and hostile despite his extraordinary service.

Even if he loved her to madness—she winced with the pain and longing attached to the thought—what would their options be? She could not marry him. Nor did she believe *this* man would offer the sort of relationship Doctor Overley had in mind. And of course she would not accept such an offer, however tempting it might be coming from Mr. Haverfield. Evidently it was not morality but merely distaste for the man himself that made her shrink from the doctor's advances. That was a lowering thought. A giggle rose from somewhere inside, and she quashed it. It must be exhaustion, or perhaps hysteria.

Mr. Haverfield stoked the fire and lit the candles on the dressing table, and then turned the big upholstered chair to face the bed. He sat down, elbows on his knees and hands clasped under his chin. "Tell me, ma'am, what you've run from."

Deborah stared at him. Did he want her life story? Which sad, ugly part of it, exactly? Maybe the part where she abandoned her mother to a monster?

"There's a hint of something in your voice—the southwest, perhaps?"

"I grew up in Devon, sir. You'd not know the place."

"You might be surprised. I've explored a great many of England's out-of-the-way places."

He couldn't possibly want to hear about this. But she was so tired. It was much easier to answer his question than to frame one of her own. "My father's property, such as it is, lies in Lydford."

"Ah yes, I've been to Lydford." He sat back in the chair. "Passed

68

through with a friend a few years ago. There is some fascinating history, and of course the gorge is fabulous. But you would know that better than I."

Deborah snorted. "Yes, all that *fascinating history*. Prisons and coffins and thievery. As for the gorge, I saw it only once, and that just from the top—we hadn't time to make the descent." Even Matilda had not dared push Deborah's father too far.

His eyebrows rose questioningly. "It's a steep climb, but an easy day's outing. Surely the young people thereabouts must make it the object of pleasure excursions."

She looked down and stroked an errant wisp of Julian's hair into place. "I wouldn't know."

He paused. "When were you last at home?"

Home? "I left when I was seventeen and have never been tempted to return."

"But you still have family there?"

"When last I heard, yes." The most recent letter had come more than a year ago. Her mother's hand was shakier, but nothing else had changed much. Young Robert had been sent down from university— Deborah's father was never mentioned. As long as *he* lived, she would never consider revisiting Lydford.

The questions kept coming, increasingly uncomfortable as he probed for details. Deborah provided the shortest possible reply to each one, hoping he would give up. But he was patient, and persistent, and seemed interested in her answers. What did he think about them? About her?

It didn't matter. Her eyes stung with fatigue. She closed them, leaning her head against the headboard, and pretended she was talking to herself.

It was easier once Aunt Matilda entered the story. "I was her charity project, I think. She was determined to remove me from... from Lydford."

"Your parents didn't want you to go?"

"My mother did." And Mama's penance had been a beating that left her dizzy and badly bruised. She'd been allowed only the briefest of farewells to her only child that day they left. Maybe it had been easier that way.

"Where did you go?"

"To Plymouth. I found it daunting. So busy and important." Her heart beat faster just thinking about it. "I was giddy with excitement when we left Lydford, but it didn't last long." All the noise, the people, sailors, and shops lined up along every street. And the sea, wondrous and frightening, the tumult of the harbor.

"Where did you stay?"

She laughed a little, without humor. "I've forgotten the name, thank heavens. My aunt said the money was better spent on clothes." They'd spent more than a hundred pounds to buy gowns, bonnets, slippers, gloves, ribbons—a profusion of luxury to a girl who had never owned more than three drab and ill-fitting dresses at one time. "We attended services at St. Andrew's and must have seen every concert and play in town." All from the cheapest possible seats.

He leaned forward again in the chair, his eyes bright with interest. "How exciting. Had you never seen such things before?"

"Never. And I'm afraid all I really cared about were the assemblies." Though they were frightening too. All those men, tantalizing yet intimidating in uniforms of one sort or another. She'd expected that one of them would fall in love with her, but why would anyone fall in love with a mouse? "After some months, we moved on to Dawlish."

"Ah! That is a place I've not seen. What is it like?"

She shrugged. "Modest, though the setting is pretty. The assemblies were small but quite genteel."

"And that's where you met Mr. Moore?"

"Yes." She rubbed her eyes. "Hartley was down from Oxford with his mother, who'd been ill. He was handsome and very attentive. I was flattered." And oh, so naïve. "My aunt caught him kissing me, or there would have been no marriage. I don't know how she persuaded him—though she did offer a bit of a dowry." She shook her head. "It should never have happened."

Deborah opened her eyes and looked around the room in a daze. How utterly bizarre that she should be sitting on her bed discussing private things with a near-stranger over the still form of her dying child. But perhaps it was not so fantastic. Time and reality seemed suspended by the situation, the three of them isolated in a soap bubble where such concepts were mere theoretical constructs with no practical application. Here, in this room, her customary barriers were like the surface of that bubble, transparent and ephemeral. Without Julian, meaningless, like everything else in this insignificant life she led.

Mr. Haverfield said nothing. But the look in his eyes, sober and intense, made her sorry she had said so much. "Please," she said, sitting forward and reaching out a hand toward him impulsively. "Please don't get the wrong impression. It was no fairy-tale marriage, but it gave me independence and a modicum of contentment, and of course Julian—"

As though on cue, Julian's hand moved to twine around hers. "Mama?" He looked up at her, weak but sentient, and curled up under the bedclothes shivering like a sapling in a windstorm.

She turned to him and rose onto her knees. "Dear God, he's soaked with sweat. Could it be—"

Together they stripped him of his sodden nightdress, wrapped him in toweling, and covered him with extra blankets. They watched while he soaked through the towels and replaced them again. Finally the shivering subsided to an occasional shudder, and he rasped out, "I'm thirsty!"

Deborah lifted his head and held a glass of barley water to his lips. Julian could manage only a few desperate gulps before curling up in the driest corner of the bed and lapsing once again into sleep. But it *was* sleep this time, his breathing markedly better, his position more natural.

CURIOUSLY SUSPENDED between joy and tragedy, Evan's eyes met hers, wide and dark. She stood motionless and silent, yet he could feel her tension, like a rope stretched taut. Then she fell apart.

Shaking, she buried her face in her hands and wept. Evan pulled her into his arms and wrapped her tight, murmuring comforting sounds somewhere above her right ear. Her hair felt soft against his lips. He pressed a kiss to her temple.

Damned fool. Thank God she hadn't noticed.

And yet he was sorry. What might have happened if she had? He imagined her face turned up to his, kissing her tears away, the feel of her lips—

No.

Best not to think of that.

❧ 10 ❧

The previous week had crawled at the speed of a snail crossing the garden. But the next morning, time jerked into another rhythm entirely, scurrying like a mouse escaping the broom. Doctor Overley examined his patient and confirmed him out of danger, prescribing a week's bedrest.

He appeared once again the morning after and presented his bill. Catching her hand as he transferred the folded paper into it, he leered at her like a cat in the cream. "If it is too much, my dear, rest assured that my previous offer still stands." He allowed her to pull her hand from his. "I am a patient man. Perhaps, after your current protector leaves Whately, you will feel differently."

Deborah stared at him. "My current…"

She clenched her teeth, looked down at the bill in her hand, opened it, and folded it again. Her heart dropped to her feet, but she refused to let him see her dismay. "You will be paid within the week." When he was gone, she checked the bill once more. It was phrased as a request, gracious and flowery, but that did not change the amount. He'd found another way to punish her.

She still did not know how, but she would pay him. And she would not let anxiety over the matter disturb her euphoria at Julian's recovery. She hugged herself and performed a pirouette in the middle of the parlor, smiling for the first time in weeks.

The boy was unbelievably fretful. On the verge of calling the doctor back again the following day, Deborah received a brief visit from Lady Reston, who assured her such behavior was normal. "It may be weeks before he's completely restored to normal, Mrs. Moore. You must bear with it as well as you can."

There seemed no end to his complaints. He wanted a buttered egg —no, it had to be poached. He wanted raisins in his gruel—no, he hated raisins. But he looked such a pitiful wraith that for now it was easy to put up with his ill-tempered whims. His sleep was deep and natural, through the night and at intervals during the day.

Deborah used that time to make caudles, and lemonade, and possets, in all the varieties Julian demanded and then refused, and to help Molly clean the bedding and nightclothes. She threw away the dress she'd worn throughout his illness, though she could ill afford to do so.

She had little opportunity to catch up on her rest but found a few minutes, here and there, for herself. On Thursday morning, basket in hand, she dallied on her way to the chicken coop. The cottage, closed up tight against errant drafts for so many days, felt like a mausoleum.

Only two eggs. She would come back later with the hatchet—those two oldest hens would do them more good in the stewpot. There was no point in feeding them all winter.

What a relief it was to breathe in the crisp winter air. Frost coated each brittle, brown stalk of nettle and lavender, a garden of ice. She broke off a few sprigs of holly and brought them indoors with her, tying them to the bedposts to sweeten their Christmas dreams.

On Friday evening, after Julian was asleep, she dragged the big washtub out of the corner of the kitchen, filled it with pots and pots of hot water, unwrapped her last bar of scented soap, and soaked and scrubbed until not a trace of illness remained. By the time she sat before the kitchen fire, brushing her long hair as it dried, sleepy and smelling *good* at last, it was past midnight.

Evan visited each day that week after spending his mornings with the viscount. Usually Miss Latimer arrived with him, lending a semblance of propriety. And whether she came or not, Evan always brought foodstuffs and other fine things: butter and eggs, or bread and ale, a dozen beeswax candles, and one day an entire pound tea, unadulterated and fresher than any she'd ever had. She split most of these items into portions and took them to other villagers more needy than she. But the tea she hoarded, to sip over her sewing or a book. It smelled too lush and earthy to taste so divine.

Deborah did not see much of Evan when he came, for his arrival signaled an opportunity to accomplish some task or other. She'd made it very clear that she did not have time to visit with him, yet he kept appearing on her doorstep. "I like the boy," he assured her, "and I hope it makes your life a bit easier."

He no longer seemed a stranger, hardly even a guest. In the aftermath of her tears that night, he had used her given name and insisted she do the same. "You can't cry on a man's shoulder and continue to call him *Mister*, you know." But now that the crisis was past, she saw that as a misstep and avoided calling him anything at all whenever possible.

For propriety's sake, Deborah carried Julian and his blankets to the sofa downstairs during the day. Evan sat with him there, and they read or played at jackstraws or cards. Evan brought Viscount Latimer's recent edition of Hoyle's to resolve rules questions on the games Julian fancied he already knew and taught him to play rudimentary forms of loo and piquet and faro. "A child's best guide to the gallows," Evan said, which made Julian laugh and then cough.

Others visited as well. How strange and inconvenient to have callers, to keep the parlor spotless and her precious tea at the ready, to make stilted conversation with the vicar, Miss Latimer, Lady Reston and her daughters. It was Mr. Haverfield's doing, Deborah was sure. They were not coming to see *her*.

On Saturday she walked to the bakery, her hood down despite the cold, relishing the chill on her cheeks, the wind riffling her hair. She hated to go into the shop, hot from its big oven, but the familiar aromas were enticing in their own way. "A loaf of the red wheat, please, Mrs. Harcourt. Yesterday's if you have one. And I'd best take two dozen of the lemon biscuits as well." Callers were expensive as well as inconvenient.

The dairyman's wife approached her as she counted out the coins for her purchase. "I'm right glad to hear your boy is on the mend, Mrs. Moore."

"He is, thank you, Mrs. Martin." No doubt everyone knew the whole progress of Julian's illness, with all sorts of details, real or imagined.

"Aye, let me add my good wishes to that, ma'am," said Mrs. Harcourt from behind the counter. "Here's a little cake for the tyke. You bring 'im in when he's up and about, I'll give 'im another."

Surprised at the woman's good will, Deborah thanked her and headed out of the shop, stopping outside the doorway to settle the cake safely in her basket. The door had not closed completely, and she caught the continued conversation between the two women. "Eh, that is good news. I've never seen 'er lookin' happier, I'm sure. She's an odd, shy one, that gel."

"And the lad too, so quiet and serious," replied Mrs. Harcourt. "But you've heard about that young man up at the Manor, he that found the lad. Do you know he's been there every day since the boy took ill? Could be *he* has something to do with her high spirits. A good-looking man like that would surely put a skip in *my* step."

"Never mind what he looks like. He's said to be worth ten thousand a year."

"He's not likely to marry the likes o' her then, is he? She'd best not be setting her hopes in *that* direction."

Deborah bit her lip and hurried away. However much she hated it, the talk was inevitable. The wonder was she'd heard no clucking about impropriety. If the doctor thought her Evan's mistress, others might, as well. Would the women be so benign without the aegis of Evan and his wealthy friends? She thought not. Rank brought many privileges, but this was the first time she had been a beneficiary. *Don't get used to it.*

❧

EVAN DEALT JULIAN ANOTHER CARD. A six. *Damn.* It took the boy a minute and several fingers to discover what Evan already knew.

"That makes twenty-*two.* It's not *fair!*" Though addition was still a challenge, Julian knew his numbers well, and Evan found his grasp of the games precocious—when he was in a good temper, which he most decidedly was not. He'd been whining and wore a red blotch on each cheek, like poorly applied rouge. The boy still grew feverish in the afternoons, and Evan reached out to feel his forehead, but he pulled away. *How in the world do they manage?* Nursemaids and tutors at least received wages for their patience. Mothers without the benefit of such help deserved far more respect than he'd ever given them.

He vetoed another game, and after a few tears, Julian consented to lie down. When Deborah returned home and looked in on them, the child was lying quietly, glazed eyes fixed on the fire, that decrepit stuffed pony clutched at his chin. Evan shook his head at her—her entrance would only delay the necessary nap—and she withdrew.

He found her in the kitchen some minutes later. The room smelled of the lemons he had brought from Latimer's hothouses, their fresh astringency warring with the succulence of pheasant fat dripping into the fire. The heat from the flames was intense, and Deborah worked on a small table at the far corner of the room, where the door to the yard stood open.

Evan crossed from heat to cold and sat down on a stool beside the table. Here the lemons were nearly overpowering as Deborah pounded them in a crock. She looked up at him, a question in her eyes.

"He's asleep, mercifully. I had to invent an irascibility clause that forces an end to the game."

She didn't even smile. Instead, she bit her lip, lowering her head to her task. "I'm so sorry. You must be bored to tears."

He restrained a chuckle and put a finger under her chin, bringing her eyes back up to meet his. "It was his irascibility, not mine." *Why the*

77

hell do I like her so much? She doesn't even recognize a joke when she hears one.

He let her go. "And oddly enough, I'm not bored."

She cast him a quick, nervous glance and focused on turning out the lemon juice and rinds into a sieve. More intently, surely, than the job required. "Will you... Should we expect you tomorrow, Mr. —Evan?"

"Is it inconvenient for you? I hope you will tell me if I'm becoming *de trop*."

Her gaze leaped to his face again, her cheeks turning red. "Oh no! No. It's only... I must call on the squire regarding some financial arrangements. Normally I would take Julian with me, but he is not yet well enough..."

He'd hoped to hear her welcome him for her own sake rather than Julian's. But even if she liked him—and he was not at all sure she did— he no longer expected her to show him any encouragement. After the story she'd told him that evening when they thought the boy would die, he could not fault her constraint. Her early years had borne no resemblance to the halcyon days of his own youth.

He straightened his cravat and buttoned his coat. In the final analysis, it was better this way. "Of course not," he said. "Just tell me what time you want to go."

Evan arrived at the appointed hour on Sunday afternoon, this time accompanied by his groom and driving his phaeton. Deborah still could not believe how easy it had been. She'd asked the favor and he had agreed, without the smallest protest.

It was time he left town—she could not afford to develop such a pleasant habit.

"Really, Mr. Haverfield, you need not have brought your carriage. I fully expected to walk."

"It was no trouble at all, ma'am."

"But I'm sure it was. I'm sorry to have imposed on you at all. Molly could—"

"Hush now," he murmured. He handed her up and threw a rug

over her knees. "You are the one performing a favor, ma'am. My horses need the exercise. Don't they, Grady?"

"Aye, that they do, sir."

They were conspiring against her. But his eyes glinted with amusement, and she gave in gratefully. She even found herself smiling back.

"Just tell Grady how fast you want to go. It will be fun." *Also faster, and warmer, and drier.* If she arrived home exhausted, it would not be from walking. The next favor she had to ask would not be so simple.

She gave Evan's man a tentative smile and a soft "Good afternoon," and would have ridden the distance beside him without uttering another word until it was time to say her thanks at the end. The man probably knew Evan as well as anyone, and there were no doubt questions Deborah would have liked the answers to, but she asked none of them. She could not even think of one.

But Grady seemed to be a friendly sort. "It's a cold morning, right enough. Will the rug keep you warm, ma'am?"

"Oh yes! Thank you."

"Mr. Haverfield tells me you come from the south somewhere?"

"Yes. From Devonshire."

"Aye, that's it. Lydford, wasn't it? He mentioned it 'cause we visited there a few years back, maybe in '13 or '14. Stayed at an inn next the castle and spent a morning climbing down into the gorge. Quite a sight. And quite a scramble to get out again."

"Yes, I—imagine it would be. I was not there at that time."

Another couple of reminiscences filled the rest of the short drive, to which Deborah could respond with no more than an "ah" and a nervous smile. Lydford was the very last subject she wished to discuss. She caught the skeptical look he gave her as he pulled the horses to a stop. He thought her mindless, and no wonder.

It was quite a novelty to arrive at the great front doors of Reston Park in a carriage with a groom and a fine pair of matched grays. The footman who descended the steps to hand her down moved with alacrity, treating her with unexpected deference as he handed her into the care of Fleming, the squire's butler.

Fleming, unswayed by her mode of transportation, made Deborah an infinitesimal bow and showed her into a small morning parlor. The coals were still warm from earlier in the day, and she seated herself as close to the fireplace as possible. She'd half expected to be left in the hall under the watchful glass eyes of stag and boar, like one of the squire's tenant farmers. "I will inquire if Sir James is at home, madam." He did not offer to take her cloak.

Half an hour later she was glad he had not. By the time Fleming summoned her to Squire Reston in his library, she was shivering from cold and nerves. The cloak helped hide her shudders. She gazed long-ingly at the fire burning in the massive fireplace but stood awkwardly where Fleming had left her, just inside the door.

"And bring me that bottle of burgundy," Sir James shouted to Fleming on his way out of the room. "I don't care what that damned sawbones says!"

It was not an auspicious beginning.

He bowed. "I beg your pardon, Mrs. Moore. I've been ill, but that's no reason to swear in your presence. Please, sit." He gestured to a chair in front of the big desk. "Shouldn't even be out of my bed, but Fleming tells me you have 'urgent business'. What can I do for you?"

He made the journey to the other side of the desk and sat down in his chair. It could have served as a king's throne. He pulled his thick brocade dressing gown tighter and adjusted the silk scarf around his neck.

"I'm sorry, sir. I didn't know... that is, I knew you *were* ill, but I thought you were better." Could she go home and forget her errand? Sir James had helped her through the necessary paperwork after Hartley died. The reduced rent he allowed her on the cottage was all that kept a roof over her head. And he'd organized the search for Julian—*that* was a debt she could never repay.

But she would far rather be obliged to the squire than the doctor.

She raised her eyes to his, forcing herself to sit straight and speak clearly. "I already owe you far too much, sir, but I find myself in another predicament. I have received the bill from Doctor Overley. It is—"

"Yes, I was glad to hear he brought your boy through, ma'am. He is a fine physician, is he not?"

Deborah doubted the doctor had much to do with Julian's recovery, but she said, "Of course, sir. Nevertheless, his bill is higher than I expected, and far more than I can pay at one time."

The squire leaned forward in his chair, leaning his arms on the desk. "Overley is a generous man. I know he is accustomed to receiving payment in installments or in kind. Do you tell me he is unwilling to offer you such terms?"

Deborah stared blindly at her hands, gripped tight together in her lap. Suddenly she felt hot. "The terms he offered I could not accept, sir." She could not be any more specific and prayed he would not ask.

"What are you saying?" He sat back in the chair, graying brows lowered over his frown. "I hope you're not implying what I think you are."

Deborah opened up her reticule and pulled out a very thin roll of banknotes, which she set on the desk in front of her. Then she compressed her lips to keep them from trembling and met his eyes. He looked very severe. "I've brought the rent for January. I can promise you a quarter again of that amount until the loan is repaid." It would take a year.

After studying her for a long moment, he threw up his hands. "All right, all right. Don't look so stricken. I can do nothing today, of course, but the funds should be in your hands tomorrow afternoon."

The relief was like an abrupt cure for a toothache. Her shoulders slumped with it. She let out the breath she'd been holding, and then drew in another, deep and relaxing. They both stood, and he shook her hand. "Don't worry, Mrs. Moore. Be assured you will have no further trouble from Doctor Overley."

"Thank you, sir. And a merry Christmas to you and your family."

Deborah hurried outside. Her sweat cooled quickly while she waited for Mr. Haverfield's carriage to be brought around, and she shivered.

As Grady turned the horses away from the gargoyles and cherubs that adorned Reston Park, she wished she were walking instead. It might have soothed her nerves.

‡ 11 ‡

"Heavens, what a beautiful day," Amanda said with a laugh, breathing hard as they trotted home alongside the Manor wall. Her hat hung down her back, and her hair was a tangle.

"Of course you'd think so—you won," complained her brother. "Sorry Lookout's such a slug, Haverfield."

"Don't be sorry. If you'd given me a faster horse, you'd have finished dead last." Evan didn't mind losing; it had been a good run.

"You think so, eh? I think it's my superior horsemanship."

The Manor gates stood at the junction of two lanes. As they rounded the corner, they were met by a racket of jangling harness and hoofbeats louder than their own. There was a screech from Amanda, a yell from Latimer, and a great deal of superior horsemanship from everyone involved.

"Whoa!" shouted the coachman in charge of the approaching carriage, hauling on the reins. Four big, strapping beasts plunged across the lane, coming to an angry halt an inch shy of the hedgerow opposite. The hapless postilion dragged himself out of the traces, white-faced, and staggered to the leader's head.

The Earl of Sudbury and his sisters had arrived.

They weren't supposed to come for a week yet. Evan scowled as the three riders preceded the carriage up the drive and dismounted to await their guests. This took a few minutes, while Sudbury's coachman realigned his vehicle and drove sedately up to the house.

Latimer grinned. "I say, what a jolly surprise for Christmas eve, eh?"

Amanda was less enthusiastic. "But the rooms aren't ready. *None* of the house is ready! And Cook is liable to give notice." She jammed her hat back on top of her head.

Evan could dredge up no enthusiasm at all. With a houseful of guests, it would be rag-mannered for him to spend half his time in the village.

He took his frustration out on the viscount. "That's a mighty inconvenient place for your gates, Latimer."

Latimer did not give up his grin. "Been there for years, Haverfield. Odd that you never complained before."

Wheels crunched to a halt on the gravel. Latimer pulled open the door and let down the steps.

The first to appear was a chit Evan didn't know. Lady Honora. The viscount took her hand and helped her down to the ground. His eyes shone with pride when he turned to introduce her to Evan and Amanda, as though she were already his.

Evan could see why he might want her. She was fair, and quite pretty, her willow-green traveling dress showing her to advantage. She seemed modest, even shy, as she made her curtsies, her voice so soft he could barely hear it.

How different she was from her sister, who now claimed Evan's hand for her own descent onto the gravel. As Lady Blythe stepped down, she managed to stumble, gracefully, forcing his other hand to her waist to steady her while her dark eyes gleamed up at him.

"*Such* a long drive we've had, Mr. Haverfield. I declare I could positively swoon from the tedium of it." No, nothing modest or shy about Lady Blythe. Evan led her away from the carriage door.

Finally, the earl clambered down and greeted his hostess. "'Tis a pleasure to see you again, Miss Latimer." Past forty and a widower

twice over, Lowell Huntingdon, Earl of Sudbury, had become ponder-
ous, both in girth and civility. He still acquitted himself like a youth
on the hunting field, though he creaked slightly as he bowed to
Amanda.

He appeared the most travel-worn of the three—even one day in a
carriage with Blythe, Evan imagined, would wear most anyone to a
frazzle. "I beg you to tell me, ma'am, if we have arrived betimes for
your house party. I thought I heard Latimer invite us for New Year's ,
but m'sister swore up and down 'twas Christmas. I hope we do not
put you to any inconvenience..."

What could Amanda say but "Of course not!"

Lady Honora's welcome was in no doubt—Frank had already led
her into the house. As the coach was driven away to the stables,
Amanda and the earl followed. But Lady Blythe, hooking her arm
through Evan's, pulled him in the other direction toward a pond that
lay in its own little vale to one side of the drive. "Oh, don't let us go
indoors just yet. I have been cooped up in that moldering carriage for
days; the fresh air feels delightful!"

Had she not just declared herself ready to faint from fatigue?
Moreover, in Evan's experience, winter travel was chilling, even in
closed carriages with blankets and hot bricks. Those bricks cooled off
far too quickly. And Blythe's pelisse, cut low and square to match the
gown underneath, left a quantity of flesh exposed to the weather. But
from courtesy, Evan accompanied her across the frosted lawn.

Lady Blythe was a vibrant soul. Like most men, Evan had found
her quite appealing on initial acquaintance. She had a fine figure,
which she flaunted beneath low necklines, raised hemlines, and
dampened skirts. All this was topped by a head of thick, black hair
and a face that should be beautiful but somehow lacked... he couldn't
put a name to it.

Perhaps it was a matter of expression, so often arch or condescending. Flirtation seemed to be her only mode of interaction with
any man between the ages of eighteen and eighty. She was a courtesan
at heart, he thought. She needed either a husband on his death bed or
one of those fashionable marriages that left each partner free to

pursue outside *amours*. And whatever else he might be, the man had to be wealthy—rumor said the family's coffers were empty.

"We've missed you in town, Mr. Haverfield. London is a cesspit in winter. The only thing worse is the country. All the mud! We sank almost up to the axles not two miles from here. And if the weather's bad, we'll be stuck inside that horrid, drafty house. But *you* are in the country, so here I am."

Stuck in the house with Blythe? He could think of few worse fates. "True, my lady."

She slanted a look at him, up and down, beneath long black lashes. *Calculating.* He could imagine the questions she asked herself, summing him up. Was he handsome enough? Would he get fat? What tailor did he use? Would he be more susceptible to her beauty, her wit, or her title? Would he be a jealous husband or let her do as she pleased?

She turned to gaze at the Manor for a moment. "Houses do offer a few interesting possibilities, of course. There must be plenty of rooms to hide away in, and no doubt Miss Latimer has planned some dancing."

"There's to be a ball in the village."

"Oh dear. I much prefer an intimate gathering, don't you, Mr. Haverfield?"

"It all depends." Lord. He'd be dodging her at meals, on the hunting field, each evening in the parlor.

The next two weeks began to sound interminable.

Evan stopped a safe distance from the pond's edge.

Laughing, she let go of his arm. "You men are all the same. You think women are delicate little flowers to be protected from every little thing." She eyed the ice extending a couple of feet out into the lake and took two more steps. He opened his mouth to warn her. Before he could do so, one dainty foot slipped on the wet grass.

She emitted a shriek and a cackle of laughter, quite at odds with her speaking voice. He caught one flailing arm and pulled her to safety against his side. He could feel her heart beating frantically.

"Are you all right, my lady?"

"Yes indeed. How exciting this is." She fluttered her eyelashes again.

Evan disengaged her gloved hands from his coat and settled one of them, very properly, on his arm. "It's time to head back to the house."

She wrinkled up her perfect nose. "Why, Mr. Haverfield." She hooked the fingers of her other hand and ran them down his chest. "Are you afraid I'll dig into you with my claws?"

He'd been thinking of talons and a sharp, hooked beak, but claws came close enough to make him laugh. "No. I'm afraid of missing breakfast."

Finally she permitted him to lead her back to the house, hanging heavily on him. Not for a minute did he believe in her renewed fatigue, but her shivers were no doubt sincere. If she were Deborah, or any other woman in the world but Blythe, he would have draped his greatcoat around her shoulders.

Once back at the Manor, Evan eyed the profusion of breakfast dishes before him with surprise. But then, he had dined with Sudbury before and figured it was the right decision. "It's a veritable banquet," he murmured, finding himself next to Amanda at the sideboard. "I trust you did not lose your cook?"

Amanda chuckled. "She muttered some nasty things under her breath, but no, she did not quit. Not yet, anyway. I don't know what she'll find to serve for dinner, though—most of it's here."

Lady Blythe picked like a bird at her baked turbot and ate—Evan counted—exactly two stalks of asparagus. She was too busy, apparently, keeping the company's attention centered on herself. She regaled them with bright gossip about Lord This and Lady That and tried her best to start an argument about the recent disturbances in Spa Fields.

The earl put away a healthy serving of ham in addition to the fish and apparently thought the dish of stewed mushrooms was his own individual portion. He washed it all down with copious quantities of the Manor's own ale, which he proclaimed to be bang-up.

"But then," Blythe confided to Evan in a stage whisper, "Lowell's taste is so often *bung*-up."

Evan gave a noncommittal grunt. He thought Lady Honora blushed faintly. Everyone else contrived to look as though they hadn't heard. Having neatly insulted her hosts as well as her brother, Blythe beamed upon them all and turned the conversation to the hunt. And while her sister adjourned to her bedchamber to rest, she led the remainder of the party to the stables to supervise the installation of the horses they had brought. Eight carriage horses plus six hacks and hunters. Even doubled up in the stalls, they took up a great deal of room.

Whatever measures of economy the earl's family might be forced to employ in other areas, their horses were apparently immune. Predictably, Evan supposed, Lady Blythe's mounts were showy and high-strung, treating the grooms to an array of tricks before finally settling down. The earl's were massive, noble beasts that looked bred to carry armored men to war. Honora's mare, on the other hand, was pretty and placid. She started munching on her hay even before her rump made it through the door.

Compliments were passed on all sides. Blythe managed to find a little disparaging something to say about each animal, however, save Evan's.

Does she actually think she might touch my heart through my horses?

DEBORAH SLOGGED her way through the not-quite-frozen muck of the high street, wishing she were riding again in Mr. Haverfield's phaeton. While her destination was disagreeable, her errand there was very agreeable indeed. She was on her way to discharge her debt to Doctor Overley.

It would have been intensely gratifying to arrive like a lady in a carriage, directing her footman—Evan's man Grady in this fantasy—to deliver her payment into the doctor's own hands so he would have to come to the door himself. Instead, she would appear on his doorstep with cloak and gown a foot deep in mire, looking like a farm wench. At least she needn't fear being asked inside in such a state.

Despite her appearance, she lifted her chin in the air and insisted on handing the packet to him personally. His butler disappeared with her card, and as the doctor approached, he rubbed his hands, his cheeks broadened by his greedy smile. It would not have surprised her to see him drooling.

"Why, Mrs. Moore. What a delectable Yuletide surprise..." He trailed off as his eyes traveled down her body to the filth around her ankles.

"I've come to pay my bill, sir."

His brows rose and his nostrils flared. "Indeed." He took the packet by one corner between finger and thumb as though it were some noxious thing. Then he counted the squire's money right there in the doorway, grumbling as he thumbed through the last few banknotes.

"If you would mark the bill as paid, please?"

Deborah caught the words "inconvenient" and "hussy" as he grumbled his way into one of the rooms that opened off the hall. He emerged again a moment later and handed the paper back to her. Squinting at it, she thought it might say *Paid*. The date, at least, was legible.

What a relief to be rid of *that* debt, at least. Grinning, she wished the man a happy holiday, though she preferred he should spend it by himself, sad and lonely. Her own Christmas might not be very festive, but at least she had Julian to share it with. She would sleep well tonight.

ANOTHER WINTER, *a lifetime ago. Snow rested between the cobbles in Oxford's Broad Street, out of reach of the frenetic feet and wheels of Christmastime traffic. Shop servants and household staff bustled about their errands; peddlers sold their chestnuts, trinkets, and baked goods. University folk and the gentry, at a more leisurely pace, pursued their rounds of visiting and shopping for holiday finery.*

She hurried to meet Hartley, a familiar face emerging occasionally from the background: Mr. Blackwell, for one, bidding her a good evening from the doorway of his lending library—surely it was on the wrong side of the street?

Sprigs of holly or mistletoe adorned every entry, fastened to knockers, knobs, or stair railings. Light spilled from windows into the quickening dusk: single candles, then double candelabra, then chandeliers, and finally a whole roomful of light flooding the hall where they were to meet—odd, she didn't remember that it had windows.

She paused outside to observe the festivities. It was merry indeed, students already rollicking and flirting outrageously with the serving maids, platters half-cleared of their delicacies, inebriated young men performing drunken country dances partnered by each other or by serving-maids pressed into service, or by one of several indecently-clad women who graced the company with generous glimpses of ankles, knees, and other various parts of their anatomies. Either she was quite late or Hartley had mistaken the time. And it was not at all the kind of party she had expected. She could see Hartley, head-to-head with a redhead, and Stuart and Forester and others of Hartley's friends. The other wives she knew were conspicuously absent.

Stuart turned and saw her, peering in the window like the little match girl, and nudged the others, and they all looked her way laughing. Incongruously, her father was there too, laughing at her, his nose bloodied by a fight; and Sir James, and Doctor Overley, and then another man who turned out to be Evan Haverfield, all laughing, heads-thrown-back laughing, doubled-over laughing, rolling-on-the-floor laughing.

She stumbled away from the window into a sudden blinding blizzard, tears frozen on her cheeks, lost on the Devon moors, nowhere to go, no one to trust, a world of white solitude punctuated by a flock of ravens gathered in one frostbitten tree, laughing at her.

❧ 12 ❧

Deborah awoke early Christmas morning, her eyes dry and gritty as though she'd slept with her eyes open. The dream hung there, muddled and stifling; so wrong, yet so real. The greenery, the carols, the tables laden with delicacies—Christmas in Oxford had seemed strange and magical to a girl who'd hardly known there was such a thing. At home in Lydford, it had meant no more than a bit of decoration in the public rooms—it would not do to be thought un-Christian.

When she looked out her window, she found the snow was quite real. It was only an inch or so, not enough to keep anyone from church. The grasses stuck their brown tips right through the white coverlet, like a ragged lace coverlet laid on the ground overnight. Children whooped and girls squawked as little bits of the stuff fell from the trees onto their best bonnets.

Deborah escaped that fate, though there was nothing best about her own bonnet. But she arrived at the church later than she'd hoped and had to sit farther forward than she liked. A smile at the old farmer in the third pew from the back earned her the aisle seat, at least. She must get home to Julian after the service.

The church was little warmer than outdoors, but the greenery made it welcoming. The congregation had fairly settled in and Mr. Hepplewhite was ascending to the pulpit when a commotion at the entry caused all heads to skew around on their shoulders. A large party walked in, dressed in finery seldom seen in Whately. Surely not strangers? No, there was Miss Latimer, and the viscount, and— Deborah swiveled quickly to face front. Mr. Haverfield gave no sign that he saw her as he filed with the others to the family pews near the altar.

And why should he? On his arm was one of the most beautiful women Deborah had ever seen. Draped in silk and fur, she laughed up into his face as they passed by. The group arrayed themselves in their seats across the aisle from the squire's household, still somewhat diminished from illness.

The service commenced with friendly greetings from the vicar to the rich and the poor, the high and the lowly, the proud and the meek. Mr. Hepplewhite was too gentle a soul to single out any in his audience for criticism, but he frowned once or twice at the continuing giggles from the mischievous face beside Evan. The vicar happily endured the fidgets of children and fussing of infants—they knew no better—but it was clear that he disapproved of such inattention on the part of an adult, however lovely.

Deborah was detained for a few minutes by the farmer when the service was over, long enough for Isabella Reston to catch her and relay her family's pleasure at Julian's recovery. As a result, she was just hurrying out through the lychgate when the viscount and his guests emerged from the carved double doors of the church.

She heard her name called but pretended she did not. When it was repeated, much closer, of course she had to turn and acknowledge Mr. Haverfield's greeting.

Public conversation with him was the last thing she wanted. She would gladly have vanished had such a thing been possible. *Surely I'm not jealous?* No, for she had no hopes or expectations where he was concerned. It was humiliation, she decided, at the reminder of how unworthy she was even to think of such a thing.

Reluctantly, she gave him her hand and responded to his polite inquiry after her welfare and Julian's.

"I must apologize, Deborah. The viscount's company has begun arriving—I'm sure you saw them inside. I'll not have much time to spend with you over the next couple of weeks."

"It's not a matter for apology, sir."

Then she saw the Beauty, finishing a brief exchange with Miss Latimer and her fiancé, turn to find Evan in close conversation with a country dowd in a worn woolen pelisse with no silk or lace or fur showing anywhere. The Beauty's red lips smirked, the lovely curve of her eyebrow lifted. Deborah flushed in embarrassment and indignation. Then she lifted her chin and met Beauty's eyes boldly for a long moment.

Mr. Haverfield glanced over his shoulder to see the woman moving toward them. He gave Deborah's hand a quick squeeze, said he hoped to see them on the morrow, and turned back where he belonged. Kind of him to acknowledge her at all.

"*Cosí, il mio caro, chi è il vostro inamorata?*" That acidic tongue that Evan had managed to steer away from Deborah was inevitably directed toward him instead.

Amanda had finished her farewells and put up the window of her carriage, and then turned to make some remark to Evan when Blythe cut in with her own ill-mannered utterance. Easy enough for her to guess that Miss Amanda Latimer of Whately Manor, schooled at home more in the ways of horses and hounds than in the accomplishments of noblewomen, would not understand Italian. Evan was far too polite to carry on a conversation in a language unknown to his hostess, even had he been fluent enough himself to accomplish it. And he was not having *that* conversation in *any* language. If Blythe had hoped to disconcert him, he was glad to disappoint her.

He regarded her for a moment, very coolly indeed. "Just a local widow with whom I have some acquaintance."

"Ohhh, a widow." A world of understanding filled the drawn-out exclamation, and then a soft gushing laugh. "Well, a man has his needs, and who better than a widow to satisfy them? I rather look forward to being a widow myself."

This accorded so neatly with Evan's thoughts by the pond on the previous day that he nearly choked. Amanda said with unusual severity, "I collect you speak of Mrs. Moore? I can assure you, Lady Blythe, you mistake the nature of their acquaintance."

Blythe raised one skeptical, perfectly-sculpted eyebrow.

The party went riding later in the day. They split up in various groups, though Latimer never strayed far from Lady Honora. Those two were joined by Sudbury and then by Evan. Sudbury entertained Evan with indelicate jokes and some anecdotes about his children. Evan could not have cared less.

Amanda and Lady Blythe rode ahead of them, deep in conversation. Then Blythe broke away with a peal of laughter and turned back to meet them. She tried to tempt Evan with a race, but he declined, and she took off at a gallop with her brother. Amanda slowed to join Evan, while Latimer continued alongside his lady-love, poking along in the rear.

"She's going to get tired of Frank," Amanda said, once they were out of earshot.

"I don't know. I haven't seen any sign yet of a superior intellect. Usually, he gets tired of them."

"It seems different this time. But I suppose it's too soon to claim her for my sister."

"I should hope so. She just got here yesterday." Evan glanced over his shoulder at the subject of their discussion. "I gather you like her?"

"I do. She seems sensible. After our game of loo last night, when Lady Blythe was throwing herself at you in that appalling way, I heard her suggest that her sister's courtship tactics were likely to miscarry. Blythe doesn't seem the type to heed advice, unfortunately. And the way she behaved in church this morning..."

"Well, she didn't want to go at all. I didn't either, but church sounded much better than a *tête-à-tête* with her at the house."

"Lord, yes."

"I'm sorry about the incident in the carriage afterward, Amanda. Someone failed to teach her manners."

"Everyone failed to teach her manners, but *you* have nothing to apologize for. It wasn't *your* job." Amanda rode in silence for a moment, a crease between her brows. "She wanted to hear about Master Moore's rescue."

Evan smacked his crop against his boot. Lookout shied at the sound. "I wish you hadn't told her. You can bet everyone else will have the whole tale within ten minutes of their arrival."

"Well, why not? It's a very flattering story. There's certainly nothing for you to be ashamed of."

"You can bet there will be, the way Blythe tells it. She makes a difficult guest, doesn't she?"

"My Aunt Chastity will be here tomorrow, but I don't suppose..."

"Chastity?" Evan had thought he knew the guest list.

"You know her, Evan. Miss Chiggerford, my chubby chaperone. Her parents had an unfortunate penchant for alliteration."

He remembered her vaguely. "Do you really think she'd say anything to Blythe?" The woman behaved like a mouse, despite her stature. She'd never exerted any influence over Amanda as far as he could tell.

Amanda shook her head. "My money's on your sister. If she can't keep you safe from that doxy, I don't know who can."

❧

ALBERTA, Countess of Witney, sat at the dressing table in Viscount Latimer's best guest chamber. She'd had grander accommodations, but it smelled fresh, the fireplace did not smoke, and a vase of flowers added color. Assuming the sheets had been well-aired, it would be tolerable.

"My dear," she said to her husband as she prepared for bed, "I agree with you completely. Her manner is offensive and her judgment questionable. Nevertheless, she would be a fitting bride for him if he wants her. She's well-bred and—"

Her lord interrupted her with a snort. "I'm sorry, Berta, you cannot call conduct like that well-bred."

"But Theo, her breeding is impeccable. She's angling for a husband, that's all, and it has led her beyond the line of what is pleasing. Once married, do you not think she would settle down?"

"It's possible," replied Theo. "On the other hand, she would have money to spend, and her family has never been known for thrift. Or fidelity, for that matter. I say she would break the bank in short order, and if he cared for her, she'd break his heart too. And you know, my dear, I'm an excellent judge of character." He plucked at the front of her nightdress and peered inside. "And some other things as well."

Alberta slapped his hand. "Do something useful," she said, giving him her comb. "Well, 'tis early days yet. I can't say Evan was very encouraging to the girl this evening."

"Lord, no. The soldier, though—Westwood, is it?—seemed inclined to flirt."

It was her turn to snort. "She'd never have him. From the looks of him, he has no more money than she does. I can't imagine how the viscount came to befriend such a rough, unpolished sort of man. He *smokes*, Theo."

He laughed at her in the mirror as he teased a snarl out of her hair. "The ultimate sin. Spent too long in America—many of 'em come back that way. His birth is genteel, I'm told. And I believe, my dear, that Latimer will befriend anyone who likes horses."

For the thousandth time, Alberta wished she'd gotten the thick curls Evan and their sister Elizabeth had. "I do wish I had inquired who was on the guest list before accepting the invitation."

He laughed again. "Come now, Berta, you know you would never do anything half so rude. You'll have great fun watching this odd assortment. I've some watching to do myself yet this evening—I'm promised to the winner of the first match. Sleep well, my love. I'll report to you in the morning." He bussed her on the lips and returned downstairs to billiards and brandy.

Theo missed his chance at the second match. Captain Westwood had won out over Latimer and was now playing against Evan, but with a variation—a partner, in the feminine shape of Lady Blythe. Men considered billiards sacrosanct to the male sex, but the lady either didn't know or didn't care. And her brother, who might have sent her to bed when her sister went up, was snoring on a sofa in the drawing room. Hardly an adequate chaperone for Lord Hartwell and his fiancée, seated side-by-side on the piano bench. Theo had heard far more snoring than music as he passed by on his way to the billiard room. At least the door was open.

In the several hours since his arrival in Whately, Theo had twice heard the captain offer Blythe his services—"whatever services you may desire, my lady." Undoubtedly he'd had a different sort of recreation in mind, but billiards looked intimate enough. The unconventional pair stretched halfway across the table to reach an awkward shot, the captain's arms close round her to guide her hands. Her bodice revealed as much as it concealed as she laughed up at Evan at the far end of the table.

Latimer appeared quite intoxicated—they'd all had plenty to drink —and seemed oblivious to her charms, though perhaps that was because he was on the wrong side of the room. Or perhaps he was thinking about his Honora, who had retired—very properly—to her chamber. At least Blythe was not insipid.

Evan welcomed his brother-in-law with a grimace and a roll of the eyes. Theo laughed at him; he was taking the whole thing too seriously. Blythe was quite entertaining—or so Theo had thought until Berta started going on about marrying the vixen to her brother. Well, he'd do what he could to deflect her schemes, but he certainly had no objection if the hussy insisted on exposing herself. And it was clear that Westwood would take whatever was on offer.

The ball missed the pocket—hardly surprising—and Evan easily ran off the three remaining shots to win the game.

"Too bad, Captain." Theo patted him on the shoulder in consolation. "You're handicapping yourself, riding with extra weight."

"Aw, she just needs a little more training," Westwood responded.

Theo grinned. "Then we can all take turns, eh?" The men were mostly drunk enough to find this hilarious. Lady Blythe laughed too, but she also blushed. That was a surprise.

Evan did not laugh, but he relaxed a fraction and chalked up his cue for a match with Theo.

Blythe left them shortly thereafter, showing her pretty teeth in an artistic yawn and rejecting Captain Westwood's offer to show her to her room. "Do you think I cannot find it by myself, Captain?"

"No indeed; but I do think you might find it more fun with some company, ma'am."

This very improper exchange seemed to cause the lady no embarrassment whatsoever.

13

The breakfast parlor was quite full when Alberta arrived the next morning. All the gentlemen were there, seven or eight of them, fortifying themselves for a day of hunting. Most of the women were doing the same. Miss Moreton, Lord Hartwell's young fiancée, had never hunted before but proclaimed herself all excitement at the prospect. With some luck, she wouldn't injure herself or her mount; Alberta was certain her inexperience would put a crimp in Hartwell's day.

Plans had been laid over tea the previous evening. Lady Honora did not hunt—she would stay at the house and write letters. Alberta did not hunt, either. And Evan, to her surprise, announced that he would keep her company.

Last night's protests resumed over the breakfast table. Lady Blythe was the most vociferous. "Really, there's nothing better than a good day's ride over good country. And there's no better country than right here."

"Why would I risk my neck chasing down a creature I have no desire to kill?" asked Alberta. "Sidesaddles are dangerous enough on the road."

"You don't *have* to jump the fences, Lady Witney. With a rank novice like Miss Moreton along, you won't be the only one. There are always grooms to open the gates for—um—the faint of heart. In fact, you could keep *her* company, and then Mr. Haverfield wouldn't need to keep *you* company."

So that was it.

"That's quite all right," said Evan. "I look forward to hearing all the family news."

Rebuffed, Blythe stuck out her lower lip and pouted, for all the world like Alberta's ten-year-old. Then she went to change her clothes. When she came back downstairs, stunning in a tightly fitted riding habit, she ignored Evan entirely. Instead, she fluttered her eyelashes at Captain Westwood, tickled his nose with the preposterous plumes on her hat, and led him out toward the stableyard, all swaying hips and flirty glances.

"Humph," Berta said as she watched them leave. "Bit early in the day for a show like that."

"How stuffy you've become," Evan murmured. "Westwood didn't seem to mind."

Alberta was happy enough to accompany her brother on a leisurely ride down the country lanes, coming back along the river road where he had searched for Julian Moore, and winding up at the cottage where the boy lived.

Alberta had heard the story of Evan's heroism, of course. Amanda told it admiringly to each successive party arriving at the Manor, while Lady Blythe supplied suggestive commentary.

His sister found it a curious tale. It was not inconceivable that Evan might have heroic potential. But his manner seemed so altered. He was not ill-tempered, but distant and abstracted, and far more easily annoyed than amused by the foibles of their fellow guests. Was this what happened to heroes? If so, it was a good thing so few men indulged in the exercise.

He'd said nothing about visiting Mrs. Moore and her son, yet Alberta had the distinct impression, as the cottage came into view, that this had been his ultimate objective all morning. He suddenly lost track of their conversation, trailing off mid-sentence to peer ahead and see who it was sweeping the front walkway.

It was a child, a boy not long graduated to jacket and trousers, wielding a broom in inexpert fashion. With him a woman wearing a long apron and carrying a bucket, preparing to follow after the broom with her scrub-brush.

Of the boy's identity there could be little doubt. He dropped his broom as they approached and jumped onto the old wooden gate that looked as though it might not survive the experience, shouting out that Mr. Haffield had come at last. The woman must have spoken sharply to him, though too softly for them to hear, for when he turned back to them, he looked rather abashed and climbed down to open the gate and greet them like a proper little gentleman. He was a slight, attractive child with straight dark hair and dark eyes that glowed with excitement despite the reprimand.

Alberta turned her attention to the woman Evan addressed as Mrs. Moore. *This* was the lady of the house? Berta had taken her for the house-maid. Closer inspection showed her error; the woman was no servant. Her voice was genteel, her curtsy perfectly calculated from one lady to a greater one. Could she really be reduced to scrubbing her own front step? And if Evan had indeed saved the life of her child, how to account for the spectacularly blank expression on her face? Was she witless?

Evan gave Mrs. Moore no opportunity to refuse their visit, swinging himself down from the saddle and lifting Alberta to the ground even before making the appropriate introductions. Mrs. Moore conjured up a smile that did not reach her eyes and said everything that was proper and civil. No, the look in those eyes was not welcoming. If it had not been ridiculous, Alberta would have said she looked afraid.

Evan either ignored or failed to notice the constraint in her welcome. He ruffled the boy's hair fondly, squatting down on the barely swept walk to converse with the child face-to-face. This left Alberta to receive Mrs. Moore's invitation to step inside for some refreshment. Left to her own inclinations, Alberta would have politely refused and ridden on her way. Clearly, however, Evan expected her to accept, so accept she did.

The boy gravely secured their reins to that old gate, and they stepped into the cottage. Heaven forbid anything should happen to spook the horses, for Alberta could easily envision them flying down the street in terror with the gate clattering at their heels.

Alberta ended up by setting down Mrs. Moore's ambivalence to embarrassment. Hers was indeed a modest establishment in which to entertain a countess, and while clean, the cramped little parlor was in a state of some disarray. The boy's mother put him quietly to work gathering books into a neat pile and placing his toys in a basket, and then excused herself.

The child's presence prevented Alberta from asking Evan the question that burned on her lips. Which was, what on earth do you want from this woman, who lives no better than our tenants at home though she might—or might not—be entitled by birth to her quiet dignity? A flirtation she could understand, but there was nothing of flirtation in her manner or his. Pity she could likewise understand, and a desire to improve the lot of the child whose life he had saved, but that would not account for the intensity in Evan's eyes when he looked at her. In Alberta's experience, charity was easily given by those who could afford it, and rarely refused by those who could not.

Master Moore finished his task and came to stand by Evan's knee. One small hand rested familiarly, almost possessively, on the leather breeches, and the serious little face looked shyly up at his benefactor. "Mr. Haffield, when will you take me for a ride on Lookout? You promised when I got well…"

"I have not forgotten. Do you think you are quite well again?"

"Yes, sir, I'm strong as an ox. Or maybe I should say, strong as a horse!"

Evan chuckled at this humorous attempt. "We shall have to see what your mother says. That's one reason I came this morning."

"What is the other reason, sir?"

"Why, to introduce my sister, of course."

Julian looked sidelong at Alberta. He said in a rather fierce whisper, "Did you say she is a *countess*?"

Evan grinned, his eyes sparkling with laughter. "Why yes, she is. But countesses don't eat little boys, you know. In fact, Lady Witney has three boys of her own. And one of them is named Julian."

Master Moore turned his head to gaze at her, round-eyed. Though disinclined to encourage familiarity, she had to smile. Perhaps that persuaded the child to risk a direct address.

"Does your Julian like horses, ma'am?"

"Indeed he does."

"I'll bet he has his very own pony." He sounded wistful.

"He does not, as yet."

A pause.

"Does he like to read, as well?"

This made Alberta laugh, and the boy looked anxiously back at Evan. But Evan was still smiling, and he turned back to her.

"To tell you the truth," she said, "my Julian is most interested in escaping from his nurses and making as much noise as he can."

Julian looked like this was an activity that had never crossed his mind, and as serious as he seemed to be, Alberta did not doubt it. In defense of her offspring, she offered, "You must understand, he is not yet three years of age, *much* younger than you are."

Another pause while Julian apparently reflected on this news. "Did you bring him with you to Whately, ma'am?"

"No, I regret I did not."

"There is a stable full of fine horseflesh at the Manor, however," said Evan. "Perhaps you could ride there with me and point out all their faults."

The two males pursued this suggestion with enthusiasm under Alberta's curious eyes. Though he stayed quite often with Theo and herself on his way between London and Northridge, she had never seen Evan behave so naturally with his own nieces and nephews. She was only slightly inclined to take umbrage at this—she supposed there might well be a quite unusual bond between saved and savior. She could certainly not accuse this sweet, soft-spoken child of putting himself forward unbecomingly.

Things were different among the lower classes, of course. When her own children appeared in the drawing room, they were there for show, not conversation. Evan saw more of them than the typical guest, but they took their meals in the nursery, and though they could often be found out and about on the estate, they were then under the jealous care of nursemaids, tutors, or grooms. Yes, her brother was acquitting himself very well—and obviously had an avid devotee in the little boy, if not in his mother.

IN THE KITCHEN, Deborah measured out her precious tea while her mind ran riot.

Lord, his sister is married to an earl! She poured the boiling water over the leaves, nearly scalding herself in her hurry.

Why would he bring her here? She took her prettiest little plate down from the dresser and arranged a small selection of ginger and caraway biscuits.

He ignores us completely for five whole days and then descends upon us with a countess in tow. What nerve! She strained the tea into the pot and put it on the tray with the sugar, the cups, and the biscuits.

Pull yourself together, Deborah... She wiped her hands on her apron, remembered to take it off, and tucked an errant hair into the knot at the back of her head. Then she schooled her face into its well-worn mask and returned to her guests.

Conversation was proceeding merrily as she entered the parlor. Julian was laughing, a rare enough occurrence, little to be seen in his face of the serious boy she knew. It was a happy sight. It took sane, stable people like Mr. Haverfield and his sister to generate gaiety.

Julian fairly danced over to her, his whole little body aquiver with excitement. He uttered "Mama" but seemed unable to proceed, over-wrought. She had to stop abruptly and step around him in order to deliver the tea tray safely to the table—she hoped that would excuse the rattling of the dishes as she set it down. In honor of the company, she did not reprove him as she might have done.

"Julian, what is it?" she asked as she began to pour out the tea. "Do you think you could take this *carefully* to Lady Witney?"

He calmed himself sufficiently to accomplish the task, but of course could not manage to talk at the same time. Evan spoke for him. "Julian has been invited to accompany us back to the Manor to inspect the stables. Please say he may come."

Deborah seated herself, sorry she had no more chores to keep her occupied. "Does not Miss Latimer have a houseful of company? She will hardly appreciate a five-year-old underfoot."

"Miss Latimer and the whole houseful are out hunting, with the exception of my sister and myself. They will be gone for some hours yet, I should think. In any case, I expect we will restrict ourselves to the stables, with perhaps a brief visit to the kitchens."

What could Deborah say that would not make her sound like a shrew?

"I promise to take very good care of him and to bring him home at the first sign of mischief."

At this Julian whispered earnestly at her knee, "I'll be really, *really* good, Mama."

And then Lady Witney added her entreaties. "'Tis not far, after all. He'll come to no harm, Mrs. Moore."

"It is time for his nuncheon. Also, there are medicines he must take. And I simply cannot ask you to take charge of him for so long a time." Now she sounded mulish.

"You don't trust me?" Evan asked her, smiling.

Deborah felt her face flood with color. "You know that could not possibly be at issue, Mr. Haverfield." Why would he smile? Had he meant it as a joke?

He cleared his throat, the smile fading. "Well then... I understand that you ride, Deborah?"

Surprised, she replied, "Why, yes. But I seldom—it has been—oh, a year and more since..."

"Then let me suggest this. My sister and I will return to the Manor while Julian has something to eat—and yes, his medicines too." He gave Julian a stern look. "We shall come back here in, say, an hour? And I will bring a horse for you as well, Deborah, so that you may supervise him yourself and make sure of his safety."

It was not safety Deborah was concerned about, it was obligation and an intimacy that had become painful. But she had been outmaneuvered. Again.

She spread her hands in a gesture of acquiescence and smiled rather tightly as she expressed her gratitude for their kindness. Evan helped his sister into her saddle, and then swung himself onto his horse. Deborah watched them go, hugging herself for warmth and fortification. Then she hurried inside to see to Julian's needs and change into her old riding habit.

❧ 14 ❧

Lord Latimer's stable was warm and redolent of the expected things—horses and manure, hay and leather. Fresh straw covered the floors, brass work gleamed, and sunlight shining through the high windows filled the space with amber light. Were all stables so welcoming? Deborah hadn't enough experience to know.

A stranger might almost imagine them a family. Mr. Haverfield carried Julian, who was full of wonder and delight. A number of stalls were empty, but many curious, long faces remained to peer out at them over the walls, which rose chest-high and showed teeth marks from generations of horses. The animals' coats gleamed from the curry brush. Little whickerings and stampings greeted them as they zig-zagged slowly down the corridors, stopping to admire each beast and perhaps stroke a sleek neck or pat a velvety nose.

The grooms were friendly and undemanding like the horses, though Evan's man, Grady, regarded Deborah with an unblinking expression she could not interpret. All were happy to answer questions as they went about their chores, talking about each horse as a companion, a character. They supplied the visitors with carrots, making sure Julian knew how to hold his hand flat so he wouldn't get nipped. His favorite was Imp, a shaggy pony whose sole purpose in life was to keep the grooms on their toes, as they told it.

Deborah, inevitably, liked Evan's lovely grays the best—and Miss Latimer's pretty sorrel mare he had brought for Deborah's ride to the Manor. The countess, to Deborah's relief, had not returned to the cottage with Evan.

A commotion out in the yard heralded an end to her brief idyll. Air currents set the dust motes dancing in the golden stable as grooms ran to take charge of the arriving horses and riders. Deborah closed her eyes for a moment and put herself back on guard.

The beautiful woman she'd seen at church entered the stable, following her horse and groom and talking over her shoulder to a mustachioed man in the uniform of an army officer. Miss Latimer was with them as well, her face as stony as Deborah's own.

The Beauty showed quite theatrical surprise at seeing Evan there in the stable. She came right up to him and laid a hand on his arm. "Why, Mr. Haverfield! Where is the countess, whose company you so desired this morning? Ah, but I see you have found a diminutive substitute. This must be *le petit garçon* you wrested from eternal rest."

Julian, who had been gazing at her, hid his face. He didn't understand her words, of course, but it seemed her insincerity was obvious even to him. She made another feigned start. "Oh! *Et la mère, la cherie.* How domestic."

Amanda stepped forward to welcome Deborah. "It has been far too long since we saw you here at the Manor. How wonderful to see your son up and about. Have you been inspecting all the horses, Master Moore?" Julian nodded vehemently. "I'm glad you like them. Did you ride here with Mr. Haverfield?" He nodded again.

She turned again to Deborah. "We are famished. You must join us for tea and something to eat, Mrs. Moore. Very informal, just as you see us in all our dirt."

"No, I'm afraid I can't possibly... I must get Julian home." Deborah looked to Evan for assistance, but it was not forthcoming. Instead, he smiled at her and performed the introductions no one wanted.

Captain Westwood returned a bow to Deborah's curtsy, his eyes lingering on her chest before returning to her face. "Now that's a pretty thing"—a ludicrous thing to say to the beautiful woman standing beside him. Lady Blythe gave him a smoldering glance and accorded Deborah a slight tilt of the head. It could not be called a nod.

"There, now everything's tidy," said Amanda. "Perhaps Julian would like to have a sandwich here in the stable." She called to one of the grooms. "Jeremy, would you mind taking charge of Master Moore for a bit? I will ask Cook to send out a sandwich, and some cakes for all of you."

Jeremy agreed readily, and certainly Julian had no objection. Deborah was left without a word to say except "thank you," uttered in a bit of a daze. How did these people bully their way so easily past her defenses? *I should have stayed at home.*

She might have enjoyed the company of Evan and Miss Latimer, but she had grave doubts about the rest of them. The dashing captain had a disturbing light in his eye and a smirk at the corner of his mouth, as though he went through life finding things to ridicule.

And she was hardly likely to enjoy any occasion where she must compare herself to the elegant Lady Blythe. Even in her riding habit, fresh from the hunt, that damsel looked as though she had just stepped out of the pages of *La Belle Assemblée*—teal velvet cut in a military style, embellished with fur, and topped by a matching shako set at a rakish angle.

Deborah's own habit dated from the early days of her marriage when Hartley had first taught her to ride. It was made by her own hand, of poor-quality wool that was originally burgundy but had discolored to a shade very like dried blood. It had no embellishment at all.

There were just two men to offset the six women in the breakfast parlor, and a number of empty chairs sat against the wall. Lady Witney was cordial enough, condescending to take the seat on Deborah's right. Lady Blythe's sister made an appearance, though for all she ate, Deborah wondered why—nor did she contribute more than a few quiet words to the conversation.

Miss Latimer's aunt, appallingly large, hardly raised her eyes from her plate and said nothing at all except to ask for the fruit compote. Captain Westwood was seated across the table but was largely occupied by his food and by Lady Blythe; Evan was on Deborah's left.

They talked of holiday observances, the following evening's ball, the weather—which promised to hold good for that event—and the quality of the ham. Miss Latimer and Lady Witney, aided by Evan, showed their good manners by changing topics when some member of the party had been silent too long—though no one made any attempt to involve Miss Chiggerford. Deborah felt similarly invisible and was quite happy to have it so.

Then Miss Latimer asked after Julian's health and his interest in horses. Lady Blythe converted this into a review of the morning's hunting.

"You ride, though you do not hunt, Mrs.—uh, Moore?" she asked.

"Yes, my lady."

"You should try out my hunter. He's a fine hack as well."

Captain Westwood snorted, and Lady Honora troubled herself to comment that Mrs. Moore would do better to stay with Miss Latimer's mare.

"Nonsense," cried Lady Blythe. "His name is Lump, for God's sake."

"An appropriate enough name, I grant you," her sister conceded, "until someone tries to ride him."

"Oh, I'd wager Mrs. Moore can ride the male of any species quite handily." This was uttered in dulcet tones, with a pointed look at Evan.

Captain Westwood chuckled. Miss Latimer stared aghast at Lady Blythe and then turned toward Deborah in distress. Honora uttered "Blythe!" in a shocked undertone, while Lady Witney looked as though she'd like to take the troublemaker by the ear and drag her upstairs for a well-deserved beating. Miss Chiggerford stopped chewing and stared at Lady Blythe. And Evan actually started to his feet, though Deborah could not imagine what he thought he could do about it.

Deborah grew hot and then shivered. Hidden in her lap, her hands shook. But her gaze held Beauty's unblinkingly. "I am quite happy with the mare, thank you. She has excellent manners."

"Oh ho, she has claws," murmured Captain Westwood quite audibly. Deborah flashed a furious glance his way and then looked down at her plate. It could have been writhing with leeches; she would not have noticed.

The meal was hastily adjourned. Leaving the room with his hand at her back, Evan murmured, "Bravo, Deborah; well done." Lady Honora hurried out behind them and rested her small white hand on Deborah's arm, delivering a brief, graceful apology for her sister's behavior. Lady Witney smiled and patted her hand in passing, and Miss Latimer insisted on walking to the stables with them, apologizing for Lady Blythe and praising Deborah with alternating breaths.

Deborah found all this attention more profoundly embarrassing than the original insult had been, and by the time Miss Latimer left them, she was almost in tears.

"Mama—"

"Not now, Julian."

Evan rested a hand on the boy's head. "Did you see her face, Deborah? I thought—"

She rounded on him. "Enough!" she cried. "The whole affair was despicable. Let's forget it, please." She had not been so angry since... well, not so long ago.

"Mama—"

"*Not now*, Julian!" She was trembling, perspiring, very aware of the grooms looking on curiously as they saddled the horses. Finally they were all mounted and on their way down the drive.

As they turned out through the Manor gates, Julian looked anxiously up into Evan's face. "Mr. Haffield?" It was little more than a whisper.

Evan responded in a similar tone. Deborah did not hear what he said—she was concentrating on the mare fidgeting under her nervous hands.

Then Julian started talking, hesitantly at first, but gaining in enthusiasm as he went on. He described each horse, and each groom, and all the tasks he had helped with, and how Jeremy had put him on Imp's back and led him down the wide corridors in the stable. Evan seemed to be listening and reacting with an occasional comment or question as if nothing had happened. As if chiding her for an unreasonable reaction and for taking her anger out on Julian.

She kicked the horse and cantered out of earshot.

When they rode into the yard behind her after their brief ride, Julian was laughing. She was still mounted, of course—if there was a way for lady to dismount without help from a man, she had yet to learn it.

Evan swung easily out of his own saddle and lifted her down. Then he took both sets of reins and started toward the shed.

Deborah spoke up sharply. "I'm sorry, Mr. Haverfield. I cannot entertain you. Julian needs his nap. Thank you for taking us."

Evan looked a little hurt; maybe later she would care. He gave her a quick bow. "I'm sorry it caused you such anguish." He climbed back into the saddle and lifted his hat in farewell. "With all the company, I'm afraid my time is not my own. But if I can't visit before then, I'll look forward to seeing you at the ball tomorrow."

She turned away toward the cottage.

"Deborah…" He beckoned her closer as she looked over her shoulder. "It's not the child's fault." He said it softly so Julian would not hear.

"Don't tell me how to be a mother," she snapped back at him. The need to keep her voice down stoked her rage, and she stormed in through the kitchen door, sweeping the boy ahead of her.

EVAN FROWNED at the closed door for a moment and then rode out of the yard leading Amanda's mare. Barely twenty minutes after he'd left it, he returned to Latimer's stable, no doubt looking as irritable as he felt.

Grady took the reins from him. "What was all that about, then?"

"It's not your business, is it."

Grady quirked an eyebrow.

He never talked to Grady that way. He never talked to anyone that way.

Evan sighed. "The truth is, I hardly know. *Thought and passion all confused.*"

Grady lifted the flap to uncinch Lookout's saddle.

"No, leave it," Evan said, suddenly decisive. "I'm going out again."

Grady gave him a leg up. "It's coming on to rain."

Evan flapped a hand in dismissal and headed back down the drive. He couldn't go back to the house yet—he didn't even want to risk running into anyone else on the estate. He was furious with Blythe, but it was Deborah who had him tied in knots. He was determined to bridge the distance she insisted on maintaining, but she made it damned difficult.

She rode happily across the moor, beautiful in its autumn adornment of gorse and heather, feeling at ease with Nugget, the sorrel mare Hartley had purchased for her use. Riding was still a new experience but one she loved; it was freeing, somehow, especially when she rode alone.

She remembered the day clearly... except it had not been the Devon moors but the fields around Oxford, and Hartley had surely been with her. But now she was alone and free, and she took her time, allowing Nugget to choose her path and nibble as she liked while her rider gazed into the distance, or looked for the lark singing his heart out somewhere in the high blue sky, or watched the ground for the nests of ouzels.

Then it was time to make her way to the ball. Inexplicably, she wore a silk ball gown of dark teal—much the color of Lady Blythe's riding habit— and inexplicably, Nugget stepped daintily from the autumn moors, through the church gate, and into the frosted high street in Whately, where Evan waited outside the inn to lift her from the saddle.

They danced, alone in the assembly rooms, no curious or sly or jeering faces to judge them from the periphery, their feet hardly touching the floor, no sound but the music, no feeling but exhilaration.

Then the room spun away and Evan was gone, and she was back on the moor, hanging on for dear life as Lady Blythe's hunter, huge and black in the nighttime, pelted through a cold, driving rain to nowhere.

✤ 15 ✤

Lady Blythe looked up from whatever she was writing, her lips pulled back in a grimace. "The *brewer?*" she exclaimed. "Please, Miss Latimer, tell me you jest."

"Oh no," Miss Latimer replied. "Mr. Nutall is—"

"Don't say the solicitor is coming as well?"

"Two solicitors, in fact." Miss Latimer's chin lifted in defiance. Alberta opened her mouth to speak, but Blythe had not finished.

"My God. It's not enough that we must dine at five. We are also expected to dance with ale-makers at this so-called ball tomorrow. Who planned this tribute to social *egalité?*"

"Why, I did," said Miss Latimer, "along with Lady Reston and several others."

"Has England not just eliminated the revolutionist element in France? How ironic that we should so encourage the rabble here at home."

"Not quite rabble," murmured Alberta. Though she would never have expressed herself in such terms, her sympathies were largely with Lady Blythe.

Miss Latimer's definitely were not. "Whately is a small community, Lady Blythe. If we restricted the guest list to those approved by you, we might perhaps manage a table of whist. As it is, we may expect upward of thirty couples on the dance floor."

"Mushrooms and toad-eaters," muttered Blythe, dipping her quill into the inkwell.

"Nonsense," said Alberta. "It will be a delightful change of pace." She might agree with Lady Blythe on this point, but she liked Miss Latimer much better. And she would welcome some entertainment other than parlor games.

"Yes, Blythe," Lady Honora admonished her sister. "No one will oblige you to dance with anyone you do not deem worthy. If only out of courtesy to our hosts, I think you should refrain from such slurs on their neighbors."

Lady Blythe rolled her eyes.

Alberta was tempted to do the same. But Theo strolled in at that moment with the other gentlemen, and she restricted herself to raising one eyebrow at him. He came to sit beside her on the brocade sofa.

"Have you had an enlightening hour, my dear?" he asked her.

"Grossly enlightening," she replied. "And it was a most generous hour. The men look particularly merry this evening."

"Latimer broke out some excellent port. Exhumed from some dungeon in Portugal after the war, to hear him tell it."

Blythe spoke up in a voice that sounded mild yet carried across the room. "I suppose we shall all be consigned to another evening of charades and music. Unless we have exhausted your repertoire, Miss Moreton?"

"Oh no, my lady," replied that naïve young woman, oblivious to the put-down. Her fiancé was off in the corner laughing with Evan and Viscount Latimer, paying no attention.

"Ah," Blythe said, her voice very dry. "Well, then. Play away." Miss Moreton moved to the pianoforte, and Blythe went on with her writing, chattering all the while with Captain Westwood.

"She could at least pretend to keep her voice down," Alberta murmured.

"Wait until we get to the charades," Theo replied. "She's excellent."

And Alberta had to admit, she was. She performed a pantomime with Captain Westwood depicting the Prince of "Whales"—hardly an original joke, but her delivery was superb. No one else could match her. She had a great deal of flair and no delicacy whatsoever.

So she had an eager audience when she announced, "I have a riddle. I've written out several copies—you may share." She passed out the sheets she had been working on all evening.

But for the crackling of the fire and the clink of a teacup, the room fell silent as everyone began reading. A little unnerved by the smug little smile on Blythe's face and the gleam in her eye, Alberta did the same:

> *A Widow lost her babe one day*
> *And thought his fate was sealed;*
> *But a Hero found the lad and bore*
> *Him home upon his shield.*

> *So Knight met Mother at her door*
> *And to the gods appealed,*
> *"What nectarous courtesan is this?*
> *I'll have 'er in the field!"*

> *The Widow threw her mourning off*
> *And to the Knight did yield—*
> *'Tis no easy task, I vow*
> *Keeping Knight and Dame concealed.*

Alberta heard someone say "Oh, that's—" and then a gasp.

Then little Miss Moreton chirped, "What does nectarous mean?" One of the gentlemen cleared his throat, and finally Captain Westwood burst into laughter. Sudbury followed suit.

From Evan, reading over her shoulder, she heard nothing at all. She turned toward him as he brushed past her, plucking Blythe's riddle out of her hands and moving straight toward its author. His face was flushed, his jaw tight. Silent as a cat, he stalked his prey, gaze fixed on her as though nothing else existed. Except that he was actually the prey, turning the tables on the predator.

She said his name and grabbed his arm. It felt like iron. But he paid her no heed at all, pulling her across the floor with him. Someone else took hold of his other arm, but by that time he had reached his target.

Blythe had retreated as he approached and stood stock-still, backed against the piano. Evan stopped not a foot away, his face thrust into hers. His voice was a growl, low and threatening. Probably no one but Alberta, and Amanda Latimer on his other side, heard his words. And Blythe herself, of course.

"If you were a man I beat you to a bloody pulp. Having better manners than a toad, I won't do it." He held up her riddle, clenched in one fist, and shook it in her face. "But by God, ma'am, you'd best keep your distance from me and the other characters in this little farce of yours, or I'll cut that malicious tongue out of your pretty head and feed it to the rats."

Then he tore the paper across, dropped the pieces on the floor, and strode out of the room.

Alberta watched him go. Had he really said those things? She could hardly believe it was the same man, her younger brother whom she had seen evolve from a happy child to a mischievous schoolboy to a charming, thoughtful gentleman. When had she last seen him angry? She couldn't remember. She realized her mouth was hanging open and closed it with a snap.

She turned to find Theo right behind her, one of the crowd surrounding Lady Blythe. She pulled him aside. "Did you hear what he said to her? Go find him, Theo."

But Theo shook his head. "Best to leave him alone, Berta."

Alberta huffed with impatience. But it was a sure bet Evan would not appreciate *her* intrusion. Besides which, she had another task to accomplish, even more unpleasant.

She made her way through the little throng. Someone had helped Blythe to a chair. She was very pale, and perspiration glinted on her forehead, but it looked like she was recovering nicely. Too nicely.

"He threatened me, Lowell," she moaned, holding onto her brother's arm. It looked too dreadfully artistic.

Sudbury patted her hand, but that seemed to be the extent of his sympathy. "I do believe you had it coming, my dear. It was very cleverly done, but—"

"Too clever by half," growled Latimer. "Did you expect him to roll over and play dead?"

Alberta put on her most imperious manner and surveyed the assembled guests. "I believe we've had enough excitement for one evening. I will stay with Lady Blythe until she feels able to climb the stairs."

As the door closed behind the last of them, Alberta turned back to Blythe.

"I suppose you want to lecture me," Blythe said, rising to her feet. They were much the same height, and Alberta looked her straight in the eye.

"Not nearly as much as I want to, er, *beat you to a bloody pulp*, was it? If this were my home, I would—"

"What a violent family the Haverfields are, to be sure." One graceful hand half-hid Blythe's yawn. "It really is too much for me. I believe I'll—"

"Not until I've had my say, young woman. You notice I do not say 'lady'. In my book, you forfeited all right to the title with your little ploy this evening."

"Isn't it fortunate for me that you are not in charge of updating the rolls of the peerage," Blythe retorted. "And you know, you have no standing to—"

"Blast my standing!" Alberta exclaimed. "As one woman to another, what on earth did you want to do? Humiliate a good man? Blacken the reputation of a woman you don't even know? Did you get the results you expected? Are you happy, Blythe?" She could hear her voice rising and hoped there were no servants hanging about in the hall. But there probably were.

Much to her surprise, Blythe folded again into her chair, her arms folded protectively as though she were cold. "No," she whispered. "It was supposed to be funny and a little bit... bawdy."

Alberta forgot about keeping her voice down. "Bawdy? Try crude, foul, vulgar. Disgusting!"

Good God, are those tears? And are they real or just an act? She watched, skeptical. When Blythe pulled a handkerchief from her sleeve and blew her nose, she was convinced. It was not done delicately.

She sat down and took one of Blythe's moist hands, patting it gently. "There, there. One of the nicest things about being high-born is that we get more chances than everyone else. But you must make what amends you can, dear. An apology to my brother, of course, and to your hostess. Can you do that?"

Blythe looked less contrite by the second. "I can think about it." She sounded like a child again, stubborn and spoiled. Alberta dropped her hand and put the steel back in her voice.

"Thinking about it does not count. One thing we can do right now is burn all these copies. Or would you like to send one to the *Gazette*? Imagine what fun they could have with it, Blythe. Society loves bawdy jokes. Is that what you want for my brother? Public ridicule?"

Blythe sighed. "No."

"Then help me collect them. How many did you make?"

By some miracle, they found all of them. Assuming Blythe was telling the truth. Alberta put them into Blythe's hands and led her to the fire. They stood side by side and watched the pages burn to ash.

Alberta, Lady Witney
Whately Manor
31 December 1816

My dear Elizabeth,

I trust, dear sister, that your Christmas festivities proceed happily, with less intrigue than we have seen thus far at Whately. It's a peculiar assortment of persons, and I do believe that Theo and I were invited mostly to stand chaperone. Truth to tell, it's a daunting task. Sudbury is here with both his sisters; why did I never realize what a shameless hussy Blythe is? She seems desperate to snare a husband, which leads me to believe the rumors about their finances. The men enjoy her, of course; but none has yet offered to become her bridegroom. She has our Evan in her eye, but thankfully he seems immune—to Blythe, that is—and her tactics would be sufficient to scare any sane man away.

There is another woman in the picture, however. How wonderful, you say! Not so. Herein lies a tale, to be told briefly: Some few weeks before our arrival, Evan succeeded in finding a young lad (aged just five) who was lost. He restored him to his mother, victim to frostbite and an inflammation of the lungs, and by all accounts, helped nurse him back to health. How romantic, you say? Well, possibly. You would think she would be falling over herself in gratitude, would you not? There is no doubt she is a devoted mother, even a bit overprotective—but she is very reserved and seems to hold the world at arm's length. She stands aloof even from Evan, which is curious. She uses no arts to attract, no flirtation or coquetry, and gives no indication that she might be on the catch for a wealthy husband, or even a protector—which speaks in her favor, of course.

Unfortunately the woman—she is widowed, as you will have guessed—is totally ineligible. My dear, she was scrubbing the doorstep when we arrived for our morning call. At least she is cleanly, you say! Yes, you can joke about it, for you have not seen our brother in his new guise. I have, and I confess to some alarm. Perhaps it is her reserve that attracts him; it is certainly not her sparkling personality. She is handsome enough, her speech is refined, and her manner dignified (far more so than Lady Blythe). Her husband was a vicar, so presumably her antecedents are respectable. But for Evan finally to lose his heart to such as she might break mine. Particularly if it means he will spend the rest of his life in an abstracted mood, walking around with a crease between his brows, unaware of the conversation that surrounds him. On the other hand, it was a surprise and a pleasure to watch him with her son, young Julian Moore. A sweet, serious child and quite an intimate relationship. It made me think, for the first time, that Evan really should be a father someday.

Theo comes to tell me 'tis time to dress for dinner. He sends his love, as do I.

Alberta

❧ 16 ❧

The mirror looked back at Deborah, slightly warped and gothic in the flickering light from the candelabra. She was reasonably pleased with what she had achieved. Her old silk ball gown was a brighter color than she would choose now, closer to peach than amber. But it fit her quite well though it was a bit loose across the bosom; she had been swollen with milk when it was made. And like all but her mourning clothes, which were more recent, it was hopelessly out of style. Why she had even kept it was a mystery, except that it was the only silk she owned.

Like some schoolroom chit playing dress-up with her older sister's wardrobe, she had readied herself for a ball she had no intention of attending. After putting Julian to bed, she had bathed, perfuming the water with lemon and cloves. Then she had donned her shift and this frippery bit of silk, and sat down at the dressing table to do something with her hair.

The possibilities were limited with only her two hands to tweak and roll and fasten it all in place, but it had come out well enough, tied up high on the back of her head and gathered into a loose knot, with a couple of locks allowed to fall to her shoulders. Too youthful a style for her now, however—people would think she was on the catch for a husband.

She owned no silk stockings or formal gloves. She clipped on her ivory earrings and fastened her cameo around her neck—it felt unfamiliar against her bare skin above this low neckline. And she was ready.

For what? She was truly a fool. However presentable she might seem here by herself in the dim light of her bedchamber, she would hardly pass muster at a public ball. To think she might dance without shame alongside Lady Blythe, or Evan's sister the countess, was pure presumption.

To think she might dance with Evan himself—he would certainly insist upon it... No, that was not a subject she wished to contemplate. Unlike that schoolroom chit trying on her sister's clothes, Deborah's future held no promise of a society presentation, no wedding at St. James's, no gleam of elegance or excitement. With some luck she might keep herself off the charity rolls, might even, with strict economy, manage some sort of tutoring for Julian. His intelligence was marvelous, and he would need much more instruction than she or the village school could provide.

The church bell tolled midnight and then pealed insistently in celebration of 1817. She must go downstairs, bank the fire in the parlor, and snuff out the candles. Then she must remove this ridiculous garb and go to bed. She would alter the gown for day-wear or, better yet, use the fabric for a new nightdress. Then no one need see her in this color.

It was difficult, for some reason, to get up from the dressing table and set these events in motion. The mirror frowned at her, as reluctant as she was to give up altogether on pretty gowns, and dancing, and—

A pounding sounded at the door downstairs, startling the night. Everyone in town should be at the ball, celebrating the hopes and possibilities of the new year. More likely than not, it was some village youths rousing anyone who might be sleeping. Another grimace at her reflection, and she went softly down the stairs in her old dance slippers.

Mr. Haverfield—Evan—waited on her doorstep in the cold. If not some prankster, who else could it have been. His narrowed eyes bored into hers, two creases cutting deep between his scowling brows. He brushed past her into the hall. She shivered in the cold air and shut the door.

"Why are you at home? I've been waiting for you."

"I—"

"You said yesterday that you would be there tonight."

Teeth clenched, she dug her fingers like claws into the silk at her hips.

"No, sir." She knew he hated it when she called him sir. "If you examine your memory, you will find I did not commit myself one way or the other."

"You did. You said—" His mouth, twisted with anger, closed tight. He turned on his heel, took two steps across the hall, and slapped his gloves down on the table. His hat followed, more deliberately. Then he hung his greatcoat on a hook and turned to face her. The scowl was gone, replaced by something bleak and somber. She would rather have faced the anger.

"I stand corrected," he said at last. "But surely you intended to go. Your gown and your hair... you look lovely. That color is very becoming."

"No, I never did. I told Molly last week that she could help out at the inn this evening." He looked alarmingly handsome himself in formal black and white, with a touch of burgundy and silver in his waistcoat. But she would not say so.

"Then why are you dressed this way?"

Deborah shrugged her shoulders and turned away into the parlor. Not only was she a fool, she'd been caught out in her foolishness. "I merely..."

"Merely what?"

"I don't know. I was curious to see if the gown still fit me. Reliving the past, I suppose."

A window facing the street stood open a couple of inches, and the room was cold. She crossed the parlor to stir greater life into the fire. Evan took the poker from her hands and did it for her.

"Shall I close the window?"

She shrugged again. "I opened it so I could hear the music."

"It's the supper break now, but they'll be starting up again shortly." Leaving the window open, he sat down on the sofa, obliging her to sit as well. She chose a chair as far away from him as possible.

He settled in, for all the world as though this was a morning call. "How is Julian? I trust he took no harm from his outing yesterday?"

"He is well, thank you." She looked at her hands, folded in her lap. They *looked* relaxed enough. To break the silence, she said, "I expect everyone is quite merry at the inn. Did you enjoy the dancing? Or do you prefer the card room?" All she really wanted to know was whether he had danced, and with whom, but she would not expose herself so patently.

"I wanted to waltz with you," Evan said.

That startled a laugh from her. "You should be glad I wasn't there, then. I would surely have embarrassed us both. I don't even know the steps."

He shifted to the edge of his seat, one hand on his knee, eyebrows raised in astonishment. "You've never waltzed?"

Anger pricked her again. Her voice sounded harsh. "Just when would I have learned it, sir?" *And why?*

"You were waiting for approval from the patronesses at Almack's, no doubt."

She examined his expression, saw the quirk of his lips and the gleam in his eyes that meant he was teasing, and smiled a little. "Frankly, I've no reason to know how to waltz, sir."

"Nonsense. It's fun. I'll show you."

He rose and cleared a space in the room. Good gracious, did he mean *right now*?

She sat frozen on the sofa. But when Evan came to her, and bowed over her hand and asked for this dance, she humored him. A bit more play-acting.

It was colder away from the fire, but his hands were warm where they touched her. She laid one hand on his shoulder as directed. Suddenly shy, she looked up into his face. How scandalous! *How wonderful.*

He talked as he set her in motion, describing the movements and counting out the time, allowing her to watch his feet for a few minutes. She compared her present teacher with Mr. Aston, her gin-soaked dancing master in Plymouth, and giggled. The sound of it shocked her. When was the last time she giggled?

Evan laughed. He lifted her chin with their joined hands. "Now look at me." He hummed a tune while she became a bit more comfortable with the steps and turns. Then the musicians returned to their labors up the street. Conveniently, they began with a waltz.

It was too soft to hear properly, and the sound drifted with the wind. But the rhythm was easy enough to catch, and she infinitely preferred dancing with him in private where no one could see her blush.

In the near-darkness, hopefully Evan couldn't either.

"That's it," he said, guiding her with his hands. "You learn quickly." She let herself relax a bit. "Now let's see what we can do."

He widened the pattern of their steps, sweeping her in spirals around the room. She locked her eyes onto his, her anchor in the dizzying whirl. His hand was a caress at her waist, her heart raced with exhilaration. Had she really thought the room cold?

The parlor was too small. They spun into a chair and tripped over Julian's toy basket. She laughed as he steadied her, and he grinned.

It was an obvious opportunity to draw the curtain on this little charade. But she did not resist when he drew her back into position and guided her into a decorous turn. His arm pulled her closer, and she did not resist that, either, though their thighs kissed as they moved and his coat grazed her breasts. In her distraction, she missed a step, throwing off their rhythm. The musicians now played a country dance, so it hardly mattered. When their feet moved again, they followed no rhythm at all.

She rested her cheek against his shoulder, and his hand spread wide on her back, pressing her closer still. She couldn't think. She pulled away, but only to lift her head and look into his eyes. They were no longer smiling.

She slid her hand from his shoulder up the back of his neck into his dark curls, and pulled his mouth down to meet hers. All movement stopped at that.

She melted into his kiss, aware of nothing but the physical sensations cascading through her body. One of his hands slipped down below her waist while the other stroked slowly up her back. She curled back against it, binding herself to him. Folded in his arms, she felt complete. She could not imagine wanting more, except... more.

He slid his hand into the hair on the back of her head, pressing her lips to his. When the kiss ended, his face was flushed and his breathing ragged.

It was too powerful. She did not even try to talk herself out of it. She took his face between her hands. "Come upstairs with me?"

His brows rose a little in surprise, but she could see desire burning hot in his eyes. She extinguished the one candle that had not yet guttered. Then she took his hand and led him up to her bedchamber. Here, too, the window stood open, and the music wove in and out of her awareness. They undressed each other, slowly. As he removed from her hair the pins that had not already fallen to the parlor floor, he asked simply, "Are you sure?"

"Completely. But," she murmured, "there must be no responsibility, no obligations." He was pressing a kiss to her throat as she spoke, and she forgot to exact his promise.

It was leisurely and agonizingly delicious, the intense and wonderful things he did with his hands and mouth, things she had never imagined. When he had spent himself inside her, she felt warm and languorous, content to lie quietly by his side, his hand on her breast, watching the light flickering on the ceiling. Had she ever felt this way?

"Your husband was a lucky man." And at the surprised face she turned to him, "Did he not know it?"

"N-n-no, I don't believe he felt lucky." Hartley, poor fellow, had been backed into a corner by Aunt Matilda. All the physical attraction and gratitude that Deborah, at least, had mistaken for love, soon evaporated.

With her lack of experience or information, and his lack of patience or sensitivity, even the physical aspect of the marriage had provided little satisfaction to either party, tantalizing with a hint of what might be but never delivering it. This much was history, and she felt quite free to offer up that chapter of her past for Evan's contemplation. He must know that tonight she was satisfied—she'd made no attempt to hide it.

Deborah spoke out of a long, comfortable silence. "How many waltz partners end up in bed together, do you suppose?"

He chuckled in her ear, sending a warm current down to her womb. "Keep in mind that most waltzes are not danced alone in the dark. *That* was our mistake."

She turned her head to look at him. "Are you sorry?"

"God, no. This has been the most extraordinary night of my life." He ran a hand across her ribs and brought it to rest on her abdomen. "I hope *you* don't feel, tomorrow, that it was a mistake."

She shook her head.

But it was. Because after another silence, he spoke again.

"Marry me, Deborah."

❧ 17 ❧

Nettled by the vehemence of Deborah's rejection, Evan stalked to the inn and left a message for the viscount. He was too rumpled, in his attire and his feelings, to rejoin the festivities.

Then he marched back again as far as Deborah's cottage, where the faint glow of a candle or two still illuminated her bedroom window. But once around the corner and out of sight, he slowed his pace and let reflection take precedence over pride.

Latimer's question rolled round in Evan's mind—*Do you love her?* He still didn't know. Proposing marriage had been an act of impulse, and if it surprised *him*, it surely surprised her more. It had generated quite an explosive recoil, which was humbling.

Yet he was reasonably sure she liked him very well. And without a doubt, he could offer her a life far better than the one she lived now. He cared very much what became of Julian, and as for Julian's mother —could he possibly leave Whately and never see her again? The prospect of marriage seemed more and more satisfying. It would take him a lifetime to understand her, no doubt, and he could think of no way he would rather spend it.

At the risk of sounding like the pompous Mr. Collins from *Pride and Prejudice*, perhaps he should not be discouraged by Deborah's rebuff. There was no question of her subscribing to *that kind of elegance which consists in tormenting a respectable man*, but it was possible that some reflection might effect a change in her feelings. He was far from sanguine, however.

Alberta tapped on his door when she returned from the ball. She heard nothing and had turned to go when he called out his permission to enter.

"Come." It sounded reluctant at best.

He flicked a glance her way but said nothing. He sat in his shirt-sleeves in a wing chair by the fire, a mostly empty decanter at his elbow. She'd seldom seen him more than a bit merry with drink; he was considerably beyond that, she judged, and did not look merry at all.

"I'm surprised you're not asleep. You left the ball hours ago."

He just grunted. She would get no confidences from him tonight. She had her suspicions. Mrs. Moore had not come to the ball, and Evan's impatient attention to the doorway had not escaped Alberta's notice.

"Are you feeling faint, my dear?"

He looked up at her under lowered brows. "No, why?"

"As far as I'm aware, the only ailment brandy can cure is faintness." She marched out again, leaving him to his brown study.

Theo was undressing in their bedchamber, yawning—as balls went, this one had been pretty dull. They had danced one waltz together, and then Theo had retreated to the card room while Alberta occupied herself with observing the antics of Lady Blythe's *rabble*—and of Blythe herself, who seemed set on making herself conspicuous. She'd romped through the country dances just like the village girls she despised, and waltzed with vigor when she could. Captain Westwood was not one to restrain himself or to encourage restraint in others, and since those two had danced most of the night together, *most* improperly, there had been ample opportunity to observe their horseplay.

Evan had avoided her entirely.

Blythe's interactions with the local populace were marked by lofty disdain, so that Alberta and others of the Manor party found themselves leaning over backward to compensate for Blythe's snobbishness. How Lady Honora had turned out so quiet and modest was anyone's guess; perhaps she had determined to distance herself as far as possible from her sister's behavior.

If Evan saw fit to court Honora now—but it seemed she would make a match of it with Frank Latimer. As things were going, Alberta would not be surprised to hear an announcement from *that* quarter before the house party broke up.

Theo listened with some interest to Alberta's description of her brother's present state and her conjectures as to its cause, but disclaimed all responsibility in getting to the bottom of the matter. "He's nearly thirty, my dear. Surely he deserves his privacy without his sister sticking her curious nose where it's not wanted—or his brother-in-law, either. If his *affaire* has gone awry, well, that's what you wanted, is it not?"

"I suppose. It seems incredible that she would reject him."

Theo cleared his throat. "You are in the habit of thinking Evan to be honorable in all things—well, we all are—but it is just possible, my dear, that what he offered her was not marriage. We know precious little of his dealings with women, after all. And if that should be the case, a rejection certainly speaks well of her morals."

Alberta grunted, frowning. She was busy taking the pins out of her hair.

"I've not met the woman, of course," Theo continued, "but judging from what I've heard, she sounds a good, serious choice for Evan. She would settle him down. I like her."

"That's neither here nor there, Theo. It would be a gross *mésalliance.*"

He shrugged and pulled out a pin she had missed. "We would have to check further into her background, of course. But I've not heard anyone cast aspersions on her breeding."

"Humph. But it's not your family, after all. Why should you care who he marries?"

Theo cried pax at that. It was all speculation, it was past three o'clock, and it was true, he did not care very much. One thing was sure: given a choice for sister between Lady Blythe and a *mésalliance*, he would choose the *mésalliance* nine times out of ten.

DEBORAH COULD NOT SLEEP, could not even persuade her eyes to close. Instead of lying dreamily, reliving and reveling in the pleasure they had shared, she turned over and back again, got up and prowled the room, returned to the bed, and fumed some more.

She'd thought to hold this night in memory, a warm interlude in a cold lifetime: the night she learned to waltz, to ask for pleasure and give it in return. But he had spoiled it. The sheets were infused with the smell of what they'd done. She pummeled the pillow, buried her face in it, but his scent lingered.

Marry him? He must be crazy, for all that he seemed so sane. She spent some time trying—realistically now, without interference from that silly girl in dress-up clothes—to picture herself in his home as his wife. Always the picture degenerated into unhappiness for them both.

She would be inept as a hostess and hopeless at managing a large household, intimidated by butler and footmen and lady's maid and omnipotent housekeeper. She had no wit and no conversation, and Evan would be ashamed to take her into society—and being the man he was, ashamed to leave her behind. Surely he would consider the future, as she was doing, and see how ludicrous it was.

She was astonished to see him walk into her parlor the next morning. Had she not been rude enough to him last night?

It was still early, perhaps half past eight. Molly must have let him in the kitchen door, confound the girl. Julian jumped up from his lessons to greet "Mr. Haffield" as he would greet his favorite person in all the world—as no doubt he was, at least this morning.

She had already scolded her son more than once, probably undeservedly. In quite his usual manner, Evan squatted down to talk to the child, laughing at Julian's description of their battle with a rat at sunrise. But he looked as though he'd had little more sleep than she had. She was glad in some way she was not proud of.

He stood up and rested a hand on her son's shoulder. "I've left Lookout in the yard. Perhaps you might beg a carrot from Molly and go keep him company for a few minutes?"

They were alone, the last place Deborah wanted to be. She remained standing by the table and did not offer him a seat. To her relief, he did not approach her but stood ill at ease, pulling his gloves through his hands as though he wasn't sure how to begin.

It would be an apology, she decided; he wanted her to know he was withdrawing his offer.

"Deborah, I— I took you by surprise last night. It took me by surprise as well, I'll admit that; you know it already. Perhaps the thoughtlessness of it offended you, and I cannot blame you for that. I suppose a proposal of marriage should be pondered and planned, not blurted out like—like I did."

He wandered restlessly toward the table and gazed down at the paper where Julian had been practicing his alphabet. "In any event, I have now pondered the night through, and I have realized there is nothing I want more."

Deborah's eyes flew to meet his for the first time since his arrival. They must clearly show her stupefaction—how in God's name could a rational man reach such a conclusion?

She turned away to the window. "You're wrong," she said.

A couple of quick strides brought him close behind her, but he did not touch her. "Deborah, this life you're living, you and Julian—I want so much more for you. I can give you a nice home, a fine library. We can go to concerts and the theatre. We can travel if you'd like. And Julian can have a family, the education he deserves to have, a pony of his own. You don't have to be alone." He spoke earnestly, even passionately.

How she wished she could allow herself to be tempted.

Her own voice was quiet and hard. "That sounds like pity speaking. Your family would certainly not approve of you marrying for pity."

"It's not pity!" he cried. Then, more quietly, "Perhaps it is, if pity is the desire to help someone. But only in part. I want to share my life with you; I don't want to leave you behind."

"You must." Silence.

"Why?"

She took her courage in her hands and turned to face him. "It's quite impossible, Evan, surely you must see that. It could never work."

"Why?" he repeated. "Is it that you don't like me well enough?"

Too much, her mind screamed, to condemn you to the marriage I see. She stared at his cravat, quelling the urge to smooth his coat, to touch him one more time.

"No, not well enough."

A short pause, and then he bowed abruptly. "I'm sorry to have been a nuisance. Good day, Mrs. Moore."

He was gone.

She stood stock-still until her lungs demanded air, but in drawing that shaky breath, her knees gave out and she crumpled to the floor. Her best hope for happiness had walked out, and she had allowed it. No, she had flung it as one might hurl a fearsome night creature, a bat perhaps, that attacked in the darkness.

She stayed, her hands clenched tightly round the stiles of a chair, until she became aware of the pain. She would *not* cry. There was this whole day to get through, and then another, and all the weeks and years of days to come. Tears would help her not at all.

By the time Julian returned to the parlor, she had regained a semblance of composure. She cut short his effusions over the horse, and the man, and the shiny new guinea he'd been given, and put him back to work at his letters.

She worked her way around the room with dust rag and polishing cloth. Whatever disappointment or resentment Evan might feel now, he would soon be offering paeans to whatever power had been watching over him this day.

In her fierce performance of chores that would keep her from thinking, she knocked the miniature of Aunt Matilda to the floor, breaking the glass. She could not bring herself to care, was almost glad to have the additional work to do. She pulled the remaining shards from the frame and stuck the picture away in a drawer, swept the glittery fragments from the floor, and brushed the past from her hands.

❧ 18 ❧

E van returned Lookout to the stable and headed toward a set of French doors that led from the gardens into the drawing room. It should be deserted at this hour, and he dearly wanted solitude. But rounding the corner of the house, he was waylaid by Amanda, just finishing some instructions to one of the workmen. She fell in beside him.

"Some of us are going for a ride after breakfast, but it looks as though you've been out already. Well, it's a glorious morning to start off the year."

Evan lifted his head and looked about him, up to the pale blue morning sky and into the gardens where evergreens and bare branches moved in a fresh, cold breeze. "It's nice enough."

Amanda regarded him quizzically. "I take it that your errand, whatever it was, did not prosper?"

"No. No, it didn't."

"And I take it you were looking for something more than—oh, a loaf of bread, say."

He stopped, gazing at their footprints in the frosted grass. "I was looking for a wife." He looked up to gauge her reaction.

Amanda's brows flew up, her eyes wide in amazement. "She said *no?*"

He resumed walking. "She did."

She stared after him and then ran to catch up. "Perhaps you should ask her again."

He grimaced. "I already did."

"Oh!" She hesitated. "Did she say why?"

"She doesn't like me well enough."

"Balderdash," she exclaimed. "You saved her son, Evan!"

He smiled, but there was no humor in it. "That hardly obliges her to marry me."

"Of course not, but…"

"I think she's afraid."

"Of what, for heaven's sake?"

His frown deepened. "Oh, *the rustling of the grass, the very shadows of the clouds.* Her own shadows. Her life has not been like yours or mine."

"Is that Wordsworth?" she asked, her forehead creased in concentration.

"Yes." Evan slapped his crop against his leg. "I think she's afraid my family would disinherit me."

"They wouldn't."

"No. But they wouldn't be pleased. No doubt they would prefer Lady Blythe."

"Oh, Lord. No, I think your sister's eyes have been opened by this little party." They were silent as they entered the comparative warmth of the drawing room. "And even if they did cast you off, Mrs. Moore would still be better off than she is now."

"I confess, Amanda, I hope she could find some better reason than that to marry me."

"I'd wager she will do so yet," she replied brightly. "Now, how about some breakfast?"

"Not just now, thank you." He did not feel hungry, and he certainly did not feel sociable. "I don't want to put a blight on your party."

Amanda snorted. "This party is growing blights like a bad case of root rot. Blythe is a blight unto herself and has alienated everyone except the captain, who positively eggs her on. I dread they will compromise themselves under my roof. Frank's making a cake of himself over Lady Honora. And my poor, devoted Charles wants more of my attention than I can give until this assortment of motley fools breaks up. Never again will I play hostess to a party of Frank's devising."

Evan smiled. His face felt rusty. "Poor Amanda. You should kick us all out, my dear."

"Hmm. Perhaps smallpox in the village?" She sighed. "I suppose not. Well, I must get to the breakfast parlor. You're sure you won't join us?"

He shook his head.

"Do you stay here? Shall I have the fire lit?"

"No, I'll not stay long. But perhaps you could ask Parker to bring some coffee?" That would take the chill off.

Evan sat down at the piano. Idly, he riffled through the stack of music to give his mind and hands something to do. Music was not a standard component of a gentleman's education as it was for a lady. But he'd been fascinated by the piano as a child, and Alberta, always the bossy sort, had happily taught him the rudiments of scales and sight-reading.

Finding a Mozart sonata that looked fairly straightforward, at least through the first couple of pages, he began picking out the notes.

The door whispered open, and he turned to see Lady Blythe slip in. Almost secretively, she pushed it shut again and came across the room with a coy smile. "Oh, you don't have to get up. I wondered where you were hiding yourself, Evan."

"How wonderful that you found me," he responded very drily.

"Oh, it was quite easy; I followed the coffee. And the music. Do you really play?"

"Execrably. What you heard was definitely *not* music."

"Good. I detest music," Blythe said. "Much as I detest boredom or virtue. Or widows." Evan picked out a few more notes, frowning. "You never did return to the ball last night, dear Evan. I suppose you found some more pleasurable pastime?"

He was silent.

"It *was* dull, wasn't it?" Blythe murmured, slipping two fingers inside his cravat and running them around the back of his neck. "I would happily have escaped with you."

Evan shuddered at the touch of her cold hand. Then he turned abruptly and stood up. "No, thank you, ma'am."

She stepped up to him and put her hands on his chest. "Why not? I have far more to offer than that insipid widow of yours. She makes me quite jealous. And jealousy makes me stupid. I should never have composed that riddle. It was rude, and I apologize."

Well, that was a surprise.

"But I'll bet you anything you like, I kiss better than she does." Another half step brought her right against him. Her arms snaked up around his neck.

Hindered by the piano at his back, Evan was impelled to rather rough tactics. He took her arms and forced her down onto the piano bench before backing away.

Blythe bounced to her feet. "You're rude, Mr. Haverfield!"

"You're insufferable, Lady Blythe. Good day."

As he reached for the door handle, one of the music books sailed past his head. "Hateful," she cried.

Evan retreated to his bedchamber.

Even here he was not left in peace for long. A knock heralded the entrance of his brother-in-law, who found him sprawled in much the same attitude his sister had seen the previous night. At least he was not drunk. Not yet.

Beyond commenting that hangovers were the very devil, Theo showed no interest in Evan's megrims. "How about a gallop? The others are riding through the village to look at the abbey ruins, but I thought we might head across the meadow and down toward the river."

Thank heaven for indifference. Evan relaxed. It was difficult to converse upon serious subjects while galloping willy-nilly across the countryside, and the last thing Evan wanted was conversation.

❧ 19 ❧

As the gentlemen made their way to the drawing room after dinner, Evan drew Latimer aside into the library. "Feels like I've hardly spoken to you since I arrived in Whately."

"It's all this company," Latimer said, shaking his head. "And before that it was your widow. Been meaning to ask, what's happening there?"

"The boy is quite recovered," Evan said, refusing a brandy, "and you'll be happy to hear that nothing else is happening at all."

"Oh… I thought maybe that was where you snuck off to last night." Frank sat down by the fire.

Evan assessed his friend for a moment and then sat across from him. "It was. But nothing came of it." At least, nothing he was going to talk about with Latimer or anyone else.

He stood up again and poured himself some of the brandy he'd refused earlier. "What of your own prospects?"

"With Honora, you mean? I don't know. It's aggravating as hell."

"I'll turn the tables on you. Do you love her?"

"Oh, she's an absolute angel, Haverfield," Frank said, leaning forward. "But I can never tell what she's thinking." He took a gulp of brandy. "What do you think of her?"

Evan pondered what to say. It wasn't as easy as discussing horse-flesh. "*Angel* seems apt. It's only… You fall in and out of love so easily, Frank. How can you be sure she's the right one?"

A harebrained question for me to be asking—I fell just as quickly.

Latimer shrugged. "I'm not sure it matters all that much. I'm an easygoing fellow, I figure I should be able to get along with any number of women."

"Hell, Latimer. Are you really content to *get along* with your wife? I want…" He let loose an explosive sigh. "I don't know what I want." Except that he did know. And he couldn't have it.

"They say if you pick a young one, you can train her up the way you want her. I only hope I can talk her out of turning the house into some Oriental fashion plate."

Evan grimaced. "I hope so too." He swirled his brandy around, fire-light through amber. He didn't want it after all. "Listen, Frank. I need to go to Shrewsbury tomorrow to see my bankers."

"Another week and we'll be done here."

"I know, but it can't wait. I'll be back Sunday. Saturday night if I'm lucky."

Latimer drained his glass. "With all the acrimony between you and Blythe, I can't say I'm surprised."

"Ha. I won't miss her, but that's not the reason."

Latimer stood up and moved toward the door. "Well, the ladies are waiting. We'll miss you. And Haverfield? If I should ask for her while you're gone, wish me luck."

Evan gripped Frank's shoulder. "Done."

Ironic that the two of them, who had talked so adamantly against marriage less than a month ago, should both offer it so soon afterward.

May he fare better than I did.

ALBERTA COULD HAVE THROTTLED her brother.

What could possibly be so important that he couldn't wait a week to see the family bankers? She wouldn't have come to this dreadful party at all if *he* hadn't been here.

"You know," she'd said when he told her he was going, "if you need some ready cash, Theo could—"

"No, it's nothing he can help with."

Neither roundabout conversation nor a direct approach elicited anything more useful. Alberta thought about packing up and leaving as well, but Theo was inclined to stay, and she didn't want to leave Miss Latimer in the lurch.

She watched Evan leave from her window as she dressed the next morning. Grady was taking him to the inn—he'd be traveling post from there. Evan *never* traveled post. So at least he had speed in mind.

The others went hunting, leaving Alberta with only Honora for company. When the girl finally went upstairs to rest, Alberta moved to the drawing room and pounded out the *Presto* from a Cramer sonata on the pianoforte.

Three and a half minutes later, she was smiling. She might not practice as much as she should, but she still had the touch. She played until she was bored to tears.

She was so glad to see Theo, she hung about their bedchamber while he bathed and dressed, listening to his report on the hunting. His valet maintained a stony silence, lips pursed in disapproval.

Alberta made a face at the door after he left the room. "What an old woman he is. Surely you could do better?"

"Are you saying you're displeased with my attire?" he teased, showing himself off. "Or the shine on my boots?"

She surveyed his navy coat and paisley silk waistcoat, the fit of his breeches, the fall of his cravat. And yes, his boots. She had no complaint with that. It was quite a nice package she'd married.

"I'm sorry, I've had an insipid day. I cannot fathom what Latimer finds to talk to that girl about. I tried every subject I could think of, and the only things that interested her at all were God and gardens. I ask you, Theo, does Latimer seem likely to appreciate either one?"

Theo laughed. "It's one of the mysteries of love, my dear." He put his arms around her and gave her a kiss. "Poor old Bertie. Tomorrow

will be more interesting. In fact, today could be more interesting..."
He cupped his hands over her bottom and pulled her tight, nibbling on her ear.

"Theo!"

"What? There's no one to see."

"Thank goodness for that."

The following day they drove to Belvoir Castle, something over an hour's journey. Theo had made the arrangements. Alberta and Theo visited with the Duke and Duchess of Rutland in their private wing while the head housekeeper guided the others through the public rooms. A light repast and visits to the stables and succession houses rounded out the excursion. Blythe seemed out of spirits, which was a pleasant change. It was the most enjoyable day Alberta had seen since her arrival.

They returned to Whately Manor for a late dinner. The final set of plates was cleared, and Alberta waited for Miss Latimer to lead the ladies from the table. But the viscount tapped his glass with a spoon and rose to his feet.

"I have an announcement to make." All eyes turned his way. Blythe yawned, making a show of it. "This afternoon, the Lady Honora honored me by accepting my offer of marriage." Honora blushed.

There was a satisfying chorus of cheers and applause. Sudbury must have known already, of course—Latimer would hardly have proposed without speaking to him first. In fact, *everyone* must have known. But the cheers were obligatory.

In honor of the occasion, the gentlemen accompanied the ladies to the drawing room and drank champagne instead of port. The evening passed away in a buzz of light-headed conversation and cards.

The rain started as Alberta headed upstairs to bed. It slapped against the windows and kept her awake half the night.

"I KNOW, DEAR," she told Miss Latimer the next morning. "Rain is a hostess's worst nightmare." It was less violent, but there would be no outdoor activities today.

With nowhere to go, they had lingered over breakfast, calling for more pancakes and topping them with an excellent compote of apricots and cherries. Theo and Sudbury were still there, finishing the newspapers. Alberta sat in the morning room writing to Mama, while Miss Latimer agonized over how to entertain her guests.

Miss Latimer sighed. "You must have some ideas, Frank."

He looked up from his admiration of Lady Honora's stitchery. She was good at it, Alberta admitted, but that hardly seemed like the viscount's line, either.

He scratched his nose. "I don't know. Games?"

Miss Latimer groaned. "If I have to play any more charades, I'll scream. And no cards, either." She strode to the window and looked up at the sky. No help there.

"Well, there's chess, and backgammon. How about dominoes?" He sounded as skeptical about the idea as Alberta felt.

Lady Honora sat up straight and dropped her sewing in her lap. "Goodness, I haven't played dominoes since I was a child. That sounds like fun!" Her eyes were shining. She looked very pretty indeed.

The viscount certainly thought so. "Where are they?" he asked his sister, suddenly enthusiastic. "Do you know?"

"No." She frowned in thought, one finger across her lips. "Perhaps that cabinet in the billiard room?"

Honora jumped to her feet. "Oh, let's go see."

The three of them traipsed out. Their voices receded while Alberta tried to decide how much to tell Mama about Evan's state of mind. *Very little. She'll find out for herself soon enough.*

A screech sounded from across the hall, followed by piercing hysterics. *That* would be Honora. And Berta would bet it had nothing to do with dominoes.

She dropped the pen and ran into the hall. She was the first but far from the only one. Theo and Sudbury emerged from one doorway,

Lord Hartwell and Miss Moreton from another, and the household staff came out of the wainscoting like mice.

The viscount and Miss Latimer stood on the billiard room threshold, mouths agape. Honora had turned away and wailed into Latimer's chest. He put his arm around her, but it was an automatic maneuver—his attention remained on whatever was happening inside the room.

Peering over Miss Latimer's shoulder, Alberta had no question at all what was happening. Or rather, what *had been* happening. Captain Westwood and Lady Blythe stood several feet apart, both of them bright red. Blythe was adjusting her bodice while the captain, for once bereft of his smirk, tried desperately to button his breeches.

Honora was finally led away, tended by her own maid and Miss Latimer's. Sudbury foamed at the mouth, quite literally, flecks of saliva spraying with each expletive as he tried to get at Westwood. What a daunting scene.

While Theo took control of that situation, Alberta put on all her authority and sent everyone else packing. She grasped Miss Latimer's hand for a moment and offered her vinaigrette—Amanda was quite white, her eyes still wide with shock. Then Latimer took her back to the morning room, saying something about brandy.

Berta and Theo herded Sudbury and the two transgressors into the library, where even Alberta accepted some brandy. It burned as it went down, but yes, it was quite bracing. Theo propped himself against Latimer's desk. Alberta sat down, hoping everyone else might do the same, but they did not.

Blythe had gone from flushed to pale, but she held her chin stubbornly in the air as she paced back and forth.

Initially she claimed rape. "What made him think he could do that to me?"

Had they been alone, Berta would have been quite happy to answer Blythe's question for her. But a choked laugh from Theo earned him a glare from both women.

"You hussy," Sudbury yelled at his sister. "How can you say that? You've been throwing yourself at him since we got here."

Blythe rounded on him. "Yes, I'm a flirt! But I never meant..." She sagged suddenly and dropped down on the sofa next to Alberta. "I never meant for him to do *that*."

Sudbury turned his spleen on Westwood. He accused the captain not only of rape but of base birth, deceit, and losing the war in America. Then he spat a challenge in his face.

Theo, who had listened to the whole diatribe with a growing gleam of merriment in his eyes, intervened. "Now, Sudbury, let's approach this rationally. Your filial loyalty is entirely admirable, and there is no question you're entitled to satisfaction. But there will be no advantage to your sister if you are killed in a duel. And the captain has proved himself a better marksman than any of us."

"By God, I will *not* be contravened! I'll kill the bastard, and then I'll make him marry her!"

"Er," said Theo, his voice unsteady, "that *would* be a trick. Perhaps the wedding should come first?"

The captain spoke for the first time since the billiard room door had opened on the scene of ignominy. "I'm more than willing, if the lady is agreeable."

All eyes swiveled toward him and jaws fell agape.

"There," Theo said into the sudden silence. "Captain Westwood is prepared to be reasonable."

"Well I won't have it!" sputtered Sudbury. "That good-for-nothing just thinks to get his hands on her dowry."

Lady Blythe gazed at her brother in frank incredulity.

"Um—*is* there a dowry, Sudbury?" inquired Theo.

"She has £2,000 from her mother, invested in the five-percents, that comes to her upon her marriage."

"And you think a fortune-hunter would sacrifice his freedom for *that*?" exclaimed Blythe. "Tell me, Lowell," she added with biting sarcasm, "why did I not know of this great bequest?"

"Because you'd have found a way to get at it without meeting the terms of the trust, that's why. And if I couldn't make use of it, I didn't see why you should."

"People do manage on £100 a year, of course..." Theo commented unhopefully. Those people were not accustomed to life in the *ton*.

"But I'm not one of them," declared Blythe. "I've been pinching pennies and nipping farthings for the past four years, and I will *not* do it for the rest of my life! I have no intention of marrying a pauper."

Theo looked curiously at Westwood. "*Are* you a pauper, Captain?"

"I wondered if anyone would get around to asking me that," Westwood replied, his smirk back in place. "I've no land to my name, though my father owned property in Sussex. I would sell my commission, of course, and with that I will have something over £1,500, with additional funds invested in gas and in shipping. And a reasonably wealthy aunt with no children and a fondness for—er, good-for-nothings."

Well, that was not *too* dreadful. Alberta had supposed the man to be impecunious and a wastrel, based on nothing more than his smirk, and a certain negligent way with his clothing, and a healthy set of side-whiskers—oh, and that nasty habit of smoking cigars. But he was quite dashing. Such means as he described were modest, but still a very pleasant surprise. Particularly for a woman obliged to marry the man.

"Well, my dear," urged Alberta, patting Blythe's hand. "Have we another betrothal to celebrate?"

Lady Blythe looked the Captain over, assessing. "Perhaps." She sounded shy, but Berta didn't believe it.

"I certainly hope Lord Latimer has more champagne in the cellar," murmured Theo.

20

Arrived back in Whately, Evan strolled into the drawing room behind the tea tray on Saturday evening but was plied instead with champagne and the news of matrimonial expectations not his own. Quite sincerely, he congratulated everyone involved, except Lady Honora, who was absent from the evening's gathering. Some of the guests exclaimed in surprise that he'd been able to travel that day with all the rain, but no one expressed the least curiosity as to where he had gone or why. That suited him just fine.

He took his champagne over to the corner where Theo and Frank stood in conversation. "I knew of your plans before I left, Latimer," he said. "But how did this other business come about?"

Theo's grin looked like it might split his face in two.

Latimer rolled his eyes. "Indeed, it's quite a tale. Can't go into all the details here," he said, casting a sidelong glance toward the unnamed couple. To Evan, the lady looked ill-tempered enough without being gossiped about in stray corners.

"You'll be sorry you missed it when you hear the whole," Theo said. "Let's just say it involved an unconventional use for the billiard table, and hysterics—"

"Honora's," Latimer chimed in. "She's still out of curl."

"—and dominoes—"

"Lord, yes, we went looking for the dominoes. That's what started the whole thing."

"—and extended negotiations, greased with generous quantities of liquor in various forms over the course of the day." Theo looked across to where Sudbury was clapping Westwood on the back, all jovial brotherhood. "Ten or eleven hours ago, that same fellow was challenging Westwood to pistols at sunrise."

Evan gazed at his brother-in-law. "How I admire you, Theo. Why haven't they drafted you into diplomatic service?"

Theo laughed out loud, and Blythe shot a look of wrath their way.

Sunday morning was still drizzly and sloppy. Deborah used that as her excuse to stay home from church. Instead, she worked with Julian on his lessons at the table in the parlor.

Julian jumped from his seat and ran to the window. "Who is that, Mama?"

She rose from her chair to get a better look at the phaeton stopped in the street. Though her reply half-strangled her, the boy ran off and reached the front door almost before the knock sounded.

She could see them through the parlor doorway, though she could not hear what they said. Evan lifted Julian and they talked for a few minutes. Then he put the boy down and ruffled his hair, and Julian trotted into the kitchen.

Evan pulled off his gloves as he came into the room but did not remove his greatcoat. Nor did Deborah offer to take it, though it dripped on the floor. He looked far better rested than the last time she had seen him—she knew the same could not be said of herself.

He extracted some very official-looking papers from an inside pocket and set them down on the table. "I beg your pardon for imposing myself on you yet again. It will not take long."

He gestured to the documents. "I know this will go against the grain for you. I have set up a trust for Julian, specifically to fund his education."

She made an involuntary movement and he paused, but she neither looked at him nor spoke.

"I don't know whether you will want to send him to school or employ private tutors, but this is designed to cover whatever choice you make, up to and including university, or so I hope. You are a trustee, of course, together with my bankers in Shrewsbury. They will keep me informed as to its use, but you need have no direct contact with me."

It was clearly her turn. She dared a quick look into his face. "I can't believe... I don't know what to say. You are far too generous, sir." Her voice hardly sounded like her own.

"You're not going to turn it down?"

Deborah gazed down at the table, at the documents he had brought and the painstaking words Julian had lettered out: book, horse, man, Mister. She hated the obligation, but she certainly wanted the schooling. "No, I'll not do that."

"It just needs your signature, then."

Quill and ink were handy. She signed twice, where he indicated, pleased that her hand was reasonably steady. Then he separated one copy, rolled it up, and returned it to his coat pocket.

"Deborah..." He paused long enough that she finally looked up. "I am not a trustee and have no say in how the moneys are used. But if you should ever want my advice, or if Julian needs a reference or a sponsor, please know that I will always be eager to help in any way I can. You can reach me at any time through the address listed in the trust document."

A strangled "thank you" was all she could manage.

"I think Julian has a birthday soon?"

She nodded. "The twenty-seventh of this month."

"I hope you won't object if I send him a little something? And perhaps a letter now and then?"

"Of course not. You—have a kind heart, sir."

Evan grunted. "According to Shakespeare, *a woman would run through fire and water* for that very thing. So apparently I still have a deal of work to do."

Bowing abruptly, he left her.

&

THE LAST DAYS in Whately passed quite pleasantly. Thankfully the weather remained fair—Alberta didn't know how they'd survive another rainy day.

With the exception of Sudbury, who didn't count, Evan was the only single gentleman remaining, and there were no eligible ladies for him to compromise.

Heaven forbid he should compromise the ineligible Mrs. Moore!

Tensions in the house were somewhat relieved following Blythe's engagement, though that lady's emotions were uneven. She would flirt with her betrothed at breakfast in quite her usual manner, and the next time Berta saw her, she was berating him for something or other, or flying from the room in a huff.

One afternoon Berta came across her in the morning room. She was by herself, sitting by the window with her feet curled up beneath her, her dainty kid slippers on the floor beside her chair. She looked up and gave Alberta a smile, but it was a woebegone attempt.

Forgetting the writing paper she'd come for, Alberta approached. "Do I intrude, my dear? If you would rather be alone…"

"No," Blythe said. "I'm just feeling sorry for myself. I don't indulge in the exercise very often, I assure you."

"I know you don't," said Alberta as she sat down nearby. "But I'd say you have some cause for preoccupation. You'll see many changes in the months ahead."

Blythe brought her knees up, wrapping her skirts modestly around them, and rested her chin on them. "He's not like *any* of the men I've imagined marrying." She turned her gaze to the expanse of brown grass and bare trees outside the window. "And all this will be Honora's, while I live in lodgings somewhere, hoping I can scrape together enough pennies to pay my dressmaker."

"Time will tell. But bitterness and self-pity will not help. You're an intelligent woman, and the Captain seems to have a good head on his shoulders." Alberta plucked a loose thread from her gown. "Am I only imagining that he treats you more gently since your betrothal?"

"No, it's true. It's rather sweet, is it not? And it could drive me crazy." She sat up, spreading her arms wide. "I need *life*. I want tearing gallops across the countryside and a good argument now and then."

She slid her feet into her slippers and stood up, straight and resolute. Then she spoke in quite a different voice, much more like her own. "If nothing else, my bedroom will be a far more exciting place than Honora's. Frank Latimer might be a viscount, but he's about as dull as men come. A perfect match for my passionless sister."

DEBORAH SAW Evan once during that week as she returned home from her errands to the bakery, the greengrocer, and the library. He was riding down the high street with his sister, the viscount, Miss Latimer, and some others she did not recognize. He doffed his hat, and he and Miss Latimer stopped briefly to greet her. The countess directed a cool nod her way. Deborah started to sweat, though she was cold, and dropped a parcel in her nervousness, but they had already turned their horses away.

Except for some of the servants, no one from the Manor attended services the following Sunday, and Deborah heard talk that the party had broken up. She also heard, over the next few days, that two betrothals had been announced. One was Viscount Latimer's, which of course generated much discussion around the village.

No one seemed sure who was involved in the second.

Evan Haverfield
Whately Manor
January 9, 1817

Dear Elizabeth,

Another year is gone, and I've precious little to show for it. I've been with Latimer since leaving Yorkshire, but I'd have done better to stay with you despite your appalling winters in Wrackwater Bridge. I cannot truthfully claim that the company here has been dull. Nevertheless, I am eager to be gone.

No, that's not right, either; I really cannot claim to be eager for anything. I suppose I am the dull one.

Latimer, at least, is pleased with the year just ended. He has engaged himself to marry Sudbury's youngest sister. You would not know her; she should have come out last Season but that her grandmother died. You know the older girl, however, who also formed an engagement while she was here. But I'm sure Alberta has written all about that.

I expect she had some choice words to say about me, as well. You hoped that I might find some lovely damsel in attendance at Latimer's party who would capture my cold heart at last. And indeed, I did meet a woman whom I thought—but she has made it clear she is not interested, so there the matter ends. I mention the lady only because I'm sure Berta did so—disparagingly, no doubt—and I felt you should know that nothing will come of the acquaintance. That will please Alberta, at least.

I leave tomorrow for Northridge, where I expect to stay some weeks. That will please Mother and Father. Do you have any notion what might please me, Lizzy? For I don't.

I would like to be warm.

Yours,

Evan

❧

Alberta, Lady Witney
At home
January 12

Dear Elizabeth,

We are home from Leicestershire, though briefly. Theo leaves Wednesday to make ready for the new session of Parliament, and I leave for Northridge the following day to remove the children from under Mama and Papa's feet. Evan will be there as well, he says. Then on to London for the Season.

I don't believe I was ever so pleased to leave a gathering. The betrothals were rather fun, and Amanda Latimer is a pleasure. One cannot call her elegant, but she proved herself a surprisingly good hostess. Her fiancé seems eminently suitable, with country tastes like her own. He should have no regrets in his choice of bride. Whately Manor will have a new mistress by the time Miss Latimer vacates the position; the viscount and Lady Honora plan to marry in April.

I expect we will attend the third ceremony—or rather, the first—as it will take place in London. Lady Blythe insists that a date in mid-February will permit enough time to collect her wedding clothes, and although she clearly feels some trepidation, she professes herself ready for the change. She has abandoned the dream of a grand ceremony at St. George's. Her status entitles her to the dream, but Captain Westwood's does not entitle her to the reality; nor do the sordid circumstances of their engagement. And Blythe was the first to say that it would be muddle-headed to spend a vast sum of money they don't have on a single day's excitement. Theo thinks that bodes well for their future, at least insofar as finances are concerned. I myself begin to think the girl is not beyond redemption.

I can't but wish that Evan's nuptials were in the offing. I would not have had him marry Blythe, however, and I am more relieved than I can say that his relationship with the widow has evidently come to nothing. He is not happy and is not himself; but the crisis has passed. What it was exactly, I still don't know. He seems quiet, resigned, somewhat distant. I think it's rather attractive, this new gravity.

Is there any chance we might see you and Philip in Town? You know you would be welcome at any time.

Fondly,

Alberta

❧ 21 ❧

Time seemed frozen like the weather, or her heart. Deborah did her best to maintain a stoic calm and continue with life as usual, and in general succeeded fairly well—she'd had a great deal of practice. But each day seemed grayer than the one before, and those that were not merely miserable were dreadful.

Julian's birthday was one of the latter. Deborah arrived home from the butcher's that morning to find chaos in her kitchen. Julian and a little dog chased each other gleefully around the room to the tune of shrieks, barks, and Molly's laughter as she tripped over them while going about her chores.

Deborah set her parcel down on the table with a smack. "What is this?" she demanded.

"It's a *dog*, Mama! Mr. Haffield sent him for my birthday."

And the chase resumed.

"Jack Martin brought him by a little bit ago," Molly said. "He said this is the dog that saved young Master's life back in December. Isn't that the best present you can imagine?"

Good God. Had Mr. Haverfield really tracked the dog down before leaving Whately? What nerve! No doubt he'd provided the big red bow as well.

Deborah exploded. "No! It's totally unacceptable. I won't have it! How dare he think he can—"

The dog peered out warily from under the work table while two human faces turned toward her in surprise and consternation. Julian, too astonished to cry, clutched Molly's skirts.

"Molly, you put that lead back on him and march him right back where he came from."

"But ma'am," Molly said, "you *like* dogs."

Deborah pressed her hands to her temples. It was true. There had always been dogs about the place when she was a child, though she'd had little direct contact with them except for one runt pup. Cook had rescued that one from destruction, and Deborah helped her nurse the little thing—in vain, for it had died after struggling through a couple weeks of life. Though she had denied more than one request for a dog from her son, those refusals had probably sounded more like "Not yet" than "Absolutely not."

Deborah clenched her teeth and read the short note Mr. Haverfield had sent along for Julian:

I hope you like your birthday present. I thought of sending you a book, but this little fellow seemed far more special; he saved your life, you know. You may call him anything you wish—he has had no other name than "Boy", and I know you can do better than that! Be sure to use the lead when you go outdoors; he is used to having the freedom of the countryside and just might forget he has a new address. Don't expect your mama to do all the work. I hope you will write and tell me what name you've chosen. Have a wonderful day!

Fondly,
Evan Haverfield

And the still shorter one for herself:

Mrs. Moore—

I hope this is not too great an imposition. He seems a smart little dog, and I'm sure he will readily accustom himself to his new life. He is part of the

Martins' dog herd and can be returned to them if necessary. I think he will do Julian good, however.

  I trust you are well—
  Evan Haverfield

I am not well! The notes did nothing to appease her anger, and they made it impossible for her to do other than accept the dubious gift.

"He's not handsome, is he." She sounded crabby, querulous, but she couldn't help it.

Julian flew to the defense of his dog, landing on his knees under the table with his arms around the creature's neck. "Mama, he's *beautiful!*" The dog wagged his tail uncertainly and gave the boy a lick.

"I do think you be stretchin' the truth there, Master Julian," said Molly, "but he's a real taking little thing, and you can see they're already the best of friends. I'll help with him, ma'am."

Deborah contemplated the wretched mongrel. He was probably as attractive now as he would ever be, for he had clearly been bathed and brushed for his big day. His hair grew every which way, with some of every color one might expect to find on a dog, all interspersed haphazardly on a misproportioned body. His legs were too long, his tail short and scraggly, and his ears stood out from his head at a rakish angle. His eyes were his one good feature, bright and questioning. He did look reasonably intelligent, for a dog. And thank heaven he was small.

"One week," she allowed. "We will try this for one week. He will live in the yard, and he can sleep in the shed with the goat. He may come in the kitchen for his meals; the rest of the house is off limits."

Julian ran to her and hugged her hard about the legs. "Thank you, Mama! He'll be really good, you'll see!"

She was skeptical. Hopefully, he would give her an excuse to send him back to the dairy... though by the end of a week, Julian would be so attached to the animal that it would take something truly egregious to justify taking the dog away. Like massacring the chickens.

She must indeed be crazy, and if she was not, she soon would be. Here was a responsibility she hadn't asked for, didn't want, and one, moreover, that would remind her of Evan—*no, he's Mr. Haverfield*—all day long. As though she needed more reminders when his face was engraved on the backs of her eyelids.

He had asked her permission to send *a gift*, like a book or a toy. He'd said nothing about a living creature. No doubt he anticipated she would say no and had not wanted to give her that opportunity.

He knew her too well.

"I suppose you'd better find a name for him." As she left the kitchen, his letters clutched in her hand, the discussion was already underway. And when she saw the mongrel again a short time later, Julian introduced him as Pelleas.

She gave up on afternoon lessons because Julian cried about coming inside. He took the animal over every inch of the little yard, introducing him to Lucifer the goat and each of the chickens. He scolded when the dog tried to jump up on the stone wall, shaking his finger in the same way she did. Fortunately, the wall was an inch or two beyond jumping range.

Then boy and dog went for a walk. Julian looked so proud and happy when they returned that Deborah capitulated then and there, though she didn't tell her son.

Before Julian went to bed, they had to spend half an hour shivering in the shed while he built a nest in the hay and persuaded Pelleas to curl up inside, covering him with an old moth-eaten saddle blanket. When she finally got him upstairs, all he could think about was whether the dog would have nightmares in his new home and what they would do together tomorrow. And in the morning, he ran downstairs in his bare feet to release the prisoner.

Unfortunately for her rules, the weather turned bitterly cold. Before Julian even asked, Deborah took pity on the poor animal shivering on the back step. She certainly was not going to let Julian spend any length of time outside. She knew from her own reluctant ventures out the door that no amount of clothing was sufficient to keep a body warm. So she sent boy and dog out into the lane for a quick run after breakfast and then allowed both back into the kitchen where they settled cozily by the fire. Julian had a cup of tea; Pelleas had to settle for water.

They hardly left the kitchen for three days. Trying to heat the rest of the house would have been dreadfully expensive and probably futile. Deborah envied Molly her little chamber off the kitchen—and Pelleas too, for he was permitted to sleep on the rug by the fire. She heated bricks at bedtime and dashed upstairs to slip them into her bed, and then grabbed nightclothes for herself and Julian and returned to the kitchen, where they changed and washed up with warm water from the copper.

Then they ran back to her chamber and slid into the big bed, where the bricks had taken off the worst of the chill.

Once there, any urge to use the chamber pot or get a sip of water—which would have been frozen in any case—was instantly quashed by the thought of freezing to death outside the covers. Deborah gritted her chattering teeth and tried to make a game of it, but she hated every minute.

The happy little dog in the kitchen seemed like the one bright spot in that dark, dismal winter. Impossible to remain hostile toward that warm, furry being who came up to her chair by the fire, rested his whiskery chin on her knee, and gazed up at her with brown eyes that said *I love you.* Impossible not to shed a few tears at the sight of that creature sitting on the hearthrug with her sober, reserved little boy, to all appearances engrossed in the story Julian was reading to him.

And somehow the knightly name Pelleas seemed appropriate, even though he was scruffy and homely. He might not fight dragons, but he knew how to vanquish the beast named Loneliness.

By early March, spring was stretching awake. It was still chilly, but each rain seemed to wash away one more thin layer of winter gray, uncovering just the faintest tint of green to be revealed the next time the sun shone.

The kitchen door stood open wide one afternoon as Deborah and

Molly scrubbed the room clean. Pelleas ran out as a carriage drove along the lane toward the high street, barking as it rounded the corner.

The knock came a couple of minutes later. Drying her hands on her apron, Deborah went to answer it. But Julian was already there, riveted, on the threshold. Beyond him she could see Miss Latimer and another woman she did not recognize.

She heard Miss Latimer say, "Good morning, Master Moore." She heard no response at all from Julian. *Where are his manners?* She hurried toward the door, a smile on her face to cancel out her son's diffidence.

"Is your mama—ah, here she is."

As she came closer, Deborah saw that the stranger held a boy's hand. Julian stared spellbound at the other child, so close to his own height.

And the dratted dog had his muddy feet up on Miss Latimer's pelisse, sniffing the basket she had brought.

"Pelleas! Get down!" He complied, transferring his attentions to the boy, who let go of his mama's hand to scratch him behind the ears.

"I'm so sorry, Miss Latimer," Deborah exclaimed, leaning down to brush the dirt she couldn't even see from the plain, dark garment. "Let me—"

Miss Latimer laughed her off. "Don't be silly, Mrs. Moore. This old thing has seen more mud than our hogs. And some worse things too. I hope we're not interrupting you?"

"Of course not," Deborah lied.

She stood aside to let her visitors into the hall, and as she took their pelisses, she tried to assess the unknown woman. There was nothing fancy about her woolen gown, but it fit her to perfection, and the fabric's luster spoke of quality. She had curly brown hair, expertly arranged, and a kind, pretty face that looked as though it laughed a lot. She looked slightly familiar.

There was nothing familiar about her name, however. Miss Latimer performed the introductions as Deborah showed them into the parlor. "This is Mrs. Dusseau, who has come to stay with me for a few weeks. And her son, Alexander."

Deborah uttered the usual mundane courtesies and ensured that Julian made his proper bows. Then she excused herself to return to the kitchen, basket and dog in tow, and removed the humiliating apron.

"Am I clean enough, Molly?" The girl wiped some dirt from her face and fingered a tendril of hair into place. "Tea and lemonade, please. And biscuits, if there are any left."

Deborah returned to the parlor. The boy and his mother sat on the sofa, while Miss Latimer had the chair by the fire. Deborah took the remaining chair, and Julian came to stand by her knee, his eyes still glued to young Alexander.

Had he said anything at all? Mrs. Dusseau must think him mute.

"You probably don't know it, Mrs. Moore, but all five of us in this room have a mutual friend," said Miss Latimer. "Mrs. Dusseau is the former Miss Elizabeth Haverfield."

Thank God the tea had not yet been delivered—Deborah would have dropped it in her lap. As it was, only her jaw dropped. She clenched it shut lest it betray her further.

Miss Latimer continued. "You met Mr. Haverfield's older sister, Lady Witney, over New Year's. Elizabeth is his younger sister."

Julian turned his attention from the boy to his mother. Shyly, he said, "I hope Mr. Haffield is well?"

Mrs. Dusseau shook her dark curls. "I regret I can give you no news of him. You have seen him more recently than I."

Molly arrived with the tea tray. By some miracle the cups did not rattle in their saucers as Deborah handed them out.

Julian subsided against Deborah's skirts once she was settled again but dared to ask Mrs. Dusseau, "Are you a countess too?"

Deborah blushed for his impertinence and opened her mouth to intervene, but Mrs. Dusseau laughed. "No, I'm sorry to disappoint you. I am merely a missus like your mama."

Julian relaxed, relieved rather than disappointed. He helped himself to a biscuit and returned to his perusal of Mr. Haverfield's nephew.

Deborah shook herself out of a surreptitious inspection of Mrs. Dusseau's similarities to her brother. Miss Latimer was speaking about plans for her friend's visit. "Oh, we shall have a few dinner parties, which I trust you will attend, Mrs. Moore. But I hope that you and Master Moore might help in keeping my guests entertained during the day."

Mrs. Dusseau looked on complacently, and the thought snuck into Deborah's head that all was going according to someone's plan.

Whose, she was not sure.

❧ 22 ❧

The following day, Elizabeth hosted Mrs. Moore and her son at the Manor. They had a small nuncheon served in the breakfast room and then went riding.

The viscount owned no ponies for children, but Miss Latimer had borrowed two from her fiancé's stables. Alexander was handling one of these, though not very well.

Julian Moore was clearly envious of Alexander's greater mastery but seemed happy enough to be up in front of a groom on a horse named Imp. When Elizabeth had extended the invitation yesterday, the poor child had been pathetically eager, imploring his mother with looks and whispers.

Mrs. Moore had been less enthusiastic. Behind an expressionless façade, her eyes were wary. If Elizabeth had not seen the mask fall when Miss Latimer introduced her as Evan's sister, she might have thought the woman stupid or unfeeling.

But in that moment, Elizabeth saw plenty of feeling. Dismay bordering on horror. Yet she had accepted the invitation readily enough. She might be cautious, but Elizabeth thought she was also curious.

The ladies rode slowly ahead of the boys. The groom was in charge of them, but until she was more familiar with him, Elizabeth preferred to stay close by. Mrs. Moore, too, kept one eye on the path they rode and the other over her shoulder.

"Have you visited often at Whately?" Mrs. Moore asked.

"Oh no, I've never been here before," Elizabeth replied. "I've known the viscount for years, of course—he and Evan are school chums from way back. And I met his sister in London. Philip and I were in town for part of the Season when she had her come-out. I like her very much, don't you?"

"Of course. She's been very kind to us."

Elizabeth caught Mrs. Moore's sidelong look of puzzlement and smiled at her. If Mrs. Moore was curious, Elizabeth was fairly bursting. She had read her sister's ruminations over New Year's and longed to know more. She had read Evan's letter, now two months old, and felt all the pain of unrequited love he had tried not to express. And then silence, though he was normally an excellent correspondent.

Mama knew nothing of his whereabouts, though he had paid a brief and thoroughly unsatisfactory visit to Northridge after leaving Whately. Alberta had heard nothing but knew he was not in London. Viscount Latimer had no news of him, either. The family's agents in Shrewsbury, who always knew where to find him, did not—at least, so they said.

These past couple of years, Evan had spent most of his time wandering, but he had never put himself out of touch. Elizabeth knew her brother as well as anyone, and whatever was going on, she was not inclined to take it lightly.

So she had written her own letter to Amanda Latimer, received a long and fascinating missive in return, and resolved to meet this widow who had spurned him.

Needless to say, she discussed none of this with the woman she had traveled so many muddy miles to meet. Elizabeth argued often with Alberta about society's inequities and would not reject out-of-hand Mrs. Moore's suitability as a sister-in-law. What did it matter that the woman had meager means and scrubbed her own doorstep? An advantageous marriage would relieve all such embarrassments.

She must be genteel, of course, in birth and in manners. Beyond that, what mattered was whether she would appreciate Evan and make him happy. That's what Elizabeth had come to determine, if she could.

"I just had to get out of Yorkshire. I love the place, but our winters are beastly. Philip couldn't get away quite yet, so I came here for a couple of weeks."

"I'm surprised you did not go to London, ma'am," Mrs. Moore asked her as they poked along. "Surely the Season is underway?"

"It is just beginning," Elizabeth replied, "and I'm meeting Philip and the girls there after we leave Whately. But to be honest, London is not my favorite place. It's noisy and it smells. The longer I'm away, the less I miss it. It's heresy to say so, but there it is. You don't seem the London sort, either, Mrs. Moore."

Mrs. Moore shook her head. "I've never been there at all."

"Oh! Well, you *must* go sometime. I complain about it, but there are so many marvelous things to see—the Tower, and the British Museum, and music, and the theatre, and the fashionable hordes with their noses in the air. Everyone should visit London once. And there is no place like it for replacing one's wardrobe and seeing old friends."

Mrs. Moore's horse tossed its head. The woman frowned but said nothing.

London would be a very different place for a widow without friends or financial means, of course. But Mrs. Moore could definitely use a new wardrobe.

She tried a change of subject. "Have you always lived in the country, Mrs. Moore?"

"I spent some months in Plymouth when I was a girl."

"What were you doing there?"

"Oh—learning dance steps and deportment."

"You like to dance? That's famous! Miss Latimer was wondering whether to get up an informal dance; I shall insist that she do so."

Mrs. Moore's eyes flared with alarm. "Oh, please don't go to such trouble on my behalf."

Elizabeth watched, intrigued, as her face went blank, her voice flat.

"It's difficult for me to get away in the evenings." Mrs. Moore turned her mount around, and they rejoined the boys.

§.

CONFUSION SET Deborah's thoughts jangling. Such slight acquaintance as Mrs. Dusseau claimed with Miss Latimer would hardly justify a two-week visit, particularly when the latter was spending most of every day with her betrothed. And Alexander's presence compounded the enigma. There were no children at Whately Manor, after all.

Was it possible that Evan's sister had journeyed to Whately to meet *her*?

Over the next week or so, Deborah found herself a great deal in Mrs. Dusseau's company. On some days she and Julian walked to the Manor, on others Alexander and his mother joined them at the cottage. They rode, sometimes with the children, but sometimes alone while Jeremy gave the boys riding lessons in the paddock. They walked or sewed while the boys did other sorts of lessons with Alexander's nurse, an inestimable woman named Miss Halley, who took them for nature walks on clement days and spun stories from around the globe on rainy ones.

At the conclusion of one of Miss Halley's tales, Deborah sighed. She picked up the mending that had lain forgotten in her lap. "How I wish there had been someone like Miss Halley when I was small."

If she had thought first, she would never have said it.

Her remark gave Mrs. Dusseau an opening to ask uncomfortable questions about her girlhood. Questions like, "What was your nurse like, then?"

Deborah looked at her for a moment, wondering what to say. Then she shook her head. "There was just Mama."

Mrs. Dusseau talked freely about her own youth as she worked her embroidery, telling stories that astonished Deborah. Most beguiling, naturally, were those that involved Evan.

Deborah worried that her face would give her away and longed for each one to end, but was cross when they did.

"My own poor nurse earned her keep, without a doubt. She raised all four of us, together with various governesses and tutors, but I was the most troublesome. When she finally retired, I'm sure I could have heard her sigh of relief from London, if I'd known just when to listen." Her expression sobered. "Dear Laney. She didn't get to enjoy it for long." But then she was bubbling again, her face so clear and bright Deborah could hardly pull her gaze away.

"I ran away when I was about twelve. We had such a fight, Laney and I, and Mama supported her. I can't even recall what it was about, but I'm sure she was right. My friend and I snuck into the stables when we thought no one was looking, saddled our ponies, and rode off. I don't even remember where we thought we were going. But Melanie didn't get her saddle cinched tight enough, and before we ever got off our own land, she fell."

"Good gracious," Deborah exclaimed, captivated as much by the woman as by her story. "Was she injured?"

Mrs. Dusseau nodded as she threaded her needle with peacock-blue silk. "She sprained her ankle. She couldn't walk, and she wouldn't get back on the pony. And I didn't want to face whatever gruesome punishment might await me at home. We argued for what seemed like hours until we were desperately hungry. We hadn't even taken any food, can you imagine? And then Evan appeared, riding over the hill-side. One of the grooms told him what we'd done, and he came to find us." She shook her head, chuckling, while the blood rose to Deborah's cheeks. "Poor Evan. Melanie and I argued all the way home, and still he tried to take the blame."

Deborah ducked her head and focused on her stitches but not in time to hide her blush. "What was the punishment?"

"Oh, my parents knew the truth of the matter all along. They just laughed at me, which of course, made me angrier still."

Mrs. Dusseau's openness made Deborah feel some obligation to respond in kind. Indeed, she *wanted* to, for she liked Evan's sister very much. But it was a behavior that was essentially foreign to her, and often she was not as forthcoming as she herself wished.

The new acquaintance was uncomfortable in other ways as well. In the middle of refusing a dinner invitation from Miss Latimer, Mrs. Dusseau interrupted Deborah to say, "Oh, you *must* come, Mrs. Moore. I don't know anyone in Whately but the viscount and Miss Latimer. I'll feel quite lost without you."

Deborah felt obliged to go. But as she expected, Mrs. Dusseau showed no sign of needing her. It was only a small group, by anyone's standards except Deborah's, comprised mostly of Restons. It was as comfortable a situation as she could have asked for, yet she felt out of place, like Romeo among the Capulets but without a mask to hide behind. She began to wish she had never met any Haverfields at all.

Elizabeth Dusseau
Whately Manor
March 12, 1817

Philip, my sweet,

I trust you are finding the fortitude to struggle on without me. It was rotten of me to steal Nurse from you, but I am sure that you and Betsy, between you, are managing to keep the girls out of harm, if not out of mischief! Betsy was excited to be given more to do with the children than simply clean up after them; she shows great promise, don't you think?

Regarding Evan's affairs, I believe it is time to put inquiries in motion. I was rather hoping to find this widow of his ugly, boorish, and loathsome. I'd prefer not to earn the family's hatred for supporting a match they are bound to find unsuitable in every way. But sadly for me, I like her very much. Few people would use 'Deborah Moore' and 'levity' in the same sentence—though I have just done so!—but she is not dour, as someone here described her. I would call her sober, and very disciplined.

She is sadly intimidated by rank and is quiet to a fault in company, which can generate a perception of severity, or perhaps even haughtiness. It is false, however. She is intelligent and good-hearted, and though she knows little about politics and less about art or music, she is well able to discuss science and nature and literature and history and education. Unfortunately, she is too shy to do so. And she has no small talk at all.

Before I proceed to a first-name basis or have any communication on the subject with Evan (assuming he ever emerges from whatever hole he's hidden himself in), I must be sure that her breeding is not totally impossible. She dislikes speaking about her family—I gather her father is a monster, and I have been unable to extract his given name or any pertinent information about her mother. Given her reluctance, I have not tried very hard. But the surname is Carlington, in the vicinity of Lydford, in Devonshire. She had an aunt, Matilda—her mother's sister, I believe—who appears to have had great influence.

Do find out what you can and let me have word as soon as may be. It will be a fine excuse for you to write, not that you need any; in fact, I expect a letter from you much sooner, bearing news of the girls and your undying love.

Enclosing mine—

Elizabeth

23

"Mama! We found a snowdrop!" Julian exclaimed, trotting into the parlor where Deborah and Mrs. Dusseau sat stitching. "At least," he added conscientiously, "Miss Halley says it *will* be a snowdrop when the flower grows." Alexander and his nurse followed him into the room.

"How lovely. Where did you find it?" Thankfully, Miss Halley had made sure the shoes of all three were brushed clean before entering the cottage; fields and lanes alike were deep in spring mud. Pelleas must have been left outdoors or in the kitchen.

"Under a tree by the river. Miss Halley says we can go back tomorrow or the next day and see the flower."

Alexander made a disgusted sound. *"Flowers,"* he groused. *"I* made a stone skip *three times."* Julian looked abashed.

Mrs. Dusseau clapped her hands together. "I never could skip stones at all."

Deborah admired the way she so adroitly praised her own son while making Julian feel better about falling short. "Neither could I." She had never tried, but she didn't say so.

Alexander's companionship was transforming her son into a quite different child. He had so little intercourse with others his age that concepts like competition were alien to him. If *"Miss Halley says"* had become Julian's new byword, *"Alex can"* surely ran a close second: *Alex can* jump his pony over a fence (albeit a very small one), *Alex can* climb way high in the chestnut tree, *Alex can* stand on his head, and do cartwheels.

When he bewailed his inadequacies at the end of a long, tiring day, Deborah pointed out that Julian could read far better than his friend, which was some small comfort. And Mr. Haverfield had taught Julian some card games his own nephew did not know, to contribute to their entertainment on rainy days.

Deborah's feelings toward Alexander's mother were similarly ambivalent. Mrs. Dusseau was like some foreign creature embodying all the happy traits she herself lacked. She was open and warm, talkative but always interested in what others had to say, comfortable in any company, and seemed always to be happy.

The days passed in a whirl, and each evening ended with a *whew* of relief. Deborah wanted time to reflect on this radical, if temporary, upheaval in their lives. Time to remember Evan's face and the feel of his hands, to recall all the reasons she could not have him, to ponder the wisdom of friendship with his sister. But by the time she saw her bed at night, she was too tired to do anything but fall into it.

They enjoyed picnic lunches with the boys or took Mrs. Dusseau's carriage to the next town for some shopping. One day they braved the dangers of a nearby fair, treating Alexander and Julian to a taste of the low life. There they drew the line at *A Giant, with All His Giant Parts on Display*, but paid the ha'penny fee to see a cat with two heads and a pig that could count, and they purchased several little books from the traveling chapman. In the daytime, with Mrs. Dusseau's coachman and groom keeping an eye on things in the background, it seemed a grand adventure for all of them.

As they made their way to the carriage, Deborah realized Mrs. Dusseau had been calling her "Deborah" for most of the afternoon.

More prosaically, the women spent a good deal of time sewing. Elizabeth was embroidering a set of napkins for Miss Latimer's wedding present. They looked very elaborate and ambitious to Deborah, who was a good enough seamstress but knew nothing of decorative stitchery. She spent her time on clothing for Julian, who was suddenly accumulating holes and stains in the garments he had not already outgrown.

"I'd be pleased to teach you some embroidery," offered Elizabeth.

Deborah shook her head. "It would be a waste of your time. I never manage to finish the sewing that *needs* to be done."

"But it's so relaxing. And it's an inexpensive way to create something beautiful for someone. Or for yourself." Elizabeth adjusted the hoop on her fabric. "And who knows, perhaps your situation will not always be as it is now."

Deborah continued with her silent stitches.

"You might marry again, for instance."

"That's highly unlikely," Deborah muttered.

"Why should you think so? You're young yet and so pretty. The physician—what is his name?—certainly finds you interesting."

"Unfortunately. But it's not marriage he thinks of, I assure you. And the idea of facing him over the breakfast table every morning..." Deborah shuddered.

"No, perhaps not. But if he is attracted to you, surely other men are as well." They stitched in blessed silence for a few minutes. "What sort of man do you dream of, Deborah?"

Evan's face, already imagined across the breakfast table, suddenly lay beside hers on the pillow, earnestly asking her to marry him.

Deborah blushed furiously and quickly banished his image from the room.

"Oh, you think I'm dreadfully impertinent, don't you?" Elizabeth shrugged her shoulders. "It is my biggest flaw. At least, so says my husband, who knows all of them and loves me nonetheless. I suppose that's the sort of man *I* dream of. As a girl, of course, all I thought about was a handsome face, and strong arms, and kisses that would make me dizzy."

Good heavens. Do women really talk about such things? Deborah did not know. She knew better how to relate to men than women, and less than nothing about either.

Elizabeth smoothed the satin stitch that formed one petal in her design. "But I am preposterously lucky because I found all of those things, and all in one man. I was afraid I might have to marry several!" She laughed as she began another petal. "At one time, I wanted a fine swordsman as well, to fight duels over me."

"How dreadful!"

"I am a little wiser now, I hope. Now don't tell me you never dreamed up a perfect man, for I'll not believe you!"

"Well... There was once a knight on a white steed—it was Pegasus, actually—who carried me away from Lydford."

"He didn't have to fight for you?"

"Heavens no. No one would have stood in his way."

"What did he look like? I'm sure he was handsome."

Deborah frowned, ousting Evan from that other knight's armor. "I suppose so. I don't think I ever saw behind the visor. But he was *not* fat," she said firmly, "and he did not wear stays that creaked whenever he moved!"

Elizabeth gave a peal of laughter. "Of course not! Heroes are not allowed to be fat. They would find it far too difficult to dazzle fair damsels or to rescue little lads from peril."

Deborah gasped as the needle stabbed her hand, and Elizabeth looked up at her. It was an assessing look, as though she had hoped to kindle a reaction. If so, she'd succeeded.

But there was sympathy as well. "I'm sorry, Deborah. Did you think I didn't know the story?"

"No." If Evan himself had not told her, or Lady Witney, no doubt Miss Latimer would have done so. But it almost seemed Elizabeth was encouraging her to hope for him. If that was so, what could be her motivation? Either cruelty or something Deborah did not dare dream of.

Elizabeth smiled gently and then returned to her work. A moment later she chuckled. "Can you imagine the good doctor crawling about under the hedge?" Deborah was too mortified to be amused.

Elizabeth wove the end of her thread into the back of her stitchery. "So what will you wear to the ball next week, Deborah?"

Oh dear. Could they not just talk about the weather or the children? The informal dance proposed earlier had evolved into a formal affair celebrating the double nuptials of the viscount and his sister.

"I have a peach-colored silk that will do." Deborah had no intention of attending, but it was far easier to play along than to say so.

Elizabeth clapped her hands—one of those happy habits of hers—and threw her embroidery aside. "Oh, do let me see it!" Before Deborah could come up with a reason not to, Elizabeth took her hand and drew her out of her chair. Chattering about fashions and fabrics, she led Deborah up her own narrow staircase.

"What a sweet room!" she exclaimed. It certainly made the best possible use of the morning sunshine with its dormer window facing east. It felt warm and stuffy.

Deborah watched her friend take the Grand Tour of her drab little bedchamber. There was no reason to take even one step—one could stand in the doorway and see everything from the threadbare rug to the water damage on the ceiling. But once she'd started, Elizabeth no doubt felt she had to finish.

She touched the locket that lay on the dressing table. Picked up Deborah's scent bottle and sniffed its contents—"Mmm. Yes, that smells like you"—and dabbed a bit on her wrist. Inspected the view of the high street and a cheap engraving of the harbor at Plymouth. Lifted Hartley's watch from its place on the bedside table. Remembering Evan's similar meanderings, Deborah almost smiled. Or cried. She wasn't sure which.

"Now, about that gown," Elizabeth exclaimed brightly, throwing open the wardrobe. She needed no help finding the gown in question. Deborah had picked it up off the floor and hung it angrily at the very back of the wardrobe in the earliest hours of the new year, hoping never to see it again. But everything else she owned was dark and clearly unsuitable for a ball, and there simply wasn't enough of it to hide the offending garment.

"Oh, it's a lovely color. I'm sure it looks stunning on you." She paused, holding the skirt out and pursing her lips. Compared to Elizabeth's pretty yellow walking dress, it looked ready for the rag man.

"And you wear it with the blue underskirt? That's very nice—or maybe a dark teal? Or ivory, of course, would be classic... but no, too boring. We can touch it up just a bit here and there: sew on a wide sash to alter the waistline and— Oh, I have ribbons just the right color to use in your hair. And by the way, I want you to spend the afternoon at the Manor before the ball. My Francine will fix you up and do your hair. I wager you'll hardly recognize yourself. You'll bring Julian, of course, and both spend the night..."

Elizabeth cut short her monologue and peered at Deborah. "You don't want to go, do you?"

Deborah sighed. "No."

Elizabeth sat down on the bed and drew Deborah down beside her, arms interlocked. "Why?"

"You've seen how I am in company. I never know what to say to anyone."

Elizabeth gazed thoughtfully at the wall. "Instead of embroidery..." she turned impulsively to Deborah, "let me teach you conversation!"

Deborah shook her head. "You'd be setting yourself an impossible task. I'm not..."

"No, listen. You have no confidence in yourself. Do you think people are born knowing how to say the right things? And the wrong things as well, of course. The greatest peers in the land, the politicians, the most successful Society hostesses, had to learn these things. And do you think none of them are shy? Of course they are! You needn't speak loudly or often. A few well-placed words are all that's necessary."

She squeezed Deborah's hand and continued. "The ball is Friday week. That gives us ten days. If you're still set against going when the day arrives, I won't even try to talk you into it. Agreed?"

"But you're leaving before then," Deborah said, dreading the separation even while she yearned for it.

"Well, I won't. Philip will have to wait."

Deborah wanted very much to say no. She was scared; scared of failing, but perhaps more scared of succeeding. The wall she had built was crumbling, and once it fell, she would have no more refuge in isolation.

Reluctantly she said yes.

"I am sure you'll not regret this," Elizabeth said earnestly, clasping Deborah's hand. "And in case you *do* decide to attend the ball, let's get busy with this gown!"

🦋 24 🦋

Deborah's lessons began that very afternoon and hardly let up for the next ten days.

They went to buy fabric for her sash, and Elizabeth made her practice on Mr. Price at the dry goods shop. They stopped at the inn to find out if she had any letters—of course she did not—and practiced on the innkeep's wife. She inflicted her stammering attempts at small talk on the unhelpful proprietor at the lending library and on Isabella Reston, who was borrowing *The Prisoner of Chillon*, Lord Byron's latest volume of poetry. But she would do no more than nod to Doctor Overley, who lifted his hat as he passed them in the street.

"Weather is always safe and always boring," Elizabeth said. "At the library, of course, books are an obvious topic, and they are useful at dinner parties as well. If you're dealing with a merchant, find something complimentary to say about his product. 'The bread smells wonderful today. You must have added a pinch of spring to the dough.' In fact, compliments always breed goodwill. Do you see the woman over there in that dreadful gown? You needn't say it's a lovely gown, but it *is* a rather gorgeous color, isn't it?

"But if you can, find something personal to say. Ask a question about where they live, their family, mutual friends. Now, what do you know about the baker's wife?"

"Mrs. Harcourt? Um—her son was sent to Botany Bay for stealing the wheels off the doctor's phaeton."

"Heavens, you don't want to mention that!" Elizabeth frowned in puzzlement. "How would one even accomplish such a thing?"

Then Deborah recalled that the Mrs. Harcourt's daughter had recently married, so she was able to inquire after her and learn that already she was in the family way.

Unfortunately, Mrs. Harcourt asked in return about "that nice young man what was stayin' up at the Manor over Christmastime," as though she thought Deborah might actually be in communication with him. With *that nice young man's* sister standing next to her admiring the hot cross buns, Deborah's face grew hot, and she stammered something unintelligible.

Mrs. Harcourt nodded knowingly.

Deborah attended a nuncheon at Reston Park and an evening party at the Manor where she practiced on the highest society Whately had to offer. These attempts were less successful.

Afterward Elizabeth devised a game, which they played with Miss Halley and the boys. The participants took on the roles of anonymous personages high and low and played them to the hilt, while each took a turn as The Innocent, whose task it was to respond with courtesy and grace to the peculiar behaviors and impudent curiosities of the others.

All of them learned a bit and laughed a lot. But how humiliating that she had as much to learn as her six-year-old!

By the day of the ball, spring was full upon them. The green tips of peas and lettuces and carrots pushed up out of the brown earth while cows and ewes heavy with young consumed vast quantities of new grass in mindless contentment. Chaffinches and robins hopped busily about in the hedgerows collecting caterpillars to fill their stomachs and twigs to cradle their eggs. Snowdrops now abounded under the trees by the river with primroses and narcissi for company. The big chestnut behind Deborah's cottage awoke one morning wrapped in a

green mist that resolved, within days, into pale, infant leaves. Strawberries were in the market, shipped north from Cornwall and Kent.
And oh, the mud…

Deborah knew days beforehand that she would have to go to the
Latimers' ball. Regardless of her performance at her lessons, she owed
it to Elizabeth. She *had* made progress and viewed the event with
somewhat less trepidation than she had ten days earlier.

Shortly after Julian's luncheon on the appointed day, she packed
what they needed into the carriage Elizabeth sent for them and
headed off for their overnight stay at Whately Manor. Julian had been
wild all morning and bounced and chattered throughout the mercifully short drive.

Alexander and his mother would be leaving Whately the very next
day. The loss of his first and only friend surely contributed to Julian's
restlessness. Alexander had all the excitement of going to London,
reuniting with his father and sisters and cousins. And when he went
home to Yorkshire, his mother had promised him his own pony now
that he rode so well.

Julian could anticipate only a return to what seemed a previous
life, circumscribed by house and yard and lessons. Miss Latimer said
he could come to Reston Park any time and ride "his" pony, but it
could not be more than an occasional event. Small wonder his mood
was uneven.

"I miss Philip and the children dreadfully," said Elizabeth as they
sat in her allotted bedchamber putting the finishing touches on their
gowns. She fingered lovingly the letter she had received from her
husband that morning.

"Well, *we* will miss *you* dreadfully," Deborah chided. She hoped it
came out playfully, but she was no happier than her son about the
prospect of a return to normalcy.

"We will write, of course. I must know how your social life
progresses."

Deborah's stomach dropped. She had already received an invitation for an evening at Reston Park the following week, and another
for a picnic by the river, and was far from sure that she wanted a

social life at all. Especially one where she had no Elizabeth looking out for her.

Later in the afternoon they took tea with Miss Latimer and some of her other houseguests. Then they went to check on the children but found the schoolroom empty. Though Deborah could have no concerns about Julian's safety in Miss Halley's capable hands, it was peculiar, and a little unsettling, to be out of touch with him.

Finally they went to Elizabeth's allotted room to rest and change before dinner. And though she had no expectation of doing so, she fell asleep immediately upon lying down.

ELIZABETH PULLED her letters from her reticule. With a glance at Deborah's still form on the bed, she gave them the attention they deserved.

> *Philip Dusseau*
> > *London*
> > *April 1*

> *Dearest Lizzy –*
>
> *I trust you have begun your packing. I have been very patient, I think! I have been cooling my heels in London for a week already. I've caught up on things at White's, practiced my boxing form and hit the target at Manton's, played innumerable hands of cards, seen a fine production of Le Nozze de Figaro—there will be nothing left for me to do by the time you arrive! The days have been busy enough, and the evenings more so. But how cold the nights with no Lizzy on the other side of the bed.*
>
> *I'm sorry it's taken so long to obtain the information you wanted. I offered the man a bonus for prompt performance, hoping to advance the hour, or the minute, when I may next kiss you; but it could not be done. It has finally arrived, however, and I judge it best to forward the whole. Now that you have it, I trust you will bring to a speedy resolution whatever course of action your pretty, clever little head deems appropriate. You are the smartest woman I*

*know, yet you seem to share with all your gender the mysterious conviction
that no man is capable of managing his own romantic affairs.*

Do come soon! –

Philip

(Enclosure)

> *Brown & Sons, Solicitors*
>
> *Exeter, March 26*
>
> *Mr. Dusseau:*

*Herewith the information you engaged me to collect regarding the
antecedents of one Deborah Moore, nèe Carlington. I beg your pardon for
failing to meet the early deadline you proposed; I was obliged to travel to
Liverpool in order to clarify some details and thus suffered some delay. The
weather was abominable.*

*The Carlingtons have held property in Lydford for over a century. The
original estate was quite respectable, and the gentleman farmers who owned it
likewise. Old Blake Carlington seems to have been a paragon: good to his
tenants, careful of his land, and sensible of his status in the community. The
incumbent's father was no such thing, however, and by the time he died, half
the acreage had been sold to pay off debts. At the age of seventeen, our
subject's father, Mr. Robert Carlington, inherited the reduced estate along
with (by all reports) the cavalier propensities of his sire. He proceeded to
gamble his remaining assets on cards and on a variety of investment schemes,
not all of which, it must be said, were abject failures.*

*In 1788 he was plump enough in the pocket to win the hand of Catherine
Winthrop, fourth daughter of one John Winthrop. Mr. Winthrop hailed from
the landed gentry but was a younger son with few expectations. He involved
himself in business and was at this period quite a prominent Liverpool
merchant. (Matilda, whom you also mentioned, was his second daughter.
There were no sons.) Miss Winthrop was twenty years of age at the time of
her marriage, and there were two other motherless daughters still unmarried.
Her father was no doubt happy to make the contract, and the settlements were
reasonably generous.*

*John Winthrop's primary source of revenue was an extensive and lucrative
sugar operation in Barbados. Together with profits from the transshipment of*

slaves and certain other trading operations, this had kept the family in affluence for some time. Unhappily, circumstances conspired during the several years surrounding Miss Winthrop's marriage to bring ruin upon them. Ships sank, an overseer absconded with funds, and the slaves revolted; the sugar plantation was lost, and bankruptcy ensued. Winthrop killed himself in 1791, never seeing his granddaughter, Miss Deborah Carlington, who was born 14 October 1790. The estate went toward payment of debt and all further payments or expectations Mr. Carlington may have had from his father-in-law lapsed. In fact, having invested funds of his own in the plantation, he himself lost a considerable sum.

From this point the tales told by townsfolk in Lydford become increasingly sordid. Rumors abound encompassing all the evils of mankind. Debt, there certainly was; adultery and natural births (including that of his heir, if the stories are true); and also cruelty to his horses and household, extending to his wife, his heir, and possibly Miss Carlington herself. Many villagers appear to have forgotten there ever was a daughter; some hint that she was murdered by her father. Clearly that is not the case, and we must question the veracity of the other claims as well. In any event, the years following Miss Carlington's birth are outside the scope of my employment.

I hope this information is of use to you, and trust that if I can ever serve you further, etc. etc.

INSPECTING the reincarnation of her gown in the mirror, Deborah was vain enough to be pleased. Elizabeth had brought her dresser to work some wonder on her hair, involving Elizabeth's ribbons and enameled combs and a ridiculous amount of time. It was nothing she could recreate for herself if she had a week to devote to the task.

More and more as their acquaintance proceeded, Deborah had seen reflections of Evan in his sister's face and never more so than this evening. Elizabeth watched as Deborah's hair was coaxed into place, offering an occasional comment or a third hand when needed. Deborah watched the sister in the mirror and wished: that he had never come into her life at all, or that she could undo all that had passed between them, or that she might find him standing at the foot of the staircase in evening dress awaiting her descent, with eyes only for her…

Well, it would not happen tonight. It would never happen. She could only hope Elizabeth would ascribe her distraction to nerves. Evan had seldom been mentioned between the two women, yet Deborah was quite sure Elizabeth knew how she felt about him. She might chatter like a sparrow, but her bright eyes missed very little.

"There now, ma'am," said Francine at last. "Nod your head and shake it just a bit… Yes, that will do."

"Indeed it will!" Elizabeth exclaimed with the clap of her hands that said *Magic has been done!* "I don't think you have any idea how pretty you are."

Deborah wrinkled up her nose in reply. She handed Francine a half crown she could ill afford, but the woman pulled back. "Oh, no, ma'am. I can't take that." Though she was happy to keep her money, Deborah felt herself blush at the misstep.

She set aside her unhappy thoughts. Tonight she must repay Elizabeth for her attention, her support, and her friendship. She pulled on her borrowed gloves and summoned the smile that would be her mask through the coming ordeal.

"Do we have time to visit the children? I promised Julian."

"No, but we'll do it anyway." Their silks rustled into the hallway and up the stairs to the Manor's long-disused nursery. "Do you think Julian will recognize you? Do you recognize yourself? Your gown turned out beautifully, I think."

Julian had no problem with his mother's identity, but it was plain he did not approve of the new look. He hugged her tightly before drawing back and looking dubiously at her. "You smell different."

"It's just perfume, sweetling. I will be back to normal tomorrow." She smoothed his hair from his forehead. He looked exhausted.

"What did you do to your hair?"

"I had it done properly, for once."

He touched it gingerly. "I don't like it."

"Well, that will be back to normal soon enough as well. Now I must run, or I'll be late for dinner. Someone might scold me."

Julian giggled. Another quick hug and it was back down the stairs to the drawing room, where they *were* late, but not last.

ELIZABETH MUST HAVE WORKED some magic of her own on the seating arrangements. On Deborah's right hand at dinner sat the vicar, who attended her as much as possible given the garrulous Latimer aunt on his other side.

"It is good to see you amongst us, Mrs. Moore. I hope your son continues healthy?"

"He is flourishing, Mr. Hepplewhite. Thank you for asking."

"I do not believe I've seen you at services recently. In my official capacity, I am obliged to chide you." He wagged an admonishing finger at her.

"I have been quite busy. I know I should—"

"You did not let me finish, Mrs. Moore," he said with a smile, laying his hand on her wrist. "In my *un*official capacity, I can say that it does me good to see you out and about. I hope you will not withdraw again from society after Mrs. Dusseau's departure."

"Thank you, sir. I hardly know..." Deborah caught the eye of Mrs. Hepplewhite several seats down on the opposite side. She flinched at the malevolence she saw there, and whatever she'd thought to say flew out of her mind. She applied herself in some confusion to her turtle soup. When she raised her head again, Mr. Hepplewhite was fully occupied with his other dinner partner.

"Ahem," came from the chair on her left. "It seems, Mrs. Moore, that we have each been deserted for another."

Deborah turned toward the gentleman. Elizabeth had introduced him before dinner as Mr. Sherill. A handsome man and a bit of a dandy with his high, starched collar and flamboyant waistcoat. She had hardly thought he would have anything to say to her. But peering beyond him, she saw Miss Chiggerford on his left.

He spoke so softly she had to lean toward him to hear his words. "I believe no one can say I did not try. She is quite devoted to her dinner." His mouth was drawn down at the corners in a mournful expression, but his eyes sparkled with merriment.

Deborah should have been offended by his mockery of the poor woman, but she found herself chuckling instead. She took another sip of wine.

"So," Mr. Sherill continued, "having done my due diligence, I may follow my preference without blame."

Deborah smiled a little. "But then, your choices are so limited."

To her surprise, he threw back his head and laughed. "At the moment they are, but in this case I believe my preference may survive one dinner and come out the other side unscathed."

Nicely said, sir. We'll see how you feel at the end of this meal when you've had no one to talk to but me.

The dinner looked to be a protracted one as the covers arrived in dizzying profusion. But she laughed too, and drank more wine. It seemed to relax her. *Ask a question, Elizabeth said...*

"I believe you are from Nuneaton?"

"I am," he said, spooning some sort of sauce over his salmon. "Met Viscount Latimer on the hunting field a dozen years ago. What about you, Mrs. Moore? Why have I never met you before? Are you a Yorkshire friend of Mrs. Dusseau's?"

That question had not gone very far. "No. I live here in Whately." Deborah withdrew into her wineglass. *Another question, quickly...*

"Lord Latimer visited friends at Nuneaton in December. Was that you, Mr. Sherill?"

"Why, yes, it was. Came with a friend of his named Haverfield. Nice fellow, rather quiet. Do you know him as well?"

Do not blush... "A little. He stayed with the viscount for several weeks. He is Mrs. Dusseau's brother."

His eyes widened in polite surprise. "You don't say! May I serve you some of this whatever-it-is? Veal, do you think?"

Deborah didn't know either and was no wiser after tasting it. Aside from the wine, nothing seemed to have much flavor. And when he offered her a rabbit cooked in pastry with its head and ears sticking out, she recoiled. She refused everything else except a small dish of syllabub.

While she sipped her wine, Mr. Sherill covered a number of subjects. He found her unqualified to discuss London but discovered she knew Oxford and talked of that instead. He told her stories of his travels in Italy and Austria. One of these involved his visit to a fair, and Deborah added a few comments about her own recent experience. He paid her handsome compliments—she laughed at them but was grateful. He kept her mind from straying, her anxiety at bay.

Before the ladies left to refresh themselves for the dancing, he bespoke her hand for the supper dance, a particularly kind gesture. Not for a moment did she take his gallantry seriously. She suspected he saw in her an unthreatening companion, attractive enough to justify a little flirtation yet mature enough to see it for what it was.

As it happened, Mr. Sherill danced with her not once but twice, and he was not her only partner. She recalled the dance figures readily enough, did not trip over her own or anyone else's feet, and did not tear the hem of her gown.

When Doctor Overley approached her as the musicians were striking up a waltz, she forced herself to stand her ground. "No, sir. I cannot." She would have been happy to insult him just a trifle, but it was safer to let him think she didn't know how. She would have rejected even Mr. Sherill, had he asked her. She would never waltz again. More than once her dreams had afforded her the painful delight of dancing again in Evan's arms, and she would not sully them by letting another man put his hands on her.

She was happy to have danced at all and was neither surprised nor disappointed at the time she spent at the edge of the room.

She spoke with the squire and Lady Reston, with Miss Reston and Miss Caroline, thanking each of them, yet again, for their loan of the pony Julian had been riding.

She listened while poor Miss Chiggerford bemoaned her imminent removal to Leicester following Miss Latimer's marriage. Poor woman, so very alone.

Miss Latimer took five minutes from her hostess duties to spend with her, and her fiancé, whose injured leg precluded dancing, was kind enough to sit with her for quite a few more.

She talked dutifully of rain and mud, found something to compliment in each woman's attire, and exclaimed with the rest of the local folk over last night's fire at the brewery. And Elizabeth appeared frequently at her side to perk up a flagging discussion or merely take her arm for a minute and smile her encouragement. The people she talked with responded readily enough, which gave her confidence that her blather seemed more natural to them than it felt to her.

The evening lasted for all eternity, but finally they were able to escape upstairs. Once changed into their nightdresses and dressing gowns, Elizabeth sent Francine away and they brushed each other's hair while they discussed the evening.

With an impish smile, Elizabeth asked, "What did you think of Mr. Sherill?"

"I think you not only seated him beside me but warned him to prepare a great deal of one-sided conversation."

Elizabeth laughed and clapped her hands. "I confess to the former charge. Knowing Mr. Sherill, I hardly supposed he would need a warning. He is what we call *a rattle.*"

Deborah brushed out one last little snarl, and Elizabeth stood up from the dressing table. Deborah touched her arm for a moment. "I don't think I can possibly say how much I appreciate all your kindness, Elizabeth. These weeks have been... I'm so tired I could sleep for a month. I don't know why you came to Whately or—"

Elizabeth took hold of her chin and gave it a gentle shake. "Hush, you goose." Then she pulled her into a hug. "You did beautifully, Deborah. Didn't I say you would? And it will be easier each time."

She pulled back to look into Deborah's face. "What occasion do you suppose your next ball will celebrate?"

❧ 25 ❧

Was it so unreasonable to want someplace warm? Warm, and far from the curious, concerned, or censorious looks Evan's family had directed toward him for the past week?

He'd intended an indefinite stay if Mama would just curtail her endless prattle about marriage. A couple of months, perhaps, until the Season was underway, and he would join the throng in London as he usually did. None of it sounded particularly appealing, but one had to be somewhere.

Home should have been a good choice. It was an Elizabethan manor house, made comfortable by modern improvements and dear by myriad memories of a happy childhood. The schoolroom, the attics, the big cupboard under the stair... here he had played with his siblings, learned his lessons, dreamed of adventure.

Now the whole place seemed overrun with people. His brother and sister-in-law were visiting, and Alberta's children, who had stayed with their grandparents while Alberta and Theo spent New Year's in Whately. They had taken possession of these indoor haunts. And any time Evan braved the cold to get away from them all, his brother

Raymond came nattering at his heels as he had when they were children.

Alberta arrived to reclaim her progeny, and his parents were thrilled to have so many of the family at home. Evan knew he should be enjoying the reunion as well. He liked all these people, with the possible exception of Raymond's wife, Clarice, who thought everyone must be as interested in her "interesting condition" as she was. He suspected Raymond sought his company as much to forget impending fatherhood as for any other reason. It certainly wasn't for Evan's scintillating conversation, because he couldn't find any.

So far from a two-month stay in the bosom of his family, he hardly lasted a week.

He pointed Grady and the horses toward Cornwall. By the time they arrived, the snowdrops might already be pushing green nubs out of the soil, and the most precocious of the birds would soon be nesting.

Evan craved springtime—it was all he could think of except Deborah—and they breezed through Warwick, Stratford-upon-Avon, and Cheltenham to Stroud and Chipping Sudbury, where they were stalled for a day by driving, almost-freezing rain. That past, they set out for Bristol, only to be held up by a thrown horseshoe in the middle of nowhere. They plodded into some village—presumably it had a name, but it wasn't advertising the fact, and one could see why. It was nearly dark by the time the smith was finished with Jory's hoof. They were obliged to put up at the nameless little town's nameless little inn.

"I reckon we're living a charmed life if we come through this night without an inflammation of the lungs," Grady complained.

Evan grunted. "We've slept in worse places. At least it's stopped raining; it won't matter if the roof leaks."

"Lord yes. D'you remember that inn at King's Landing where we'd've needed a dozen buckets to catch all the drips? Wasn't enough roof to keep one bed dry, much less two." He got no response. "Might be bedbugs, though." That earned another grunt and a grimace.

They survived the night with nothing worse than a few fleabites and arrived in Bristol the following afternoon. There they stayed the weekend and inspected the impressive fossillary at the library on King Street.

Heading west along the north coast of Somerset, an appalling spell of weather trapped them at the Hood Arms near Watchet. The roar of the wind made it easy to imagine Mr. Coleridge sitting in some room nearby writing of the storm that carried his mariner all the way to the Antarctic. Evan despaired of ever being warm again. It was hardly reasonable, but he blamed it on Deborah.

He also despaired of regaining his equanimity, and *that* he could lay at Deborah's door. Virgil insisted that *'Time bears away all things, even our minds'*—well, Evan was losing his mind right enough, yet his discontent remained firmly entrenched. It had been five weeks since he'd last seen Deborah, but he was still mired in remembrances, from the sheen of her hair to the decaying boots she wore, and every sweet inch in between.

FINALLY THE WEATHER began to improve. It was no help to Grady. If his master's mood had improved as well, that would have been one thing. But the thaw meant mud, which slowed their progress, setting Mr. Haverfield's nerves on a feather edge. At the end of each day's drive, Grady spent an hour and more washing the horses and the phaeton, only to have them sullied again minutes after they hit the road the next morning.

It was a relief when they came to rest near Barnstaple at the home of an old friend from Mr. Haverfield's university days. Mr. Allan Woodyard's residence was just the informal sort of place where Grady enjoyed staying. Make that *Sir* Allan Woodyard, for he was now a baronet, though neither the man nor his staff seemed to set much store by it.

At Sir Allan's, he was glad to spend less time in his master's cheerless company. The love affairs of gentlemen were mighty uncomfortable for their manservants, as Grady could now attest. Since leaving Whately, he had been treated to silence and irritation from his usually easygoing employer. And as far as he could tell, this widow of Mr. Haverfield's was in no way worth all the trouble.

❧

EVAN's own feelings about the visit were mixed. Woodyard was easy company, and like Latimer's, his was a bachelor household, with not even an Amanda to disturb the careless habits of its owner. But Evan feared he'd be a rude guest, even for so undemanding a host. With humiliation, indignation, and bitterness all battling for the upper hand inside, merely being civil was sometimes a challenge.

He tried to warn Woodyard over their port on the evening of his arrival.

"Gammon," Sir Allan replied. "You've already apologized for being late, which you cannot be since we never set a precise date. You don't need to do the pretty. If you don't want to talk, don't talk. Tomorrow I thought we'd take out the pointer bitch I've been working with, see if we can find anything to shoot. And a couple of friends from the neighborhood are coming in to dinner and cards. Other than that, I've nothing planned for your entertainment. You want to walk all day by yourself, you're welcome to it." Though Evan did not take these words entirely to heart, they were good to hear.

They passed the evening contentedly enough, reminiscing about Rugby and Oxford, bringing each other up to date on their own lives and those of various mutual friends and acquaintances.

"So who is this bride of Latimer's?"

"She's Sudbury's youngest sister."

Woodyard sat up straight. "What? Not Blythe the Bitch?"

"No, though she's to be married as well. Honora's quite different. Pretty enough and fair. Latimer always did go for blondes. She missed her debut last season—some relative or other died—so you'd probably not know her. Rather too godly for me, which I'm sure redounds more to her credit than mine."

"Ah, poor Latimer. She's just a chit, I gather—will he be able to reform her, do you think?"

Evan shook his head. "I doubt it. By the time he realizes he wants to, it will be far too late. She may rule by vapors and hysterics, but rule she will."

Woodyard himself disclaimed any interest in marriage. Evan was truthfully able to say, "I know exactly how you feel"—hadn't he felt the same three months ago? He fancied that his friend looked at him rather searchingly, but there was no objection when he moved on to the safe topic of horseflesh.

The next morning they found some grouse to shoot and in the afternoon they fenced. They had often dueled each other at school, being well-matched and similarly fascinated by the sport. Woodyard had added an unfortunate amount of weight to his frame, which slowed his movements; on the other hand, he was in better practice. The sweat, and the scrape of steel, and the intense concentration cleared Evan's head of the detritus, and he actually enjoyed himself.

The evening looked to be more arduous, particularly when the two invited neighbors turned up for the predictably excellent dinner with a friend apiece. Evan found, however, that the larger numbers worked in his favor. It was a raucous group, and with so many voices, the reticence of his own was hardly noticed.

And when, later, he found it impossible to concentrate sufficiently on his cards, it was easy enough to withdraw from the game. Instead, he searched Woodyard's shelves for *The History of the Kings of Britain* and sat down to review Geoffrey of Monmouth's version of events surrounding King Arthur's birth—he expected to find himself at Tintagel at some point on this journey.

They were discussing the innocuous, impersonal topic of Arthurian legend in the course of a leisurely ride the next morning when Woodyard expressed an inclination to join him on his visit to Tintagel. "I've not been down that way since I was a lad. And St. Ives as well. And Penzance. We could do the Grand Tour of Cornwall together. Gads, that would be something! Like being twenty again. Except we know what to do with a whore now, eh?"

Evan could think of nothing to say. Certainly nothing encouraging. On some days he could hardly resign himself to poor Grady's company. Hell, on some days he could not bear his own. "Well, I must warn you that I intend to take my time. I want to spend time at Bideford and perhaps Clovelly."

Woodyard laughed heartily. "And you can't stand the thought of it. Pining away after some female, no time to spare for your old friends."

Evan shook his head. "I find I'm angry, actually."

"That's the ticket, Haverfield! Don't let the filly bring you down. You're in luck, in any case; I can't do it. My sister's coming next week, and I have some other obligations I can't miss. Tomorrow, though, you're mine. We're going to see a fight. I got word today there's a match out east of Barnstaple. Then we'll go to the best inn in town for some sustenance. Who knows what the evening might bring."

It brought a fine dinner of duck stuffed with apple and sweetbreads and glazed with plum jelly. "But you know, Woodyard, your own cook would do it better."

"Mm. She *is* a gem, ain't she?" Evan suspected she warmed her employer's bed as well as his ovens. "But she deserves a day off now and then, and besides... Well, there's a house a couple of blocks from here where the girls'll knock your britches off. There's a pretty blonde, name of—hell, I forget her name. If she don't make your pecker stand up, then you're only good for the stewpot!"

Evan tried to look interested.

"I can see you don't believe me. But trust me, it'll do you good. I'm paying... I'll even let you have the blonde!"

What the hell. Clearly Woodyard had his heart set on it. Or some part of his anatomy. And perhaps he was right. It was Deborah he craved, but it would be a relief to get her out of his mind for an hour.

The young woman in question—Portia was her name, or at least the name she used—was everything Woodyard had promised. She was young enough, pretty enough, curvaceous enough, and eager enough.

But he felt no inclination to take her upstairs. "I guess it's the stewpot for me, old friend."

Sir Allan shook his head in disgust, but he got the blonde after all while Evan sat in the parlor and got drunk—quietly, unhappily, inexorably drunk.

A dark-haired girl brought his third glass and a bottle to refill it from. She seated herself beside him on the sofa and introduced herself as Rose. She wore a low-cut bodice, barely laced across her breasts, attached to a thin muslin skirt, and nothing else at all. Beyond thinking that she must be cold, Evan hardly noticed.

"Wouldn't you like to forget your troubles upstairs?" Her voice was soft and, either by breeding or training, genteel.

"What makes you think I'm troubled?" Evan responded, annoyed at her intrusion into his brown study.

"I'm sorry, that looked like a cloud over your head. But perhaps you're one of that rare breed? A loyal husband just keeping his friend company?"

Evan snorted in self-derision. "I would be if I had a wife. Unfortunately, she's rejected me." He took a gulp of brandy and gasped as the fire ran down his throat. "Twice."

Rose curled her legs up beneath her and gave him a frank appraisal. He was not at his best in any way—dressed for a boxing match, drunk, and disagreeable. But Evan supposed a prostitute developed the ability to assess a man, both for his wealth and his character. Oddly enough, it seemed she was pleased with what she saw.

"Looks to me like you'd have plenty to offer a girl."

"A widow, say, one step up from the workhouse? You'd think so, wouldn't you." He spoke in bitterness, and she scrutinized his face quizzically.

"Did she give you a reason?"

He grunted. "Said she doesn't like me well enough."

"You seem quite a nice man."

"I *am* a nice man," Evan replied. "It hasn't got me very far. Into her bed once. And she's not the type to take that lightly." It was cheap brandy, and it burned like gall all the way down. He drained the glass. "I must have been mighty disappointing."

"I have a hard time believing that." Rose nibbled on a finger. "Do you love her?"

"Love her?" He turned toward her abruptly, really seeing her for the first time. "I suppose I do. I can't seem to live without her."

"Have you told her that?"

"I asked her to marry me, for God's sake."

"It's not the same thing though, is it?"

Evan opened his mouth to say something rude. How could a whore expect anyone to take seriously her advice on romance?

Mercifully, Woodyard appeared before he could do so, looking happier if no more sober than his guest, and Evan had a moment to collect himself. Instead, he apologized for his temper and thanked Rose for her company, slipping her a sovereign. He'd been quite aware of the proprietress, scowling upon their conversation. Couldn't blame her. The girl's time was worth money, after all, whether he used her in the conventional way or merely talked her ear off.

Evan left her well-satisfied, disbursing a generous sum to pay for the liquor he had consumed and the flesh he had not.

When Grady arrived in his room late the next morning, he was still sitting on the bed, dressed only in his breeches, his head in his hands.

"Bad night, sir?"

"I can't remember the last one that was not. Did I used to have good nights?"

"I believe so, sir. But sad to say, I have trouble, too, these days when we're on the road, sleeping in a different bed every night."

"That's part of it. We're aging, Grady."

Grady busied himself assembling his master's morning attire and shaving gear. "It's right comfortable here at Sir Allan's, though. I've been sleeping like a babe."

That sounded like heaven. But no amount of walking or wine seemed to help Evan sleep. On the road, he dreamed of ruts and potholes that rattled his teeth and woke him with a headache each morning. In the absence of those grievances, he dreamed of Deborah. It was torture of a different sort, but it was still torture.

"I'll give you one more night's sleep, Grady. But only because it's nearly noon already. And it's raining. We leave tomorrow."

Grady *tsked* his disappointment but asked cordially enough, "Would you like me to shave you this morning, sir?"

"I would, thank you. Just don't cut my throat. Not that I would entirely blame you for doing so."

🦋 26 🦋

Maybe because Grady had complained about changing beds every night, the master followed a more relaxed timetable upon leaving Barnstaple. They spent several days in Bideford, and in Clovelly, and a couple in Bude as well. Grady would have liked to say they extended these visits because Mr. Haverfield found so much to see and do there.

It probably looked that way from the outside. The scenery was breathtaking, right enough, and they climbed the steep stone stairways to hike along the clifftops where primroses bloomed. But Grady wasn't sure Mr. Haverfield saw any of that. And there wasn't a thing he could do about it. He just rolled his eyes again and followed along, except when the master declined his company.

Distraction had a powerful hold on Mr. Haverfield, making him forget all sorts of things that should've been second nature with all the traveling they'd done. In addition to his regular duties, Grady found himself doing things the master usually took care of himself: putting his boots outside the door for blacking overnight, bespeaking his breakfast at an appropriate hour the next morning, keeping a wary eye on the weather and roads as Mr. Haverfield drove too fast and too far.

And at the end of the day, ordering ale to counteract all the wine and brandy his master drank, sitting alone in the private parlor of some inn, staring into the fire or pretending to read.

EVAN FELT LIKE MISTRESS MARY, quite contrary. Having found fine weather at last, he wished it were foul. Not cold—heavens, no. And rain would have barricaded him indoors, which would not do at all. But dreary weather befits a dreary mood, and heavy dark clouds, with perhaps some bluster, would have suited him better than the bright sunshine that reflected painfully off the water and made everyone in these damned picturesque villages smile so damned happily.

At Tintagel, at least, the weather was cooperatively miserable. How *could* one contemplate all that passion and duplicity on a sunny day? Evan suspected it was always windy on this desolate rock so tenuously connected to England—the elements had certainly done their worst on whatever fortress had been Igraine's refuge here.

A poor enough refuge it had been, no match for Merlin's cunning, or Uther's determination to have her at whatever cost. How did she feel, later, when she learned the truth of that night? Had she hated the man who had fooled her so completely? Had she been forced to marry him? Forced by convention, of course. But quite possibly she had been thrilled to trade old Gorlois for a young, forceful king whose son she was carrying. To a more modern mentality, the notion that magic could have disguised Uther so thoroughly seemed like nonsense, in which case it must be inferred that Igraine had known of the deception all along.

It was harder these days to force a woman into marriage—and what man would want an unwilling bride in any case? But in fact, the conventions had not changed very much at all. An unmarried woman, finding herself with child, was still compelled to marry, if she could—

He stopped short in his restless perambulations among the rocks. He had not allowed himself to think of it: Deborah could be carrying his child. Would she feel compelled to marry him, if so? Would he *want* her to, if that was her only motivation?

He was no Uther, and he had practiced no deception. But saving the life of her only child, and then gifting her with another, might well back her into a corner between obligation and trepidation where she felt she had no choice. As much as he wanted her, he did not want to get her that way. Yet he, too, would be compelled by the need to protect her and their child.

Would she let him know? He had received one scrupulously polite note two weeks ago, ostensibly from Julian, thanking him for the dog... No, this was not something she would set down in a letter. By the time he arrived back in Whately, it would be three months from conception. So easy to calculate, it would be hard to forget.

The first night of every month would be an anniversary of sorts, and every New Year's eve— Well, that did not bear thinking of. Surely three months would be soon enough. She must know he would be back for the weddings, and it would be a blackguard indeed who would not make certain of her welfare. There was nothing to do about it in the meantime except worry.

THEY HEADED SOUTH AGAIN, still trying to outrun Mrs. Moore's ghost as Grady saw it. He figured they'd stop at St. Ives or Penzance. Both were good places to spend the rest of the winter.

Indeed, they visited both towns but neither for very long. Mr. Haverfield seemed incapable of staying still. He had friends in the vicinity and had sometimes stayed in their homes, dined or hunted with them. This trip he saw none of them.

He was at least talking more, which Grady supposed was progress, though sometimes he sounded more like a madman than a rational being. After stewing for what seemed like hours, he would suddenly start up on something like the scenery, or Cornish history, or that damned King Arthur again. His talk was almost fevered at times, though he seemed intent on Grady's participation. Like as long as someone was responding, he was having a conversation; otherwise he was just ranting. Then he'd lapse into silence again. Then perhaps he'd recite a few lines of poetry, which maybe related to something he was thinking about but meant nothing to Grady.

WITH A LAUGH that didn't ring true, Grady asked if their goal was to see every insignificant fishing village along the coast of Cornwall.

Evan had no goal at all.

Grady diffidently pointed out that it was the middle of March and supposed they would head north soon.

Evan hardly heard him and made no reply.

When they arrived at Plymouth, Grady breathed a sigh of relief. "Good roads north from here. A day or two to rest the horses, and we can be in Whately in good time for Lord Latimer's wedding."

BUT EVAN FOUND himself assailed by the thought that *she* had been here, in Plymouth, when she first escaped her home. He did not know precisely when or for how long. But he knew that she had shopped for clothing here, and learned to dance, and attended church and assemblies. He saw a production at the Theatre Royal and thought of her there—it wouldn't have been the current building, which had been open just a few years, but its predecessor at the far end of George Street. He attended a concert and wondered if she would have enjoyed it. He purchased new gloves and imagined her doing the same.

But for most of the three days they spent in Plymouth, Evan stood in the drizzle and watched the harbor. No doubt she had walked on the Hoe, where he stood now, marveling at the roiling gray-green ocean and engrossed by the frenzied activity in the harbor.

Things were probably quieter these days—neither Napoleon nor anyone else was likely to invade any time soon. But still it was an exciting and cacophonous place, with ships sailing in and out, cargoes loading and unloading, sailors and soldiers and dockhands lifting, sweating, swearing, and swaggering in all directions. Even on Sunday, the motion barely slowed. Given Deborah's previous seclusion, the scene must have been awe-inspiring, if not downright frightening.

He thought about the exotic places those vessels might be going and considered the possibilities. He did not think India or the East Indies would be to his taste; dying of yellow fever did not sound adventurous, merely wretched.

He was not daring enough, he decided, to attempt Africa. Although, like most men of his generation, Napoleon had denied him the Grand Tour, Europe seemed almost too tame, though somewhere off the beaten track, like Norway, or Iceland... No, too cold. Farther east then, Prague, or Buda, the Black Sea.

Or he could sail west. South America sounded marginally more civilized than Africa, and Canada likewise, though still mighty wild considering it belonged to England. And cold.

But probably he would choose a ship bound for Philadelphia or Charleston. Surely America could offer adventures to last him the rest of his life, and if that proved not to be so long, that would be all right too. He could sign over his inheritance to Raymond and never return to England at all. He'd have to spend some time with his family first, endure their bewilderment and tears and recriminations. And he must see Frank Latimer through his wedding because he had promised to do so. And no, he could not leave the country without seeing Deborah again. He would need a fresh memory of her to hold in his mind.

Rose had told him to talk of love. He would do it. And if that didn't work, *then* he could sail off to the New World. It would be a suitable expression of anguish. Or would it just look like pique?

Whatever Grady might think, Evan was fully aware that time was running short. But for some inscrutable reason, it seemed crucial to follow Deborah's footsteps before he solicited her for the last time. They left Plymouth on the direct road toward Exeter and pushed the grays hard.

&

GRADY WONDERED at the cause of it, but speed—and in the right direction—was all to the good. Mr. Haverfield had stopped talking again, but that was all right too. Grady hummed to himself, took his turn with the reins, and spent some extra time getting Jory and Bess settled in when they finally stopped for the night.

So he was dismayed when they left the main road the next day and headed east, back toward the coast. Grady had seen enough coastal scenery to last him—well, until next winter. And it was raining again.

"I thought we was headed north for sure now, sir." He sounded petulant, even to his own ears.

"We've another couple stops to make, I'm afraid."

More silence. Clearly the master was not going to volunteer anything more. "D'you mind telling me where?"

Mr. Haverfield took the time to negotiate a sharp turn and then to pass a farm cart before answering. "Dawlish first. And Lydford on the way north."

Grady grunted. He didn't know about Dawlish, but Lydford was Mrs. Moore's home town and he figured she must have something to do with Dawlish too. "Damned pilgrimage," he muttered.

"I beg your pardon?" It was spoken quite sharply for his good-natured master. Except he wasn't so good-natured anymore.

"Sorry, sir. I was just sayin', Lydford ain't precisely in our way."

"Nevertheless, that's where we're going." And silence fell again, except this time Grady felt it was directed at him. He ground his teeth and fretted. Might be time to look for a new employer. Some placid country squire, a confirmed bachelor—or at least long married—somewhere down here in the south. But *not* on the coast! Maybe Sir Allan could use a new man in one capacity or another.

It was a damn shame. He was not likely to find a job that suited him so well. Mr. Haverfield might get over his megrims sooner rather than later, particularly if he could get the troublesome widow to marry him. But whether she said yea or nay, life with Mr. Haverfield was bound to change.

27

Evan awoke to what could have been a fantasy world. Early morning sunlight flickered through the budding branches outside his window, the new leaves wet from last night's rain and so vivid, that exuberant shade of green seen only in the springtime. A blackbird sang just out of sight and won a response from somewhere farther away. Passion in the treetops. And in the fields and forests and barnyards as well, no doubt. *Does me no good.*

The flies were certainly breeding. He made his third attempt to swat one pesky youngster who was after his breakfast. The whole extended family was much in evidence in the stableyard as he awaited the phaeton. But once the luggage was loaded and they were underway, this annoyance was left behind. Jory and Bess, who had plodded half-heartedly through the previous afternoon's rain, were in high spirits this morning, tossing their heads and nipping each other fondly. If Evan could not claim such high spirits for himself, he at least felt alive, and that felt pretty damn good.

The rain had stopped them short of their goal the evening before, but an hour's easy drive along the cliffs brought them into Dawlish. Evan wasted no time in seeking out lodgings and took rooms on the Marine Parade, a few doors away from Dawlish Water and The Strand that ran alongside it, up the hill away from the treacherous coast. The main part of town lay inland with its inns and shops. But when they left Dawlish, they would leave the sea behind, and who knew when he would see it again—unless he sailed for America, in which case he would surely get his fill of it.

"Aye, I've a suite vacant," said Mrs. Puddlemire. "I only let by the week, as a normal thing, but being as there's just three days left in the week and that's all you're wanting, I can let you have it at a discount." She also promised "a full breakfast between eight and half past. And I c'n do dinner for ye as well, sir, ye just let me know the day afore."

If Evan had felt Deborah's presence in Plymouth, how much more so in Dawlish, where one could traverse the whole town in an easy morning's walk and meet all its inhabitants in the course of a few days' stay. He strolled out that afternoon and found her everywhere. Every street might have seen her pass. Every shop owner might have sold her bonnets or books, every tea room might have served her. The assembly rooms, the library, and the church had surely held her within their walls. The people he passed might have seen her, met her. Some of the gentlemen might have danced with her at assemblies. Would they remember her? A dark, pretty girl, naïve and serious, graceful and shy?

His vision of her was so real, it took a moment for his brain to register surprise when he saw her, pointing out something in a shop window to her companion. Her height, her figure, the color of her hair, that particular shade of the gown she had *not* worn to the ball on New Year's Eve...

His heart stopped for a moment, leaving him disoriented. It could not be her, of course.

It wasn't. The face she turned to her escort was too young, too round, and far too happy.

Somehow he found the way back to his lodgings. It was a wonder because he could not remember doing so. He must have earned wary looks from passersby as he staggered down the hill. Probably they thought him drunk.

Grady seemed to know better. He jumped up from a chair at first sight of his master's face.

"Why, sir! What's happened? You look like you've seen a ghost!"

Hit the nail on the head, Grady. "No. Just a… a bit of the headache."

Evan let Grady help him out of his coat as he spoke and stripped off his cravat, which felt like a noose around his neck.

"Let me get you out of your boots, an' I'll get you a headache powder."

He didn't need the powder, but it was far easier to comply. He took it with a brandy, drunk much too fast. "Thank you, Grady. I'll just lie down for a bit."

He made the effort to smile reassuringly, though judging by the look on Grady's face, he failed in his objective. Well, it was the best he could do.

He went into his bedchamber and shut the door. *Dear God.*

Had he really thought he'd need to see her again to sear her face into his memory? Right now, her image burned so clearly in his mind that the fixtures and furnishings of the room appeared as faded, nebulous things.

He pressed his hands over his eyes but fancied he could smell her scent on them, that compound of citrus and rosemary and other things he could not name. He cradled his elbows in his hands, but instead of the fine lawn of his shirt, he felt the silk of her gown and the silk of the skin beneath as he peeled the fabric away, inch by intoxicating inch.

Leaving the support of the door, he threw himself prone across the bed. He could, possibly, have shaken off the delusion, but he had little desire to do so. He would take what he could get of her, though it be fallacy. And after a time, the waking vision followed him into sleep, where most any delusion could be deemed sane.

HE SLEPT the clock 'round and then some. Grady must have come in at some point, removed his shoes and laid a blanket over him—he remembered none of it.

He woke early, too early for Mrs. Puddlemire's breakfast. The smell of it wafting up from the kitchens belowstairs was not encouraging. He stepped outside. The dawn air felt dull and thick, like his head.

In the cobbled street, vendors peddled gingerbread and oysters, newspapers and rags. A milk man trudged homeward leading a tired horse and wagon. Two housemaids emerged with shopping baskets from the house next door.

Farther along, a carriage was being loaded with a quantity of trunks and bandboxes for a journey, apparently one of some length. A dog sniffed hopefully for leavings along the pavement but ran off, tail between its legs, when one of the footmen aimed a kick in its direction. Across the street the bathing machines were drawn up on the strand for use later in the day, and two women with their skirts tucked up trolled for anything saleable that might have washed in with the overnight tide. And the sound of the sea rolled over it all, in and out, Aeschylus's *myriad laughter of the ocean waves*, restless yet soothing.

Breakfast was executed every bit as poorly as Evan had feared. The eggs had the consistency of India rubber, the sausages were cooked to some stage beyond either flavor or succulence. The kidneys he did not even attempt. The toast was cold, but it generally was. He could not fault Mrs. Puddlemire on that score. He dabbed some apricot preserves on a couple of slices and ate them with his coffee. Surprisingly, his fellow guests seemed to have no complaints.

He supposed, uncharitably, the hefty fellow at the end of the table would eat most anything, and there was a trio of youths—on some sort of walking tour, he gathered—who probably fit the same category. He could not account for the rest of the company. It was possible the difficulty lay with him rather than them.

He climbed the stairs back to his rooms. Grady, he hoped, was somewhere in the kitchens overseeing their laundry. Evan pared a fingernail that was bothering him and scanned the newspaper he had bought outside. Little enough of interest there.

In his other life as a thinking man with some curiosity about the workings of society and politics, he would no doubt have followed the progress of the bill to abolish sinecures. And in his former guise as a good-humored man who found amusement in the foibles of his fellows, he would have chuckled over the activities of the Princess of Wales, parading herself through Munich in Turkish costume. As it was, he could hardly have cared less about any of it.

He picked up his book instead, but Emma Woodhouse had no power to hold his attention. That was occupied by another sort of woman entirely.

Despite the threat of rain, he decided to go riding. He walked up the hill to the livery stable, where it seemed at first he would be obliged to find some other way to fill his afternoon.

"I dunno, sir. Y're come a bit late, y'see. A party o' gents from Lunnon, they took all the best early this mornin' to ride out Teignmouth way. An' I've got a real nice gelding what's got a spavin an' another that needs 'is hooves seen to." He looked Evan over critically. "Got a mare should be up to your weight, though. Not much to look at, an' I've not rid her meself, she not bein' here long. Groom says she rides nice though. Would you be wantin' to see 'er?"

Evan would. As the proprietor had warned, she was no beauty—not quite white but not gray either, not dappled but blotched. She was too thin, and her mane looked like it had been hacked off in segments and was trying to grow back. Her conformation was better. She looked like she might be capable of some speed.

"Looks a durn sight better 'n she did when she come in here. Them saddle sores are most healed up, and she's fatted up a bit."

She rolled a long-suffering eye as Evan swung into the saddle, reminding him of Grady. He smiled and turned her toward the street. "You're the lucky one, lass. You only need to put up with me for a couple of hours."

He headed in the direction *the Lunnon gents* had rejected, north along the clifftop toward the Exe estuary. He was hardly a demanding rider this afternoon, and the mare took full advantage of the slow pace, snatching at leaves or grass as the opportunity arose. He let her as long as she kept moving. There was no hurry to arrive nowhere.

They followed whatever road or track took them closest to the cliff's edge. This allowed plenty of fodder for the horse, and for the rider there were plenty of views out over the busy gray sea. Occasionally a ray of sunshine would pick out a gull and give it life as some sort of spirit gleaming white against the darkening clouds, but none of those rays touched ground. If any breeze blew off the water, it did not scale the cliff to rustle the trees or relieve the weight of the air. There were few travelers in evidence. Not more than a handful of times did Evan need to acknowledge another rider or carriage.

The Langstone headland came into view, guarding the Exe estuary, unmistakable from the description given him by the fellow at the stable. And at length, when he began to think he'd missed it, Evan found what he was looking for: a horse-worthy path that dropped down to the strip of sand below them.

The mare was reluctant to tackle the steep slope but succumbed to his urging without much of a fight. They had to scramble at one point as they dislodged a patch of earth, sending soil and pebbles rolling down the cliffside. But they emerged unscathed and reached the bottom safely.

The tide was well out. They rode clear around the broken promontory and passed through the tunnel carving its way through the rock. Then they turned south, back toward Dawlish.

Down here on the strand, out from under the trees, Evan expected it to be brighter. In fact there was not much difference. The sky had turned leaden, the air had come alive. As horse and rider left the shelter of the rocks, wind and water vied to win their attention from whatever grim thoughts preoccupied them.

The horse began to curvet in excitement. Evan realized he had moped far too long and was doomed to a wetting.

She wanted to run. He gave her her head.

Along the beach she galloped, in and out of the shallow water as the waves rolled up. Wet sand flew in clods off her hooves. The storm winds blew sand and salt spray in their faces. Evan leaned low to avoid the worst of it; the mare snorted and tossed her head in glee. Then the clouds opened above them. There was no shelter, nothing to do but laugh and urge the horse to still faster speeds, and laugh some more.

By the time they reached Dawlish Water and made their way to Mrs. Puddlemire's establishment, the horse had just about spent herself and so had the rain. Fat droplets collected on eaves and leaves and railings, falling as they achieved some certain mass onto the heads passing below.

Evan was wet to the skin with sand crusted in all sorts of unlikely places. He might as well have rolled in the stuff. It was extraordinarily uncomfortable, far more so than he'd realized as he sped up the beach cackling like a madman. But the despondency that had paralyzed him lifted. For the first time in months, he felt energetic, engaged in the world.

He brushed himself off as well as he could, but still he shed sand all the way up the stairs and into his rooms. Grady was folding a stack of freshly laundered cravats.

"I see you got caught in the rain, sir."

Evan grinned. "I did indeed. I've ruined my new gloves and lost my hat, and if you can salvage the coat and breeches, you're a miracle worker."

"We'll see. Stop there now, sir, before you get sand all in the rug. Let's get those clothes off you, and then I'll order up a bath."

"Already done; I saw the maid downstairs. It can't possibly come too soon; my hair feels like a broom." Off came the coat, the waistcoat, the cravat, the shirt, to drop in a gritty pile on the floor. "I need you to take my mount back to the livery stable. She's tied out front, an unprepossessing white thing." He picked his coat out of the pile again and reached inside for his pocketbook.

"And Grady? Buy the horse. Make sure she gets cleaned up. We'll take her with us tomorrow."

Grady's eyes widened in surprise. "Tomorrow, sir?"

"It's time," Evan said, "as you've been telling me this month past. We have weddings to attend." And under his breath, as he peeled off his stockings, "Who knows, one of them might be mine."

❦ 28 ❧

He had neglected his correspondence. Badly. There were letters from Frank Latimer, from both his sisters, and increasingly petulant ones from his mother, dutifully forwarded from Shrewsbury and left unread. These he determined to answer with no further delay. The scratch of quill on paper filled the parlor all evening, the sea murmuring on the strand as background music.

Latimer must be advised that Evan would miss the ball, and almost certainly Amanda's wedding as well. But he would brave hell itself, Evan wrote, to be there for Frank's own nuptials. Given the hell he'd inhabited since the year began, the expression seemed apt.

His letters to the women of his family consisted mostly of travelogue. It wouldn't satisfy them as to the cause of his long silence, but it was the best he could do. His mother made a peculiar reference to Elizabeth visiting in Whately, so implausible he ignored it. Her handwriting was sadly deteriorated in the past year or so, and her mind not always as clear as one might hope. Elizabeth's own letters made no mention of such a thing.

Reading over what he'd written to Alberta and his mother, Evan decided he'd managed well enough. The tone was lighter than he could have hoped to achieve at any other time these last three months, and although *he* knew it was pretense, he did not think the recipients would recognize it as such.

To Elizabeth he had let his guard down somewhat without noticing as he wrote. He included many of the same passages, copied more or less verbatim, but interspersed with these were rather too many mentions of the miserable weather, the miserable roads, the tedium of traveling every day. Likely she would read quite easily between those lines and come to the wrong conclusion—that is, the right conclusion, but not the one he wished her to draw. It would have to do. He was too tired to start over.

THEY GOT to Exeter late the next afternoon and checked into the White Hart. The master had behaved almost normal on the drive, as near as Grady could recall what that meant. He was cheerful and talkative. Maybe too talkative. If Grady had not known better, he might have thought he'd drunk more than just an ale with breakfast.

Mr. Haverfield drummed his fingers on the mantelpiece in his private parlor and gazed thoughtfully into the fire—yesterday's stormy weather had left much cooler temperatures in its wake. Grady hefted a trunk and headed into the bedchamber to begin unpacking.

"By the way," the master called after him. And when he reappeared in the doorway, "You won't be needing much here, Grady. We're parting ways tomorrow."

Grady's jaw dropped. Mr. Haverfield was still looking at the fire. Grady lurched toward him, ready to plead for his job, if he could make his mouth work.

"I want you to take the phaeton and the horses and start north. I'm going to—" He looked up. "Why, Grady, whatever is the matter?"

He felt faint with relief. Yes, he'd thought about leaving, but he didn't mean it. "I'm sorry, Mr. Haverfield. I thought you meant—that is—I know I've set up your back, sir, spoken out more than I should, but I—well, I thought you was turning me off, sir."

"Heavens, no. Sit down, man, before you fall over." Having pressed Grady into a chair, he continued. "I've been quite incredibly aggravating, and if you've shown any disrespect, it's no more than I deserve. But before I leave Devon, I must go to Lydford—no, sit down. It will just be a quick visit, and then I'll travel post back to Whately. I'll be there before you are, with any luck at all."

Grady felt unable to object as he otherwise would, and probably should. Now, when it was so nearly over, this damned pilgrimage threatened one last time to swallow the master whole—and Grady would not even be there to pull him out of its maw. This mania that had overtaken him yesterday could not be expected to last, and poking around in that infernal woman's home town seemed a sure way to hasten a relapse of depression.

"I can see what you're thinking, Grady, and I laud your self-control. I assure you I will survive without you."

Grady opened his mouth to object but closed it again.

Mr. Haverfield gave him a sympathetic smile. "No, I'm afraid it would do no good."

LATE AFTERNOON SUNSHINE glanced through the clouds twenty-four hours later as Evan dismounted with a grimace in the stableyard at the Castle Inn. Lydford seemed unaccountably busy, and he was lucky to get a room at all. There were no private parlors to be had. A harried maid led him up the stairs to a drab little chamber at the far end of the corridor.

"Ye'll be wantin' dinner, sir?"

"Yes, but not immediately, I think. Tell me—do you know where I'll find the Carlington estate?"

The girl's eyes opened wide. "Well o' course, sir. It's just up the road out Morehampton way, a mile or maybe a bit less. *Everybody* knows it *now.*"

It was Evan's turn to show surprise. "Why is that?"

"Oh!" She looked as though she'd like nothing more than to keep chatting, but an impatient call from downstairs recalled her to duty. She bobbed a quick curtsy and ran off down the hall.

Evan poured water from the cracked ewer into the chipped bowl, the first decorated with pink rosebuds, the other with a pastoral scene of cows and stone walls and a young couple flirting by a stile. He rinsed his face and combed his hair. What he wanted was a bath, but it could wait until evening.

He had brought only such clothing as he could carry on horseback, so his unpacking took all of a few minutes. Then he set out on foot *out Morehampton way.*

It had been many years since he'd spent a full day in the saddle, and he had enjoyed it. His hired mounts had been willing enough, the moors intriguing, and the company—well, solitude was still his safest bet. But his legs felt stiff and his backside bruised, and they would be worse tomorrow. It felt good to walk.

The road was lined on both sides by the ubiquitous dry stone walls, and by springtime flowers that grew up alongside or sprang from the crevices. The traffic, both wheeled and pedestrian, continued heavy as he headed out from the center of town. Evan frowned. Why were there so many people, and what on earth had the maid at the inn been all agog about?

The crowd made it a simple matter to find what he was looking for, though he would have preferred having the place to himself. Not all passersby stopped at the house, but nearly all slowed down to point and talk in whispers and shouts and all gradations of volume in between. They'd apparently been collecting here for some time—the road surface, and as much as he could see of the drive, showed a confused mess of wheel tracks, foot- and hoofprints, and other, more malodorous evidence of equine activity.

When questioned, two matrons confirmed this was indeed the Carlington estate, though he'd had little doubt. It wore just the aura of neglect he'd imagined. The stone wall was in disrepair, the gateposts crumbling, the gates themselves rusted and certainly unusable. The drive had once been graveled, but many a year had passed since then.

A tarnished sign on one gatepost read "Greenwood Hall," but it was laughably out of date. Though the house was well-situated on a slight elevation, the moors that formed such an arresting backdrop had long ago reclaimed whatever wood or lawns might have originally adorned the approach. Where the ground supported anything at all, it was only the rough grasses and gorse of the hills beyond. Beautiful in their own way, of course, but they did nothing to enhance the façade of Greenwood Hall.

The house was built of local stone. Though not especially large, its dimensions were pleasing. Several windows had been filled in, no doubt to reduce the taxes, and this had apparently been done at different times, for different materials had been used in different windows. The result was a hodgepodge. And this was on the *front* of the house. No telling what the back looked like.

Even from the road, damage to mortar and roof and chimneys was evident. The place hardly looked livable.

The gathering of the curious had the advantage that he could linger without being conspicuous. By the time he was ready to turn back toward town, most of the others were already headed home to chores or dinner or whatever evening activities awaited them. A disinterested farmer and his dog herded a flock of sheep back to the fold, the jackdaws flew down to evaluate the day's leavings, and the light grew dim.

Whoever said that dusk falls had it wrong in this case; it seemed rather to rise from the earth. The ground where he stood was deep in shadow while the sun still shone on Deborah's roof and the hills behind it. He took a last look, thinking of all Deborah had said and not said, trying to imagine a childhood spent within those crumbling walls. He shook his head and started walking.

He had not gone a hundred yards before a gig came up alongside, driven by a young man of twenty or so.

"Evening, sir," said he. "Care for a ride into town?"

"Much appreciated. Thank you." Dusk had now fallen—no, risen—with a vengeance.

Evan hauled himself up into the rather extraordinary vehicle. It had once been a gig, but evidently its owner had larger ambitions.

Somewhere he had obtained a set of wheels from a high-perch phaeton, which raised the height several inches above the expected. Then the body had been painted the color of claret, and the wheels picked out in dark blue and yellow. Tasteful enough. It would hardly be noticed in London, but here in Lydford it was quite out of the common way.

At a guess, the youth driving it *was* the owner, for he himself was tricked out in similar fashion. His otherwise ordinary outfit had been embellished with a checked silk waistcoat in vibrant greens and blues, a cravat with which he'd attempted a complicated knot, perhaps meant to be a Mathematical, and a very high-crowned hat. The scion of one or another family of local gentry, Evan supposed, doing what he could with a modest allowance. Certainly the horses pulling the contraption were nothing special.

"I expect you're in town for the inquest tomorrow. Nothing like a killing to bring in the curious."

"I confess to the curiosity. Something to do with the Carlingtons, I gather?"

The young man looked surprised. "Well of course! I figured you to be a solicitor or maybe a newspaper man—but then you'd know all about it, surely. And," he continued in some awe, "you'd not be wearing a coat like that, much less those boots you've got on. Are they Hobys?"

Evan chuckled. "They are. And no, I'm a friend of the family, passing through."

"Didn't know they had any friends, quite honestly. Must be queer to come visiting and find all this going on. I'm sorry if—"

"Don't be. Actually I'm only a friend of a friend. I've no reason to mourn."

"Well, I'm glad to hear it 'cause you won't find much grieving going on here. They aren't much liked, sorry to say."

Evan introduced himself. His handshake was reciprocated warmly. "Tell you the truth, I'm not clear on what's happened."

Geoffrey Radnor was only too happy to fill him in. "Old Mr. Carlington took a spill on Sunday an' broke his neck. That's no particular surprise, mind you. Everyone knew it was bound to happen sometime, the way he crammed his horses."

So it was the father. No loss to anyone.

"That hardly sounds like murder."

"You wouldn't think so. But the son, now, keeps telling anyone who'll listen that his mother killed him."

Evan frowned. "How would she have done that?" From the information he'd gleaned from Deborah, he could easily imagine why she might want to.

Radnor shrugged. "Don't know. But you can bet I'll be at the inquest tomorrow to hear what he has to say."

"You and the rest of Lydford, I'll be bound."

Radnor grinned. "Hell yes. This is the most exciting thing to happen around here since—well, since I can remember."

They arrived at the inn and Radnor turned his gig into the bustling yard. "Sorry, sir, I should have asked where you was staying."

"Oh, here at the Castle. It seems to be a popular place this evening." Any of the inn guests desirous of an early bedtime—like himself, say— would be out of luck. Sleep would be an impossibility in all the uproar of horses and carriages coming and going and voices in the tap room.

Radnor was hailed by some friends and diffidently invited Evan to join them. "Unless of course you've friends of your own, or we're too rackety for you?"

"Oh no. I'd be delighted."

Radnor beamed. Evan liked the lad. He was open and friendly, yet knew his manners, and notwithstanding his penchant for high style, he was unaffected and down-to-earth. That waistcoat of his drew guffaws from the table, which he received good-naturedly. "You're all jealous, that's what." The barmaid came by with ale and the promise of Evan's dinner.

He found he was ravenous. He'd had next to nothing since a very early breakfast. So he was quite happy to eat and listen to the various conversations circulating around the room. No one was talking about anything except the "murder." Natural enough, he supposed.

And Radnor was right in his assessment of the town's frame of mind. One red-faced gentleman was congratulating himself that *he* had recently sold Carlington the horse that killed him failing to clear a hedge. Evan did not hear whether or not the horse had survived the event.

"I wouldn't sell either of 'em any horse of mine," replied another fellow. "Be more humane just to shoot the poor beast. That stable's full of ruined mouths and mean tempers. Decent grooms don't last a month."

"Not likely you'd get paid, anyway. Did you ever get what he owed you, Charlton?"

"Not more 'n a farthing or two. But it's worth it to get rid of the scoundrel."

"You sure won't get anything out of the estate, either."

No, Radnor had not exaggerated. Evan profoundly hoped people would not talk about *him* that way after his death. More likely they'd shake their heads in wonder at his stupidity: "Fool went stark staring mad 'cause a woman rejected him. Can you believe such a thing? Never was the same again." Well, stupid was better than wicked. Surely Deborah's father had had *some* good points?

"He treated his son all right, didn't he?"

Headshakes all around the table. Young Robert Carlington must be a few years older than these lads but near enough to be familiar to them. "If you call it 'all right' to give a boy a gun but no instruction or etiquette on how to use it. He used to go up on the moor and practice on the sheep, for God's sake."

"Gave him a horse, too, when he was 'bout ten. Too big and much too spirited. That one ran away with him and got shot for his pains."

"Well, I'd 've run away too."

"That's exactly the point, Mick. You put a stupid, mean ten-year-old on that stallion of yours, what would you expect him to do?"

"His father beat him too. M'brother said he used to show up at school—when he showed up at all—with black-and-blue marks all over. Just laughed about it like he was proud, like his dad could take on Gentleman Jackson himself 'cause he could beat up his own son."

"Surely," Evan suggested, "Mrs. Carlington must have had some-thing to say about that?" She wasn't his mother, of course, but as far as he could tell these boys knew nothing about that. And surely any woman—any *person* of compassion—would protect a child from a bully.

Shrugs and more headshaking. "Rumor is he beat her too." That one was true.

"Nobody's hardly seen her in a long time."

"Must be mighty uncomfortable for her at the house just now," Evan commented.

"Oh, he's already thrown her out," Radnor informed him. It was news to several at the table, it seemed, and they happily added more black marks to the tally against Deborah's brother.

"Where is she then?" Evan asked. "Surely she's not been jailed?"

"She's staying with old Mrs. Maddox at the Doll House."

"The Doll House? Does she make them?" Evan wanted to know.

"No, no," replied one of Radnor's friends. "Just that the place is hardly bigger than a little girl's dollhouse. So it's come to be called that."

Mrs. Maddox, Evan was told, had been housekeeper to the Carlingtons "since before God was born." She had retired—or been fired by Mr. Carlington in one of his rages, no one seemed quite sure —a year or two ago. "Before God was born" might encompass little more than ten years to these youths, of course, but even at that she would have known Deborah at least briefly before she'd bolted from her prison.

It seemed odd that none of the conversations rippling around the room had anything at all to say about Deborah. Considering all the old and new infractions the good people of Lydford were eagerly using to flay Robert Carlington, abuse of his daughter would have seemed a natural addition to the litany.

Evan wasn't about to mention the subject—he had no desire to aim their curiosity her way. But later, when the bar had closed, he took advantage of his guest privileges to order an expensive brandy as a nightcap. He engaged in some obligatory small talk with the innkeep as he cleaned up the evening's mess and then asked if the Carlingtons had not had a daughter in addition to the son from hell.

"They did indeed. But she's not been heard of in years, so far as I know. Got well away from it, and good thing for her. Funny thing, though. Another gent was in here asking about her two or three weeks back. Talked to some of the patrons, and I'm sure he didn't get anything but speculation. Guess they used it up back then. It's been so long, a lot of folks've pure forgot."

Evan put himself to bed and lay in the darkness, listening to the crowd below, the waves of laughter and excitement. What could be better than a sudden death with a rumor of foul play—and no need at all to conceal their glee? No one to grieve, no one with any regrets except one pitiful old lady, whose biggest regret must be that it hadn't happened years ago.

✢ 29 ✤

By half past five the next morning Evan was awakened by all the bustle of a new day at an inn packed to overflowing. He had managed only a few short hours of much-needed sleep. He felt like an old man as he clambered out of bed and rang for hot water. He never had gotten his bath the night before—the staff had been far too busy, and this morning would be no better.

Resigning himself to another day coated in dust, he washed as well as he could, shaved, and donned a clean shirt, cravat and waistcoat. Someone had found time overnight to brush his coat and polish his boots to something approaching a shine, so he at least looked human when he appeared in the coffeeroom for breakfast.

He hoped that was still true at nine when he stood before the door of the Doll House.

Evan knocked, despite having no clear idea what he could say or do. He had no standing, was not even a resident of the county. He was laughable as a character witness, having never met Mrs. Carlington until now, three days after her husband's death. Most likely Deborah's brother was just blowing hot air about her involvement, but Evan hoped to have a clearer opinion after meeting her.

The woman who opened the door was definitely *not* Deborah's mother. She was a lummox of a woman, nearly as tall as he was himself, with little of grace or beauty and, just at the moment, an aspect so forbidding that Evan found himself wanting to turn around and walk away.

"You must be Mrs. Maddox?"

"Aye. What's your business?"

"I understand Mrs. Carlington is staying with you?"

If she'd been a dog, she would have growled. "We don't need no tourists."

Evan managed to get his elbow in the door. It would be bruised the next day, he was sure. "Please, ma'am... I'm a friend of her daughter's."

"Of Debby's?" The growl altered somewhat in timbre. She took the card he offered and looked at him skeptically.

"Please ask her if she'll see me. I promise I'll leave you in peace if she says no."

Mrs. Maddox must have been reasonably sure what the answer would be, for she admitted him to the little parlor—"Do watch your head, sir"—rather than leaving him in the street.

There was little enough here to occupy him while he waited; the room was smaller than many closets. It boasted a fireplace that heated the whole cottage and opened through to the kitchen. A kettle hung on a pothook over the little pile of wood that burned there. Two simple upright chairs, a small table, a wooden chest, and a well-used broom constituted all the furnishings. The place was immaculately tidy; any sort of clutter would quickly push the inhabitants out the door, and she had been a housekeeper, after all... now housing her former mistress. What a strange world.

He could hear the murmur of voices, thought he heard Deborah's name. Then came the tread of uneven footsteps.

His first thought was that this could not be Deborah's mother, either. Surely she was too old, too small, too frail, too drab. It was impossible to say what color her eyes or hair had been; the former were clouded by cataracts, the latter showed only gray where it was not covered by her cap.

Leaning heavily on a cane, she limped to the nearest chair. Not until she was settled there, a ragged shawl arranged around her shoulders and another draped across her lap by Mrs. Maddox, did she so much as glance at her visitor.

She offered coffee, mostly, he thought, to cover a certain nervousness. He accepted, mostly for the same reason, and Mrs. Maddox stepped out into the kitchen.

"I'm sorry. Won't you sit down?" A gesture of the hand, surprisingly graceful despite the deformities of arthritis, invited Evan to the other chair, so close to hers that their knees nearly touched. What he'd found most unsettling as she entered the room was the total lack of the natural elegance of movement that characterized her daughter. But it was unfair to expect anyone to limp gracefully. Seated, it was just possible to believe they were related.

She peered at his card. "So, Mr.—Haverfield, is it? My daughter sent you?"

Evan was forced to deny it. Perhaps she thought he was a solicitor or some such, as Geoffrey Radnor had done; but whereas Radnor knew full well that precious few solicitors could afford to entrust their feet to Hoby, Evan felt sure Mrs. Carlington had never heard of England's preeminent bootmaker and would certainly not recognize his boots.

"No, ma'am. She doesn't know I'm in Lydford. I've not seen her in —a few weeks. And as far as I'm aware, she knows nothing of your— er, situation."

"I wrote her on Monday about her father's death, but not—well, I expect you've heard what's being said."

He smiled at her apologetically. "Within two hours of my arrival yesterday. I'm sorry to say, you're rather a celebrity."

"Humph." She turned her gaze toward the little window. Evan had the impression that whatever she saw was something else entirely.

"I plan to attend the inquest this afternoon. I want to know what happened."

She turned back to him, brows raised in inquiry.

"Surely you know of the inquest?"

"Oh yes. But I am surprised that a stranger, apparently passing through Lydford merely to see the gorge, would waste half the day at an inquest into the death of a hated man in a hateful village. It makes me wonder, just what is your relationship with my daughter?"

He studied the floor between his boots. "I hope to persuade her to marry me, ma'am."

There was a moment's silence. He looked up.

"Well." She spoke matter-of-factly, almost disinterestedly. "You seem to be a nice enough young man." Pointedly she inspected his attire. "Judging solely by your clothing, I would guess that you're reasonably well-to-do. And I see nothing in your appearance to disgust a young woman."

Evan grinned and murmured politely, "Thank you, ma'am."

"Surely you're not here for my approval?"

"No, no. I had no intention of making your acquaintance at all, quite honestly."

"You don't seem very sanguine about your prospects."

"She's already refused me once, you see." *Twice, to be honest.*

"Good for her!" She waved a hand back and forth. "I've nothing against you personally, mind. I am not a great believer in the institution of marriage, however."

"I quite understand—"

"She was not merely being coquettish?"

Evan almost laughed. "Coquettish? Deborah? You don't know her very well if you think—"

He broke off abruptly as Mrs. Carlington flinched, coloring up in a way that seemed all wrong in an old woman. Touching her knee, he apologized in a softer voice. "I was forgetting how long it's been since you've seen her."

Mrs. Maddox could have chosen no better moment to appear with the coffee. Without doubt, she could hear all that passed in the parlor —had she been awaiting her cue?

The coffee was poured and distributed, the sugar and cream offered and stirred. Mrs. Maddox seated herself on the chest under the window, rather like a guard dog.

Evan didn't mind.

Mrs. Carlington had regained her composure. "If you want to know what happened, you could save a lot of time and bluster. Why don't you ask me?"

"I feared it would be an unwelcome intrusion." But her tone was resentful. An intrusion, but also an insult, as though *her* thoughts on the subject were of no account. He gestured toward her with one hand.

"Please, ma'am, tell me."

"He was brought home rolled in a blanket, dead as a fencepost. Neck broken, one side of his head bashed in. I'm told the girth snapped."

That was Deborah's voice, the cold, hard version.

"And no," she continued, "I had nothing to do with it. I'm sure you're wondering and too polite to ask." She did not make it sound like a compliment.

"To be honest, ma'am, it wouldn't matter to me." With some surprise, he realized it was the truth. A moral failing, no doubt, but there it was.

"Not that I haven't thought about it a hundred times."

Evan finished his coffee. "Tell me, would your son be likely to listen to reason?"

Both women shook their heads.

"He's no blood o' hers," asserted Mrs. Maddox. "And he got all his father's worst traits." She stood up and collected the coffee cups. "But if ye go, sir, ye might ask if someone could pack up her clothes. That is, if he ain't burned 'em already. *He* don't want 'em, it's sure, and she's got naught but what's on 'er back."

Mrs. Carlington seemed to be blushing again. Embarrassment, perhaps, at having all her dirty laundry aired—quite literally—in front of a stranger.

HALF AN HOUR LATER, Evan was admitted to another house by another reluctant servant. This one was not protective so much as lazy. He was also soiled, smelly, and shifty-eyed. But given the price of a couple of drinks at the Castle, the fellow shambled off with another of Evan's calling cards.

Mr. Carlington was apparently in no hurry to discover what his visitor wanted. Evan was left to cool his heels for half an hour in the chilly, threadbare parlor.

Surprisingly, the place seemed clean enough. Mrs. Carlington had been in residence until very recently, of course, and presumably some other housekeeper had taken the place of Mrs. Maddox when she retired. Someone was doing the best they could with a bad lot.

Bright rectangles showed on the walls where paintings had been removed for sale. What rugs remained on the floor were too worn to be worth anything, and the draperies should have been replaced years ago. What had been a fine plastered ceiling—not an actual Adam, surely, but a well-executed copy—was cracked and flaking. Furnishings were sparse; probably the best of those had been sold as well, along with whatever *objets d'art* might once have graced mantel and sideboard. It was a sad place, even the memories musty with neglect.

When had a happy sound had last been heard here? Someone whistling, perhaps, or some female Carlington accompanying herself on a long-gone instrument. It was hard to imagine her singing anything but a lament.

He was in a mood to pity the proud new owner of this ruin rather than despise him. Accounts were uniformly negative, but accounts could be wrong. Certainly his father had done him no favors, of blood or upbringing. But that same blood ran in Deborah's veins, to quite different effect.

Subduing his impatience with the long wait, Evan smiled at his host when he sauntered into the room and offered his hand. Carlington shook it, though his expression was wary.

"Afternoon, Mr... Sorry, I didn't get your name. What can I do for you?" His voice was curt. "The household is in mourning, you must know."

Evan made the obligatory noises of sympathy. Carlington was dressed not for grief but for riding, in breeches that needed a good brushing, a well-worn blue coat, and a handkerchief knotted around his throat. Leaning negligently against a table, he could have been one of his grooms. But he had Deborah's eyes, and Julian's too.

"I am here in some sort as your mother's representative."

"Ha! Where'd she get the money to hire a *representative*? Running scared, is she?"

"Would you allow yourself to be charged with murder, Mr. Carlington, without making a reasonable effort to avoid it?" Evan exercised his tension by strolling around the room, hands clasped behind his back. "What makes you think that frail old woman is capable of such a thing?"

"Doesn't take any particular strength to cut partway through a strip of beat-up old leather."

"I doubt she could even hobble as far as the stable. Tell me, when did you last inspect your saddles for safety?" Evan asked.

"There are grooms to do that," Carlington spat, his chin jutting belligerently.

"Mm. Quite a succession of them, I hear. And was your father careful about such things?"

Carlington looked mulish. Evan stopped his perambulations and confronted him. "It seems to me two reasonable men should be able to reach a reasonable agreement in this matter."

"I suppose you're bound to tell me."

Evan smiled. Couldn't expect the man to give in happily. "Let it go, man." He infused as much persuasion into his voice as he could muster.

Predictably, it wasn't enough.

There was some bluster, and then some negotiation, and finally Evan walked back into Lydford. His pockets were lighter, but so were his steps.

❧ 30 ❧

Evening found Evan back at Greenwood Hall, peering out the window of Deborah's old bedchamber toward the moors, just a darker blackness beneath the night sky.

All he could see in the glass were the candles that had lit his way to the third story and the ghost of his own face. He shivered. The fireplace had been boarded up many years ago, by the looks of it, and there would have been no fire laid for him in any case. Mrs. Carlington herself had received an embarrassingly cool greeting from her own servants, and he received none at all.

The same surly fellow who had admitted him earlier in the day—the butler, for want of a more suitable term—had let them in, though grudgingly. A housemaid greeted Mrs. Maddox with some affection and showed a proper respect for Mrs. Carlington, dropping a small curtsy as she took her cloak and bonnet. She offered her assistance with their packing, as well, but was whisked away by the new housekeeper. Young Mr. Carlington might not be a generous or congenial master, but the staff could expect nothing at all from his mother.

A half crown—ostentatiously bitten to assure its authenticity— persuaded the butler to retrieve a dusty old trunk from the attics. It looked like it had come to Lydford with Mrs. Carlington upon her marriage.

How well she had known her new husband? What hopes had she held for the future? Judging by his son, who was said to resemble him closely, Mr. Carlington must have been a fine looking young man. He would have displayed whatever charm he possessed in courting his chosen bride. He might have seemed to be all a young woman could want. And he'd had hopes too, no doubt. Evan's imagination failed to construct a scenario to explain how so many things had gone so wrong.

Young Robert Carlington had stayed away from the inquest, turning the event into a dismal anticlimax. He was absent from the house this evening, too, as he had promised Evan. "I don't want to see her, that's sure. And I ain't worried about her stealing anything 'cause there's nothing left that's worth sixpence." He seemed disgruntled about this but also sorrowful. If the place were not so far gone to wrack, Evan might have thought he cared enough to put things to rights. If it were even possible.

He seldom spent an evening at home in any case, according to Mrs. Carlington. "What's to keep a young man in a gloomy place like this? His father wasn't here either, more often than not, and if he was, they'd just fight about one thing or another. And he certainly took no pleasure in my company. Nor I in his," she added hastily. "It suited me best when they were both out of the house."

She spoke quietly as she and Mrs. Maddox set about their packing. There was pitifully little of it as far as Evan could see. Her bedchamber was bare and shabby, with a narrow bed, threadbare curtains, and not even the comfort of a rug on the floor.

The women did not need his help and probably did not want him watching as they worked. Little as Deborah's mother would miss this place, it must still be a bitter leave-taking. And she was far from comfortable with his plan for her immediate future. When he asked to see Deborah's room, Mrs. Maddox found a branch of candles in Mr. Carlington's dressing room and gladly sent him off up the stairs.

Deborah's little chamber was even more desolate than her mother's. A bank of shelving had been built all along one wall, and there perforce it remained. Otherwise there were no furnishings but a small bed with a concave mattress, covered with a wool blanket that showed evidence of moths.

No rug softened the floor, no curtains graced the window—it was a small miracle they hadn't boarded up the window as they had the fireplace. A poorly-executed sampler hung on the wall, and Evan smiled to think of Deborah hidden away up here, doing something so normal as sewing a sampler. Little enough of her life had been normal; how in God's name had she occupied her time?

It was no wonder that the girl growing to adulthood in this arid place should be reserved, fearful, and slow to laugh. The wonder was that she had grown to be curious about the world, to be kind, to care for a child. She bore little resemblance to the woman he'd imagined he would love, but he loved her nonetheless and wouldn't want her to be different—except happier. He definitely wanted her to be happier. And he wanted the chance to make her so.

Uneven steps approached down the corridor and interrupted his thoughts. He felt jealous of this place, resenting Mrs. Carlington's intrusion.

"You've finished your packing?" It came out more curtly than he intended.

"I left Maddox folding a few last things. I just wanted to come up here and see..." She made a circuit of the room, much as he had done. Her finger checked a shelf for dust, and he realized what had seemed incongruous. It was far too clean for an abandoned room. The rest of the house was tidy enough, but that was a matter of doing one's duty. If anyone had kept this room spotless, it had been this old woman, and it had been out of love.

She would see Deborah again soon enough. In the meantime *she* needed to say her good-byes far more than *he* needed whatever it was he was looking for here.

His irritation evaporated. "Shall I leave you alone?"

"No, stay. If you don't mind." She continued to hobble along the shelves. Heaven knew there was little enough to see.

Mrs. Carlington reached the window. "She used to sit here for hours."

He wanted to know so much more. "Reading?"

"Some. Mostly dreaming, I think. When she was small, she would tell me—oh, whole stories about people who lived in the clouds. With unicorns, and birds that came to eat out of her hand, and foxes that would roll over to have their bellies rubbed, like a dog. All gentle goodness, poor dear." She gazed out of the window into the darkness. "Later, I think she couldn't pretend anymore. At any rate, she stopped talking about it."

"Natural enough as a girl grows up, I imagine."

She shrugged. "And no sisters to talk to, or friends. Just the birds. For years she would put breadcrumbs on the windowsill for them."

"And they came?"

"Sometimes. They'd always fly away if anyone else came into the room. I think she liked to keep them to herself in any event. Something no one else had, and no one could take away from her." She turned toward him. "Does she still like birds?"

"I don't know. It's not something we've talked about. But she has a couple of prints on her walls, and a natural history." The book had been in deplorable condition; he suspected the framed prints were merely pages that had come loose from their binding.

"I taught her to read and write and speak properly, but there's so much I don't know, and my time was not my own. From my sister she learned some science—birds and all sorts of animals. And—oh, many things, I don't know what." She bent awkwardly to lift up the window seat, revealing a storage space underneath. From it she pulled a basket covered with what looked like a child's dress. Crossing to the bed, she sat down, and Evan joined her, the basket between them.

With reverence, Mrs. Carlington lifted the little gown. For a doll, or Deborah's own? Even this, Evan noted, was quite free of dust. It had been protected inside its hiding place, of course, but he suspected nonetheless that Deborah's mother had been through this same ritual fairly recently.

"Her treasures," she murmured.

There was little enough of it. A disintegrating bird's nest and a few desiccated feathers, a mended china figurine of a sparrow, a broken piece of china painted with tiny flowers, a small doll sewn from muslin and wearing a faded blue gown. Below these a pair of knitted booties, a scrap of lace and another of velvet ribbon, a small geode and a handful of other stones, and a coin slipped inside a fraying fabric pouch. Only the coin was of any possible value; it looked very old and was made, surely, of gold.

"She should've taken that with her when she went," said Mrs. Maddox from the doorway. "'Twas meant to bring her luck. It's from the old Lydford Mint."

At some level Evan had heard her footsteps in the hallway, but he'd been so absorbed in Deborah's *treasures* that her voice startled him. Mrs. Carlington spoke calmly, however. "I think she's found her luck now. But you might as well take it to her, Mr. Haverfield. The rest of this is rubbish."

"We'll take it along, nevertheless," said Evan. "Julian might like to see it."

Besides, he himself wanted to unpack these pitiful mementos as Mrs. Carlington had done, to hold each piece in his hand and let his imagination conjure what it would.

❧ 31 ❧

The only vehicle available for hire on short notice was a cumbersome old beast with, it seemed, no springs at all. It would have served well enough for luggage, but the idea that he and Mrs. Carlington might need a separate conveyance for their luggage was laughable. He was damned if he'd pay what the innkeep was asking. Argument was getting him nowhere—certainly not to Exeter.

The room was far less crowded than it had been the previous evening, and Geoffrey Radnor, again engaged with his friends, evidently overheard Evan's travails. He stood up and walked over.

"Are you leaving us so soon, sir? I couldn't help but hear—I need to get over to Exeter myself. Could you stand some company? We could take my phaeton or just ride. Got a couple of good mounts in my stable could use a good run."

Evan smiled at this patently spur-of-the-moment idea, but shook his head and explained his need for a chaise.

Radnor was not about to give up so easily. "Why then, we'll take m'father's carriage. It'll be a far sight more comfortable for Mrs. C than that piece of rubbish Pidgeon's trying to rent you. Though ours probably ain't what you're used to, either. And you and I can still ride.

I'll show you some of the sights off the road, and we'll still beat the carriage to Exeter by hours."

This wasn't a perfect plan, either. Evan was still sore from his previous ride—Lord, was it just yesterday?—and it seemed rude to leave Mrs. Carlington alone all day in the carriage. But it was better than the alternative.

Radnor's papa was conveniently to hand at a table across the room and, clearly approving of Evan's errand, granted permission and assisted as arrangements were finalized.

The morning of departure brought a setback—it was raining. Compared with a rollicking ride across the moors, young Radnor understandably found the prospect of a long carriage ride in company with an old lady pretty dull. But his father had committed the carriage, with or without his son, and a couple of days in Exeter out from under the parental eye was a boon not to be turned down.

Evan worried that Radnor's presence would make Mrs. Carlington uncomfortable. He talked with Radnor about horses for the first hour, while she looked quietly out the window. Radnor then began to pester Evan with questions about London, quite in the manner of a child.

Mrs. Carlington relaxed and even posed a few queries of her own.

After that Radnor launched into a description of the activities he expected to pursue in Exeter, complaining good-naturedly about all the little commissions imposed upon him by his mama. "I ask you, ma'am, would *you* trust me to match this ribbon? 'Raspberry,' she says, 'not cherry or burgundy.' They're all just *red* to me!"

Deborah's mother actually laughed at this, though she seemed rather shocked to hear such a sound coming out of her own mouth, and suggested that he might do best to leave the matter in the hands of the milliner.

By the time they reached Exeter, she was no longer inclined to laughter. Indeed, she seemed quite uncomfortable. She never complained, but she leaned heavily on his arm as they walked from the carriage into the White Hart, her face pinched and pale. Radnor happily shared dinner with Evan in his private parlor, but Mrs. Carlington retired to her room.

෧

THEY HAD a choice of carriages to take them north, and Evan reserved the best of them. Then he found a bank and replenished his purse. He hadn't planned on buying a horse, much less paying out bribes. Then he fretted until they were on the road.

It became clear early on that the speedy journey Evan had envisioned was not to be. Though at first she took an interest in the country they passed through, by the time a couple of hours had passed, Mrs. Carlington was squirming again, shifting her position repeatedly in an effort to relieve whatever discomfort she was feeling. She said she felt stiff; they stopped to change horses and walked around a bit, but it didn't help for long.

They put in just six hours before Evan called a halt. He'd hoped to reach Whately in three long days, but at this rate it would be double that. Irritating, but he could hardly blame her. She had traveled nowhere since she was twenty years old—an unimaginable thought— and could not have known how her aging, damaged body would respond to sitting still for so long. She apologized each time they stopped and each time they started out again.

Evan did his best to hide his impatience and pretend he was happy with their pace. Barring floods, an unseasonable blizzard, or an apocalyptic attack by the minions of Satan, they would still arrive in time for Latimer's wedding, perhaps with a day or two to spare.

In Cirencester Evan paid an overdue visit to a barber. And he had plenty of time in Bristol to buy a magnificently illustrated edition of *Gulliver's Travels* as a gift for Julian.

What could he get for Deborah? He considered a gorgeous necklace of garnets with earrings to match, but if she refused him again, he would have to consign them to the Atlantic Ocean on his way to America, and what a waste that would be.

Finally, in Coventry, he found a fine copy of Bewick's *History of British Birds*. It would do. All in all, he had far too much time to twiddle his thumbs, becoming more anxious each day.

Mrs. Carlington seemed to share this affliction. They had begun by conversing a fair amount as they sat together in the chaise and shared dinner in their private parlor. They talked of various things but very little of Deborah. She was there with them, though—perhaps that was why conversation became more difficult as they drew closer to Deborah herself. Evan found it harder and harder to think about anything else and suspected the same was true of his companion.

On the final evening before their arrival in Whately, in his bedchamber at a pleasant inn in Coventry, he yielded to temptation and began to sift through Deborah's treasures. But somehow it felt like rapine, so he stopped and replaced those items he had removed with even greater care than he'd used taking them out.

MRS. CARLINGTON WAS EVEN QUIETER than usual all that last day. She said she had not slept well, and she had eaten no more than a mouse's portion at breakfast.

His body thrumming with tension, Evan watched out the window as they crossed the bridge at Dellford in mid-afternoon. "Just a few more miles, ma'am."

"Oh my. I must… I have a confession to make."

It was breathless, almost whispered, so that he had to lean forward to hear it.

Then he sat back abruptly, surprised and angry. This would make the situation harder for everyone. But she was so pale, and looked so unhappy, that there was really nothing he could say. He considered depositing Mrs. Carlington at the inn while he went to talk to Deborah but decided against it. He smiled at her instead, and though she did not return it, he thought she relaxed just a trifle.

Julian was sitting on the front step when the carriage pulled up in front of the cottage, shelling peas into a basket. He and the dog looked to be eating their share now rather than waiting for dinner. What had they named the mongrel? Oh yes. Pelleas.

Evan grinned. He'd been so focused on Deborah these past months, he hadn't even realized how much he'd missed her son. He jumped down as Julian and dog ogled the carriage and had the reward of seeing the boy's face light up in jubilation. He swept him off the ground for a hug but was promptly recalled to his other obligations by a couple of sharp barks from the vicinity of his knees.

A quick acknowledgment for the dog, and then the coachman must be told which of their luggage to unload here and which to take on to Whately Manor. Finally, Evan turned to help Deborah's mother down from the carriage. Her eyes, wide in her lined face, drank in the sight of her grandson.

"Julian, here's someone I want you to meet."

"Is she a countess?" Julian looked skeptical as he got his first look at her.

"No, she's not a countess. She's even better. This is Mrs. Carlington." Clearly the name meant nothing to the boy, and she was only a missus, after all, but he made his bow very properly.

"She is your grandmother, Julian."

Julian's eyes flew to Evan's face and back to Mrs. Carlington's. Evan thought Mrs. Carlington might faint as she underwent that grave and dubious scrutiny. Instead, she stepped away from his supporting arm. Her voice broke, but she got the words out. "I am so glad to meet you, Julian." She offered her hand, and after studying her face for another moment, the boy shook it.

First hurdle cleared, thought Evan. "Where is your mama?"

"In the kitchen I think, sir."

Evan picked up the basket of peas and ushered the whole party into the house. "Your grandmother needs to sit down, Julian. Would you take her into the parlor? You can introduce her to Pelleas."

He watched them enter the room and then turned toward the kitchen. He set the peas on the hall table and closed his eyes, taking a long, shaky breath. He was, he supposed, as ready as he was ever likely to be.

She was setting a bucket down on the floor as he crossed the threshold. She must have just brought it in from the yard, or she would surely have heard the commotion in the hallway.

She picked a teacup from the clutter of dishes on the counter for washing and saw him. Her jaw dropped and so did the cup. Oblivious, she stepped through the broken pieces and into his arms.

She felt better, so much better than he had remembered or imagined. His lips sought hers but found only hair. Her face was pressed into his shoulder, her hands gripped the sides of his coat. He thought he must be hurting her and eased his hold ever so slightly. She moved and took what he could swear was her first breath.

"Did you miss me?" Evan wasn't sure whose voice it was; it certainly didn't sound like his.

She seemed to gurgle. With laughter, perhaps? Her gaze was on his cravat. "I suppose you'd not believe me if I said no?"

He freed one hand and tilted her chin up. "No."

Now came the kiss. He forgot all about being gentle and was suddenly glad that Mrs. Carlington had not written to advise her daughter of their arrival. Forewarned, Deborah would no doubt have armed herself against such a show of emotion.

Unfortunately, that thought reminded him of the hurdle still to be faced. With reluctance, he divided himself from her. Hand on her back, Evan turned her toward the table.

"Sit down, Deborah."

She gestured toward the mess on the floor. "I need to—"

"Later. I've something to tell you." He urged her onto a bench and sat across from her. He tried to think of some way to mitigate the shock of his news, but failed.

"I've brought your mother with me."

Deborah stopped breathing again. She stared at him, frozen.

"What?" It was hardly audible.

He shook his head. "I'm sorry. She was supposed to write to you. I found out just this afternoon she had not, or I would have written myself."

"You were in Lydford?"

Evan nodded. "I went south when I left Whately in January and stopped in Lydford on my way back here for Latimer's wedding. Your brother turned her out of the house after your father's death. She didn't want to stay in Lydford, and she has nowhere else to go."

Deborah still had not moved. Evan pried one of her hands from the tense grip of the other and folded both his own around it. Her gaze dropped for a moment to their clasped hands on the tabletop, a crease between her brows. Then she stood up. "Where is she?" If her expression was not eager, it was at least determined.

"In the parlor with Julian." It could certainly cloud a man's confidence to note how precipitately her attention had shifted away from him. "I must tell you, she is afraid you won't want her."

Deborah made no reply to that but strode through the door and across the hallway. Evan saw her stop in the parlor doorway, one hand on the jamb.

When she moved out of sight into the room, he found a broom and dustpan and bent to pick up the broken china.

32

Whately had always meant Viscount Latimer. Now, Deborah was the center of town, the center of Evan's world. And that world was askew.

He stayed for less than an hour following their arrival, carrying Mrs. Carlington's meager belongings up the stairs and depositing them in Julian's little room under Deborah's direction. "He can sleep with me," she said.

Not for long. Evan caught her in his arms and kissed her rather fiercely, but she was resistant. He hoped to God she was merely constrained by the presence of her mother downstairs. He loosened his hold and murmured reassurances in her ear until she relaxed, pulling back to give him a quizzical little smile.

"What is it?" he asked. "You're not angry with me for bringing her?"

She shook her head. "No. But I must go back to her."

He'd taken his leave of them all and walked a brisk mile to the Manor.

His definition of Whately may have changed, but Evan still owed allegiance to his old friend. Among all the houseguests and wedding preparations the following day, a brief visit to the cottage was all he could manage. Already Julian's curiosity was outstripping his natural reserve. He seemed to be courting his grandmother's attention and preened under the small caress Evan witnessed. Mrs. Carlington was plainly enthralled with the child. And Evan could not tell how Deborah felt about any of it. She certainly evinced no delight at finding *him* on the doorstep. Had yesterday's kiss been a figment of his desire?

❦

DEBORAH WAS glad to see him go on that first day. Kissing her on the landing upstairs in full view of anyone below? Was he crazy?

She was caught up in a whirlwind of confusion. Her mother needed help she did not know how to give, Julian needed restraint and explanations, and Molly needed assistance with dinner. She could not possibly think about Evan until later. When she was alone.

Through the evening, the tension pulled tighter, like a thread about to snap. She tried not to inflict it on anyone else. They were not to blame.

By the time the house was quiet and everyone else asleep, she knew that she was angry, sickeningly angry. She wanted to scream. Cry. Break something valuable. Tear out her hair. One of those trite ways people react to rage and frustration. How *could* she have been so stupid, running into Evan's arms as though—well, as though something had changed.

Nothing has changed. She had met his sister, and his sister had been very kind to her. That was all. Marriage remained as impossible as it had ever been. She and

Elizabeth had talked about many things, but Evan was not one of them. Only once was his name mentioned in conjunction with hers. That must indicate pretty accurately how Elizabeth felt.

And the night before her departure, when Deborah tried to ask why she had come to Whately, Elizabeth silenced her.

Seething quietly as she listened to Julian breathing beside her, she had another depressing thought. As Evan said, he'd had no choice but to bring her mother here. What if that had been his only reason for seeking her out at all? Then she assaulted him, and he felt honor bound to pretend an emotion he did not feel.

It was hard to imagine. Was it possible to fake such a look as she'd seen in his eyes? He looked thinner and a bit haggard, but there could be many reasons for that. He'd certainly seemed enthusiastic. But maybe that was merely lust. What did she know about these things, after all? It would be humiliating. But it would also make it far easier to turn him away.

In any case, there was a new member of the household to consider. Evan expected her to welcome her mother into her home. She expected no less from herself, though it would be a financial hardship. Well, he could hardly expect that she would walk right out again to marry him, leaving Mama to fend for herself.

Though she ached to see him again, she was sorry when he arrived the next day. She was purposely cool to him, and when he left, it was Julian who saw him out the side gate. She did not want to be alone with him. She was not prepared for the necessary conversation and could not allow further intimacies under the circumstances.

When Julian returned to the parlor, he was full of the new mare Mr. Haffield had brought. "She ate a lump of sugar from my hand, Mama!" Deborah pretended an interest and wished "Mr. Haffield" had not returned to Whately.

The third day he was occupied with Lord Latimer's wedding and did not come at all. She was glad of it and spent the day on the verge of tears. She resented the viscount for keeping him away, though she was not so uncharitable as to hope the evening rain had ruined the festivities.

She hardly thought to see Evan the following day, either. The rain continued its onslaught all morning until the yard and roads were a quagmire. But he appeared at the kitchen door sometime after noon, mud on his boots and rain dripping from his greatcoat.

He apologized for all that. "I thought my mess might be more welcome if I confined it to the kitchen."

It was her place to confirm that welcome, but it came instead from

Julian, from Pelleas, from her mother, and even from Molly. She turned back toward the chicken she was cleaning while the hubbub went on behind her back.

"Will you take some coffee, Mr. Haverfield?" inquired her mother. Deborah pressed her lips together, holding in a screech of frustration. She thought he hesitated a moment before accepting the invitation.

She tried to shoo them all into the parlor, but they seemed stubbornly obtuse. Instead they milled about, discussing Gulliver's adventures that Julian had been reading to them, haltingly, before Evan's arrival.

Her mother prepared the coffeepot while Molly took down the cups, spoons, and sugar and ladled a bit of cream from its stoneware crock. Julian climbed onto a stool to reach down the tin of biscuits. And Evan appeared at her side.

Her hands were wet with chicken juices, but he laid a gentle hand on her forearm. A curious warmth ran up her arm and all through her chest and belly. So very distracting.

He spoke softly, taking advantage of the chatter to snatch a few private words. "What is it, Deborah?" When she still did not look at him, he repeated her name.

She had to look then. But she had insufficient mastery of her face, and whatever he saw there caused his expression to change from concern to wariness or even—if the thought were not ludicrous—dread.

He cleared his throat. "We need to talk. Will you ride with me in the morning?"

Her attention returned to the chicken. "I can't possibly. I have far too much to do here to go pleasuring about the countryside."

Her voice came out sharper than she intended, catching the unwelcome attention of her mother. "Nonsense, Deborah. We can manage quite well without you for an hour or two."

Deborah clenched her teeth.

"Can I come too?" asked Julian.

Evan released her arm and turned away, but Grandmama beat him to a plausible excuse. "Oh dear, Julian, I was counting on your help

254

finding all your mama's sewing supplies and reading your new book to me while I work on my gown."

Evan smiled first at Mrs. Carlington and then at Julian. "Let's plan on the day after, then. Will that suit you, Master Moore?"

Julian giggled. "Yes, that will be excellent, my good sir."

They shook hands on it.

❧ 33 ❧

Deborah arrived at the Manor early. Her mother had all but pushed her out the door.

After the conversation they had last night when Julian had gone to bed, Deborah could be in no doubt where her mother stood on any issue involving Evan Haverfield—on his side.

"Is he not the most agreeable man, Deborah?" They were cutting the pieces for a sorely needed dress. During the morning, they had picked apart one of Mrs. Carlington's old gowns to use as a pattern. "So obliging and patient. So good-natured."

"Yes, he's very nice. He's been more than kind to us." *Nice. Kind.* Stupid words. *Gentle. Considerate. Generous.* Oh, just say *perfect* and be done with it!

"Why do you not like him?"

"Of course I like him, ma'am."

"Do you?" Squinting, she paused to negotiate a sharp corner with Deborah's scissors. "It doesn't show."

"I'm not one to wear my heart on my sleeve, Mama."

"And I'm not one to advocate marriage for its own sake. You know that." They were silent for a few minutes, cutting and pinning. "But if you had any thought of marrying again— Well, you'd be a damned fool to turn him down. You could look for the rest of your life and not find—"

"I know that, Mama." It was a struggle to speak.

Her mother peered at her through clouded eyes. "There, there. That's all I'll say. Except that the man deserves honest dealing, whatever you decide."

"Yes, ma'am," she muttered. She could hardly disagree. With all he'd done for them, honesty was the least she could give in return.

But it was with gritty eyes and a heavy heart that she greeted Julian's friend, Jeremy, in the stableyard this morning. He and another groom were readying a traveling carriage for a journey; the guests would all be leaving today, Deborah supposed, since the weather had been so inclement yesterday. The roads were still messy—her boots were proof of that—but they seemed passable.

She knew from Miss Latimer—no, she was Mrs. Charles Reston now —that the viscount and his bride planned a honeymoon in Paris and Vienna. "*Her* choice, not his, you may be sure!" she had said. Had they gotten away or were they still stuck at the Manor with all their guests?

"Good morning, Jeremy."

"Mornin', missus. Where's your young man, then?"

With Evan on her mind, for a moment Deborah thought he meant *that* sort of young man. But he must be referring to Julian. She shook her head, more at herself than at Jeremy. "I hardly supposed you'd have time today to keep him out of trouble."

He looked ruefully at the carriage he was working on, with its crest and gilt trim, and at another, more ordinary vehicle that was pulled out into the yard as they spoke. "Well, he's never a mite o' trouble, but it's sure I couldn't give him the attention I'd like."

Their riding lessons had ended, perforce, when the pony Julian had been riding was returned to the squire's stables after Miss Latimer's marriage. Jeremy had encouraged him to spend "all the time your mama can spare you" haunting the Manor's stables, but Deborah could not imagine that Viscount Latimer and his new bride would relish miscellaneous urchins hanging about the place.

"Has Mr. Haverfield come down, Jeremy?"

"No, ma'am, I've not seen him yet. I know Grady has orders for your horses, though. You'll find him inside." He motioned with a jerk of his head.

Deborah left the bright morning outside and entered the welcoming, fragrant dimness of the stable. She roamed at random, stroking a soft nose where it was offered and murmuring inane endearments. Every stall was occupied, some twice over, with the hacks and carriage horses that had brought the wedding guests to Whately. But Lookout was already saddled and drowsing patiently in the corridor. Miss Latimer's mare that Deborah had ridden during Elizabeth's visit was gone, but Evan's grays were there, and she found Imp sharing space with another horse she did not know.

By the rear door of the stable where it opened into the paddock, Grady stood grooming a big white mare. Deborah smiled at him, a little shyly. He and Evan had a long history together, and he groomed his master as well as his master's horses. Likely he knew how Evan felt about things... about her. He himself had always seemed to regard her with skepticism, as though he thought her not good enough for his master.

Well, she wasn't. She could not argue with him there.

He greeted her cordially today, however. "G'morning, ma'am. Beautiful day for a ride."

"Hello, Grady. Is this the new mare my son told me about?"

"It is, ma'am. Master picked her up in Dawlish."

She stroked that smooth neck, averting her face. *Dawlish? As well as Lydford?* "What's her name?"

"Doesn't have one. I believe it'll be for you to decide."

"Me?" She gazed at him in surprise.

He smiled back. "She ain't much to look at, ma'am, but she moves real well, and she's real sweet-tempered. She's meant as a wedding present, if I ain't mistaken."

Deborah blushed furiously at this. "He hasn't even asked me," she muttered.

"He will. An' I hope you don't mind me saying, I trust you'll say yes and put the man out o' his misery."

"Has it been so bad?"

"Worse, ma'am. Much worse."

Deborah felt the pressure of tears behind her eyes.

She had come to the Manor this morning prepared to give Evan that honest dealing her mother had spoken of. But she had convinced herself that he had arrived in Whately with no intention whatsoever of renewing his offer, so that all she need do was persuade him she neither wanted nor expected it. Instead, she must persuade him of what *she* already knew—that however he felt about her, he would be better off without her. It would be a far more difficult task.

She followed Evan out of the stable yard and they rode across a meadow dotted with oaks and anemones. Deborah had been over most of the Manor grounds with Elizabeth, and she recognized this route. It would lead them through a shady stretch of woodland and then downhill to a stream, not far from where it tumbled into the river.

Their conversation was strained. Perhaps he, too, was reluctant to come to grips with the subject that lay between them. Deborah thanked him for the book he had brought her, and Evan asked after Mrs. Carlington, and Julian, and how they were getting on together. Obvious, innocuous things. She asked how the viscount's wedding had gone.

Then he solicited her opinion on the mare. She commented on the intelligent look in her eyes and her happy disposition. And since they had done no more than amble halfway across the meadow, she could legitimately request a chance to try out her other paces before rendering judgment.

The horses needed little encouragement to trot, which was not conducive to intimate discussion. The canter that followed was so smooth, Deborah might have imagined herself to be floating on a well-behaved magic carpet had the circumstances been happier. And still conversation was averted.

She was very glad she'd ridden recently with Elizabeth, but she had to demur when Evan suggested a gallop. "It scares me," she confessed. Feeling wretched, she pulled the mare back to a walk.

"I can vouch for her gallop, in any event," said Evan. "We had a mad, glorious race with the rain along the strand."

"Who won?"

"Oh, the rain. By many lengths."

"That was in Dawlish?"

"It was," he replied. This was followed by silence. When she risked a glance at his face, he was frowning.

Honest dealing. She was perspiring, and her stomach hurt.

She launched into the alternative oration she had outlined in her head the night before long after the household was asleep, pacing the small, unoccupied space in her little parlor where she had once waltzed in the dark with this perfect man. She'd hoped not to need this version at all.

She talked about her mother and the need to care for her.

"I've been assuming she would live with us. I like her."

She talked about his family.

"They will have their doubts, but they'll come around."

She talked as they rode through the woods about his position as heir to his father's estates and how untrained she was to manage such a household.

"*Untrained* implies a learnable skill. You could learn all that. If you wanted to."

She talked about her ineligibility as a Society hostess—her shyness, her ignorance of politics, her social ineptitude.

"I'm not looking for a Society hostess."

In desperation, as the stream came into view, she attempted to paint for him the dread picture in her mind of her continuing failures, his gradual disillusionment and discontent, and deep unhappiness for them both.

"There is risk in everything." His voice sounded harsh. "I can't speak for you, but these last few months have been absolute hell. I never—"

She could not let him continue in *that* vein. "I know, Evan. But look at this future I'm seeing. Better to spend a few months in hell than the rest of our lives in misery. You'll get over this soon enough and find some totally worthy woman with none of the deficiencies I would inflict upon you. *She's* the one you want, Evan. *She* can make you happy."

He stopped abruptly and grabbed her reins below the bit. Both horses sidled nervously. "Oh no, Deborah. Don't cast this back on me. If you don't want to marry me, say so. But don't tell me I don't want you. I want *you*, Deborah. I want you in my bed at night. I want you to raise my children. I want you to stir my damned coffee. I want you to stir my blood when I get old. I want us to grow old together." She could feel herself gaping at him. "I want you, by God!"

He slid from his saddle and pulled her from hers, willy-nilly. She fell against him and slid down onto her feet, her skirts catching on his clothing so that his leather breeches pressed against her bare legs. He tugged her hat from her head, scattering pins amongst the grass, and tossed the hat itself after them.

So much for her powers of persuasion. *His* were far more potent. She wrapped her arms around his neck and thrilled to feel herself crushed against him. Between the pressure on her lungs and the pressure on her mouth and the pain of her love for him, it was very difficult to breathe.

She was sorry when his mind reasserted control over his instincts. He loosened his grip fractionally, removed his hands from the quite improper parts of her anatomy where they had been, and rested his forehead against hers. He too was having trouble with his breathing— he sounded rather like Pelleas after a good rabbit chase. She pulled her head back and looked up into his face.

The first unsteady words out of his mouth—predictably, she supposed—were apologetic. "I got a bit carried away. I'm sorry, Deborah."

"No," was the only word she could get out of her mouth.

It hardly produced the expected reaction. Evan gripped her by the shoulders, hard. His voice was furious, but his expression was so hurt.

"Don't tell me 'no' any more, Deborah." And then a pleading, "I can't stand it."

"No!—I mean—I just meant... don't apologize."

He pulled her close again, but it was some different emotion this time. After some minutes, he heaved a sigh and held her at arm's length.

"So—*will* you marry me, Deborah?"

"I will." She poked his chest with a finger. "But only because I need new boots. And probably a new riding habit as well." She'd not been aware of it at first, but the ground where they stood was sodden from the rain.

Evan looked down at her in surprise. "Deborah? Am I mistaken or was that a joke?"

She blushed and peered up at him anxiously.

"I tell you what I'll do, sweetheart. For every joke you tell me, I'll give you a gown of any sort you wish... No, make it two. And a kiss." This one was tender. "Or maybe three."

"Evan?"

"Mmm?"

"Are your feet not wet?"

"Hush. Don't spoil it."

❧

She dried the last of the plates and set it on its shelf on the dresser. Then she crossed to the fireplace and swung the pothook out so she could stir the strawberries that simmered there, becoming jam. Julian and Pelleas played by the door, which stood open to let in the sunshine.

Julian threw a soiled towel repeatedly over the little dog, who battled his way out from underneath and barked with excitement. "Look, Mama, he's wearing a judge's wig!" Julian shouted. "Look, Mama, he's wearing a shawl!" As he wrapped it around Pell's neck: "Look, a cravat!" Piled on his head: "a turban!"

Deborah laughed too. It was a perfectly ordinary, perfectly perfect spring day.

"Come, children, let's go for a walk." Julian cackled with glee at her inclusion of Pell as one of the children and jumped up to put on his coat and grab the dog's lead—though they never used it anymore—while Deborah pulled her shawl and bonnet off the hook.

They went to the door—now mysteriously closed—and she opened it to...

Nothing. No steps, no yard, no chestnut tree, no bright sunshine. Boy and dog were swept into a black void, soft and velvet, the sound of Julian's laughter carried back to her where she stood in the doorway of the dark kitchen.

She looked over her shoulder. A single candle on the table shed its meager light on the familiar surroundings. From the hallway beyond came the sounds of a beast, snuffling and roaring as it searched out its prey, coming closer.

Deborah turned back to the darkness outside and stepped off the threshold.

She was riding the white mare, Evan mounted behind. His arms came around her; he kissed her, and then they were riding the moors in the sunshine while Julian and Pelleas gamboled around them. They took their time, allowing the horse to choose her path and nibble as she liked, while her riders gazed into each other's eyes, or looked for the lark singing his heart out somewhere in the high blue sky, or watched the ground for the nests of ouzels.

A perfectly ordinary, perfectly perfect spring day.

SHE AWOKE, later than usual, to the smell of strawberries burning.

She hurried into her morning gown—*not* the pretty sprig muslin she had worn in her dream; no telling where her imagination had pulled that from, but certainly not from her wardrobe—and ran down the stairs to deal with Molly's mess.

34

It would not be so easy, of course. There were no perfect days, and no perfect man, and certainly no happy-ever-afters, at least not for her. Even quite simple things sounded daunting.

While the idea of having new gowns to wear was intoxicating, Deborah found it very hard to picture herself visiting a modiste, pretending to be a lady of fashion, while seamstresses in the back room did the sewing for her. One thing about making her own clothes, it encouraged her to settle for fewer of them! If Elizabeth, say, had to stitch her own gowns...

Deborah Moore
Whately, April 15

Dear Elizabeth—

I know I am not the first to send you the news, as Evan pronounced that he would spend yesterday evening writing to all his relations. And I know he did so, for he stopped here before taking his letters to the post. And then he brought my post to me, which consisted of your letter! So the secret of your visit to Whately is out. To be sure, you never said that it should be secret, but clearly you had not informed him of it, and I did not feel it was my place to do so. It was bound to come out sooner or later, however; Julian has been distracted by other events, or I feel sure he would already have mentioned something about you or Alexander. Evan was taken aback, without a doubt; but then he laughed and made me tell him all about our doings and really seemed quite pleased.

For myself, I would have preferred that he wait to make his announcements for a day, or a week, or perhaps a year—but that is because I am craven.

What will they think? What do you think, Elizabeth? You have been so kind to me, that I almost dare to hope for your support. Even if it must be given from a distance, still it would ease my mind knowing that not all of Evan's family will mourn the occasion as I fear your sister and your parents must.

I hardly even know how to brave modistes and milliners—as I must do quite urgently—without your assistance. If you do not renounce me entirely, please send me your best advice in this matter; and I hope that you will come to the wedding and stand my friend, if you feel you can. It will be held at Northridge, not later than the end of May.

With best wishes,

Deborah

After the wedding, there would be other horrors to face.

They had talked, riding slowly back across the meadow, about where they would live. And about other things, most too silly to mention, or even to remember, except when she hugged them to her heart at night while waiting for sleep to take her.

Wherever they settled, there would be a household far larger than Whately's vicarage to be kept clean and organized, servants to hire and supervise, menus to plan, gardens and dairy and henhouse, possibly a brewery or bakehouse. She knew how to clean and cook better than she knew how to direct a staff whose job it was to do those things. Would her hands someday become soft? The hands of a lady?

Beyond their own household, there would be a whole community to meet, callers and dinner parties and other sorts of entertainments to attend—and to host, whatever Evan said. Thank heavens he had no desire to locate in London! He talked of visiting there in the fall and of introducing her to the *ton* the following spring—but that was very far away. There were many, many things to worry about first.

One of these, to which she had not yet given any thought at all, was the mystery of how to make him happy. She had failed conclusively with Hartley and was determined that Evan should never regret his decision.

Elizabeth Dusseau
London, April 17

My dear new sister,

Of course I will come to your wedding, Deborah; it is Evan's too, after all! Philip will be there as well, and all of the children. And of course I will stand your friend, you silly goose! I wanted to talk with you about Evan, but he had disappeared, and I could hardly broach the subject with you until I could ascertain his feelings. I admit I've been anxious over how he would react to my "interference" as my husband termed it, and am relieved that he did not take umbrage. I did try very hard to do nothing that would influence the outcome—though if I had found the two of you mired in misunderstandings and silly qualms, I would have had to employ some aggressive tactics. I like you both so much!

I will write a letter to Mama as soon as I finish this one. Philip and I will leave for Northridge as soon as we can make all the arrangements and pack up the family, nursemaids, &c. We can be there within two weeks. If you do the same, we will have time to visit those dreaded modistes together; there is an excellent woman nearby whom we have used since I was a girl, who will be delighted to put forth her best efforts on your behalf. What fun I will have —and if you do not, you're a very unnatural woman!

Leave Mama and Papa to me, and my sister as well. I'm sure you are worrying about all sorts of things. Don't! It's a time for excitement, not apprehension.

Yours, truly—
Elizabeth

❧

EVAN DROVE TO NORTHRIDGE, leaving Deborah and her mother to their sewing and packing. Would he have to persuade her all over again when he returned?

They were sewing dresses, not for Deborah but for her mother, whose need was desperate. Deborah had bought some fabric from a peddler that they were making up for the older woman. Evan would have been delighted to pay for Mrs. Carlington's clothes as well as Deborah's, but they united against him, insisting that they would have plenty of opportunity to test his generosity in the future. He gave in.

He had arranged for one of the viscount's footmen to transfer his allegiance for a few days. Deborah had objected to that as well, but he overbore her. With Latimer away on his honeymoon and Amanda moved to her new home, there was little enough for the servants to do at the Manor, and Evan did not want her run off her feet.

The man would have plenty of idle time at the cottage, during which he would be quite dreadfully in the way. But however small it might be, the place was full of furnishings and dishes and clothing and books, all of which had to be disposed of in one way or another.

Evan was eager to start a fresh life with his bride, choosing china and all the frills and necessities that would adorn their first home, and hoped she would elect to leave behind most of what she owned. But he left those decisions to Deborah. She knew how worthless most of it was. He promised to buy her all new books, but there she dug in her heels. The footman's first task was to crate them all up for transport, even the stack of little chapbooks she had accumulated for Julian.

At Northridge, Evan traded his phaeton for the family's traveling carriage, his grays for four strong carriage horses, and Grady for the coachman and a couple of outriders. And he talked at length with his mother and father.

They'd had his letter, of course. Predictably, they were less than thrilled with his impecunious widow and all her baggage. Well, they could be forgiven for thinking her a fortune hunter, though it made him grit his teeth when all his protestations met with disbelief.

And when his mother threatened tears and began lamenting his failure to oblige her years ago by offering for Melanie Littleton, who was so eligible and such a dear friend to the family and had kept her hopes alive for so long that she was now practically on the shelf and whose property marched with theirs, he became uncharacteristically severe. "It's not going to happen, Mama. And however you feel about Deborah, I expect you to treat her with every consideration. My wife deserves no less."

"All right, son." It was his father's turn. "We'll have to accept that. But this other business: Why in God's name do you feel you need to make this boy the heir to Northridge? The world does not expect such a thing. And there's no reason to think you and this woman—"

At a blazing look from Evan, he held up his hand in apology. "No reason to think you won't have children of your own blood."

"It doesn't matter, Father. Julian is smart and serious and loyal. It would be impossible for me to love my own children more. Northridge could not have a better master."

"So make him—I don't know, make him steward, or something."

"If I adopt him—and I will—he will be my eldest son. I can hardly appoint him steward. Might as well name him head groom, for God's sake."

"I can cut him out of the succession, you know!"

Evan sighed. "You can cut me out too. Do what you must." He had never been so exasperated with them. "But do tell me this evening, please, if that's what you plan to do. It will certainly affect our wedding plans and where we choose to live afterward."

He strode to the door and pulled it open. "I leave tomorrow at first light."

35

A week later Evan conducted his new family through the countryside that was so intimately familiar to him, so entirely strange to them. He tried to see it through their eyes as he pointed out this Roman bridge or that Norman church, but he'd traveled this road too many times. It was home, and a deep elation grew inside him at the thought of bringing his wife here. It was not five months since he had first seen Deborah and pulled Julian from under that hedge. How quickly life could change.

She was not quite his, of course. Not yet. He knew she still harbored doubts; he caught her a few times watching him with trouble in her eyes. As soon as he looked up, she tried to superimpose her old mask, but she was not fast enough. Riding in the chaise with them all, he could do little more than smile at her from the seat opposite. That seemed to provide some reassurance, as the furrows in her brow relaxed and her mouth softened. He wanted to kiss both of those places and many more, but it would have to wait. She would probably have doubts on her way to the altar.

Though it was not a long journey, they spent a night on the road for the sake of Deborah's mother. Evan judged that they all needed some relief from Julian, too, who had never been more than three miles from Whately, had never traveled post, had never seen a city even so large as Wolverhampton, and had so recently acquired a grandmother. With his whole short life turned on its head, it was no wonder he was a bit frenzied.

When he started bouncing up and down on Mrs. Carlington, however, Deborah reprimanded him sharply. This sufficed to keep him quiet for perhaps four minutes. Evan opened a book to read with him, and that worked for five more. Then he was bouncing again— not on his grandmother, it was true, but from one seat to the other, one person to the next, asking unanswerable questions of each one in turn. Thank heaven Evan had relegated Pelleas to the baggage wagon following somewhere on the road behind them!

"Julian!" Evan's sternest voice cut the chatter. "Be still now. You're becoming a pest." He felt like a beast at the dismay in the boy's face. But he stood quietly at Evan's knees, peering out the window at the misty world they passed through.

It was unfortunately too wet to take the boy up on horseback. Deborah's mare, christened Cirrus, trotted behind the chaise, brought along for just that purpose. But the weather did not cooperate.

The ladies, too, had questions for him. Mrs. Carlington asked about Evan's family: his parents, his siblings, his nieces and nephews, all the relatives who might be expected to attend the wedding. The more names he produced, the more daunted both she and Deborah looked, so he brought the list to a premature conclusion.

On the second day, as they drew closer to Northridge, Mrs. Carlington asked useful questions about the gardens and the village nearby. Was the dressmaker there, or would they need to go farther afield? Was there a lending library? A cobbler? A grocer? One inn or more? Did the mail coach come through there?

Evan laughed at her. "Why, ma'am? Are you planning a journey to someplace exciting?"

"What? Oh! No. Heavens no!"

He thought her nerves were making her talk, rather like her grandson. He was not even sure she heard his replies. But after all, her life was changing as radically as Julian's.

Deborah's nerves produced quite different symptoms. The nearer they approached to her new home, the less she opened her mouth. She had been looking out the window, but now she pressed herself back in the seat and pulled self-control around her. She was pale, her hands held rigid in her lap, and something perilously close to fear looked out of her eyes. Evan traded seats with Mrs. Carlington so he could take her hand. Her questions were almost whispered: for the third time, reminding herself of the name of the butler, the housekeeper, the footmen...

He wanted to say something to make her laugh but couldn't think of anything. She took a comb from her reticule and used it to straighten Julian's hair. She moved it toward her own head, but Evan took her hand and held it.

"You're beautiful," he said softly.

Unexpectedly, she laughed at that. It was a bit hysterical but better than all that tension. She put the comb away.

They turned into the gates, and three pairs of eyes turned to the windows. Deborah gulped. Evan surveyed his wife, and her mother, and her son—*his* son—and was happier than he had ever been.

A scant half-mile brought them onto the graveled sweep in front of the house. To him, of course, the place looked warm and welcoming despite the mist, but judging from the expressions on the others' faces, they did not share the feeling.

A footman—"That's Henry," Evan murmured—trod down the steps with a wide smile on his face and headed for the carriage but was forestalled by a whirlwind that flew through the front door with a shriek and ran toward them in a blaze of red silk. Evan chuckled. "What a hoyden she is."

"Oh," Deborah breathed, and the color rushed into her face. "It's Elizabeth, Mama."

Evan sent Mrs. Carlington a smile. She was nearly as white as Deborah had been, and she clutched Julian's hand—for whose reassurance, he was not sure. After talking all the way from Whately, Julian had gone suddenly quiet, reluctant to leave the safety of the carriage. Evan climbed down first, clapped Henry on the shoulder, and gave his sister a quick hug. Then he turned to help Deborah down the steps.

"I guess I don't have to introduce you," he said. Elizabeth wrapped Deborah in a hug far warmer than the one she'd given Evan.

"Oh, Elizabeth, I'm so relieved you're here," Deborah murmured.

"I told you I would be. And here's Julian. How was your journey, Master Moore?" He smiled shyly up at her, holding his mama's hand.

"Where's your bow for Mrs. Dusseau, sweetling?"

"Stuff," said Elizabeth. "I'm Aunt Elizabeth now—well, almost—and aunts prefer hugs." She proved it by giving him a quick one.

"And you must be Deborah's mother." Elizabeth reached out to clasp one hand in both of hers. "I am *so* glad to meet you!" As Evan performed the introduction, he thought what a talent his sister had. Already Mrs. Carlington had regained a little color. He could safely leave her to Elizabeth's care.

He turned with Deborah toward the house. She hesitated for just a moment, resistant to his guiding hand on her back, and then started forward.

He murmured, *"How easy is a bush supposed a bear."*

Deborah looked at him in astonishment.

He grinned and wiggled his eyebrows. *"A Midsummer Night's Dream.* They're not monsters, Deborah. They won't eat you."

She blushed. "No, of course not. I'm sorry."

DEBORAH NEVER COULD RECALL what Evan's father and mother said to her or what she replied. Did they smile at her or sneer? Did they wear cloth-of-gold or rags? Did she speak the King's English or bark like a dog?

She must have said everything that was proper because Evan kept smiling at her. How shameful that she had thought of them as monsters, still more so that she had let him see it. Yet he had understood and taken no offense, had even joked about it in an attempt to set her more at ease. Perhaps there was just one *nearly* perfect man…

Worse awaited her. They entered the hall and found a line of servants stretched from the doorway to the bottom of the imposing staircase—more servants than Deborah had ever seen in her life—all gazing at her, curious, assessing, judging. Evan's hand clenched into a fist. He muttered some word she did not know.

A tall woman with an angular face and twinkling eyes stepped forward from the front of the line. The keys at her waist proclaimed her the housekeeper. She greeted Evan with the familiarity of long service and then smiled and curtsied to Deborah.

"I am Mrs. Jacobs, ma'am, and I am that pleased to meet you. And this would be your boy? What a fine lad!" Then she drew Deborah reluctantly away from Evan's supporting arm and led her down the line. Deborah found time for one desperate glance behind her where Evan was making sure Julian and Mrs. Carlington were spared the same ordeal.

A commotion from the stairway announced the arrival of the schoolroom party. Deborah caught a glimpse of Miss Halley and of Alexander, who dashed forward to greet Julian, but had to return her attention to Mrs. Jacobs.

Here was Forby, the butler, whom Evan said had been at Northridge a mere dozen years. Here was Henry again, and Georgie, the second footman. Then came all those whose names she didn't know: housemaids and parlormaids, cook and pastry-maker, dairymaids and charwomen, and others Deborah had forgotten by the time she reached the end. How could one household need so many? If she'd thought her legs would obey her, she might have run from the place screaming.

An unfamiliar gentleman leaned on the newel post near the end of the line, smiling at her with an expression at once amused and sympathetic. He came forward to shake her hand as the servants melted off into the woodwork. "If you think you can possibly bear one more introduction? Philip Dusseau at your service!"

Evan arrived at her side then, still aggrieved. "What on earth possessed them to do that?" he inquired of his brother-in-law. "She's not my wife yet, much less mistress of Northridge. And we're moving out again as soon as we find a place to rent nearby."

Mr. Dusseau shook his head. "Believe me, we tried to talk them out of the grand gesture. They'd have none of it. At least they spared you the grooms and gardeners." He looked over Evan's shoulder toward the front doors. "Here comes Mother."

Deborah couldn't help thinking Evan's parents wanted to embarrass her.

Elizabeth and Mrs. Haverfield joined them. She might not be a monster, but she terrified Deborah nonetheless. So stiff and unyielding, her face like marble. Her eyes were the same color as Evan's but with no smile in them. At least, no smile for Deborah.

"Where have you put Deborah, Mama?" inquired Evan.

"She's in my old room," interjected Elizabeth. She pulled Deborah's arm through her own. "Come, Deborah, I'll take you up. Your mother is just across the hall. She seems *such* a sweet lady! Perhaps a bit overwhelmed at the moment—" Deborah had no doubt about *that*, "—but we'll soon have her feeling at home."

She nattered on as they climbed the stairs. Somehow it was soothing. "And Miss Halley has taken Julian up to the school room. He'll be well-occupied, you may be sure, meeting his new cousins and learning his way about."

Such a huge house! Would she ever see her son again? At Northridge, it was certain, children did not sit down to table with the adults. They did not do their lessons in the parlor, and they did not sleep in cold little closets next to their mothers' bedchambers. Julian could vanish into the upper reaches of the house and reappear for show like a prize heifer in fancy clothes his mother had never seen.

The thought was ridiculous, of course. She was sure Elizabeth raised her children as part of the family. And they would not be at Northridge long enough for any such appalling habits to become entrenched. Or so she hoped.

Her bedchamber—*Elizabeth's* bedchamber—was far and away the finest she had ever been privileged to inhabit. It smelled of beeswax and lavender. Carpet stretched nearly from wall to wall, thick and soft underfoot. The walls themselves were papered in a tracery of leaves, the green repeated in the bed linens shimmering of silk on a four-poster bed that looked like mahogany. Two big windows looked out over the front lawns and the plantings that stretched down toward the road, enveloped in mist; a cheerful fire banished all possibility of gloom. An exclamation of pleasure escaped involuntarily.

"This is too beautiful. Why are you giving up your room to me?"

"Now, don't you worry about me. Philip and I need more space and a dressing room."

More space? "Are you sure there's no garret you can put me in? I would feel more at home, I assure you."

Elizabeth regarded this as a joke and let loose a peal of laughter. "You *are* a goose, Deborah. If you think for half a minute that Evan would countenance such a thing—"

"Such a thing as what?" Evan ambled through the doorway, looking around at the renovations with approbation. "It looks like a new room. Mama did a fine job of obliterating all the damage you did, Lizzy."

"Oh, stuff," Elizabeth replied, snapping her fingers. "No more than any child, I daresay, and rather less than a certain brother of mine, who shall be nameless. But yes, it's a beautiful room now. Eminently suitable for its new occupant."

Evan's smile made Deborah blush clear down to her toes.

"No," he said. "We would need the Taj Mahal for that." She felt as though he had kissed her on the high street.

"You just wait until her new wardrobe arrives," Elizabeth said. "I wager you'll hardly recognize her. Deborah, I'll send Francine to do your hair, and I'll be here at five. We'll go downstairs together." And Elizabeth nipped out of the room, leaving the door just slightly ajar.

"She leaves me nothing to do," complained Evan. "*I* was going to escort you down for dinner."

"Oh! Well—the hairdresser is part of the deal, you know. Does Grady do hair?"

Evan laughed. "I'd like to see his face when I ask him. And that's two more gowns, by the way. Are you trying to ruin me?" He took a long, lingering kiss in lieu of any reply.

Deborah took refuge in his arms for some minutes. Then she drew back to look up into his face. "Will you tell me how to get to the schoolroom?"

"No. But I'll take you there."

❧ 36 ❧

Whenever she could escape her obligations, Deborah made her way back to the schoolroom. It was her refuge, where no one expected anything of her and she could remove her mask. She missed Julian—heaven knew she saw little enough of him at any other time. And despite his playmates and Miss Halley and all their activities, Julian seemed lonely for her as well, clinging rather too long when she had to leave.

In good weather Miss Halley took the older children outdoors, and Deborah would find only Betsy, the nursemaid, and Elizabeth's youngest, recently turned two. Even then she would stay for ten minutes, or thirty, and play with little Lucy or just sit in one of the little chairs and look out the window or read one of the books that filled the shelves.

How envious she was of the children who had grown up here with all those books. She would pick up the copy of *Robinson Crusoe* that Julian was looking at yesterday and find Evan's name inside, run her thumb over that inexpert signature, and contemplate the difference between his childhood and hers.

He had brought that pathetic basket of things from her room in Lydford—had he really thought she might want them? But for the gold coin, she would have tossed the lot into the fire, but Julian insisted not one item should be thrown away. So the basket resided at the back of Deborah's wardrobe behind the expanding rows of gowns and shoes and bonnets, reminding her of loneliness and desolation. Reminding her to be wary.

Often Deborah found her mother in the nursery when she arrived. With fewer dress fittings and less obligation to meet the neighboring gentry, and no role at all in searching out a suitable house, she had more time at her disposal. And once she had struggled up the stairs, she was loathe to come down again.

Elizabeth was a frequent guest as well, and Philip occasionally poked his head in, though he and Evan were more likely to accompany the children on their outings, riding or playing a rudimentary game of cricket or just kicking a ball around the orchard. Pelleas, barred from the house like all the dogs on the estate, participated in these activities too. Sometimes the women would sit outside and watch them all at their sports, the men casual in their shirtsleeves, dirty and disheveled just like the little ones, and enjoying themselves just as much. To Deborah's eyes, they looked more handsome than ever in disarray, though Mrs. Haverfield, when she deigned to join them, sat stiff and disapproving.

And if Evan did not find Deborah downstairs, he knew where she would be. She loved it when he came. Whether she was happy or troubled or wistful, he always had that smile for her. It made her feel beautiful and desirable.

Deborah found the place very quiet one afternoon a week before the wedding. The smell of cheese and ham still lingered from the children's nuncheon, but Miss Halley had taken the three older ones outside. Betsy moved about the rooms while Lucy napped, putting away the toys and brushing out the children's clothes, checking to see what needed laundering or mending. When she sat down with her needle, Deborah offered her help, but the girl refused it. "Och no, mum, it's just a little tear, see?"

Evan and Deborah had spent the morning exploring another rental property. It would not do. But she had reveled in his company. He was teaching her to drive and had let her take the reins for part of the drive home. Handling his beautiful grays bore little resemblance to the single beast that had once plodded in front of her gig.

She had not wanted to come back at all, but the dressmaker was coming at three o'clock, and Evan had promised to ride out with his father to visit one of the tenants. And later in the afternoon, Evan's older sister, the countess, would arrive with her family.

Deborah sat down by the open window, lulled by the cool breeze and birdsong and the smell of freshly scythed grass. She thought, reluctantly, that she should seek out her mother, or Evan's, when Mrs. Haverfield appeared in the doorway. Deborah and Betsy both jumped to their feet, and Deborah hardly prevented herself from curtsying as Betsy did.

"Oh!" exclaimed the older woman upon seeing Deborah. "Mrs...."

"Please, ma'am, do call me Deborah." Several times she had asked Mrs. Haverfield to use her given name, but she never did so. It must surely be meant as a set-down; certainly she called her other daughter-in-law *Clarice*. In a week, Deborah would no longer be *Mrs. Moore*, and for the woman to call her son's wife *Mrs. Haverfield* would be ridiculous.

But then, Deborah could not imagine calling Evan's mother *Mama*. Nor had she been asked to do so. *Ma'am* would have to do.

Mrs. Haverfield looked around the room rather vaguely. "I was hoping to find the new boy... What is his name?"

"Julian," Deborah said. She should be offended—Mrs. Haverfield knew his name perfectly well. But her manner seemed so peculiar. Perhaps she had been sleeping. "Won't you sit down?"

She did, choosing the old sofa pushed up against one wall. She ran her hand over the brocade in some surprise. "I thought this was in the morning room."

Deborah could not enlighten her. The condition of the piece made her think it had been relegated to the nursery long ago. "Why did you want Julian?"

"Julian? Oh! I merely thought I should see how he's settling in. He's quite a nice-looking boy, isn't he? And very well-mannered. If he's going to live here..."

He wasn't, of course, not for a few years yet. Mrs. Haverfield knew that, too, but Deborah did not press the issue.

"I want him to be happy here," she continued. "But I wish Evan would not... We don't *want* some strange boy to be master at Northridge."

"There is no question of that, ma'am."

"But there is! Evan insists. My husband was just livid. But Evan said if the boy can't inherit, then he'll cut himself off, go to America or some other godforsaken place."

Deborah stared at her. "Did he really say that?" Surely not.

"Indeed he did. You would think he despised us," she said, running her fingers up and down a seam in her skirt. "He's always been such a good boy. Oh, a bit of a rover, but never any of that devilry so many lads get up to." Her face puckered with anxiety.

"He loves Northridge, I know he does. I don't *want* him to go to America!" She sounded like an old woman, shrill and querulous.

"Of course you don't, ma'am," Deborah soothed.

"He'll regret this mismatch, I know he will. I did so want him to marry our Melanie. Such friends as they've been since they were—oh, just little things. Playing games, and riding, and learning to swim in the lake. It just breaks my heart. And that woman he's chosen to take her place. So aloof and awkward. And her circumstances so peculiar!"

Dear God. Does she have no idea who she's talking to?

It seemed impossible. She could not blame Mrs. Haverfield for feeling the way she did, but to hear it spoken so plainly...

"Mrs. Haverfield, let me get—"

"She was not raised properly, that's clear for anyone to see. No conversation, so glum and uninteresting. My husband calls her 'mechanical'. Why Evan cannot *see*... But he'll listen to nothing his father or I say about her."

Deborah sat very still. *Glum?* She'd had a smile plastered on her face since she arrived at Northridge. *No conversation?* She had plied all the tricks Elizabeth had taught her, the compliments and questions and all the rest. She'd listened for the leads Evan and Elizabeth gave her and followed them up, sometimes at the risk of inanity. She'd been spouting drivel for three weeks. And she had tried particularly hard with Evan's father, deeming him slightly more approachable than his wife. Evidently, though, she had not performed her part as well as she'd thought.

Footsteps sounded in the hall, and Mrs. Haverfield's abigail appeared in the doorway. A pent-up breath escaped Deborah's lungs.

"So here you are, ma'am. I've been looking for you all over the house."

"I'm sorry, I—" Mrs. Haverfield stood up. "I've been having such a comfortable coze with—" She gazed myopically at Deborah. "What did you say your name was?"

Betsy gaped from across the room. As well she might!

Richards replied cheerfully, "Why, that's Mrs. Moore, ma'am, who's to—"

"That's all right, Richards," Deborah rushed to intercede. She could see no good reason to embarrass the poor woman by making her aware of her own rudeness. "I think perhaps your mistress needs to rest?"

"I'm sure that's it, ma'am. And Mrs. Dusseau says I should remind you about the dressmaker, ma'am."

"Yes, Richards. Thank you." *God, the dressmaker!* When all she could think of was locking herself up in her bedroom. Her hands went to her hot cheeks, and she looked at Betsy. The girl should not have seen or heard any of that. Had it actually happened?

"Oh, mum. I never seen such a thing before. She's been comin' up here a lot, but she's—"

"Has she? I've not seen her."

Betsy looked uncomfortable, but she plowed ahead. "I think she's been avoidin' you, mum. Your mama's been here with 'er, though, a couple o' times."

"Does she play with the children?"

"Play? No... But she'll read a story, or brush Maddy's hair, or tell about when my mistress was growing up here, or when she was a girl herself. An' t'other day she was talkin' to Master Julian about—well, about you, mum, and about your mama."

Deborah frowned. "About what sorts of things, Betsy?"

The girl shrugged. "About where you lived before you came here—your house, I mean—and what sort of carriage you kept, and how many servants. Things like that."

Deborah wagered she hadn't gotten much pleasure out of *that* exercise.

"But she's always been all right—right in her mind, I mean. Oh, she might call one o' the children by the wrong name, but that's nothing. Me own mum is right bad about that. O' course, there's nine of us…"

Deborah *hoped* she had not been in her right mind. Otherwise, Evan's mother must have devised this deceit to warn her off.

She thought she might vomit.

37

Elizabeth knocked for the third time. "Deborah!"

She still didn't answer. She made no attempt at silence, but she did not want to talk. She wasn't sure she could.

"Deborah? Mme. Georges is waiting for you."

"Send her away, if you please." Her voice worked after all.

"Your wedding gown is stunning. Come out; I want to see it on you."

"I don't need a wedding gown." She laid a pile of shifts and night-dresses in the trunk. Without her new things, it was a very small pile indeed. "I don't need *any* of those gowns."

"What on earth... Please let me in, Deb."

Deb? No one had ever called her that.

Against her better judgment, she opened the door but turned back to her packing without looking at Elizabeth.

"What are you doing, Deborah?"

"I'm packing."

"Where are you going?"

"Back to Whately, I suppose." She had nowhere else to go.

"Why? What's happened? Did Evan say something stupid?"

"No."

Elizabeth took her hand and turned her face-to-face. Deborah willed her mask into place, but it wouldn't come. "Oh, Deborah. Whatever it is, we'll sort it out. You're overwrought. Why don't you lie down and rest? Evan will be home soon, then we'll see—"

"No!" She sounded childish, even to herself. She attempted a more reasonable tone. "Please leave me, Elizabeth. I have a great deal to do."

Elizabeth looked at her for a moment. "All right. But it's far too late to think about leaving today. And I assure you, you will not leave this house without some explanation."

As soon as the door closed, Deborah slumped onto the bed. What sort of explanation could she possibly give? *Your mother was mean to me?* Or alternatively, *your mother's out of her mind?*

Neither of those was an option. And in the end, it made no difference, at least to Deborah.

EVAN PULLED the door shut with a snap. A maid passing in the hallway gave him a knowing smirk—not yet married and visiting his bride in the middle of the afternoon!

He ground his teeth. Let her think what she liked. If she'd listened at the door, she would know the truth of the matter. Deborah would not let him touch her at all, for pleasure or for comfort. It had been an exceedingly unsatisfactory interview.

He had declined Elizabeth's presence, thinking he could talk Deborah around easily enough—that in fact, his sister might be very much in the way. After all, he had fully expected that his chosen bride would need reassurance all the way to the altar. But she was resolute. Elizabeth seemed sure that *something* had happened to overset her, but Deborah would not tell him what that something was or even concede that there *was* a something. She just reiterated that she "could not go through with it" and went on filling her trunk with Julian's things. He growled and crossed the hall to her mother's room.

"You're packing, too, I see." He'd expected it, yet it galled him.

"Of course." Mrs. Carlington looked at him mournfully. "I feel as though I've done nothing but pack and unpack for the past six weeks."

"She shouldn't be putting you through this. And for what? She certainly won't tell me!" He strode angrily about the room. "Is it just a case of nerves, ma'am?"

She shook her head decisively. "No, it was something very sudden and specific. But she won't tell me, either."

Evan stood at the window, watching love fall apart. By rights it should be raining, but the sun still shone, brash and selfish.

"You know, ma'am... if you refused to go, she would have to stay. At least a few days, to give us some time."

"Dear Evan. I am sorry about this. I suspect Deborah's making a mistake. But I don't know her reasons, and I... She's all I have, she and Julian. Can you understand?"

He could, he supposed. "How is Julian doing?"

"I've not seen him. But—I think she hasn't told him yet. It will be hard on him."

Yes indeed. What a pleasure it had been to watch the boy open up, run and laugh and play with Elizabeth's children. And his other cousins would be arriving any minute, come for a wedding that seemed more and more like a rainbow. Approach it too closely, and it disappears.

"There has to be a way through this muddle," he muttered and left the room without ceremony.

Elizabeth was waiting for him in the hall, trying to look nonchalant for the benefit of passing servants. Every room in the house was being readied for the influx of wedding guests, which entailed much coming and going with sheets and brass polish and the like. But she was biting her nails, a habit that her governess had broken, with great difficulty, when she was twelve.

"Oh, Evan! Do come with me. Betsy—you know, our nursery maid?—heard something."

Nothing pleasant, evidently. Elizabeth led him to the bedchamber she shared with Philip in the other wing of the house. Here Betsy sat at the very edge of the most uncomfortable chair in the room.

Elizabeth sat down across from her. "I'm sorry to make you go through this again, but I want my brother to hear it. All of it, please."

The girl glanced up at him nervously. He sat down.

"Well—Mrs. Moore came up to the schoolroom earlier. The children was all gone out with Miss Halley, but she sat down like she sometimes does. We talked a bit—she wanted to help me with the mending, God love her—and then Mrs. Haverfield come in and things got right peculiar, sir. She was as friendly as could be, but… said she was looking for Master Julian, but she couldn't remember 'is name."

Evan leaned forward. The narrative had not proceeded very far before he was back on his feet, pacing around the Aubusson carpet. It was hard to believe. He didn't *want* to believe it. But either it was true, or the girl had a phenomenal imagination—as well as some nefarious motivation he could not even guess at.

Parts of the conversation she related word for word, she said, and she seemed as upset by the whole scene as Elizabeth was—as he was. By the time the story ended with Richards escorting his mother downstairs and Deborah turning to Betsy—"Oh, white as a ghost she was, sir, and her eyes so big, and hurt, like she'd been hit…"—he was quivering with rage. He threw the door open, knocking a Sèvres vase off the spindly little table that stood behind it, and stormed out.

"Evan? Evan! Do you think she's sick or something?" Elizabeth ran after him.

He failed to break any precious *objets* when he burst into his mother's sitting room, only because there were none so poorly placed. Richards was helping her mistress into a chair, a shawl ready to spread across her lap. Both looked up in considerable surprise. Even with the grandchildren visiting, such displays of emotion were rare in this part of the house.

"Why, Evan!"

He stood over her, hands clenched into fists. "Pray explain your-self, Madam."

She gaped up at him.

"Sir!" Richards plucked ineffectually at his sleeve. "Remember who you're talking to!"

"Oh, I remember. If only *she* had remembered that she was talking to *my wife*. Upstairs? In the nursery? Do you remember that, Mama?" She quailed before his attack.

"Please, sir!" Richards tried again. "She's had a very difficult day."

Evan threw the woman's hand off his arm. "*She's* had a difficult day? So am I having a difficult day! Because *she* can't keep her mean-spirited thoughts to herself, *my* life is blown to hell. You promised me, Mama. I would never have dreamed that you could be so rude to a guest in this house. *Particularly* when that guest is the woman I was to marry. Yes, I said *was*. You achieved your purpose. You've driven her away. But if you imagine you'll ever see *my* face again, you're dreaming."

A gasp and a flurry of movement at the door, and Deborah was there. A shriek sounded somewhere farther away, and several pairs of feet could be heard in the hallway. But Deborah, for whom Evan was fighting this battle, was first into the fray... and on the wrong side.

"Evan, don't!" She ran to him and slipped between him and his mother, pressed back in her chair bewildered and frightened. Hands against his chest, she looked into his wrathful face and said more softly, "I'm convinced she didn't know who I was."

"That's rubbish, Deborah. She remembers *my* name. She remem-bers *Elizabeth's* name. She remembers *Melanie's* name, for God's sake. It was all an act, a ploy to—"

"No, Evan, I'm sure it wasn't. She's known you forever, of course she remembers you." Finally he yielded to the pressure of her hands and backed off a step or two.

His father's voice barked from the doorway, pushing through the crowd that had gathered. "How dare you talk to your mother that way!"

Deborah turned away from him and went down on her knees by

his mother's chair. She held her hand and stroked her arm. Her lips moved, but in the approaching confusion of voices, he couldn't hear what she said.

Hands attached themselves to both his arms and guided him from the room. *Dear God, was I wrong?*

38

The room was very quiet by the time Deborah stood up again and turned her attention from Evan's mother. Between the smelling salts Richards waved under her nose and the brandy someone made her drink, Mrs. Haverfield had regained some composure and the color returned to her face.

The servants had been dispatched to their various duties, and Deborah was alone with Mrs. Haverfield, Richards, and Lady Witney, who had evidently arrived in the midst of the uproar—quite a welcome that must have been. Richards wanted to dose her mistress with laudanum and put her to bed, and the countess endorsed the proposal.

"She certainly should not attempt dinner downstairs. I hope she will sleep through the night and feel more herself in the morning. Come, Mama, we'll help you to your room... Oh, Mrs. Moore, please stay. I'll just be a moment."

Trapped, Deborah stood and waited.

Pulling the bedroom door closed behind her several minutes later, the countess smiled at Deborah. It was a social smile, not warm, but kind enough, her eyes assessing, perhaps curious. "Thank you for your help, Mrs. Moore. It was most... filial of you."

Deborah flushed and curtsied. "It was nothing, my lady."

"Oh, none of that formal stuff. We're to be sisters, after all. I was most surprised to hear that you will be joining the family."

And not pleased, Deborah was sure. "No," was all she said.

"No?" Alberta's eyebrows went up in surprise. "Well, I confess I have no clue what all the commotion has been about. But we are to join the others in the drawing room now that we're finished here, and no doubt it will come clear." She put her hand on Deborah's elbow and started toward the door.

Deborah hung back. "You've no need of me, Lady Witney. I have some packing—"

"I'm sorry, Mrs. Moore, I was most strictly adjured to bring you along. I was given to understand you are a party to whatever is happening. In fact, I suspect you are the very crux of the matter."

Deborah wanted to slide under the rug with the dust and the little bugs that always managed to thrive there no matter how hard one tried to keep a place clean. Though at places like Northridge, they probably did not dare. But since she could not do that, she followed meekly and entered the drawing room in the countess's wake.

She sought out Evan, who stood in the far corner chastised and unhappy, like a small boy enduring a well-deserved scold. Their eyes met briefly, and then he turned away to the window.

Her attention was claimed by a stranger who approached her with a practiced smile very like his wife's and introduced himself as Theo Packard. He was also, of course, Earl of Witney, though he did not say so. "It's a pleasure to meet you, Mrs. Moore."

She curtsied again. "My lord." He gestured her to a seat beside Elizabeth's husband.

Elizabeth, one swollen ankle propped on a footstool, spared only a quick glance for her sister and Deborah. It did not seem the right time to ask what had happened to her. She was staring intently at her father, who was seated across from her and looked a decade older than he had that morning at breakfast.

The earl seemed to have been appointed moderator of the

proceedings. Evan had said he was politically inclined, so presumably he was good at that sort of thing.

"We've been discussing the... rather extraordinary conversation that apparently took place this afternoon. Evan and Elizabeth heard the tale from—as I understand it—the nursery maid? But as neither of them was actually present, and you were, Mrs. Moore—"

Elizabeth broke in. "Papa, you were saying there have been previous incidents? Why have none of us noticed? Why have you not told us?"

Mr. Haverfield clearly did not want to discuss the subject. Who would? He must have known Elizabeth would not let it go, however. "None of you live here, that's why you haven't noticed. And there's been nothing like this, merely a certain vagueness. She has occasionally forgotten about some social event or which neighbor she's going to visit, little things like that. Nothing that's not easy to remedy or gloss over."

Deborah thought back over the past three weeks. It would explain a few peculiarities of the visits they had paid and received.

"How did she seem to you, Deborah?" Elizabeth wanted to know.

Deborah looked at her doubtfully and then glanced at Mr. Haverfield, who seemed inexplicably absorbed in a glass paperweight he held in his hands. Everyone else in the room was watching her. "I don't want to—"

"Please, Deborah," Elizabeth cried. "Was she well? Sick?"

Deborah shook her head. "Not sick in any obvious way—in any way that I could recognize. She was not herself, though. Her hair was untidy, her shawl trailed on the floor—I met her only recently, but I have never seen her looking less than perfect. I thought perhaps she awoke disoriented from a deep sleep, as one sometimes does." She thought back for a moment. "The sofa that's in the schoolroom? It looks old, but she seemed to think it belonged in the morning room."

The countess looked her amazement. "That old thing? It's been upstairs for ten years, at least."

"She'd forgotten your name, I gather," said the earl.

Deborah looked up at him earnestly. "The name itself is nothing.

What disturbed me was that she didn't know me at all—that Evan and I were to... Why would she say such things to someone she thought to be a stranger? And with a servant in the room?"

Elizabeth waved that away. "She was never as discreet with the servants as you thought she should be, was she, Papa? She always said they knew everything anyway, it was silly to think we could keep secrets from them."

"What did you do after the events in question, Mrs. Moore?"

"I went to see my mother. Then I rang for our trunks."

"You did not tell Evan about your conversation with his mother?"

She shook her head unhappily. "There didn't seem to be any benefit in doing so. But if I had, it might have spared everyone... all this."

The earl shook his head. "It's been more unpleasant than it might otherwise have been, that's all. But I'm curious," he continued. "If you were persuaded that Mrs. Haverfield was not in her right mind, then you must know that she intended no personal insult to you. Why then are you determined to leave us?"

She spoke to her lap. "I was not persuaded, at first." She swallowed hard and looked up at Lord Witney, at Evan, and back again. It was safer to talk to the earl. "But don't you see? It doesn't matter. Whomever she thought she was talking to, she meant what she said. I've been alone for a long time. It doesn't frighten me. But how could I detach Evan from his world and expect him to..."

"How sacrificial of you," Theo said drily.

Deborah eyed him indignantly. "Not at all, my lord. When his—whatever he feels for me turns into resentment because of all he's lost, how does that help me? In any case, why on earth should you try to talk me into staying? This is the only happy family I've ever known. I walked in the door three weeks ago and already it's falling apart. The sooner I leave, the better it will be for everyone."

A few quick strides brought Evan to stand in front of her. "For everyone, Deborah? How about you?"

She opened her mouth, but he forestalled her.

"How about Julian?"

She bit her lip.

"How about me, Deborah?"

She looked down and spoke with difficulty. "I told you from the start you would do better without me."

He started to speak again, but his father rose from his chair and touched Evan's arm, enjoining his silence. Philip stood, surrendering his seat beside her.

Mr. Haverfield seemed a smaller man than he had been. He sat quite close to her, and mostly what she felt was sadness. What was it she had found so intimidating?

"I want to apologize, my dear, for the rather Turkish treatment we have meted out to you. We have always prided ourselves on our hospitality at Northridge, but we have certainly failed in your case."

"Sir, I—" Deborah tried to object, but he took her hand and patted it.

"Let me have my say, if you will. It's seldom enough I admit to my own inadequacies, as my children will no doubt attest." He spoke very quietly. The rest of the room was silent. "I concede that we—Cecily and I—were not best pleased with Evan's news. Does that seem unnatural to you?"

"No, sir." *Heavens, no.*

"No. Well. I must also confess that after your arrival, I said some things—in private conversation with my wife—that would have been better left unsaid. That she should remember those unkind words yet forget far more important things…" He sighed. "Be that as it may, my opinion of you has undergone substantial improvement since those first days. I thought Cecily's had also, but perhaps I was mistaken. Whatever the case, my dear, I hope you will find yourself able to forgive us. And that you will reconsider your decision. For my son's sake, of course, but for the rest of us as well."

There were tears in her eyes by the time he finished. She wanted to say something but couldn't seem to formulate a reply.

"There, there." He patted her hand again. "There's no hurry, no hurry at all."

Of course there was! Guests would begin arriving tomorrow, and the wedding was only a week away. If there was one.

"Oh, Papa." Elizabeth wiped away tears of her own. "If I could get up, I'd come over there and hug you."

Mr. Haverfield gave her a tight little smile. "Alberta, perhaps you would ring for Forby. Ask him to move dinner to the breakfast room and serve as soon as it can be accomplished. We will not dress for dinner. Mrs. Moore, let me take you down."

❧ 39 ❧

Dinner! The very last thing Deborah wanted. But Mr. Haverfield gave her no opportunity to bow out, escorting her downstairs to the drawing room to wait until the cook had everything ready. No one laughed, and they spoke in undertones.

Evan had been sent to fetch her mother, so she perched on the edge of the sofa beside Elizabeth. "What happened to your foot?"

"I fell chasing Evan." Deborah bit her lip. "Don't worry about me, it's just a little sprain."

By the time her mother made her way downstairs, Forby had announced dinner. Evan's father led Deborah into the dining room and made her sit in the place of honor at his right hand. Evan wound up on the other side of Philip in the only chair Deborah could not see. She could see his plate, however—he ate little, though the footman refilled his wine glass at frequent intervals. And he said no more than she did.

Dinner could not be conducted in silence, of course, but neither could they discuss the topics most on their minds. So it was fortunate that Lord Witney and his family had arrived so recently. They were introduced to her mother, and then there were all sorts of logical subjects to pursue with them: their doings in London, the children, the earl's activities in the House of Lords during the session just ended. As all these topics dealt with persons and matters largely unknown to her, Deborah allowed her mind to absent itself while her eyes observed the family she might—or might not—become part of.

Philip and Mr. Haverfield asked most of the questions, though they had little enough to say otherwise. Even Elizabeth, that habitual chatterbox, was preoccupied. Lord and Lady Witney responded quite naturally, or so it seemed to Deborah. She supposed Society leaders might need masks as much as she did, though theirs would show a different expression. Her mother, who had kept aloof from most of the afternoon's upheaval, earned Deborah's gratitude by contributing more than usual to the conversation.

Since Elizabeth could not leave the table without assistance, the men did not stay at table when the ladies withdrew, and the whole party drifted apart. Elizabeth professed herself ready to retire; her husband and the countess helped her upstairs.

Evan's father went to check on his wife and doubted that he would make any further appearance that evening. When Evan followed him, Deborah was torn between pique, relief, and a feeling of abandonment.

"Ladies?" Left alone with Deborah and her mother, the earl gestured toward the drawing room with well-hidden reluctance.

Deborah repressed a shudder. "What was that word, Lord Witney? *Sacrificial*? Thank you, no; we are in the midst of packing." She frowned. "Or possibly unpacking. Good night."

The earl bowed. Deborah felt his gaze follow their slow progress up the stairs.

❧

EVAN LOOKED RATHER DESPERATELY at Deborah, but her head was bent to hear something her mother was saying. Whatever happened, she would not be going anywhere until morning. He would rouse her from her bed if need be. He chased his father up the stairs.

"Sir!" he called softly.

Mr. Haverfield stopped, his hand on his bedroom door. "Well?"

"I need to see her too."

"You don't think you've done sufficient damage for one day?" The words were caustic, but his tone was milder than Evan felt he deserved.

"I owe her an apology."

"You do indeed. But you'll probably get away without one. My guess is that she'll remember nothing of it in the morning. So I will accept your apology on her behalf, and you will make amends to *her* in another way. And though *she* may not know why, I will."

Evan waited.

"You will remain at Northridge, Evan. If you will not stay without Deborah, then you must persuade her to stay as well."

"I fully intend to do so, sir. I wanted to thank you for—what you said to her earlier. I know it must have been difficult."

"Yes. So you will give up this notion of renting another house. It's a ridiculous expenditure. And your mother's going to need help running this place. It will be the perfect way for your wife to adjust gradually to her responsibilities here."

"Ah." Evan deflated a bit. Deborah was counting on their separate space.

His father grasped his arm for a moment. "You'll make it work, son. We could not stand to lose you; you know that."

Returning downstairs, he found Theo and Philip in possession of the brandy. His need being acute, he joined them.

"How is your mother?" Philip asked.

Evan shook his head. "Sleeping. I didn't see her." It took him but a moment to down half a glass. "Father seems to think she won't remember any of it."

"Well, that's a blessing," said Theo.

Evan grimaced. "If you call losing your mind a blessing…"

"When my memory goes, I certainly want to forget the unpleasant things first."

"I'm trying," said Evan, and drained the glass. Theo poured him another. "How is Lizzy?"

Philip frowned into his own drink. "Don't recall when I've seen her so upset. Alberta is—er—applying balm."

"Laudanum for her too?"

"Oh, I don't think it's as bad as that." Philip poured another round for all of them. "Have you talked to Deborah?"

Evan's jaw clenched. "Not yet." He lifted his glass. "Fortification."

"He made her a nice speech upstairs."

"My father? Yes, he did. But he wants us to give up the idea of hiring a house in the neighborhood. She won't like that at all."

"Advice from Iago. *Honesty's a fool and loses that it works for*," offered Theo. "Deal with it after the wedding."

Philip was not so sure. "Bound to cause trouble later on."

Theo had a riposte, of course. *"Honesty is praised... and starves."*

❦

PHILIP'S ADVICE won the day, despite his lack of erudition. Evan knew some quotes too: *That soul that can be honest is the only perfect man.* Well, he could make no claims of perfection, especially after today. But surely one should aspire to it?

Deborah opened the door promptly but would not let him in. She was fully dressed, except that she had removed her shoes and taken the pins out of her hair. A very familiar desire rose within him; he shoved it firmly to the back of his mind. They talked in the doorway in near whispers.

"Did you see your mother?"

"No. My father thought tomorrow would be soon enough. Deborah, we need—"

"Is he very angry with you?"

"Yes. But he understands it, I think. We need to talk."

"Oh, Evan. We've been through all the arguments before. I can't do it."

"There are new facts in the case. I won't touch you, Deborah. Let me come in."

She did, reluctantly, and sat down at the dressing table, her back to the mirror. He eyed the chestnut hair flowing down her back and wanted her.

He turned away and told her about the loss of their house. He presented it as his father's request rather than an ultimatum and made much of the advantages his father had pointed out.

Unfortunately, those advantages accrued more to the benefit of Northridge and less to Deborah.

"And I wouldn't expect to spend all of our time here in any case. We can travel, we can spend days or weeks or months wherever we please." He turned back to her as he finished speaking.

Her lips were pressed together, her hands clasped tight in her lap. "And you agreed to this?"

"Surely you know I would not commit to such a thing without your approval, sweetheart. If you leave me, it's moot in any case." She was silent. "I did not have to tell you, Deborah. Theo advised against it."

She snorted. "That seems in character." She rose and walked to the door. "I thank you for disregarding his advice. Now if you'll please leave me to—"

"Just one more thing. I don't know if I've said... do you know how much I love you? I cannot imagine life without you. And I won't give you up easily. You'll have to go a lot farther than Whately if you want to get away from me. Japan might do, perhaps, if they'll let you in—I believe they're very restrictive. But I don't think Julian would much like it there. And the voyage would be very hard on your mother."

If he'd hoped to lighten the mood, he failed dismally. Being honest with himself, as he'd been with her, he supposed that had not been his intent. He could have spoken the words lightly—had *meant* to do so!— except that he was so damnably frustrated. Strange to think that six months ago he had been appalled at the thought of marriage. Now the only thing he could think about was getting the knot tied, binding her safe to his side.

He went to his own room and rang for a bottle of brandy—he had no desire for another chat with his brothers—but left it untouched. The night stretched out before him, troubled and unfriendly. He should have taken himself off for a long walk through the darkness, but having now stripped down to shirt and breeches, he could not summon the will to put even his boots on again. So he paced round and round his room instead, pausing now and then to drag a hand through his hair and look out the windows at things he could not see.

The hall clock struck midnight, and finally Evan broached the brandy. Someone knocked softly at his door. He figured it would be one of his sisters... No, with the injury to Elizabeth's ankle, she would send Philip.

He could pretend to be asleep. But what if it were something important, about his mother...

He strode to the door and pulled it open.

Deborah cast a quick glance back down the dark hallway and slipped inside. "I was afraid you might be sleeping." She looked very pale; he thought she'd been crying.

"You're joking." He closed the door softly. When he turned back to her, she walked straight into him and clung to his shirt, her hands like ice through the fine linen. She wore a dressing gown over her night-dress, but both were designed to be alluring—at which they succeeded admirably—rather than warm, and her feet were bare. His arms closed around her with no prompting from his brain.

"Why are you so cold? Come over to the fire." He released her reluctantly, half afraid she might disappear while he stirred up the coals. But she was there, nervously fingering the ribbons on her dressing gown. "Don't move," he adjured her and stepped into his dressing room.

She did not move except to turn around so she could watch him, her eyes dark and unreadable in that pale face. He knelt in front of her and held a heavy woolen stocking in readiness for one foot.

"Oh, that's not necessary!" she objected. "How embarrassing."

"Humor me."

She rested her hands on his shoulders for balance and lifted a foot. He rolled the stocking over her heel and pushed it gently up her calf. Sliding on the second one, he succumbed to the temptation of rubbing the back of her knee in a brief caress and was gratified by a responsive quiver of surprise and—he was almost sure—pleasure.

"You know, my love," he said, looking up and taking her hands, "perhaps while I'm down here I should just start over."

"What do you mean?"

He kissed one hand and then the other. "Deborah, will you marry me?"

"Oh, do get up!"

"But you've given me no answer."

She looked at him somberly for a moment, and then she, too, went down on her knees. "Evan—Are you quite certain that's what you want?"

"I can't believe you're asking me that."

"I promise I'll never ask you again, but—"

"You should never make a promise you can't keep." He did his best to quell the tremor of amusement in his voice.

She frowned and shifted her gaze to his chest for a moment. "I promise to *try* not to ask you again."

"In that case… Yes, I am *quite* certain." He placed her hands on his shoulders and his own at her waist. "What sort of pledge would you like?" Even in the dim light, he could see that she blushed. The candlelight sparkled in a tear that slid down her cheek. He kissed it softly.

"I still haven't said yes."

"You said yes weeks ago."

"So you get to start over, but I do not?"

His hands slipped inside her dressing gown and down to her hips, not six inches from his. "Only if you give the right answer," he replied roughly.

She rested her fingertips beside his mouth. "Poor Evan. I haven't made it easy for you, have I?"

"You have not. Unfortunately for my peace of mind, that has had no effect whatsoever on the way I feel about you." He moved those few precious inches until their bodies touched from knee to lip. Yet the three thin layers between his skin and hers seemed intolerable.

Forcing himself to move slowly, he untied the silken ribbons that fastened her dressing gown and pushed it off her shoulders and down her arms till it slithered to the floor behind her. Lightly, he traced the low neckline of her nightdress. She shivered.

"Are you still cold?" he murmured.

"Oh no." With one hand, she touched the hollow of his throat. Then she slid her fingers under the collar of his shirt.

Minutes passed in increasing delirium. Nightdress followed dressing gown to the floor, and Evan had just pulled his shirt off over his head when another tap sounded on the door. Evan groaned and Deborah's eyes opened wide, disoriented and dismayed at the possibility of discovery. She started to say something, but Evan put his finger on her lips and wiggled his eyebrows at her.

"I must answer it; it could be something about Mama." He stood up and dropped his shirt into her arms. She clutched it tight.

"Sorry to disturb you," Philip said softly. "Saw light through the keyhole..."

"Do you often go peering through keyholes?"

"Didn't have to do any peering. Just thought I'd pass on an idea of Lizzy's. Make living at Northridge more palatable, you know."

"I appreciate the thought. But your timing is—um—awkward." A sound from inside the room brought Philip's head up. It sounded to Evan like Deborah had bumped into something.

"Aha! Cerberus is guarding something!"

Evan shook his head. "Not Cerberus. Must be Saint Peter. Because this is definitely Heaven."

Philip grinned. "Told Lizzy months ago you didn't need any help from her. But it really is a diverting idea. A cottage somewhere nearby, where you can escape for—er, tête-a-têtes..."

"Philip?" Evan pushed him gently away from the narrow breach between door and jamb. "Go away."

Philip chuckled. "Tally-ho, then."

Deborah had moved into a chair; easier on the knees, without a doubt. She still held his shirt over her nakedness. Since she had not dressed, presumably she was not planning to leave him to his cold bed.

"Just Philip. Don't think anyone's getting much sleep tonight." He rummaged in a pocket of his coat that hung over a chair and pulled out a handkerchief. This he stuffed into the keyhole. "Maybe the next intruder will think I'm asleep."

"Is there no key?"

"No, it's been lost for years. But I think we'll have to rectify that." He sauntered over to her. "Did you hurt yourself?"

"Just bruised my ankle a little."

"Shall I kiss it?"

"No." She reached for him and began to unbutton his breeches. *'Tis Heaven indeed*, he thought.

It was the most cogent thought he had for quite some time.

40

As she completed her preparations, Deborah's mind ran back to the last ball she had dressed for, in Whately. Had it been only two months ago?

Some things had not changed. The trepidation that gazed out of the mirror at her looked much the same, though it felt subtly different. Elizabeth was with her again, and again she had set Francine, her dresser, to the task of arranging Deborah's hair. Every other circumstance was different.

In place of the unlamented peach silk was a gown of deep dusky blue, perfectly fitted and styled to suit her.

Her mother was there, and Julian, giggling as the funny curls were released from confinement and his mama was transformed into a lady of fashion.

There, too, was Bethan, the shy young under-housemaid Deborah had adopted. Evan had fully expected to hire an expensive dresser to take care of his wife and her wardrobe, but she wanted no part of that. She was comfortable with Bethan, which Deborah considered crucial, having discovered just how often Society women changed their clothes. And the girl quite worshipped her new mistress, which Deborah could not account for at all. Eager in her new trade, she had already spent time with Francine and with Mrs. Haverfield's Richards, learning all she could in a short time about hair, and the care of fabrics, and fashions and colors. But she had natural good taste and a sense of style all her own.

Then there was the exciting, frightening, ineluctable fact that tomorrow was her wedding day. What she had ever done to deserve a man like Evan was a mystery to her, and he was no help in solving the riddle. He just shook his head and chuckled. If pressed, he would say that love and merit had nothing at all to do with one another, and it was a silly question in any case because they deserved each other, for better or worse. She thought it was a joke, but she could get nothing more from him but kisses, which inclined her to forget all about it.

This time, he *would* be waiting for her at the foot of the staircase, handsome in evening dress. And she would waltz with him again, though the surroundings would bear no comparison. Whatever her wishes in the matter, this time there would be no tripping over the furniture in her dark little parlor. This time they would dance under the brilliance of the chandeliers, surrounded by close to two hundred people in full regalia.

Northridge had been teeming all week. There were aunts and uncles, cousins and others in residence, plus friends who were putting up in the vicinity but came to the house for picnic breakfasts, boating parties on the lake, rambles about the grounds, and of course, for dinner and long evenings of stilted conversation, musical offerings, and cards.

It was a frenetic and formidable week for Deborah with hardly a let-up from the time she woke up in the morning until she climbed gratefully into her bed near midnight or beyond. The nursery was too full of children to qualify as a refuge, even if she had found time to go there, and Bethan was sleeping on a trundle bed in her room to make space for the visiting servants, so she had hardly a moment alone.

Evan complained about the crush, but at least he knew everyone. Deborah knew only the family and a few of the neighbors. Like Melanie Littleton, whom Evan had been supposed to marry but who was nevertheless impossible to dislike. *So few familiar faces among such a crowd!*

Yet she could have none of the comforts of anonymity, for she was Haverfield's Bride, and everyone must have their pound of flesh. Had they not been setting out for the Lakes on the day following the wedding—just the two of them, plus Grady and Bethan—she must have run mad. Evan delivered her to her bedchamber each night with words of love and praise, and her mother came in each morning to count down the remaining days of torture and talk her into getting out of bed.

Fortunately Deborah had nothing to do with the arrangements for the week. The countess had taken over Mrs. Haverfield's responsibilities with aplomb and astonishing efficiency, leaving the older woman to do only what she most wanted to do, what would cause her the least anxiety, all under the watchful guardianship of her husband or children. She spent most of the time in her rooms, often attended by a select group of family and friends. Amidst the assembled multitude, sometimes she knew Deborah and sometimes she did not—with one look into her eyes Deborah knew which times were which—but there were no more distressing incidents.

Indeed, on this evening she knocked at Deborah's door and offered not only compliments on the gown but best wishes and a cool kiss on the cheek as well. The room seemed to hold its breath, releasing it with a sigh as she departed.

Not many minutes later another knock sounded, and again Elizabeth went to answer it. "I was about to give you up," she said to whoever was outside, but that was all Deborah could hear of the muffled conversation. When she returned to Deborah's side, she held out a jeweler's box.

Perturbed, Deborah looked from the box to the bearer. "What is it?"

"Open it, goose," Elizabeth said fondly. "I don't think it will bite."

Deborah took it reluctantly and lifted the lid. A note was tucked inside that said merely *Tomorrow! E.* Removing this with reverence, she sat looking at the necklace and earrings that glistened underneath.

They were the most gorgeous things she had ever seen, gold and amber and a few perfect pearls. She burst into tears, and the ladies of her court burst into action.

"Oh, no tears!" cried Elizabeth. "They'll ruin your face!" Francine jumped to the rescue with cotton wadding, Bethan handed her the powder. Mama took the box from Deborah's shaking hands and detached the baubles from the silk pillow that cushioned them. Then Elizabeth took over, carefully guiding the chain beneath the curls that kissed Deborah's neck and hanging the earrings in place.

"Oh, ma'am," Bethan breathed, not far from tears herself.

Elizabeth drew Deborah to her feet and surveyed her critically. "Perfect," she pronounced. Francine applied a couple extra dabs of perfume. Her mother kissed her cheek. Bethan helped her pull on her gloves and handed her the fan Mrs. Haverfield had given her. Julian was attached to his grandmother's skirts but came shyly forward as his mama knelt down—carefully—and held out her arms. A near-tragedy had brought them here; and if she still could not believe in happy-ever-afters, she finally felt ready to accept what happiness might be granted in the here and now.

She and Elizabeth left the room and made their way to the stairs. Several steps down, Elizabeth abruptly dropped Deborah's arm, exclaiming brightly, "I forgot something! Do go on, I'll be down directly."

Clustered in the hall, awaiting the ladies who would join them in the receiving line, were the men of the family: Philip, and the earl, and Mr. Haverfield, and Evan's Uncle Frederick, a fatherly type who was to give her hand to Evan tomorrow… and yes, Evan as well. Deborah faltered, but she could hardly stop now that their eyes had turned toward her.

Another lady would have made the most of her moment. But Deborah did not know how to strike a pose or amend her posture to emphasize her womanly assets. What she wanted was to fly back to her room and hide under the covers. She could see nothing but admiration in the faces arrayed below her, but appearances could be deceiving. So she found Evan again and concentrated all her attention on him.

In her dreams of this moment, his eyes always crinkled up in that smile of his, but he was not smiling now. He looked stunned.

EVAN HAD ALWAYS THOUGHT her beautiful. But tonight! Her gown was superbly flattering, draping around her legs in a damnably seductive manner as she descended the stairs, in a particularly delectable shade of blue that made her skin glow, with copper-colored trimmings that answered the gleam of her hair. And yes, the amber necklace as well—Elizabeth had been right. He realized his mouth was hanging open and made a conscious effort to close it.

From one of the men came a low whistle of appreciation; Evan was fully sympathetic to that. It made Deborah blush, though, and he dredged up a smile to reassure her. He kissed both her hands as she reached the foot of the stairs, and she curtsied, giving him a shy smile of her own. As he turned her away from the group, he heard Elizabeth murmur in her husband's ear. "That went rather well, don't you think?"

Evan laughed softly. When Deborah looked up at him in inquiry, he shook his head.

"My sister should have been a puppeteer. She manipulates us all."

SO MANY EYES as she gave Evan her hand. So many gawkers as they faced each other at the head of the two columns of dancers. They watched Evan, of course; but *she* was the mystery, the one none of them knew, the subject of so many murmured comparisons to Evan's smiling, easy manners; to Alberta's poise and confidence; to Elizabeth's *joie de vivre*.

She failed all those comparisons, failed them miserably. She would be better suited to a family of misfits.

Those who were staying at the house knew this already, of course, and all the neighbors she had met. The remaining guests would know it soon enough. Deborah had never felt so exposed as she did that evening. Coming down those stairs by herself had been one of the most difficult things she had ever done. Almost, she could wish she had fallen and broken her neck.

For the hundredth time she thought about putting an end—yet again—to the charade. But it would be too dreadfully rude to those who had put so much into the preparations or traveled long distances to be here when Evan took a wife. And to Evan it would be worse than rude.

He looked marvelously happy as they stood waiting for the musicians to strike the first chord. His smile could be seen by all; the love in his eyes was for her alone. She blushed and bit her lip.

They came together in the first figure of the dance. He squeezed her fingers. "You're frowning, my love."

She tried on a smile, but it must have been a poor effort because he chuckled. "I'm thinking this might be the worst evening of our wedded life. Well, *almost* wedded. After tomorrow, things will start falling into place, Deborah, I promise. We'll be away from all these people, just the two of us."

That was intimidating too, but only a little. They took a turn around another couple.

"You will love the Lakes. I've chosen out-of-the-way places, so we'll not be too crowded by other summer travelers."

She did want to see the Lakes. In fact, she wanted to see anyplace Evan would take her. It was a dream she had never allowed herself. They danced a figure with the next couple and then returned to each other.

"And then we'll be at Elizabeth's, in Wrackwater Bridge."

That made her smile a little. She was eager to see Elizabeth's home in the town with the peculiar name, learn something of how she managed her household. Philip and Elizabeth had invited Julian and Mrs. Carlington to travel north with them and await the newlyweds there. Julian, who had been quite agonized at the idea of not seeing his mama for an entire month, had greeted this new notion with relief and enthusiasm. His grandmother, who found most of the Haverfields rather daunting, felt the same.

Deborah's smile widened. "Julian told me he's glad Aunt Elizabeth is not a countess."

Evan laughed. "As though she would be anything other than a hoyden, whatever title she might hold. But there's no question he will be happier there than with Alberta and Theo."

No question at all.

Deborah was exhausted by the time Evan came to claim her for the last waltz. She had danced the first with his father, stately and staid. He'd apologized for being old and creaky, but she was glad to review the steps in his sedate hands. Because the second waltz, with Philip, was not stately at all. She had no time to think about steps as he took her twirling and laughing around the room.

Evan's style, she supposed, would be somewhere between the two. But from the moment she laid her hand in his and looked up into his eyes, she forgot to notice. She forgot her fatigue as well.

"I swear I've danced with every woman in the room," he complained.

"You couldn't possibly."

"It feels like it, anyway. I've missed you dreadfully." He guided her through a couple of turns. "You look happy, my love. Are you enjoying the evening?"

"I'm enjoying *this*." He smiled down at her, and she forgot to move her feet.

He chuckled as he set her in motion again. "Much as I'd like to send all these people to perdition, and blow out all the candles, and waltz you into bed, I'm afraid it's not time yet."

DESPITE THE COUNTRY hours they kept, the clock struck two before the last of the guests departed. Servants milled around, cleaning up the mess that became suddenly so apparent once the rooms emptied of the silks and satins, the colors and the elegant coiffures, the chatter and the laughter, the cadence of the music and the movement of the dance.

Evan lingered in the hall with the rest of his family, except for his mother and Deborah's, who had retired long ago. Theo, disdainful of the punch and champagne served during the ball, paid a visit to the library and brought out brandy for the men.

He and Alberta seemed wide awake—they were accustomed to the social whirl of London where two o'clock was still an early hour. Everyone else showed the effects of exhaustion to a greater or lesser extent. Philip had yanked off his cravat, which now hung over his shoulder; Elizabeth held her shoes in one hand.

Mr. Haverfield took just a sip of his brandy before setting the glass back on the tray. "I'm for bed. Glad this is the last of these infernal affairs I'll ever have to host." He gave his eldest daughter a kiss. "Thank you, my dear. Everything was splendid."

"Hear hear!"

"Yes, Berta," affirmed Evan. "It was a superhuman effort. A wonderful wedding present." A hug for her and then for Elizabeth. "You as well, Lizzy. I cannot thank you enough for all you've done for Deborah."

"She looked quite ravishing tonight, my dear," said Philip. "*Almost* as lovely as you."

Elizabeth laughed and received his kiss with pleasure. "She *is* pretty, is she not?"

Theo addressed himself to Evan. "Acquitted herself better than I expected, your Mrs. Moore."

Evan grunted. "I'm glad to know that after today I need never hear that name again."

"She even *talked* with some of her partners," Theo added, "though I'm not sure how they managed the feat."

Evan rounded on him. "Could be they gave her some reason to *like* them! You might try doing the same."

Theo held up both hands in conciliation. "She certainly demonstrated endurance tonight. Danced every dance, I believe?"

"Every one," Elizabeth confirmed. "She said she didn't know how to refuse. I think she was gratified, though." She yawned.

"I expect all the champagne Philip brought her helped a bit," said Alberta, dryly.

"I saw that!" Evan exclaimed. "No wonder she's collapsed."

Philip held up a hand to absolve himself. "Just acting on Lizzy's instructions. And it was well-watered. How did she get upstairs without saying her good nights, I'd like to know."

"I'm here," came a small, disembodied voice from behind them. As the last guest walked out the door, Deborah had wilted on Evan's arm, and he had deposited her in one of the tall upholstered chairs that stood in the hall. It was turned away from the group by the stairs, and none of the others had noticed her there.

"Deb!" exclaimed Elizabeth. "Why are you hiding? We would have toasted you!"

"Not hiding," Deborah murmured. "My feet hurt."

"I'm not surprised, my dear." Evan smiled and squatted down to pull off her shoes. "I don't think she needs any more champagne, Lizzy. Tomorrow will be soon enough for toasts."

Evan carried her up the stairs, the others trailing behind. "We'll catch her if you fall," called Philip.

"Who will catch me?" Evan asked over his shoulder.

"You're on your own, old chap," Theo replied.

At the top of the stairs, Philip bowed low and handed Deborah her shoes. "Your glass slippers, Cinderella." She giggled and then yawned. Good nights followed all round.

Bethan was curled up asleep in the big chair in Deborah's room. She jumped to her feet when they entered, rubbing her eyes and stammering in apology. "I didna mean to fall asleep, ma'am!"

"I'm asleep myself," Deborah said with a groan. "Oh, do put me down, Evan. You can't marry me if your back is broken."

"I would manage somehow, sweetheart. And don't think you'll get out of it by sleeping through the day tomorrow!" Deborah gave a gurgle of laughter. "Would you give us a few minutes please, Bethan?"

"Yessir." The girl curtsied and disappeared into the corridor.

Evan set Deborah on her feet. Another huge yawn escaped, followed by a sigh of contentment as she snuggled against him. He began pulling the various clips and combs and ribbons out of her hair, relishing the weight and thickness of it as it fell over his hands. Then he commenced the delightful task of removing her clothing. Fortunately he was more awake than she, or the tiny buttons and hooks might have frustrated him entirely.

Her nightdress lay across the bed, the covers turned down in readiness for their mistress. He let her shift drop to the floor and permitted his hands the luxury of a journey over her skin. She murmured something unintelligible. He slipped the nightdress over her head and regretfully allowed it to slide down between them. Then he helped her to sit on the bed while he pulled off her stockings. He kissed the top of each tired foot and slid her legs between the sheets. As her head nestled into the pillow, she reached for him and pulled his mouth down on hers, but a moment later she was lost to sleep, and he was kissing an effigy, soft and warm, yet inert. He smiled, aching for her, and stroked a curl from her cheek. "Sweet dreams, my love."

Tomorrow she would be his, and he would be hers. She would learn about music, he would learn about birds. They would read to each other, they would read to their children. He would see her when he woke in the morning, when they rode and dined and danced. He would make her moan, he would make her laugh—there was nothing in the world he would rather hear than Deborah's laughter. When darkness blinded him, he would know her by her scent, by the taste of her skin, and by the way she felt in his arms and in his heart. He would show her the beauties of the lakes and all his favorite places. And she would show him Paradise.

MORE FROM KERRYN REID

WRACKWATER BRIDGE, YORKSHIRE
Mending broken hearts

Book One
ANNA'S REFUGE

The London Season
April 1817

ANNA SPAIN HID HER SMILE—easy to do in the dark carriage. She was not ready to reveal her secret, especially to Mama.

It had happened so fast! When they first danced together, she'd known Gideon Aubrey was the one. And this Adonis had fallen for *her*, the shy daughter of a Bristol manufacturer, whose best marriage option had been old Mr. Wexcombe.

"You look pretty tonight," Mama said, begrudging. "No match for the Season's diamonds, but you'll do. Thanks to Putnam."

Anna heard a cluck of disapproval from Putnam, Mama's maid,

seated across from them. Or perhaps it was an involuntary grunt as a wheel dropped into a chink between the cobbles.

"At all events, Mr. Aubrey can have no doubt about your interest. You present a convincing show of true love."

"It isn't a show, Mama. It's *real*."

"Of course it is, dear," Mama said, with a perfunctory pat on the arm. "Very wise."

Anna huffed in frustration. Could Cedric and Evelyn Spain possibly be her true parents? Surely neither of them ever had a romantic notion. The only poetry in the house Anna had borrowed from the lending library or written herself. However had they managed to conceive two children?

"It's time to bring Mr. Aubrey to the point, Anna. I've let him haunt the house, even given you time alone with him. Your father will settle the finances, of course, but *you* must seal the deal."

Mama talked of it as a business arrangement, but that was the tiniest part of it. If Mama had ever loved Papa the way Anna loved Gideon Aubrey, she would understand.

Well, Anna had done all she could, and more than she should, to *seal the deal*. Next week Gideon would go to Bristol to see her father. Then the whole world would know how fortunate she was. Nothing else in her eighteen years had made her think so, but now! Now she was promised to the perfect man, the man who'd filled her dreams since she first thought about men as anything other than father, uncle, or brother.

They joined the stream of guests entering the grand house in Brook Street, hired by Sir John Wedbury for his daughter's first London Season. Miss Cassandra Wedbury officially celebrated her coming-out tonight, after six weeks of balls and routs. She had welcomed Anna into her circle though *she* was a success and Anna was not.

So strange to have a friend—almost as exciting as a fiancé. Both of them overflowed with confidence that bolstered Anna's fragile self-assurance. She no longer shrank when she walked into a crowded ballroom like this one.

Two hours later, for what was surely the hundredth time since she arrived, Anna looked toward the door where Gideon must enter. It lay invisible beyond a sea of people, but Gideon stood half a head taller than most of the men in the room, with broad shoulders and splendid dark curls arranged across his brow. In any case, his presence made a room thrum with expectation. She would feel it in her bones when he arrived.

Anna dragged her attention back to her partner as they awaited their turn in the dance. Mr. Hudson was no Gideon, droning on about the functions of the Colonial Department, but he deserved her courtesy. So she smiled, admitting her ignorance while pretending interest.

Gideon was late, but he would come in time. The waltz would be next—*their* waltz, arranged yesterday during a private moment in the shrubbery at Kew Gardens. All the hours since, she'd looked forward to being in his arms.

When the set ended, Mr. Hudson returned her to Mrs. Worley, whom Mama had enlisted as Anna's chaperone before absconding to the card room. No sooner had he walked away than Miss Cassandra Wedbury took possession of her arm.

"May I borrow Miss Spain, ma'am?" Miss Wedbury asked. "Mr. Aubrey is looking for her."

The woman's thoughtless wave showed her disinterest in the matter. She had no reason to care whether Anna danced with someone Mama had approved or with the devil himself.

"Mr. Aubrey?" Had Gideon sneaked past her guard? Naturally, he would first seek out Miss Wedbury at her debut ball to pay his respects—it was only polite. Their families were neighbors up in Yorkshire, after all. Not York itself, or anyplace that anyone had ever been, but some primitive village hardly worthy of a name, to hear Gideon speak of it. "Why do you think I live in London, my sweet?" he'd said, laughing.

Anna had laughed too. He had such a droll way about him.

But Gideon was not Miss Wedbury's target. Instead, his younger brother watched their approach with Miss Wedbury's own brother Jack.

Mr. Lewis Aubrey stood almost as tall as Gideon but thinner, his hair a lighter shade of brown with a tendency toward disorder, his expression serious and guarded in contrast to Gideon's infectious grin. Miss Wedbury named him her best friend and confidant although she was so lively and he so quiet. Like Anna herself.

He was handsome in his own way and rather sweet. He'd spilled lemonade on her gown at Almack's once, and she forgot to be annoyed as she soothed his mortification. She had liked him and flattered herself that he returned the sentiment.

Then Gideon had claimed her attention with jokes that made her laugh and compliments that made her blush. Swept away by his gallantry, she'd almost forgotten he had a brother. Which was not nice of her, but there was nothing she could do about it now, except show him she still liked him, though in a different way.

She greeted Mr. Wedbury politely and then shone her nicest smile upon the man who would be her brother-in-law. His eyes widened in surprise—yes, he had noticed her neglect these past few weeks.

"Has your brother been delayed?" she asked him after the obligatory courtesies. "He claimed this waltz when we talked yesterday."

"I'm sure he…" began Mr. Lewis Aubrey, a blush creeping into his cheeks. "Miss Wedbury's ball, you know. I mean to say…"

"Here he comes." Mr. Wedbury's voice sounded hoarse as he scowled at something behind her.

Anna spun around to follow the direction of his gaze. Exhilaration tingled from her fingertips up her arms, all through her chest, and down to her toes. Her voice vibrated with it as she greeted her betrothed.

"Good evening, Mr. Aubrey! I knew you would not miss our waltz." As she spoke, she noticed the possessive way Miss Landrum gripped his arm and the challenge in her blue eyes as they met Anna's own. Poor Miss Landrum thought Gideon could be hers.

She would learn her mistake soon enough.

Gideon raised his brows and surveyed Anna coolly before making her a formal bow. "I'm sorry, Miss...Paine, is it? This dance is promised to Miss Landrum." He fondled the gloved hand resting on his sleeve and smiled down into Miss Landrum's face. Anna blinked. Such a tender expression, so like...

"But don't you remember?" she blurted out. "We agreed yesterday—"

"But Miss Landrum," Mr. Wedbury said at the same time. "You said you—"

"Oh!" Gideon looked up with a start, as though he had not seen the rest of them standing there. "You know Miss Landrum, do you not? Miss Landrum, this is Mr. Wedbury and his sister, who was so kind as to invite us to her little party. And Miss...Sprain, is it not? And this," he continued, giving the younger Mr. Aubrey a slap on the shoulder that knocked him off balance, "is my own baby brother."

What was wrong with Gideon? He knew her name very well, and they'd all met a hundred times. He had a swagger about him tonight, and his eyes gleamed with devilry. Almost with evil.

Anna forced a laugh and shook her head. It was only a bit of mischief. "Oh, you're teasing again, Mr. Aubrey."

She would have gone on, making light of it, but Miss Landrum tossed a careless smile at no one in particular and tugged on Gideon's arm. "Listen, they're striking up for the waltz."

"Beauty calls," Gideon said with a grin. He stepped toward the dance floor with Miss Landrum.

"But, Mr.—" Anna couldn't breathe. She lurched forward, reaching out to him. He never looked back.

Miss Wedbury put an arm around her waist, drawing her into the protection of their little flock. "It won't do any good, I'm afraid. No, Miss Spain, you may *not* faint."

"But I... He..."

"Shhh," Miss Wedbury hissed at her. To the others, she said, "People are starting to notice. I'd best take her to the retiring room. Or to her mama."

The words hurtled by as in a dream. Surely Anna must awake in her bed at any moment with the ball yet to come, the waltz, her whole future secure in Gideon's love.

His brother spoke through clenched teeth. "And I'll have to watch him gloat for the rest of the evening? I think not." He took Anna's hand and set it on his arm. "Come, Miss Spain. We're going to waltz."

"I can't," she mumbled. "I must—"

"No, you must not." So fierce and hard-hearted. She'd thought him a kind young man, but his expression showed no sympathy as he led her in amongst the dancers.

Instead, he *smiled*. How could he, when her world was crumbling to dirt around her feet?

He bowed. She curtsied.

What am I doing? I must talk to Gideon, alone.

The younger Mr. Aubrey put his hands in the right places and set her in motion.

Why would Gideon play such a trick on me? When they next met he would chuckle, and call her a goose, and reassure her with kisses and words of love, and—

"I must apologize for my brother, Miss Spain. He has always been an inconsiderate fellow."

She glanced at Lewis Aubrey, desperate to get away. To scream, to cry.

It would cause a scene. Break all the rules, embarrass him and herself, Miss Wedbury and her parents.

She missed a couple of steps, slewing around awkwardly in his arms. He righted her, his grip strong and secure.

When he spoke again, his voice was gentle, coaxing.

"Let's play a game, Miss Spain. Pretend nothing's wrong. My brother likes to *see* the misery he's caused."

She stared him in the eye. "I don't believe it. He *can't* have feigned it all." *Could he?*

"I've known him a long time, Miss Spain. He enjoys it even more when there's a room full of gossips to witness his triumphs."

He was wrong. Of course he was wrong. To say such things of his own brother! Rivalry must drive him, or jealousy. Sour grapes.

"Miss Spain?" She returned her gaze to his. He grinned, ridiculous and exaggerated.

It was the hardest thing she'd ever done, far more difficult than walking into Almack's the first time among all those people who belonged there.

But it was necessary.

He squeezed her hand, and for the rest of that dreadful waltz, they competed to see which of them could out-smile the other.

He won, but by heaven, she held up her end. He nodded his approval.

She wanted to cry.

❦

The silence hissed in Anna's head as they descended the grand staircase. *Smile, Miss Spain. Smile, Miss Pain, Miss Plain, Miss Stain. Smile, smile, smile.* She dared not meet her mother's gaze.

It was getting late and they were not the only party awaiting their carriage. The voices rumbled through her head, sound without meaning. Still she smiled, in debt to Gideon's brother, a rock standing obdurate in a roaring ocean of color and light. She forced the smile wider as her heart cracked open, spilling blood and dreams all through her body, leaving her dumb and teetering.

Anna found brief solace in the darkness of the carriage. Putnam's presence precluded conversation beyond the obvious comments on the evening. In fact, it could not be called conversation at all.

"Quite a crush, was it not?" Her mother's voice grated like sackcloth rubbing against a rash. Anna tugged off her gloves. "There was hardly a seat to be found in the card room. And I was winning, I'll have you know. Why you must have the headache tonight, of all nights."

A pause while Anna gnawed the inside of her cheek and fixed her gaze on the drizzle wetting the streets as they passed.

"Mr. Aubrey seemed keen on getting his waltz with you when we saw him yesterday. Did he not come after all?"

"He came." *As you would know, Mama, if you had done your duty.* But perhaps it was better she had not. If Mama had been there when Gideon had appeared, Anna might have gotten one final waltz with him. It would not have changed the outcome.

In any case, it was too late for Anna to wish for a proper chaperone. Two weeks ago, she'd been delighted to be left entirely alone with Gideon.

The carriage stopped, the door opened. Despite the footman's helping hand, Anna slipped as she set her foot on the wet step. Grasping for the edge of the doorway, she dropped her gloves into the muck.

"You go ahead, miss," said Putnam with a *tsk* of annoyance as she climbed down behind and then bent to retrieve them. Anna hurried to the house under cover of the footman's umbrella.

Mama followed her to her room, denying her even a moment alone. She began the inquisition as she undid Anna's gown.

"That was Mr. Aubrey's dance. Why did *he* not see to your comfort rather than that brother of his?"

"Mr. Aubrey cares nothing for my comfort." Anna choked on the words.

"What?" Mama yanked the gown off over her head and then tossed it across a chair. "Speak up, girl!"

"Mr. Aubrey danced with someone else." Anna's voice sounded dull, inert, even as the shards of love and pride sliced her heart into mincemeat. To be treated with such contempt after all his declarations, his poetic recitations. '*A lovelier flower on earth was never sown,*' he'd quoted. '*They sin who tell us love can die.*'

She would never trust poetry again. However deeply the poet might feel the words he wrote, the man reciting them need not feel anything. He might in fact feel quite the opposite. Mirth and mockery.

"Someone else?" Mama snapped, her tone scalding. "And you did nothing?"

"I reminded him, though I'm sure it was improper. But Miss... The other girl was on his arm." Anna swallowed the anger boiling up in her throat. "He pretended he'd forgotten my name."

How could he be so insulting, so heartless? Her mother tugged at her stays, cutting off Anna's sob. She clamped her lips tight and held her breath until Mama was finished.

"And Mr. Lewis Aubrey? What had he to say to anything?"

"He helped me avoid making a spectacle of myself."

"*Humph.* If he wanted to help, he should have brought you to me. I would have made sure Gideon Aubrey fulfilled his promise."

Oh, a marvelous sight *that* would have been. Her mother, torn from her card game, plowing her way through the dancers to drag Miss Landrum from Gideon's arms. Maybe she would beat him with her reticule.

"Now, let's put our heads together and figure out how to get Mr. Aubrey back. He's the best you're likely to get."

"I don't want him back." Anna's heart cried out that she lied, but it was the only possible decision. A man who would betray her after— *No.* She must not think of that until she was alone. She sat before the mirror but quickly averted her gaze, horrified at the face she saw there.

"Nonsense," said Mama, jerking the pins from her hair. "It was merely a ploy to make you jealous, I'm sure of it. Or a test to see how much you really want him. Or perhaps nothing more than a wager at one of his clubs. We just need to play our cards right."

Anna buried her head in her hands. She'd heard that men bet on all sorts of things. Had he wagered she was too love-struck to see through his charade? What if he'd wagered on how quickly he could...?

She fought the panic smashing at the foundations of her sanity. Her problems went far beyond heartbreak. She must get rid of her mother, and then she must *think*.

"How about Mr. Jack Wedbury, then? He's nothing to look at, I grant you, but worth more, and a baronetcy into the bargain."

"No, Mama." Anna groaned, lifting her head. It felt heavy, like a rock. Mr. Wedbury was nice enough, probably, but he'd left no impression whatsoever. Nor had he shown any interest in her.

"So you admit defeat, girl?" her mother accused. "You'll trudge home and marry Mr. Wexcombe? He has a grandchild nearly your age!"

Anna's hands shook with the compulsion to cover her ears. The words bit deep, bitter and degrading. She had all but forgotten Mr. Wexcombe waiting in Bristol, drinking port with Papa as they discussed marriage settlements, waiting for her to fail. Mama had negotiated for this one Season, one chance for Anna to find someone better, a man who was both wealthy and youthful. Handsome too, if possible.

And Anna had found the man of her dreams. Or so she had thought.

"My God, Anna!" Mama's gaze bored into Anna's, her tone piercing. "Were I you, I would kiss Gideon Aubrey's feet to get him back. Masculine perfection, or that old man? You just think about that, miss!"

Oh yes, Anna thought long and hard after the door slammed shut, though there was not much that was rational about the process. Mr. Wexcombe! She had known the man all her life. He had brought her sweets when she was small, trinkets as she grew older. Now he carried liver spots on his hands and decay on his breath, but he was not a bad man. He would treat her well. At his age, why should he even care that she was no virgin, as long as she gave him what he wanted?

But to have intimate relations with him? How could she bear the comparison with her memories of Gideon? His touch, his kiss, his murmured endearments. His hand slipping between her thighs, her heart soaring with the knowledge that he had chosen *her* to share his life. His plea that they should hold their love between themselves a short while, their own delicious secret.

Ha! No wonder he wanted to keep it secret. If his brother was right, it had all been fiction. Only a game.

Was it possible for a man to be so base? Was it possible for a girl to be so blind? Not only blind but stupid. All his talk of love, of their future together. He couldn't live without her, couldn't wait to make her his. Never once had he mentioned marriage, only implied it. And never once had she noticed! Why else should he visit her father, after all?

He wouldn't. He had lied. She had heard what she longed to hear.

She dropped to her knees by the bed, but no prayer came, and no tears either. Fear stared her in the face with Gideon's eyes, crinkled at the corners with the crooked smile that told her she was the most desirable woman in the world. The only woman he would ever love.

Except he had not loved her at all. If his brother was right.

Prove him wrong, Gideon, please prove him wrong!

She would give him one day. If he came tomorrow and begged her pardon, and pledged his heart, and told Mama of his intentions… If he did those things, Mr. Wexcombe did not stand a chance.

ABOUT KERRYN REID

~Winner of Chanticleer Books' Chatelaine Award for Best Regency Romance
~Silver Medalist for Romance in Florida Authors & Publishers Association's
Book Awards

Raised in a New England college town, Kerryn inherited her mother's passion for the British Isles. At seventeen, she roamed the Rock of Cashel after-hours with her first love, a local Irish lad. So illicit, so romantic… and so unsustainable. Instead she married her college sweetheart and wound up in Florida, where they've lived long enough to feel like natives.

But a piece of Kerryn's heart still lives "across the pond" where so many adventures took place—as well as the Regency romances she loves. So when the itch to write needs scratching, that's where her imagination goes to create a tender, heartfelt historical romance about love, fear, and persistence. Enjoy the journey to another happy-ever-after!

Sign up to receive Kerryn's monthly Letter from Wrackwater Bridge with the latest news. https://kerrynreid.com

facebook.com/KerrynReid.Fiction
twitter.com/Kerryn_Reid
pinterest.com/kerrynareid
amazon.com/author/kerrynreid
bookbub.com/authors/kerryn-reid
goodreads.com/kerrynreid

www.ingramcontent.com/pod-product-compliance
Lightning Source LLC
Chambersburg PA
CBHW051951240626
47153CB00005B/1707